KEN GALLENDER

TRAILS SOUTH

A New Beginning

SILVERSMITH
PRESS

Published by Silversmith Press – Houston, Texas
www.silversmithpress.com

ISBN 978-1-967386-04-8 (Softcover Book)
ISBN 978-1-967386-05-5 (eBook)

This book is dedicated
to the memory of Marie Downs,
without whose guidance and
help my success would not be possible.

Thanks goes to Betty D. Gallender
whose devotion and collaboration
help make this and all other books possible.

CHAPTER 1

Dawson Stewart stood out on the balcony of his small Calgary bachelor condo and took a puff on his cigar. In his hand he held a silver whiskey flask containing Jameson Irish whiskey. He put the spout to his lips, took a large sip, and let it swirl in his mouth before swallowing. It was always a trade-off between the taste and the effect as opposed to the burn in his throat. The Jameson was an excellent compromise.

It was bitter cold, the weather app on his phone showed minus twenty and the wind chill put it at minus forty degrees Fahrenheit. His Columbia jacket had a mirror lining reflecting the warmth of his body back to himself, and it performed the function very well. His thick, black beard helped protect his face, but his cheeks stung.

He looked up at the clear winter sky and watched the strongest aurora that had ever been witnessed by mankind in recorded history. He wondered if it could be visible in the southern hemisphere. The only aurora approaching this magnitude was what was known as the Carrington Event back in 1859. The government officials confidently stated that only minor communications interruptions were possible and the public should enjoy the light show. The bright river of charged particles streamed by overhead.

It was unfortunate he didn't have anyone to share the

moment. He had several serious girlfriends since college. All had been ready to settle down, but he always had an excuse for not taking the plunge. He was single, forty years old, and lonely.

He had been between jobs and girlfriends when he had received a phone call from a friend who knew he was available; the idea of getting out of the country for a while was appealing. The money was good, and he had always wanted to spend some time in western Canada.

He watched the amazing sight until the biting cold forced him back inside. He kicked the heater up a notch and set his alarm for 5:00 a.m. The mile-and-a-half walk to work would be cold in the morning, but he had the clothes, and if it became intolerable, there was always the bus or taxi cabs. It was snow-cold outside, a feeling hard to describe. He had only been in Calgary for a couple of months, but he had learned to tell when it was going to snow; the air somehow felt colder. If he were a betting man, he would bet there would be fresh snow on the ground by morning.

The people in the condo upstairs had finally settled in for the night. Several nights a week it sounded as though they were rearranging their furniture. Maybe the cold had them settling down early for a change. Sleep came easy.

The alarm jolted him awake; Saturday was normally a day off, but there was a project that management wanted knocked out in short order. He put on his jeans, long-sleeve tee shirt, Carhartt shirt, and wool socks. His sunglasses were wraparounds and sometimes frosted over from the inside in these frigid temps. When he headed out, he had on his Columbia jacket and ski pants with the mirror lining. He also wore his waterproof hiking boots to protect his feet from the cold and snow.

As he had predicted, there were several inches of snow and more falling. He put on his Merino wool tuque, as the Canadians called his toboggan cap, pulling it down over his ears, and pulled the hood from his jacket over that. A scarf around his neck sealed out the cold around his collar. The wool gloves finished off his cold gear.

The walk took him through a memorial park with bronze statues on granite pedestals. Each step brought squeaks from the snow that was as dry as powder and had the consistency of fine sand. The wind blew the snow around in drifts along the buildings and curbs; evergreen fir trees held it on their boughs. The panhandlers would still be in their shelters in this weather.

A shortcut through the parking garage got him out of the wind and into the elevator heading up to the eighteenth floor of the office building. He was soon at his desk; the Calgary Tower stood just up the street. He could see the steam from the gas furnaces in the buildings rising to the sky; it and the snow looked like a fog across the city from his vantage point. The fog from exhaust stacks of the shorter buildings also enveloped the building, further diminishing his view. He fired up his computer, and while he waited for it to reboot, he went to the break room for his morning coffee. Several of his coworkers were filtering in when the lights unexpectedly went out. His cell phone started overheating in his pocket, so he tossed it into the sink out of fear it would set his clothes on fire.

He and his coworkers stood around the office when he glanced down at his automatic mechanical Seiko watch. It had been six hours since the lights went out, and it was obvious something was wrong. His cell phone sat dead in the break room sink where he left it when its battery overloaded. His computer was toast, as was his laptop and everything else in the office.

The team manager had insisted everyone stay put to make sure they all received full credit for the day's work. In the six hours the lights had been off, the building had started to cool. Several of the ladies were putting on their coats; one was already wearing a scarf around her neck. A trip to the men's washroom was only accomplished with the aid of a butane lighter. When he hit the flush button, he heard the sickening gurgle of the almost nonexistent water pressure. He knew the toilets would soon be full of human excrement that had no place to go. The elevators were dead, and he did not look forward to walking down eighteen floors in the darkened stairwells. For some odd reason, even the emergency lights had failed. If he waited much longer, he would be walking back to his condo in the dark. At least at his condo he had some food, extra clothes, and an extra comforter for his bed. He could easily survive the night without freezing.

He started to add up in his mind all the things that had quit working. The wireless mouse no longer had the little red glow from its optical reader on the bottom. The wall clocks were dead, and the only sound was the wind whistling past the windows. This was normally never heard over the din of the office, the whir of fans and the almost silent computers. He recalled, around the corner, was the supply and mail room for the building. The swipe cards were no longer necessary as the electromagnets holding the doors closed no longer held them captive. He was the only one who realized he had full access to the entire building.

He quietly walked down the hall between the now non-functioning elevators and wondered if anyone was trapped inside. The thought of being entombed in an elevator until he died made him shutter a bit. He went into the supply room, flicked on his lighter, and looked around. Neatly placed on row after row of shelves were all the supplies necessary to run a large insurance company with several thousand employees. Luckily this was a special weekend project, and the building was largely empty other than the two dozen or so employees on the team. The question in his mind at this point was, What can I use in this room in the event the lights don't come back on?

The light from his butane lighter cast shadows over the shelves. He stopped looking when he realized the little lighter was all he had to light his way down the dark stairwell. Eighteen floors of unlit stairs would be difficult for him and his coworkers to negotiate in the dark.

He went into the lunch room, inventoried the cabinets, and finally the dishwasher. He found a long metal serving fork and a long knife used to slice the occasional birthday cake for office parties. On the wall was a bulletin board with a long metal tray to hold the dry markers and eraser. The four-foot-long metal tray easily detached from the wall board. In the large coat closet, there was a damaged office chair. Dawson used his small pocket knife, removed the cloth seat covers and wound them around the end of the tray using the cords from some damaged phone headsets to secure them.

He rummaged around in some of the office vacant desks. In one desk he found some female hygiene products belonging to one of the regular employees who was off for the weekend. He impaled tampons on the fork and sanitary napkins on the knife. He now had three torches he could disperse among his fellow employees that would enable them to negotiate the dark stairwell.

He walked over to his manager's desk. Jane Hinson was a woman in her mid-fifties, divorced and fighting the effects of time. She was still a beautiful woman, but the years of smoking and hard work had toughened her features.

She looked up at Dawson when he walked over to her desk. "Miss Jane, I think you need to consider dismissing everyone for the day. It's going to be dark outside soon. I think we need to head on out of here so that we can get home while it's still light enough to see. I'm only about a twenty-minute walk from here, but a lot of the folks here will have a long walk if they can't get a cab, train, or bus."

"Why wouldn't they be able to get a cab, train, or bus?"

He beckoned her to the window. "Come see." She walked over to the window and gazed down with him. "Look, all the lights are out including the stop lights. Every car is dead in the middle of the road. A bus couldn't get down the road, even if they were still running. I think we need to go if we're going to go."

She thought a minute. "No, if we leave, they are going to dock us for the day's work."

"I hope you don't mind, but I'm heading on down. I made a couple of torches that you can use to get down the dark stairwell. All you have to do is use your cigarette lighter to light them."

She gave him an indignant look. "If you leave, I'll have to doc you the day's work."

At first Dawson was irritated, but on reflection thought better of it. She was the manager because she followed and enforced the rules.

He smiled and nodded. "I understand. The torches are at my desk. Be careful and don't let the burning fabric drip on you. Take the entire box of feminine napkins in case one of them doesn't burn long enough."

"You're serious, aren't you?"

"Yes, mam, if the lights come on, I'll see you on Monday. If they don't, good luck."

He went back to his desk, pulled the ski pants from his backpack, and pulled them over his jeans. The pants felt good as the office building was noticeably colder. The other employees who had been sitting around visiting noticed he was preparing to leave. Olivia came over to his desk.

Olivia Watson was a few years younger than he and from the Calgary area. She was a shy beauty who worked hard and kept to herself. She was one of those women who didn't realize she was beautiful. She didn't flaunt it; she didn't know that she could.

6

Olivia asked, "Are you leaving early?"

"Yes, mam, I want to get back to my condo before it gets dark."

"I overheard you talking to Jane; are they going to doc your pay?"

He grinned at her. "I'm afraid so, but I can afford to miss a day's pay every now and then."

"I wish I could afford to miss a day."

"Olivia, I tell you what I'll do. If you want to join me, I'll pay your lost day, but you'll have to join me for dinner this evening."

"I can't ask you to pay me for today."

"You didn't ask. It's worth it to me to spend some time with a lovely lady."

"That's sweet of you, but I can't."

"I'm not taking no for an answer."

"OK, let me get my things, and I'll tell Jane that I'm joining you."

He winked at her. "Good choice, I'm looking forward to it."

As she walked across the office to Jane's desk she thought to herself, Finally, he asked me out.

CHAPTER 2

Hawks stood at the railing of the ferry boat adjusting the straps of the life vest to his body. An attractive woman, somewhat younger than him, had difficulty with her life vest. She had made small talk with him earlier when they were on the second-level observation deck. He secured her vest as she smiled. "Thanks, I would have never figured it out. I hope I don't have to use it."

He nodded in agreement. "I hope we stay high and dry."

He found himself drawn to her, but as was his custom, he kept the conversation strictly casual. He had very few friends and never allowed himself to get close to any woman. The last thing he wanted was a relationship at this time in his life. The thought of having a relationship at his age frightened him. He thought to himself, My friends and family would think I am just a pitiful old fool trying to date and carry on. I can hear my buddies at the hunting camp, ribbing me about a new girlfriend. No, I just need to mind my own business. There's no way I could ever face my children.

The wind across the open water was bone cold as the temperature hovered in the forties. From where he stood, he could see Salt Spring Island behind him and the town of Crofton on Vancouver Island before him. He watched as the shoreline slowly drifted by; the current carried the floundering ferry northward.

His rental car was parked in the line of cars waiting for the ferry to dock and unload, useless now. The crew scrambled to get all the passengers in life vests when the engines on the ferry went dead. He overheard one of them say the radios were out, and no one had a cell signal. His phone didn't have a signal either because it was dead, and so were the phones of everyone around him.

Just north of the ferry boat landing in Crofton sat a paper mill. A huge flotilla of cedar logs was anchored at the edge of the bay waiting to be taken into the plant for their conversion into paper. On its current path, the ferry would float into the massive raft of logs. The question was: Would the logs stop or sink the ferry? There was also the chance that the ferry would break up the flotilla from its anchorage.

If the ferry sank, the life expectancy of anyone caught in the cold black waters of the passageway would be measured in minutes. The temperature of the water around Vancouver Island hovered near fifty degrees, which would give someone caught in it only thirty minutes before they succumbed to hypothermia.

Staring into the deep, cold water, he wondered, If the Aurora from last night makes an appearance tonight, will I be alive to see it?

Passengers crowded the side of the ferry where the collision was about to occur. No one wanted to miss the spectacular event about to take place. Hawks wasn't an engineer, but he had an understanding of how things worked. That's why he was hired as a consultant on problem engineering projects. He knew and could explain why something would or wouldn't work. He also knew what could happen when a huge ferry runs into a flotilla of logs. It would all depend on the depth of the water. If the water was deep, the logs would simply pile up upon one another and dampen the collision. If the depth was shallow, they would pile up on the bottom and form a wall. If they were lucky, it would be gradual and stop the ferry. The problem was the sides of the ferry weren't as thick and robust as the ends of the ferry. The ends were designed to push up against the landing, so like an egg, the ferry was weaker on the sides. If the sides were ruptured, the ferry would go to the bottom in short order since the engines and the pumps weren't running. The prospect of piles of logs spilling over onto the decks and the sound of tearing metal was not something he wanted to experience first-hand. After realizing what was about to occur, he made his way back across the ferry to the side of the vessel away from the logs.

As he passed the pretty woman walking to join the others, he touched her arm. "I don't think it's a good idea to be over there when the collision occurs."

She looked at him surprised. "You may be right; I'll hang back away from the rails and crowd." He continued crossing the deck until he located the life rafts and studied the diagram on their deployment. In short order he understood how to deploy and inflate them. He heard a gasp from the crowd as the ferry made contact with the raft of logs. He could feel no slowing of the momentum of the ferry, but in his mind's eye, he could see the logs tumbling over one another while others were being shoved under the vessel. They would soon reach a point where a combination of the weight of the logs and the resistance to the bottom of the harbor would either stop the ferry or rupture the hull.

A low moan of bending and tearing metal could be heard emanating from somewhere below deck. Then the steel tore with a screech as a portion of the hull gave way. The captain of the vessel came out and tried to bark orders to the crew, but his voice was drowned out by the sound of the breaking logs and the screeching metal. The crowd panicked and ran to the opposite side of the boat where Hawks busied himself releasing the life boats. The crew quickly came to the realization the vessel was going down and proceeded to deploy them as well. The ferry settled deeper in the water as the cold, black water poured in.

Hawks went to his rental car and retrieved his backpack from the back seat. The backpack contained some basic items he always kept nearby. In spite of the panic and confusion, the crew was doing a good job of deploying the life rafts. The problem was getting the passengers into the rafts while the vessel sank. A loaded eighteen-wheeler, tour bus, and gravel truck were on the damaged side of the vessel. They, along with the rush of water, made the ferry list to that side. This exacerbated the crew's effort to load the passengers. A number of passengers wound up in the cold water, and they were unceremoniously pulled over the sides of the life rafts to join their fellow passengers. Hawks held back and waited as the life boats filled. He watched as his lady friend made it safely aboard. He wasn't certain how deep the water was; it was unlikely the water was deeper than the ferry was tall.

He climbed the stairs leading to the observation deck. When he arrived, he found the captain barking orders from the railing. The captain looked around. "What's the matter; aren't you afraid of drowning?"

Hawks grinned. "If we were out in the channel, I'd be down there in line. We should be hitting bottom pretty soon. I'm glad the ferry didn't completely break up when it hit. I figure as soon as the panic subsides, I'll get in a lifeboat or walk across the logs to shore. Have you guys figured out what happened to the engines?"

"We have complete electrical failure; everything electronic quit working, even our cell phones."

Hawks looked up at the sky. "I wonder if that strong aurora has anything to do with our electrical problems."

The captain glanced up. "According to the news, they were

only expecting some radio interference. It'll be dark soon; I'm curious to see if it will be as strong as it was last night."

The ferry soon settled to the bottom with the water covering the tops of the cars on deck. All the passengers were secure on the lifeboats. Hawks, the captain, and remaining crewmen climbed in the last boat, shoved off, and paddled to shore. They climbed out on the dark sand where most of the passengers gathered waiting for rescue personnel. Hawks didn't wait. He would notify the car rental company where their car was once he found a working telephone.

He was staying in a basement of a friend's home a mile or so away while vacationing on the island. He walked up the beach until he found a boat ramp that reached the water. The surface was slick, and he almost lost his footing. He was soon on the road leading back into the small town. He came upon vehicles dead in the road. A couple of the vehicles had their hoods up; a man was attempting repairs on another.

Once he was in the town, he headed down past the local pub. People stood out on the deck of the bar drinking. One of the regulars recognized him. "Hawks, come on up, the beer's still cold."

Hawks waved back. "I may be back later; I have to drop my stuff off at the house."

As he hiked down the street leading to his basement apartment, he smelled the aroma of meals being cooked on grills that would normally be stored until warmer weather. The sun was setting, and he noticed there were no street lights or lights in any of the windows. When he reached his basement apartment, he went in, and as expected the lights were out. He dug around in his backpack and pulled out the old Maglite flashlight. It was an old flashlight that used a filament bulb and was powered by two AA batteries. It faithfully illuminated his surroundings.

The den in the basement had a small, freestanding wood

12

heater, so he loaded it with firewood and soon had the walkout basement warm and a pot of canned beans warming on top. The only thing he had in the small refrigerator was a half-gallon of milk and some yogurt. While vacationing on the island, he had been eating most of his meals out. The beans were in the cabinet, along with other various canned goods, when he had moved in. All in all, he only had about two days of food in the basement and a few trail bars in his backpack. If the lights didn't come on soon, he'd be going on a crash diet. With the curtains open, the aurora lit the room. A glass of bourbon whisky filled his hand as he sat staring at the fire in the wood heater. He considered the ramifications of what was taking place. If this was a localized event, help would be arriving within days. If the event was nationwide or global, then things would get ugly very fast.

Bill Hawks was a sixty-year-old widower. It had been three years since the death of his wife. He had sold his home and traveled in his work as a consultant. A cabin in the Ozarks in his family for years awaited the occasional vacation getaway. His son was single and living in Atlanta; his daughter was married and living in Houston with one grandson. If the lights didn't come back on, they would be in dire straits. After three days, any semblance of civilization would come crashing down. Luckily, his children took after him and were extremely practical and self-sufficient. The challenge for them would be surviving the starving masses and finding food. He stoked the stove and climbed into his bed. The only sound this night would come from the logs shifting in the heater as they were consumed by the fire.

CHAPTER 3

Dawson and Olivia walked down the dark stairwell with the improvised tampon torch. Olivia laughed at the fork/tampon torch. "I hope we don't run into anyone we know."

"Maybe you should be the one carrying it. After all, this is a female contraption of sorts."

They laughed and continued down the stairs until they reached the floor that would take them out the back hallway to the rear of the building. The corridors and passages looked strange with only the light from the windows. The most disconcerting part was the complete silence inside the building. The last leg of the journey through the building took them down a long, dead escalator to the ground floor. Several of the local homeless had already discovered the back doors were no longer locked by the electromagnetic locks and congregated in the rear lobby. It would be just a matter of time before they burst into the locked coffee shop located to one side.

Dawson held the fork low and simply said, "Good day, gents," as he pushed the door open for Olivia to go through. They were out in the cold and heading toward his condo before the bums could even respond.

Olivia glanced back. "Where is security when you need them?" Dawson looked back as well and was relieved they were alone on the sidewalk. Olivia asked, "What did you have in mind for dinner?"

"That depends. How hungry are you. There's a great hamburger place near my condo with good poutine, and there are dozens of restaurants up and down 17th Avenue."

She thought a moment. "Some good warm poutine would be good on a cold night like this. Then maybe we could walk down 17th Avenue and find a spot for a hot totty."

People walked and the roads were littered with abandoned vehicles. Olivia glanced into several pubs along the way. "You know, we may not be able find a place to eat; you may have to come to my place for dinner."

Dawson asked as they continued to walk, "How far a drive is it to your house?"

"I live in the Northwest part of the city. It's about a thirty-minute train ride."

"The trains and buses aren't running; it would take us six or seven hours to walk that far. We can see if my truck will crank, but if it's dead like all the other vehicles we have a problem."

She looked worried. "Surely the lights will be back on soon. If not, what are we going to do?"

"I've got a ton of canned goods at the condo. I hate to go shopping, so I stocked up when I went out last night."

She was still worried. "I'm serious. What if they never come back on? Look up, the aurora is brighter than it was last night, and it's not even completely dark yet." They stopped in the park and looked up; the river of light was beautiful, but they suddenly realized it was deadly as well.

Dawson glanced around; he was pretty sure a naturally occurring EMP was taking place. "Let's get to my place; it's only about a half mile from here. We can get out of the cold and eat something. At least we won't freeze inside out of the weather."

Olivia chided him. "If I didn't know better, I'd say you had all this planned just to get me in your condo."

He grinned back. "You'll never know." They made their way through the park and up 4th Street where they passed the little hamburger shop. Through the window, they saw the man who owned it sitting at the bar with a candle. Dawson took Olivia's hand. "Let's see if he happens to have anything cooked."

The old man recognized him as a regular customer. "Come in and get warm."

Dawson asked, "Are you still cooking?"

The man grinned. "Yes, my stove is gas, so I can cook, and it's keeping the shop warm."

Olivia smiled. "I'll have the poutine."

Dawson pulled out his money clip. "Make that two if you please. I'll pay cash since your credit card machine isn't working."

The owner nodded. "Thanks."

Because he had a feeling the lights wouldn't be coming back on, Dawson felt a little guilty paying the man with useless paper money. He asked the man, "While you're cooking, can you make me four more orders? I want to take some home to freeze and eat later."

"Sure thing."

Dawson and Olivia went over to a table by the window and waited. Olivia spoke low under her breath, "What if the lights don't come back on?"

"If the lights don't come back on, we'll need the extra food. If they do, I'll have poutine for a couple of weeks. If they don't come back on, this shop will be cleaned out and the owner killed if he resists. You won't recognize this city in three or four days if that happens."

She squeezed his hand. "I hadn't thought of that; what'll we do?"

The owner delivered the poutine and thanked them for the business. They took the poutine, stepped out into the cold, and crossed the street. A shortcut through a parking lot took them to the drive leading to the back entrance of the condo. Dawson took out his car keys and hit the fob. The lights on his truck didn't flash. He walked over, unlocked the door, and found it was dead, just like all the other vehicles in the city. Dawson looked around at Olivia; the only thing showing was her eyes. "I'm afraid we're in trouble. Let's get inside out of the cold and eat while our food is still warm. I have a backpack with some gear in it under the cover in the back of the truck. Let's get inside, eat, and decide what we're going to do."

He grabbed the backpack and pulled out a flashlight. "Cross your fingers."

He clicked the button and it lit. He could see her eyes light up from the grin hidden behind her scarf. "Follow me." He opened the back door and climbed the stairs with the flashlight lighting the way.

The condo was small, only one room. It held a bed, a couple of chairs, and a small table with two chairs. The bathroom was off to one side, and at the other end of the wall sat a very compact kitchen. Dawson dug around in his pack, produced a small candle lantern, and sat it in the middle of the table. He lit it with his butane lighter and killed his flashlight to save the battery. "Olivia, do you have any family here in Calgary?"

"No, it's just me. I'm from Edmonton. My parents are down in Scottsdale, Arizona, and my sister is in college in Ogden, Utah. I have a roommate, and she has a cat, so it's just me. How about you?"

"All my family is scattered; I've never been married, and I don't have any children. My parents died in a car wreck when I was still in college. I'm not close to my brothers; we only see each other every year or two. One's in the army, and the other is in the Air Force. The closest thing I have to a home is a fish camp near Grand Isle, Louisiana, and I haven't seen it in a year. I guess home is where my truck is."

Olivia shivered in the cold room. "That's got to be lonely, but I know how you feel. I've given up on meeting anybody."

Dawson grinned. "If this is the end of the world as we have known it, I can't think of anybody else I'd rather survive with."

She smiled. "Me too."

While Olivia opened two of the poutine dinners, Dawson retrieved a carton of milk from the fridge and two glasses from the cupboard. "I hope you're a milk drinker. The only other thing I have to drink is Irish whiskey. I don't spend much time cooking. I only have what I can throw in the microwave."

"No worries, I love milk, and besides, we may need the whiskey before this over." They finished the meal and watched the aurora through the balcony sliding door. Olivia asked, "What are we going to do? We only have enough food for a few days, and that food is going to be frozen solid by this time tomorrow."

Dawson thought about their situation for a few moments. "Our choices are real simple. We can wait and see if they restore the power. If the power is restored, life may return to normal. I don't believe there's any way possible to repair all the automobiles, trucks, and busses that are now broken down. My truck wasn't plugged in, and it is dead as a door knob. I can check and see if the battery is dead by putting on a set of jumper cables and seeing if I can get the opposite ends of the cables to spark by touching them. If my battery is still hot, that will mean that the computer and other electronics are fried. If the trucks that deliver all the food and supplies to the stores are broken down, it won't matter if the electricity comes back on, we'll starve. Our only other option is to be proactive and gather as much food and supplies as we can right now to either ride it out, travel south or across the mountains into British Columbia to where we can find a warmer climate."

Olivia put on her gloves and coat as they sat. The cold was already starting to penetrate the condo building. "What do we need to do right now?"

"I'll go check the battery in my truck. If it's hot, we'll know that the electronics in the truck are probably fried. You sit tight and I'll go check; it won't take but a few minutes." He pointed to the candle lantern in the middle of the table. "I've had this since I was in the scouts. My dad gave it to me when I started camping."

Olivia sat next to the candle lantern in the condo as Dawson went out and checked on the battery. He came back in after a few minutes carrying his sleeping bag and shaking his head. "The battery is still holding a charge, the truck won't crank, and none of the lights are working. I assume that everything is controlled by the onboard computers, so if they are fried, then nothing is going to work."

"Is there any activity outside?"

"I didn't see anyone; this bitter cold has everyone staying in trying to keep warm. This sleeping bag along with the extra comforter in my closet should be enough to keep us from freezing. We can always put on our ski pants and coats and get under the cover in the bed and stay warm. But I think we need to take action before we're caught flat-footed. We are only one mile from the hiking and mountaineering store. I think we need to go there and stock up."

She gave him a puzzled look. "The store is closed this time of day, and besides, their registers won't be working. Do you think they'll be open in the morning?"

"I think we need to go shopping right now before anyone else gets the same idea. I bet they have a window we can break or a door I can break through."

She looked away and then back at him. "I don't know; that's breaking and entering."

"I know it is, but I figure that the cops will be busy with all the bums breaking into the liquor stores and coffee shops, and I would rather us be outfitted than sitting around starving to death. You don't have to go in with me, but I'm going to go shopping."

She thought for a long moment. "I guess I can add felon to my resume; let's do it."

Dawson went to his toolbox in the truck and retrieved a ball peen hammer, screwdrivers, linesmen pliers, electrical snips, and a hack saw and put them in his backpack. They headed down the streets leading to the store using the candle lantern to light their way. The vibrant aurora overhead would distract anyone watching; it was almost mesmerizing in its intensity. It took them about thirty minutes to reach the store, and as expected it was closed and locked. There was no activity of any kind, so they went around to a window on the side at ground level.

Taking his ball peen hammer, he struck the window on the lower left-hand corner. The safety glass instantly burst into a thousand fragments all held in place by the plastic inner layer. He punched at the corner until he had a man-sized opening they could step through.

He was very familiar with the layout of the store as this was one of his favorite places to shop. His plans were to take a few weeks or months off to hike, camp, and explore the Canadian Rockies once this work assignment was complete. Once inside, they went straight to the section of the store displaying the flash-lights, lanterns, and candles. After trying several LED flashlights, he found some that worked. He attached them on the bill of their newly acquired caps so they could walk and carry things with their hands free from holding a flashlight.

He pointed up the stairs. "The clothing section is upstairs. I want you to go there and find yourself some ski pants, a heavy parka, sweaters, wool socks, and a stocking cap. Also gather up a week's worth of undergarments and clothes. Try to find one of these Columbia jackets with the mirror lining like the one I'm wearing as well. If you run into anyone, scream out, and I'll come running. I'll start gathering up the other stuff we need. Look for a good pair of waterproof hiking boots. All I need in the way of clothes is a heavy parka."

She took his hand and said, "Hold me a moment. I'm getting scared."

He took her in his arms, and they kissed. "Just do what I say, and it will be OK." This was the first time in several years he really felt good about a girlfriend. Every other relationship seemed superficial. He felt different this time. He hoped she had the same feelings.

He went over to the checkout counter and grabbed a handful of the recyclable bags all the stores in Canada sold. He handed them to her and looked in her eyes. "OK, partner, get upstairs and start shopping, I want to be out of here in thirty minutes. Get whatever you need. Pretend that you will not to be able to get back to your apartment for more clothes." She disappeared up the stairs, and he proceeded to the section of the store with the back-packs on display. He soon had two backpacks filled with all the various camping gear he thought they could use, along with two low-temperature sleeping bag systems, canteens, camelback-type water bladders, and several fire-starting kits. He loaded two duffel bags with freeze-dried food. He stashed them near the broken window and grabbed an ice axe and sprinted up the stairs where he met Olivia decked out in her new outfit that included their best heavy parka. She was carrying a man's parka. "Try this on. It's the best one they carry."

He took it from her and tried it on. "It's a perfect fit."

They started back down the stairs when they heard voices from somewhere inside the store. They killed the lights and waited. Several men could be heard talking, a flashlight came on, and they realized that some of the homeless had found the busted-out window.

Dawson whispered, "I have all our stuff stashed near the window. Follow me, and we'll slip out past them. They're making a lot of noise talking and rummaging around. I think we can slip out without being noticed."

Gingerly they slipped down the stairs, being careful not to trip and fall. Suddenly a bright light illuminated them, and a man said, "What do we have here?"

Dawson spoke up, "We're just doing a little window shopping, hope you have a good evening."

The man called out, "Hey, Larry and Slick, get over here; I think I just found our evening entertainment."

Dawson was frozen for a moment. His first instinct was to just try and talk his way past the man. The problem with that was they would have to walk past the man on the stairs. He knew he didn't want to get within arm's length of him. Dawson was a fit, vigorous man, but he was not a street fighter.

Before anyone could answer, he threw the ice axe into the face of the man holding the light. He screamed and dropped the light. Dawson took Olivia's hand and proceeded at a fast walk toward the window. He scooped up another ice axe as he passed the rack holding them. He shoved Olivia through the opening and then threw out the backpacks, bags of clothes, and duffel bags before stepping out into the cold himself.

He handed her a backpack along with the bags of clothes. "Hang on to these until we get clear of this place." He hefted the new backpack onto his shoulder and grabbed the two duffels, then they ran across the street and ducked into an alleyway. They switched on their cap lights long enough to transfer the contents of his old backpack into one of the new ones.

Olivia said, "My hands are shaking."

He clasped her gloved hands. "Take a deep breath, we're OK."

He took a long breath before he rolled up his old backpack and stuffed it into one of the duffel bags with the food. He helped Olivia put on hers and soon had both adjusted for the walk back. Dawson held the duffel bags in his hands after clipping the ice axe to his belt with a carabiner. Fog steamed from their breath through the scarves around their faces. It wasn't long before the outside of the scarves were covered with ice around their noses and mouths from the moisture of their breath. Because of the load, it took them forty minutes to cover the distance to the condo. They didn't talk, but the adrenaline rush helped lighten their load.

Once inside the condo, Olivia burst out crying. "I've never been so afraid in my life. How bad was that man hurt?"

"I'm not sure how bad he's hurt; I tried my best to put him down when I threw the axe. When he said he had found the evening entertainment, I knew what they were planning to do. I wasn't going to fight or reason with him. If he survived, they'll be taping up his head or face from where I hit him. You can't worry about him; it was his choice. We made out like bandits tonight and we just multiplied our survival odds a thousand-fold. I could sure use a gun; I don't like the idea of using an axe or a hammer for self-defense."

"Do you think it was a good idea to hit that man in the face like that?"

"I realize that we were looting the store, but we were confronted by looters. If they were just getting supplies like us, they would have tried to hide or avoid us. He decided to confront us and then made a threatening statement. His overconfidence led to him getting hit."

Olivia nodded. "I agree; you made the right move. We've got to be careful."

"Things are only going to get worse as this unfolds, and we can't let our guard down for a minute. Don't let anyone know that we have food."

"I understand; if anyone knows we have food, it will only make us targets." A knock at the door caught them by surprise.

CHAPTER 4

Hawks woke to the sounds of the local Canadian Geese putting up a ruckus in the neighborhood. For a moment he forgot the electricity was still out, but the digital clock on the nightstand was blank and immediately reminded him. Scrounging around through the kitchen cabinet, he located some stale crackers and some canned soup. He added some wood to the stove and, using the same pot the beans were cooked in, warmed the soup and dumped in the stale crackers. The water pressure was dead in the sink, so he was only able to wipe out the bean pot with a paper towel. The soup and crackers were filling, but he quickly realized his food supply was drying up fast. He heard the geese once again and started thinking, In a couple of days everyone around here will be hunting geese, stealing food, and looting stores.

There was a secondhand shop on Main Street where he did his laundry, and just down the street from there was a small hardware store. His thoughts turned to survival. He broke into his friend's storage shed behind the home to hunt for tools. Rummaging through the tool chest, he loaded his backpack with a claw hammer, screw drivers, pliers, and box cutter. The box cutter would serve as a pocket knife until he could locate one. He drained some water from the tap on the hot water heater and filled a couple of empty water bottles he retrieved from his garbage. The bottles neatly fit on either side of the backpack in elastic mesh pockets. He put on his long underwear, jeans, and canvas shirt. Over this he put on suspenders in addition to a heavy leather belt. A stocking cap, leather jacket, and hiking boots completed the outfit. He would be walking, so he would forego his heavy parka for now.

It only took about fifteen minutes to walk over to the main street in the little town where the hardware store was located. There were a few people on the streets, and the two grocery stores were open but were taking cash only. He went into the first grocery store and managed to procure beans, bacon, flour, cooking oil, and a quart bottle of bleach. In addition, he bought salt, pepper, popcorn, sardines, toilet tissue, paper towels, honey, chocolate bars, peanut M&M's, and the last six jars of peanut butter on the shelf. He concentrated on getting calorie-dense foods. The store was already out of water, drinks, bread, and milk.

The owner of the little hardware store lived above it and had also opened his store. His planned felonious break-in attempt wouldn't be necessary. Hawks had a little over fifteen hundred in emergency cash left. He carried all his groceries over to the hardware store, where he picked out the largest rolling trashcan in the store. It held all the groceries and the other things he would be buying and would keep them hidden from prying eyes.

After making a quick run through the store, he settled on a plan. He bought pieces of PVC pipe in quarter inch, half inch, three-quarter inch, and one inch. He also bought everything he could possibly ever need. It took five trips for him to gather his supplies and transport them to his house. His last purchase was a garden cart with large wheels. He exhausted all but two hundred and fifty dollars of his cash, but he could now survive in his basement long enough to find out what was going to take place.

That afternoon he went to work organizing his equipment. The first thing he did was build a water filter using two of the five-gallon buckets he bought and a solid brick. He epoxied the brick over a hole in the bottom of one of the buckets. Any water poured into the top bucket would seep through the brick and drip into the bucket below. All he had to do was pour the water from the lower bucket into a container. A small stream ran down to the bay near the house, so a trip a day would keep him in drinking water. He would add eight drops of the bleach to each gallon as a precaution. As he worked, he felt a tinge of guilt: If they can't get the lights back on, I just robbed a couple of stores.

The second task was the construction of a bow and arrows from the PVC pipe. He cut the PVC pipe and a fiberglass fence rod to length. After a couple of hours of work with the hacksaw, propane torch, and paracord, he had a working bow. Using the lag bolts as arrow heads and the fiberglass fabric as fletching, he prepared two dozen arrows. A can of Rust-Oleum paint provided the camouflage. After a couple of hours' practice in the back yard, he was reasonably certain he could take game and defend himself.

The sun was getting low, and there were more people in the streets now. He watched from the window while his beans and rice simmered on the wood heater. People were heading in the direction of the grocery on Main Street, and they were all returning empty-handed. It had been a little more than twenty-four hours since the event started. In another twenty-four hours, these same people would be entering the unoccupied houses of their neighbors and friends looking for food and water. Fortunately, he hadn't been here long enough to meet any of the neighbors. He only knew a few of the regulars at the two pubs in town. It had been his habit to have dinner and a cocktail every evening at one or the other. He had been here about six weeks and was scheduled to depart the country in another week, but if things didn't change, he would be doing good to not be departing this life within a week. Tonight would be wing night at the Brass Cannon, and they would be having fish and chips over at the Blue Gull, but he was certain all the beer had been drunk and most if not all the food eaten or carried away by now.

Just as he understood how things worked, he also understood human nature, and he could accurately predict the sequence of events that would start to unfold. He had been on a construction site many years earlier in Argentina working in a remote area as the country's economy collapsed. He saw what took place and made it out on a workboat with the rest of the crew. He knew the authorities would not be coming to help. He also knew the authorities would not hesitate to arrest you. A police boat tried to confiscate their boat. Luckily, they had enough US dollars to buy their way past. The Argentina currency was worthless.

The one thing in his life he possessed was a gut feeling that was never wrong. In the first twenty-four hours things would be normal, everyone would act normal. In the next twenty-four hours, people would get concerned and start to look for things to bridge the gap. At first it would be bottled water, milk, bread, diapers, etc. There would be no panic, just frustration. The crooks and thugs would start looking around for easy pickings. After seventy-two hours almost all the food on hand would be gone. The water and drinks would be disappearing, along with virtually all the food in the houses. Uncooked food in freezers would start to rot, and the first instances of panic would begin. After four days the grocery stores would all be looted, and every available scrap of food will have been taken. Most of the feed and animal supply stores would also be targeted as most animal food could also feed people. Any cooperation between neighbors would start to crumble as the realization set in that there was no help and more importantly no food on the way.

From this point forward the breakdown of civilized society would proceed at various speeds depending on the location. In the big cities it would breakdown rapidly as this was where the welfare state recipients, gangs, and homeless would be congregated. This was also where the majority of the third-world refugees would be housed. These refugees would do better than the local population because they already understood the ramifications of what was taking place. They would be the first ones in the store to get food, water, and supplies; in fact, most of them already had on hand several weeks of food and supplies.

Night came and the aurora was no more. It was a cold, clear night; the stars were bright as there was no light pollution to dim their beauty. Hawks' plan for tomorrow would be the construction of crab traps from the large roll of poultry wire. He stoked the fire and dialed down the vents so the fire would last the night. Once he was confident the doors and windows were barred and no one could enter without waking him, he went to bed. He slept well as he knew this would be the last night of relative safety. Tomorrow would decide if he would have to flee or if he would hunker down and see what happened. If he could hold out for a couple of months, most of the human population would be dead.

The next morning, he woke with the dawn and headed upstairs to the main part of the dwelling. He jimmied the lock on the door and managed to break in without damaging the door or the lock. He gathered up the food in some plastic bags and cleaned out the refrigerator. He looked around the upstairs residence to see what his friends had that he could use. His friends had left on vacation to Australia, so it was unlikely Hawks would see them anytime soon, if ever. Out of respect for them, he had resisted the urge to enter their home and pilfer their belongings, but now things were different.

In the guest room he was elated at what he found in the walk-in closet. A gun safe sat bolted to the floor with space on either side where his friend had hunting and outdoor gear stored.

The electronic combination lock was exactly like the one he had on his safe in storage back in the Ozarks. Only six numbers stood between him and the contents. He had plenty of time to go through the numbers, but the big question was if the EMP had knocked out the electronics in the lock. He punched in six random numbers and hit the pound key. Nothing, it should have emitted a long tone indicating the code was wrong or it had been entered too quickly. He tried once again, and it was silent. He pulled the face of the lock off and removed the battery. He touched the nine-volt battery to his tongue and found it was dead. He looked around the house and found a container in the utility room with batteries of various sizes. An unopened pack of nine-volt batteries produced one that was still hot.

Hawks replaced the dead battery, punched in six random numbers, and hit the pound symbol. A long beep came from the keypad. Maybe the metal of the safe coupled with the fact the battery was dead enabled the keypad to survive. He now had the arduous task of methodically going through all the numbers starting with 000000#, 000001#, 000002# until he discovered the code. He took a legal pad and jotted down numbers as he reached the hundred marks.

After several hours of sitting in front of the lock, the battery went dead. He replaced the battery, but by that time had developed quite a headache and backache. In the bathroom he found some aspirin in the medicine cabinet, and just as he was closing the door he noticed six numbers written in small letters on the inside of the door. He smiled; the combination of his own safe was written in the bottom of a dresser drawer in his bedroom. He returned to the closet, crossed his fingers, and punched in the numbers. A satisfying click brought a grin to his face. He turned the spoke handle retracting the bolt and pulled the heavy door open.

His friend had never mentioned his interest in hunting and firearms. Most Canadians were very low-key when it concerned firearms. The extreme restrictions in the country tended to intimidate their population into not discussing the matter. Hawks pulled the weapons from the safe and lay them out on the bed so he could see what his friend owned.

He found a Beretta 12 gauge his friend probably used to hunt ducks and geese. There were a number of boxes of steel shot shotgun shells on the top shelf. There was also a Winchester 1873, made by Umberti. Also stored on the shelf was Schofield pistol, both chambered in .45 long colt. Hanging in the closet was a Western outfit, period holster, cowboy hat, and boots. It was obvious his friend was into Western shooting competitions.

There were five hundred rounds of the .45 long colt ammunition. The Schofield pistol was in a cross-draw shoulder holster. A cartridge belt that would hold twenty-five rounds of ammo was easily adjustable around his waist. The Winchester 1873 had a period correct sling comprised of a leather pocket the rifle butt rested in. It was laced tight and attached to it was a leather sling with the other end attached to a sling loop clamped to the magazine tube.

He loaded the cartridge belt, the pistol, and the rifle. He adjusted the shoulder holster and the length of the sling on the rifle. The cowboy hat was an oilskin drover hat that fortunately fit. The long oilskin coat from the closet and a Bowie knife in a leather scabbard completed the outfit. The other two weapons in the safe were .22 rifles. He put the other guns back in the safe and locked it before heading downstairs wearing the pistol, the rifle slung over his shoulder, and the four bags of groceries. Just as he reached the bottom of the stairs, he could see through the window next to the door the beautiful lady from the ferry walking up the sidewalk.

CHAPTER 5

Dawson called out, "Just a second." He looked at Olivia. "Quick, put the duffel bags and backpacks on the other side of the bed out of sight." They quickly hid their gear before Dawson went to the door. "Who is it?"

"It's Tom Strahan; I'm one of the condo board members."

Dawson opened the door and looked into the eyes of a man wearing a heavy sweater and looking back through a pair of wire-rimmed glasses. He wore one of the goofy looking knit hats that had the long ear flaps hanging well below his ears and almost to his shoulders.

"Mr. Stewart, we have an emergency in the building. As you know, we've lost power and water pressure. The pipes will be freezing solid within hours, and the building will be uninhabitable for sanitary reasons. Everyone will have to leave the building until the situation is resolved." People had already started to leave the building, several people with packed bags headed down the hall toward the exits.

Dawson gave him a concerned look. "That's terrible; we'll get our stuff together and will be right out. We'll head over to my girlfriend's house."

"We'll give you a call; we have your cell number."

Dawson closed the door and Olivia asked, "What do we do now?"

"Simple, we stay put and let all the idiots go outside to freeze. Those idiots have their condo rules and their bylaws to live up to. They spend endless hours in committee meetings thinking up rules for everyone to live by. This is as close to being government officials as most of them will get, and a lot of what they come up with makes about as much sense."

Dawson put a note on the outside of the door that read, I have traveled to my girlfriend's house in the Northwest, call my cell phone if you need me. He closed the door and looked at Olivia. "I suggest we get all the covers on the bed and sack out for the night. The candle light can easily be seen from the window at night, so we'll have to blow it out."

Olivia gave him a serious look. "OK, I'll go to bed with you, but I'm not ready to sleep with you."

"You do realize that what you just said is a bit confusing, don't you?"

"You know what I mean."

Dawson stripped off his outer layers and was down to just his long johns and wool socks. "This is from Victor's Secret."

Olivia started laughing. "I am wearing almost the same outfit from Victor's as well."

They crawled into bed under the two comforters and snuggled to keep warm. Sometime in the night they woke long enough to add the sleeping bag from his truck on top. The next morning Dawson awoke to the wonderful feeling of Olivia cuddled in his arms. If this wasn't the end of the world, the moment would've been perfect. They rose and quickly dressed. Their breaths fogged even though they were inside the room. The milk in the refrigerator had not frozen. The insulated box of the refrigerator had slowed the temperature exchange slowly taking place. The milk and a box of pop tarts made a good, filling breakfast.

They could hear activity in the hall as people came and went.

Dawson opened the drapes and let the light stream in. They emptied the backpacks and lay out their bounty on the bed and on the breakfast table. In short order they had both packs loaded and adjusted so that the weight was riding on their hips.

After inventorying the freeze-dried food in the two duffel bags and including the food in the cabinets, they estimated they had about six weeks of food. If they were frugal and limited their calories, they could stretch it out to eight weeks. The problem they faced was the lack of heat. In the condo they were out of the wind, but the below-zero temperatures had already penetrated the building and made it almost intolerable. They needed to figure out a way of heating the room.

In their raid on the mountain hiking supply store, he had grabbed a couple of dozen candles and an extra candle lantern. He also procured a liquid fueled stove that would burn white gas or even unleaded gasoline. "I grabbed this one because I knew that there was a parking lot full of cars with gas in them. We can't use it inside unless the windows are open. There's a danger of carbon monoxide poisoning otherwise."

From his window they could see the alleyway behind the condo was getting busier. He recognized some of the people who had moved out the night before were returning, as he suspected there was nowhere for them to go. He called to Olivia, "Come see, there's no sense in us trying to leave. Here comes our neighbors who left last night."

"You were right. Unless we have a place to go or are forced out, our best bet is to hang out here for a while. At least we don't have to worry about getting up early to go to work tomorrow or maybe forever."

Dawson grinned. "I guess there's a silver lining to every cloud. How much cash do you have on you?"

"I only have eighty dollars, why?"

He pulled out the pouch from his daily pack that held his passport and wallet. He thumbed through the bills. "I have eleven hundred and fifty left; give me your eighty. There will be some people who will still accept cash for payment." He took her money and added it to his. "You stay here with the door locked and hand on the ice axe. Things won't start to get desperate for a couple of days, but I don't want to leave our food unguarded. I want to make a last run to see what I can buy or find. If I don't make it back, try to stay hidden, and if you have to go out to gather snow or fuel, do it only at night; the later the better."

"Hurry back, I don't think I can do this all by myself."

"You can do it; just remember you will have to do whatever it takes. By this time next week, you won't recognize the world we'll be living in."

Dawson took his money pouch and put the strap around his neck and dropped in under his shirt out of sight. He took his day-pack and dropped in a couple of the freeze-dried meals and his flashlight as he got ready to head out the door. Olivia hugged his neck and they kissed for their second time. "Please, come back soon."

"I will. If you get cold, get in the bed, but keep the door closed and stay back from the window. I don't want one of the bums to spot you and think you're vulnerable. Never appear vulnerable; they can sense weakness." Olivia closed the door and thought to herself as she reached for the lock, I am so lucky that Dawson is with me. I knew I was attracted to him for a reason.

He waited in the hall until he heard the dead bolt and slide lock close. He headed down the stairs and out of the back door. He first went to the little burger joint to see if the old man was still there. The old man was there, and he had a baseball bat lying on the counter. His wife and children were camping in the back room behind the kitchen. The old man lit up when he recognized

Dawson. "No cooking today, my friend. I'm hanging on to my food and keeping warm as long as the gas is flowing."

Dawson agreed. "I don't blame you; maybe you can help find something else. I'm looking for a firearm, and I can pay with cash, trade or both."

"I can't help you; all I've got is a baseball bat."

"Good luck, can I stop back in to get warm?"

"Sure thing, the heat's free as long as the gas holds out."

Dawson felt sorry for the man and his family. He knew they would probably be dead within the week unless they had some-where to flee. Dawson headed back down 17th Avenue. There were secondhand stores and pawn shops a mile or so down the road past the restaurant section. All the restaurants were closed, but one of the secondhand stores was open with a sign that said cash only. He pushed the door open; a bell rang. The bell hung on a hook suspended so that it would hit the top of the door when opening and closing. A short, middle-aged, Asian lady grinned as he came in. "Come in, cash only please."

Dawson grinned. "I've got cash; I just want to look around." He soon spotted an imitation black thorn walking stick. This one was made of a heavy black polymer and was quite stout. It would make an excellent defensive weapon if the need arose. Hefting the walking stick, he asked the lady, "How much for this?"

"Ten dollars."

He opened his pouch and pulled out the wad of cash and thumbed through it until he found a $10 bill and handed it to the lady. "Do you know anyone who would like to sell a gun?"

"It is illegal to own a gun unless you have permit."

"That's what I understand. I'm interested in an illegal gun."

She thought a minute while eyeing the roll of cash. "How much are you willing to pay?"

"Well that all depends on what kind of gun it is and if there is any ammunition with it."

She grabbed her parka. "Let me lock the door, and you come into the back with me. My uncle died last year, and he had a collection. My family is afraid to sell them or tell the government about them."

She led him through the store and out the back door. They walked up the alley, between two buildings, and across another street into a residential area. A half a block or so down the street she turned into a driveway next to an older home. In the back was a small apartment that was once a garage. The outline of the garage door opening was still there but an inset wall with a window was in its place. She dug around in her pocket and came out with a large ring of keys. She fumbled through them and produced a well-worn brass key and inserted it into the dead bolt. She pulled on the door and twisted the key. The lock opened with a thunk. She kicked the snow away from the door with her boots and said, "My uncle lived in here until he died last year. Most of his stuff is still in here. He was a very old man, and he did not trust the government. He came over from China with my parents back in 1949 when they escaped the communists. He never married and has no children. My brother and sister think I threw the guns in a dumpster."

The room had a warm feel; the walls were real wood paneling and the floor was large ceramic tile. The stove was an old Okeefe and Merritt gas stove. The room needed a good dusting, but the furniture was covered with spreads. She opened the drapes to let in some light and produced an old silver flashlight from a desk drawer. The room wasn't much bigger than his condo, but the gas stove was working in the small kitchen. One of the stovetop burners was burning on low to keep the pipes from freezing. Without speaking, she went to the closet and came out with several long guns and pistols and lay them on the small kitchen table. One of the long guns was a double-barreled, 12 gauge coach gun. The second was an old Remington bolt action .22 rifle, and the third was a Chinese SKS rifle. He turned to the pistols and held them up to the light. One was an old Smith and Wesson revolver in .38 caliber and the other was an H&R .22. The .22 was in a nylon holster that would fit on a belt. He asked, "Did he have any ammunition for them?"

"Yes, the box is heavy; you will have to lift it."

He hefted the large wooden crate and set it on the other end of the table. They opened the hasp and then the lid. Inside he found an unopened Spam can of ammo for the SKS, a five hundred round brick of .22 bullets, a twenty-five-round box of buckshot for the shotgun, and a box of fifty cartridges for the .38.

He looked around at the lady who had been patiently watching him look at the guns. "How much do you want for all of them?"

She put on her negotiating face. "These are very rare collectable pieces and are very valuable."

He smiled. "I'm from the southern US, and I've shot and owned many guns in my life. I have a sizeable collection in storage back home. These are good weapons, but none of them are rare or valuable. Each of these has been produced by the millions."

"How much you offer?"

"I'll give you five hundred dollars for the weapons, two hundred dollars for the ammo, and I want to talk to you about renting this apartment for me and my girlfriend."

"I'll take seven hundred dollars for the guns and two hundred and fifty dollars for the ammo. And I want five hundred dollars a month for the apartment rent."

He reached out his hand to shake. "It's a deal. If I can pay the apartment rent with a check, I'll give you three months in advance."

She shook on the deal, and he paid her the cash and wrote her a check that she could never cash. She gave him a key to the apartment. "If you need me, I'll be in the house or at the shop. My name is Angie Hang, but everyone calls me Henry because that's the name on the sign of the secondhand shop. I couldn't afford a new sign, so I kept the name, so my nickname is Henry."

"I'm glad to meet you, Henry; my friends call me Dawson."

She headed out the door. "Come see me if you need anything."

He loaded the .38 pistol and dropped it into the front pocket of his coat. He dropped twelve additional rounds into the other pocket and worked his way through the snow back to the condo. Olivia was waiting anxiously. "You weren't gone long; did you find anything?"

"I sure did; let's get packed up. I found us a small apartment with working gas heat. I'm not sure how long the gas will keep running, but for now it's warm."

Excitingly, she gave him a big hug and another smack on the lips. "I can't wait to see it."

They loaded up the backpacks and duffel bags and headed out the back door and down to the street to the new apartment. Once inside, they went about setting up housekeeping to see what else they needed to bring from the condo. The queen bed was missing the top mattress, but the kitchen was fully equipped. They stowed their gear and made two runs back to the condo. The stolen mattress from the condo along with the sheets and comforters wouldn't be missed anytime soon. The toolboxes in the back of his truck were large polymer boxes with dolly wheels built in. It was easy to transport them back to the apartment as well. The only thing they were missing were toiletries for Olivia. Once his truck and condo were emptied of everything usable, they finished setting up housekeeping at the new place.

Dawson spent an hour showing Olivia how to load and operate

the weapons and finished by letting her dry fire them. Unfortunately, there was no way he could conduct live fire practice in the city. He led her back to the secondhand store where Olivia, with help from Henry, bought a few missing items for her wardrobe. While she was shopping, he spotted a pharmacy just down the street being looted by some of the local street people. He walked inside and went straight to the first-aid section and grabbed the largest first-aid kit they had. Using a shopping basket, he filled it with feminine hygiene products, dry shampoo, toilet tissue, aspirin, acetamin-ophen, ibuprofen, toothbrushes, tooth paste, deodorant, cough medicine, butane lighters, and large trash bags. The last items he grabbed were in the birth control department; he was certain their relationship was going to move to the next level pretty soon.

Once he had stolen all he could carry, he headed back with everything in heavy-duty reusable bags. The streets were busy with people looking for food and drink. He kept to himself and didn't make eye contact as he made his way back to the second-hand store where he found Olivia waiting. Henry let them out of the back door, and they retraced their steps back to the apartment. Once inside they locked and bolted the door. Olivia was delighted to find he had procured a generous number of tampons and other items. When she got down to the birth control items, she held up one of the packages and gave him a look. "What is all this?"

He grinned. "Trade goods?"

"Don't you think you're pushing your luck, mister?"

"I figure that sooner or later you are going to catch me at a weak moment and seduce me." She punched him on the arm, and they kissed once again. He thought to himself this is the best first date he had ever had in his life.

CHAPTER 6

Hawks leaned the rifle behind the door and zipped his jacket, hiding the Schofield in its holster. He waited until she knocked on door, then waited a moment before opening it. Once again, he found himself drawn to her, and he desperately didn't want to feel that way again. She smiled. "I'm glad to see you again. I live across the street and recognized you from the ferry."

Hawks put out his hand. "I'm Bill Hawks, most people just call me Hawks."

She shook his hand. "I'm Carolyn Bishop. I don't want to bother you, but I just wanted to let you know that I live in the blue house across the street. I don't have much food in the house, but if you're hungry, I'm cooking the last of the meat from the freezer on the grill a little later."

Feelings he didn't want surfaced, and he couldn't bring himself to say no. "I look forward to it. What time do you want me to come over?"

"I'm not sure of the time, all my clocks have died. How about I come get you when I'm ready to put the meat on the grill? I'm sure you're better at grilling than I am." She smiled and turned. "I'll see you this afternoon."

He watched as she walked away. She was in her late forties to mid-fifties and a little more than five feet tall. Her hair was dark brown and fell almost to her shoulders. She was suntanned with dark eyes and a figure that was at one time athletic but was now softer in places. Her smile would be burned into his memory forever.

He closed the door and continued to watch as she crossed the street and disappeared through the gate on the side of the house. He was nervous and couldn't think. This was a turn of events he had not anticipated. He went into the small den and added a stick of wood to the heater. He poured himself another glass of bourbon and sat down for a few minutes to collect his thoughts, You're a grown man, an old man. What's wrong with you, you aren't a sixteen-year-old kid. He was consumed by guilt; it was almost as though he were running around on his wife.

The bourbon soon did its job, and he was once again at ease. Hawks was not a heavy drinker but had gotten in the habit of having a nightcap after dinner. He had decided to stop drinking as the breakdown of civilization was now underway. Today would an exception; despite the distraction, he had to get back to the business at hand. He spent the next few hours building crab traps from the poultry wire. The traps wouldn't last long in the salt water, but they would make good trade items and might even provide a few meals in the coming weeks. He retrieved his daily five gallons of water, ran it through his water filter, and drew the remaining water from the water heater and took a navy shower. He trimmed his beard and shaved all the scraggly patches of whiskers from around the edges. He looked in the mirror, Oh God help me, I feel like I'm trying to put a tuxedo on a mule.

He put on fresh clothes and his best pair of shoes and went into the kitchen where he mixed up some batter for biscuits. He fried some of the bacon on the stove in a cast-iron skillet and then fried the biscuits in the grease afterward. He took the Schofield, rifle, and ammo and stowed them back in the gun safe upstairs. He wasn't sure how Carolyn would feel about the weapons. Weapons were no big deal where he grew up and lived his entire life, but this was Canada.

Through the open drapes he saw Carolyn crossing the street and coming up to the door. Once again, he waited for the knock and let her in. Again, he was weakened by her smile. "I have the meat ready to go on the grill. I want you to do the seasoning."

"I have some fried biscuits with honey; give me a second to grab them." He considered retrieving the Schofield and hiding it under his jacket but decided not to. He wasn't that far away, even though the third day of the event was just starting to unfold. He threw another log in the heater so the basement would be warm when he got back. He let her carry the plate of biscuits and the jar of honey while he locked the door. He was nervous about leaving the basement unattended. He didn't want to take the chance of losing his food and gear.

As they walked across the street, he noticed he could still smell the aroma of people preparing meals outside. There were more and more people walking up and down the street. When they got to her house, she opened the door, and he went into a house that was clean and cozy. The kitchen was at the end of the hall and out from it was a deck with a gas grill. He noticed the house was warm and there was a candle lit in the kitchen. A large tray filled with pork chops and chicken was on the counter. She said, "If we don't cook it, it's going to all go bad."

"We can't let that happen. Where are your spices?"

"I don't have a lot, and I don't like hot spices." He produced the Maglite from his pocket and looked in her spice cabinet. He found a can of Greek seasoning in the back and with the addition of some salt had the meat seasoned and on the grill. The sun hadn't gone down yet, so while the meat smoked on the grill, they sat and talked.

Carolyn asked, "Hawks, are you a drinking man?"

"I take a sip every now and then."

"I have a small assortment to choose from. What do you like to drink?"

He smiled. "I always seem to enjoy the free stuff."

She laughed. "I have some bourbon, gin, Irish whiskey, and Scotch."

"I'll just take a shot of straight bourbon."

She gave him a big grin. "I knew it. You look like a bourbon man. I'll be right back."

She came back with a bottle of Wild Turkey and a bottle of wine. "This is my last bottle of wine, but I'll split it with you if want some."

"Oh no, I prefer the bourbon. Tell me about yourself."

"Well, there isn't a lot to tell. I'm fifty-four years old, divorced for fifteen years, and I work at the paper mill in the receiving department. I lived here with my dad until he died three months ago. I don't have any children and no brothers or sisters. I have some aunts and uncles, but none live here on the island, and I seldom see or talk to any of them. I don't do much outside of work. My off time was consumed taking care of my father until he passed. What's your story?"

He grinned. "I know what you're thinking; what's a handsome debonair man doing by himself living in a basement in a small community on Vancouver Island, so I'll tell you. I am a sixty-year-old widower, with two grown children and a grandson. I work as a consultant for construction companies and for industry. When they run into problems or anticipate problems, they call me to give them advice. I get paid whether they take my advice or not. I sold my house and land when I lost my wife and divided the rest of my belongings between my kids. I have a cabin in the Ozarks that I go to from time to time, but I don't have a home to speak of.

I usually make it to one kid or the other's place at Christmas, but they have their lives, and I don't want to be in the way."

She looked concerned. "That's so sad."

"It doesn't sound that bad, does it? I travel around when I'm between projects. I became good friends with some folks I worked with over in Calgary. They invited me to stay in their basement while I toured the island and relaxed for a while. I was planning on leaving for the Ozarks this week, but that was before the lights went out."

"It's sad that you're alone. Being alone is a terrible feeling. It wasn't so bad living here and taking care of my father. He was in reasonably good shape until the very last. He could get around and had his hobbies to keep him busy. He had a stroke and fell. He never regained consciousness and died within the week."

"It's never easy losing your parents. Mine have been gone for a long time now. My wife died of cancer. They found it during a routine office visit, and she was gone within the month. It was quite a shock, but there was little suffering. So I hung around and grieved for a few months and decided to just get on with living until something popped up. I have or had enough money to retire, but I figure what's the point?"

She gave him a puzzled look. "What do you mean you had enough money to retire?"

"I know you've noticed that the electricity's been off, but have you wondered why virtually every other electronic device has failed? Have you tried to crank your car, use your mobile phone or laptop?"

She said, "Of course I've wondered, but I figure I could get them looked at when everyone gets their power back on."

"Have you been enjoying the aurora?"

Carolyn glanced up. "Of course, they say it was the strongest one in recorded history."

"The last time an aurora of this magnitude struck was back in the 1800s. They called it the Carrington Event. Back in that time about the only thing electronic were the telegraph lines. It burned down telegraph offices, caused forest fires from the overheating wires, and there were reports that the operators could send and receive messages even when their batteries weren't hooked up. This aurora has dwarfed that one, and if what I've read is true, the electromagnetic pulse created essentially burns out virtually every integrated circuit. If the entire electrical grid in the northern hemisphere is knocked out, along with virtually every vehicle, then I am financially destitute. I have two hundred and fifty dollars cash money in my pocket that is only good so long as there are people willing to accept it; otherwise, it is only good for starting fires."

Hawks got up and turned the meat on the grill. "I assume you have gas heat from space heaters in your house; the gas pressure should last a while since most of it is directly fed from high-pressure gas wells. The problem is going to be food; how much do you have on hand?"

She thought for a moment. "I went to Walmart after work on Friday and bought my weeks' worth of groceries. With what I had on hand, I have maybe nine or ten days' worth. I have to buy milk and bread midweek; how about you?"

"I bought what I could for cash yesterday at the local grocery up the street. I have a six- or eight-week supply."

She unconsciously raised her hand to her throat. "Do you know what this means?"

"Yes, if the ferries aren't running and the food trucks aren't rolling, you are going to witness hell on earth starting in another twenty-four hours. Most people don't have a week's supply of food in their homes. Most will be running out after tomorrow."

She looked around. "Let's eat, then we've got to make plans.

We're going to have to get out of here." They helped their plates and ate their dinner at the kitchen bar to the light of a single candle. Carolyn started thinking out loud. "We've got to gather our food and head up the island to a more remote area. I have a friend that has a farm about a hundred and twenty-five miles from here in the interior of the island. If we can get there, we can make it for a while. There's tons of deer and wildlife to hunt. We can use my dad's hunting rifle."

Hawks asked her, "Do you have any idea how long it will take us to walk a hundred miles on this mountainous island?"

"If you can crank my dad's Model A Ford in the garage, we can ride."

"Model A, when's the last time it's been run?"

"We used it at his funeral. He and a group of his old buddies dressed up as clowns down at their club and would go around in it and entertain folks at the rest home and at schools. They ran it in the Christmas parade and other activities."

The talk of the running Model A Ford peaked his attention. "Do you think the battery is still charged?"

"It should be; we've always kept it on a battery maintainer. It never fails to crank right up."

Hawks perked up. "Can we go look at it?"

"Sure, bring your flashlight."

They went through the kitchen door out into the garage. There sitting on one side of the garage was the old Model A Ford. Hawks quickly gave it a once over. The tires were tight, and when he popped the hood, he discovered it had been upgraded to have hydraulic brakes and a twelve-volt starting system.

He said, "Our prospects have started looking up." He awkwardly realized that for the first time in over three years he used the term "our" when talking with Carolyn. He reluctantly told her, "I have to apologize, I don't want to be forward, but I don't expect you to include me in your plans. We've just met. I'll help you anyway I can, but please don't feel obligated to include me."

She smiled. "Let's get something straight. I've had my eye on you for the last six weeks. You've been quietly minding your own business coming and going. You helped me with my life vest, and you were nice enough to visit with me up on the deck. When the boat was fixing to crash into the logs, you cared enough to warn me to get away from the danger. No one else on board, including the captain and crew, had a clue about what was going to take place. You had every opportunity to get fresh with me when you helped me with my life vest and you didn't. The icing on the cake was when you ask for the bourbon. If you had requested the Scotch, you would be sitting over there in the basement by yourself. My ex was a Scotch drinker and the two or three other men I've been around since were Scotch drinkers. In my opinion, only real men drink bourbon. My dad and grand-dad were bourbon drinkers. I've laid out my cards, I'm a strong woman, and I've decided to take a last stab at happiness. Since this seems to be the end of the world as we know it, tell me why you are here?"

"Hell, I don't know. If I had that figured out, I probably wouldn't be here. You bring me comfort. I seemed to be drawn to you for reasons that make no sense to me. In fact, I have taken great pains to avoid getting myself into a position to be attracted to anyone ever again. I guess you might say that you're a gut feeling. My gut feelings are never wrong, so I am going to trust them one more time. So what do we do from here?"

She said, "If what we think is taking place is actually taking place, I don't want to stay alone. Do you know how to shoot guns?"

He grinned. "I'm from the southern United States; I'm familiar with guns."

"Good let's go look at my father's guns and see if there is anything we can use."

She led the way with a candle and went down into the basement where her dad had a workshop. The basement was a walkout that led out to the backyard. In one corner was a metal cabinet with a small lock. She fished around behind the workbench and retrieved a key hanging on a nail out of sight. She unlocked the cabinet, and he shined the light in. Her dad had a Browning Auto 5, 12 gauge made in Belgium. He carefully laid it out on the table. The next rifle he pulled out was a British .303 Enfield rifle. There was a single shot .22 rifle and on the top shelf a S&W .38 revolver and a S&W .22 revolver. There were belt holsters for both of the pistols. She opened a drawer in his workbench and brought out boxes of ammunition. There was a box of fifty bullets for the .38, two twenty-round boxes of hunting rounds for the .303, two boxes of bird shot for the 12 gauge, and five boxes of bullets for the .22 rifle and pistol.

Hawks turned to her and asked, "Have you ever shot any of these?"

"My dad let me shoot the pistols and the .22 rifle; he said the others would kick too hard and hurt me."

"He was right. You are a small person. The others would bruise you. You can easily shoot them from the waist, but I wouldn't want you shooting them from your shoulder unless it were unavoidable."

She took his arm and looked at him with her killer smile. "It's settled; I have a nice guest room. Go get all your stuff and bring it all over here. Tomorrow we'll make our getaway plans."

He gave her a serious look. "What do we do if the lights come back on?"

She never quit grinning. "How many couples do you know are fortunate enough to be able to lay their cards on the table within two days of meeting one another? I like you and you like me. We've got that part out of the way; the rest we can figure out. And besides, we can't do it the old-fashioned way."

He squeezed her arm. "You're right, I was never any good at all the courting and stuff. This really simplifies things. It'll take me a few trips to get my stuff moved. I've been accumulating a lot of stuff."

"No worries, I'll help."

It took them a half dozen trips to get all his stuff moved over. He would have to inventory her dad's shop before moving the tools from his friend's storage room. The last trip was bringing over the weapons and ammo from the gun safe upstairs. She watched as he jimmied the lock and got into the upstairs portion of the home. "Are you sure you aren't a cat burglar or something?"

He laughed. "No, I just understand how most things work." He pulled out the weapons and selected a Ruger bolt action .22 rifle for her to carry. "We'll take all the guns. We can use them for trade if the need arises. But I want you to pack something you can easily shoot. This Winchester rifle is too long for you, but this .22 has a shorter stock. You need to be able to hit with what you're packing. Tomorrow morning, I'll go through your dad's shop and through my friend's shed and put together a toolbox to travel with. That Model A doesn't have a lot of cargo area, so we'll have to see what we can lash to the top."

He looked back at his friend's house, See you around old basement, it's been fun.

He moved into the guest room and stacked all the food in the kitchen. He then put the shoulder holster with the Schofield back on. He asked Carolyn, "What are you doing for water?"

"I have rain barrels hooked to the gutters. Water is so expensive here on the island, we set up rain barrels for water in the garden and such. I've drawn off enough to heat on the stove and pour it over my head in the shower. I also use it to flush the toilets as needed." They were just settling in when there was knock at the door. They both looked at one another; he slipped on his jacket to hide the Schofield. When they answered, they were greeted by a man with a clipboard.

Carolyn asked him, "How can I help you?"

The man quickly went into his oft recited speech. "I'm Gregory Mitchell with the City Council. Because of the ongoing emergency, we are asking everyone to come to a town meeting in the gymnasium of the high school tomorrow morning at nine a.m. You will need to bring a list of the food that you have on hand as we are setting up a food bank that everyone in town will be drawing from until the crisis is over. We have lost all communication with the outside world and with each other for that matter. We suggest that you bring what food you can carry when you come. We will then redistribute the food. Also please jot down which houses are vacant so that we may enter those dwellings to see if there is any food available."

Hawks touched Carolyn on the arm and spoke, "Thank God y'all are getting geared up to help us. We are just about out of food. We normally go for groceries on Saturday, but our cars died."

The man stammered a bit. "Anyway, bring what you can, and we'll see you at the meeting."

Carolyn closed the door and looked at Hawks. "What do we do?"

"We aren't going to the meeting, and we aren't giving away our food. It didn't take them long to figure out that they were all going to starve to death. If everyone does what he is asking, they will all be starving to death inside the week, and we will all die together with the exception of the councilmen and the police enforcers."

Carolyn said, "It's decided. We pack up and leave in the morning. I'm not going to the meeting, and if anyone tries to stop us, they'll have a problem."

Hawks admired her spunk. "Let's get some sleep and get up early to pack."

She put her arms around his neck. "Give me a kiss. This has been a memorable first date." This was his first kiss in a very long time.

Gregory Mitchell continued down the sidewalk with the aroma of the meal from the Bishop's house still in his head. His meal tonight had been a can of cold Vienna sausage. He recounted the council meeting in his mind as he made his way down the sidewalk to the next house. The mayor was nowhere to be found, so the first order of business was to elect an acting mayor. Mohammed Igthus was elected by a unanimous vote. He thought to himself, No one would dare vote against him for fear of being labeled an Islamaphobe. Igthus was probably the most unqualified person on the board, and if it weren't for the generous welfare system, he would probably be living on the streets.

The main topic of the meeting was the loss of power and communication. The meeting quickly turned to the matter of food. Everyone at the meeting was close to running out. A consensus was quickly reached that an inventory of the community food would have to be made. After it was decided that an inventory must be made, the next topic was a warehouse and distribution system. The local high school was the logical place because of its size and central location.

A hierarchy of distribution was quickly developed. The council and police force would have to be fed first since they were in charge of managing the disaster relief. Then the people on welfare because they would be the most in need. What wasn't said out loud but what was foremost on everyone's mind was the fact they couldn't let their most loyal supporters go hungry. The next group would be the families with children. Single people and couples would be next, and the elderly would be last as they were expendable and would die soon anyway.

The police were already looking for running generators to commandeer for the public good. He thought, I may need to start collecting what food I can as I go door to door. I need something to eat for breakfast in the morning. He walked up to the door of the next house and knocked.

CHAPTER 7

When Olivia woke the next morning, she found Dawson standing at the front door looking out the window. She thought to herself, This has to be one of the fastest courtships that has ever taken place. If this weren't the end of the world, would I still be sitting alone every night reading romance books?

She stretched and asked, "What are you seeing?"

"Trouble; the streets are already filling up with people. This is the third day; the pantries are beginning to go bare. I imagine all the grocery stores are being looted about now. We are going to need to lay low. I think we need to have our backpacks loaded and ready to go in case we have to bug out. If things start to get out of hand, we won't have time to stop and pack. I figure in a couple of more days it's going to bust loose around here. Let's keep the coat pockets loaded with the power and protein bars from our stash from the backpacking store."

Olivia wrapped her nude body in a blanket and joined him at the window. "I can't believe there's that many people out in this kind of cold."

Dawson let the curtain fall back in place over the window. "The lights aren't back on, so you know they aren't going to work. They're looking for food, water, and heat."

She took his hand. "Let's get our stuff together. I don't want to get caught flat-footed."

They quickly dressed and laid out the contents of their backpack once again to make certain they had the essentials. The backpacks would be worn over their coats. The parkas and the extreme cold sleeping system would be strapped to the outside of the packs. The camelback water system was filled with the boiled water from melted snow. Each pack would have enough food for the two of them for seven days. Dawson would have the .38 in his pocket with loose ammo in the opposite pocket. Olivia would wear the .22 on her belt with the ammo for it in the opposite pocket as well.

They lay the layers of clothing in the order they would be put on. If they had to move, they could be up and out in less than five minutes complete with packs, guns, and ammo. He told her, "I'll carry the SKS rifle, and you carry the 12-gauge coach gun. It kicks like a mule, but you have a better chance of hitting your target. Just be ready to hand it to me if I ask for it. I have a lifetime of hunting and shooting; I hope you won't have to learn by shooting at people." He had found an ammo pouch in the dead uncle's belongings in one of the bureau drawers. It would fit over his head and held two hundred rounds of ammo for the SKS on ten round stripper clips. They were surprised when they heard gunfire in the street outside. Dawson couldn't see anything through the window, so he went back to the chore of organizing their gear. He took the toolboxes and emptied them of their contents. All the freeze-dried food not in their backpacks was placed in one of the toolboxes along with the canned goods. They then added the canned and packaged food items from the condo along with the .22 rifle and the .22 ammunition. He also included a basic set of tools along with a bolt cutter and a small shovel. The box was heavy, but if worse came to worse, they could ditch it. Until then they left it open and concentrated on eating the canned goods because of the high weight-to-calorie ratio. There would be no need to carry metal cans unless they had no other choice.

They spent the rest of the day staying inside and watching from their windows. Other than seeing people passing on the sidewalk across the driveway, it was by and large quiet. The clear weather turned back to heavy snow. This slowed the movement of people. Dawson was certain the city was filling with people who were now freezing to death. Even in a region where people were accustomed to subzero temperatures, people would be freezing. Most modern people weren't prepared for the utilities to fail. Their ancestors had wood heat and supplies of firewood on hand and lots of cover for their beds. Even though most of the people in this modern city had warm clothes to brave the cold, it was only enough clothes for a short walk to work or a dash to the nearest doorway where warmth awaited. People would have to wear their outdoor clothes and cower under their covers in beds to survive these temperatures without heat. The cold would also cause their bodies to burn more energy to stay warm. Hunger would force them out into the city to look for food. The inevitable bounty of corpses would soon be a source of food once the supply of cats and dogs dried up.

They were quietly playing a game of cards when a knock came at the door. With his .38 revolver in his hand, Dawson peeped through the curtain. Henry was at the door all bundled up. He opened it up and let her in. "Mr. Dawson, I need you to do me a favor."

"What's up, Henry?"

"I have not heard from my husband since all of this started. He was in Toronto, so I imagine that he is stuck there. My daughter and grandchildren made it here last night.

"We have plenty of food, but I am very afraid. My husband

took one of my uncle's guns and kept it in the house, but I don't know how to use it."

"Sure thing, where is it?"

She opened her large purse and pulled out a Colt 1911 pistol. It was in a holster that could be put on a belt. Dawson took the pistol and hit the button to eject the magazine. It was loaded with full metal jacket bullets. He cocked the hammer, pulled back the slide, and saw the chamber was empty. He turned to her and asked, "How many bullets do you have for this?"

She dug around in the purse and came out with a full fifty round box and four loaded magazines. The big semiautomatic pistol dwarfed her small hand. He unloaded the S&W .38 and handed it to her. "I want to show and explain some things to you about guns and shooting. I want you to pick this gun up and aim it, and then I want you to pick up your husband's gun and aim it." Henry picked them up and aimed them.

When she sat them down, he asked, "Did you feel the difference in the weight and how they felt in your hands?"

"Yes, my husband's gun is very heavy and harder for me to get my hand around."

"The important thing to remember is that these are tools, just like a hammer or screwdriver or a knife. You need to be able to hold and manipulate it to use it properly. I'm going to show you how to operate both guns. The main thing I want you to remember is that bigger does not mean it's better. Being able to fire it and hit with it is the most important thing. I can't stress to you how important that is. Do you have any idea how a gun works?"

She looked at him. "Only what I have seen on TV and in the movies."

"OK, well, I'm going to start from scratch. Olivia, I want you to listen with Henry as I explain and show you guys the mechanics of this."

He spent the next hour going over the components of a cartridge and how the guns worked. He let Henry dry fire the weapons. He showed her how to load and charge the Colt and how to load the S&W .38. She had great difficulty operating the Colt because of the dimensions and the strength of the slide spring. Although he knew the answer, he asked, "Which of these two guns are you more comfortable using? Both will kill a man and both will shoot through doors and walls unless they are made of brick or concrete."

Henry pointed at the S&W .38. "This one is easier; will you sell it back to me?"

Dawson shook his head. "No, I will not sell it back to you, but I will trade you for your husband's gun. My hand is bigger, and I have one just like it in my collection back home."

"My husband might get mad at me if I trade his gun."

Dawson agreed. "I tell you what I'll do. I'll trade back any time you want to. If your husband comes back, I have no problem swapping them back."

Henry put out her hand to shake. "It's a deal."

Dawson told Henry, "I recommend that you not only lock your doors but you need to put some warning devices such as jars of marbles or empty cans on any ground floor or basement window that you can't barricade. The pantries are going bare, and people are going to get desperate. I hope you have plenty of food. You also need to prepare to leave with your daughter and grandchildren if your house becomes uninhabitable. I recommend that you put together some backpacks for each of you. Think about what it will take for you to survive until you can get to a relative's house or to a friend's house where you can take shelter."

Henry took the loaded .38 and the box of ammo for it and put it in her purse. "Mr. Dawson, you are scaring me; I have to start thinking like you."

Olivia interrupted. "If I hadn't followed him, I would be eating my roommate's cat about now."

Henry laughed. "My father and uncle called the dish Little Tiger. They said that cat was quite delicious. I don't want to find out. My father and uncle lived through World War II in China; they knew starvation. My basement is full; if you and Olivia stay and help protect us, you won't go hungry."

"Thanks, Henry. I appreciate you making me the offer, and I will protect you as long as I'm here. But I need to also caution you on something else. If anyone outside of us were to find out about the food in the basement, we will be overrun and murdered. From outward appearances, we need to appear to be destitute and starving. If anyone shows up, ask them for food or offer to pay them for food or animals. Don't buy any raw meat unless you can identify it. The city will be starting to fill up with corpses now. There are over a million people in Calgary and about 95 percent of them will be missing their first meal today. Do you have everything back at your shop that you and your daughter may need?"

"Nobody but you know about my food and supplies. I have some backpacks that I bought last year that I need to go get. I'm afraid to go by myself. Will you go with me?"

"Sure thing, let's go while it's snowing. Let's show your daughter how to use the pistol, and we'll go."

Olivia spoke up, "You guys hurry. I don't like staying here by myself."

Dawson gave her a hug. "I won't be long; you know how to use your pistol. Remember if you have to shoot someone, don't stop pulling the trigger until they are down, and then put one through their head for good measure."

"I know."

Dawson put on his Columbia outer gear and wore the Colt on an extra leather belt over his ski pants. It was hidden under his jacket but was easily accessible. He and Henry stepped out into the cold, and he waited until he heard Olivia lock and bolt the door. They crossed the driveway and went up the steps into the side door leading into the kitchen of Henry's house. The kitchen was warm as it had a similar gas stove with the burners running. Henry's daughter was a strikingly beautiful Asian lady that looked like he imagined Henry to have looked twenty years earlier. The young lady was all of five feet tall and maybe a hundred pounds. She had two small children who looked like little Eskimos with their heavy sweaters and stocking caps.

Henry introduced her. "This is my daughter, Cathy, and her four-year-old twins, BC and Lucy. And guys, this is Dawson, who is staying in Uncle's room with his girlfriend Olivia." She pointed to the twins. "You two, go play; we adults have something to do." She reached in her purse and pulled out the S&W .38.

Henry turned to Cathy. "I want you to let Dawson show you how to use this."

Cathy interrupted. "Mother, you know how I feel about fire-arms. I would rather die than use one of them."

Henry gave Dawson a disgusted look. "See what I am dealing with?"

Dawson pulled off his coat, hung it on the corner of the kitchen chair, and looked at Cathy. "Would you use it save your twins' lives?"

Cathy smartly answered, "I don't believe in violence."

"Me neither, but I want you to answer my question. Would you consider using violence to save your children's lives?"

"Of course, I want to protect my children."

"I'm not going to show you how to go out and rob people on the street or get in a gang war; I simply want to show you how to use a simple tool."

"You don't understand. I don't think I could shoot anyone."

"I understand, I'm not sure I can shoot anyone either. I haven't been put in that situation as of yet. But tell me, do you think you can shoot the gun up into the ceiling?"

"Yes, I can do that."

Dawson then asked, "If someone were trying to break in, do you think you could shoot the ceiling to let them know that you are armed with a gun?"

"Yes, I can do that."

"Now, let's assume that they are trying to break in and you fired your gun but that didn't deter them; can you assume that they are crazed lunatics? Only a lunatic would keep trying to break in. Would you allow someone, who is no doubt a crazed lunatic, kill your children?"

Cathy sat speechless. Dawson continued, "Of course, you wouldn't. This pistol is neither good nor bad. It's an inanimate object. It is no different than a hammer or a baseball bat or the boots on your feet. All can be used to defend yourself. You are a beautiful one-hundred-pound woman; unless you have a black belt in karate, you can't defend yourself against a two-hundred-pound lunatic or several of them. This little piece of steel is a tool, nothing more. There are over a million people in this city who have just missed their first meal; what do you think this city is going to be like in three more days?" The twins came running back into the room.

Cathy looked over at them. "Oh God, I never thought of that. Show me how to use it."

He took a few minutes to walk her through using the gun. He reloaded it and told her, "Don't let the twins play with it."

"Don't worry."

Henry and Dawson donned their coats and headed down the driveway through the driving snow. Dawson looked around in every direction as they proceeded down the street. He was glad the snow was quickly hiding their tracks. They went through the alleyway and into the back of Henry's shop. She quickly gathered up the used backpacks and camping gear. She turned to Dawson. "I thought I made a mistake by buying all this stuff. Some college guys brought all this stuff in about six months ago. I didn't think I could sell it. Nobody was interested in it."

In addition to the backpacks, she had some sleeping bags, lanterns, and camping utensils.

Dawson made a quick walk through the shop and gathered up all the candles and some candlesticks. He asked, "Do you have any quilts or comforters?"

"I took all of those home already."

He looked over in the corner where he found the imitation blackthorn walking stick. There were several more of the black polymer walking sticks. One looked like a fireman's axe, one was a Kubaton, and the last one was a long blackthorn walking stick. He also found three pairs of hiking walking sticks that would come in handy if they had to make a long trek in the snow. He almost overlooked several plastic sleds with rope pulls. He grinned. "What do we have here?"

Henry looked up. "I forgot about those; they have been here so long. The bums around here bring in all sorts of things to sell. I bought all three of them for fifteen dollars."

"They are exactly what we need." He took a step ladder and got them down. "We can gather up all our gear and carry it back to the house in these. And if you need to evacuate, you can put the twins and supplies in them and move quickly and quietly."

"Mr. Dawson, you are so smart. I am so upset; I can't think straight."

"Henry, most people don't have to think about what can happen. I happen to have lived through Hurricane Katrina when it blew through the Gulf Coast. I know first-hand what happens when society collapses. I saw how people reacted and acted after it hit. Help was on the way, but many of the people turned into savages. I have no doubt that the same thing is starting to happen here. The weather is forcing people inside right now, but that is going to change and change fast. Do you have any straps or cordage around here?"

"Sure, look in the tool section. I have cargo straps and a big roll of green shoelace cord."

He gave her a questioned look. "Shoelace cord?"

"That's what the man who sold it to me said it was. I'll show you."

They went over into the small tool section where she pointed to the roll sitting on the shelf. Dawson took one look. "That's called paracord. It is what they use to make parachute lines." He took his pocket knife and cut off a piece and pulled out the seven strands of the inner cords. "This cord can suspend five hundred pounds. Each of the strands inside can be used for thread or twine or whatever you can think of. This is very useful to have around. We'll carry this back." While they were back in the corner, he flipped on his LED light and peered into the shelves. He spotted a propane torch and some extra disposable propane bottles. "We'll take these as well."

Henry asked, "My husband bought all this. I didn't know what it was."

Dawson squeezed the trigger on the torch and it spouted a sharp blue flame. Henry grinned. "We might need that."

They finished loading the sleds and were about to drag them out into the alleyway when they heard a crash in the front of the store. Dawson said, "People will be breaking into all the stores now. We need to get out of here before they see us."

Henry was angry. "There's nothing in here worth dying for. Let's get out." They pulled the sleds into the alley, and she locked the door behind her. "This is a dead bolt; it will take them a few minutes to break out through this door."

Dawson looked both ways and started up the alley. A group of men were walking down the alley from the opposite direction. Dawson and Henry turned to cut through the walk between the buildings taking them over to the street where they lived. "Henry, I want you to lead the way. If they turn to follow us, I want to be where I can shoot." Without question she turned and headed up the walk. The sled made a smooth groove in the fresh snow. They were about halfway up the walk when Dawson looked back and saw the men turn and head in their direction.

One of the men called out, "Wait up, and we'll help."

Dawson called back, "Stay back, we don't need any help."

He could see the grin on the man's face. "You don't understand. We said we are going to help."

Dawson told Henry, "Keep going, and don't look back." He already had the Colt in his hand and concealed behind his pants. "Guys, please don't come any further."

One of the guys raised a baseball bat that had been concealed under his coat. "Beg some more, buddy."

Henry did as she was directed and doubled her efforts, heading along the walkway dragging her sled. She almost leaped out of her skin when she heard seven loud gunshots.

CHAPTER 8

After a long embrace, Hawks told Carolyn, "There's no way I can go to sleep right now. I want to start getting ready tonight if that's OK with you."

"I'm with you. I don't want to wait and get caught up in all this. Come out back and I want to show you what my dad was working on out in the shed. He put a hitch on the Model A and was working on a period camper."

They went back down the basement stairs and out through the back door. They followed the walkway back to the shop in the back. Carolyn raised the rolling garage door to reveal a period travel trailer. He quickly went around the little camper using the light from the Maglite. It appeared to be almost complete. The camper was only about fourteen feet long. Its bathroom was a sink and a portable toilet. The kitchen had a small ice box, sink, and propane stove. A double bed was in the back and a small dinette in the front. It would provide shelter and the extra cargo area they needed to make it to the farm. The only thing he could see that it needed was some trim work and paint.

He came around to the front and looked at Carolyn, "Let's get her loaded up. We should be able to get everything we need in the camper and in the Model A. I would like to be pulling out at day-light in the morning. I don't trust these people; I assure you they aren't interested in whether we're OK or not. They will be feeding themselves and their families first. I promise you; we are low on the food chain as far as these idiots are concerned."

"I don't trust them either."

"I think they will be successful in keeping themselves fed. There are enough naïve people that will willingly turn over their food to them. But nothing is going to stop what is ultimately going to take place. Can you imagine what will take place if the starving population of Victoria make it this far?"

Carolyn said, "Let's make a list of priorities. After that we'll make a wish list."

Hawks said, "Just remember we are escaping in vehicles that are over eighty years old with a small engine and limited weight capacity. I don't want to destroy the transmission, blow a tire, or burn up the engine. We'll have to go slow, and we may have to stop often. We may be on foot before it's over, so we need to plan on how we're going carry what we need in the event the Model A breaks down."

They went back to the kitchen, where under the light of the candle they started their list. They decided they had to carry all the food, all the weapons, ammo, and medicine. They also needed to outfit the camper with pots, pans, dinnerware, cutlery, napkins, toiletries, and dry goods. All of Hawks' clothes fit in a rolling suitcase, so Carolyn would have plenty of room for her stuff. Carolyn asked, "Can I take some of my family mementos in case I can't come back?"

"Sure, I recommend that you put the photos in envelopes. We can always find or make frames in the future."

"I have all but a handful in albums."

"I think we can tuck them away somewhere."

They spent the next four hours loading up the Model A and the camper. A bicycle hand pump in the garage was used to top off the air in the camper tires. He took the battery from Carolyn's dead SUV and hooked it up to the little camper to power its lights and water pump. He told Carolyn, "Cross your fingers that it will last until we get to the farm."

While going through the mementos, Carolyn came out with her grandfather's gold pocket watch. "This hasn't been wound in years; see if it still works. We can at least get some idea of the time of day. It gets daylight at around 8:00 a.m. this time of year. If it works, we'll set it at 8:00 a.m. as soon as it's light enough to see."

Dawson gently wound the stem and watched as the little round dial with the second hand came to life. He looked to see Carolyn grinning. She said, "So far so good. I can remember my grandfather pulling it out to let me listen to it tick."

"Looks like it's found a new life."

She rubbed his shoulders. "I'm tired. Let's go to bed. Tomorrow's going to be a big day." They headed down the hall toward the bedrooms. She opened the door and watched as he headed toward the guest room. "Don't I get a goodnight kiss?"

Hawks grinned. "I guess I could part with one more." She threw her arms around his neck and tiptoed to reach his lips. He stooped down and received a toe-curling kiss. She thought for a minute, then took his hand. "I don't want to sleep alone."

"Me neither, I'm sick of being alone."

Hawks was almost overcome with guilt and fright. His first impulse was to say no, but he could hear his old bachelor friend, Heston, giving him advice. There had been a number of widows and divorced women attending the Christmas party last year. Several of them latched on to him, and it was a chore to escape their attention. He could just hear the advice he received, "You better go for the gusto while you still can, old boy. You ain't getting any younger, and after all, you are single." This was somehow different. This didn't feel like he was taking advantage of a desperate woman. He took a deep breath and decided to throw caution to the wind.

The next morning, they woke early, and although they had very little rest, they were alert and ready for their escape. She went into the kitchen and retrieved the bacon and eggs from the ice chest on the porch. The forty-degree weather kept the food cold, so while she cooked breakfast, Hawks went into the garage to get the Model A cranked.

His father's hobby had been buying and restoring old cars. Back in the nineteen sixties his dad had restored a Model A. Hawks mostly held and fetched the tools, but his dad showed and taught him how to do it. He explained how and why he did things and explained how the cars worked.

The first thing he did was check the oil and the fluid level in the radiator. Next, he emptied a can of gas into the fuel tank until it was topped off. He then siphoned the gas out of the SUV into the can and into a couple of other empty ones. The siphon hose was then coiled up and secured to the top of one of the cans with some cordage. He secured the three gas cans to the top of the rear bumper. It wasn't the ideal way to transport them; but they only had a hundred or so miles to go, and he didn't want the gas riding with them inside the car.

With the hood open, he reached down and flipped a large lever switch above the starter, closed the hood, and then slid into the driver's seat. He reached under the dash and turned the valve that let the gas flow to the carburetor. The valve was just off center of the dash on the passenger side. Here was also located the choke and idle adjustment screw. The carburetor on the Ford Model A was located on the passenger side of the engine. Digging through his memory, he recalled it was a requirement the spark advance lever had to be all the way up until the engine was cranked and that it helped to have the throttle lever pushed up a bit to make it idle fast.

He set the hand brake and got out to un-chock the wheels and make one last walk around. He slid back in the seat, crossed his fingers. He depressed the clutch and shifted the car into neutral and turned the key to the on position. He pulled out the choke nob and stepped on the starter button. The engine spun and caught. He closed the choke and pushed the spark control down until the engine smoothed up a bit, then adjusted the idle knob until the engine purred. He hopped out and opened the garage door before the fumes built up to the point of asphyxiation. Releasing the hand break and putting the transmission in low gear, he pushed the accelerator pedal and eased off the pressure on the clutch.

The Model A pulled out of the garage and out into the cold air. He pulled out into the street and shifted into reverse where he backed down the drive to the shop where the little camper awaited. Carolyn waited with a flashlight and directed him so that the trailer hitch ball and the hitch on the camper were aligned. He killed the engine and set the handbrake.

He slid out to be greeted by Carolyn smiling, "You backed it up like a pro. I think we're going to make a great team."

"What are you talking about? I think we are a great team."

She grabbed him and gave him a hug and kiss. "C'mon in, our breakfast is getting cold."

They spent the next two hours packing and securing their cargo. He strapped a large wooden toolbox to the top of the Model A. He gritted his teeth as he realized the damage the box was doing to the paint on top of the car. "I'm sorry, Carolyn. I don't know of any other way to do this without damaging the paint."

"Don't worry. This is a tool for us to use to get to a safer location. If times return to normal, you'll have a project to restore if that's what you want to do. If we die, it won't matter if the paint is undamaged on the top."

"Thanks for understanding."

Carolyn fried the rest of the bacon and put it in a jar, then covered it with the hot grease from the skillet and sealed the top. She then sacked up bread and biscuits she had baked that morning so they would have something to eat while they traveled. Empty milk jugs were filled with filtered rain water and several drops of chlorine were added before sealing. Hawks came through the back door with the .38 pistol on a leather belt. "Strap this on and put a handful of the cartridges in your left coat pocket. You're right-handed, aren't you?"

She gave him a mischievous look. "Think about it for a minute."

He thought and blushed. "Like I said, put these in your left pocket because you'll be holding on to the gun with your right hand."

He made a quick run back through his friend's storage shed, unlocked the basement, house, and gun safe. There was no need in leaving them locked. They would only be kicked in by looters and/or the government.

When he got back to Carolyn's, she was finishing up. "I'm leaving the place unlocked. The doors will only get kicked in if they find the place locked up."

The sun started to light the horizon as they climbed into the Model A. Hawks cranked the car and pulled the camper out of the shed. Once out, he took canvas tarps, covered the toolbox on the top of the car and the cargo strapped to the top of the camper, and closed the rolling door on the shop. He commented as he handed her the gold watch and climbed in. "Set the watch at 8:00. We are now on island time. I think we look like the pictures on the internet of the people in the dustbowl back in the nineteen thirties."

Carolyn waved at the house. "Goodbye, old house, I hope to see you again one day. I hope we didn't forget anything important?"

"I don't see how. We have fuel, water, food, clothing, and shelter. I just hope we can make the trip without trouble or a breakdown. We'll have to go slow and easy. Just follow my lead if we are stopped or attacked. Just do what I say when I say it. My job has taken me all over the world, and some of the places were not exactly resort areas. I've been in three all-out firefights while working for military contractors in the Middle East and Afghanistan.

"It's not anything I'm proud of, but I've shot at and killed men. It was us or them. I didn't follow up on the men I shot. I simply stopped them where they stood and then ran for my life. Your new boyfriend is basically a coward. When Winston Churchill said that one of life's most sublime experiences was to be shot at and missed, he was right. I'm not telling you this to tell you that I'm some sort of macho man. I just want to let you know that I am not the type to panic.

"We'll keep our fingers crossed that we can quietly weave our way up through the country without incident." The Model A pulled the camper up the driveway and out into the street. He kept the engine slow and quiet; he didn't want to advertise their departure. They stopped at the intersection, turned left, and then took the first right. It was downhill to Main Street, so he depressed the clutch and let the car and camper coast to the bottom of the hill. They took a left and, without stopping at the intersection, slowly proceeded up Main Street past the grocery, hardware, and second-hand shop. Hawks thought for a moment. "Do you know what we didn't hear this morning?"

Carolyn gave him a questioning look. "What are you talking about?"

"We didn't hear the geese waking up. They usually wake up the entire town."

"I imagine they've been harvested."

"No doubt. I made my bow and arrow set with the idea of doing just that."

"The geese are so accustomed to being fed; they probably walked right up to the hunters."

Hawks agreed. "Just like all the welfare recipients around here. They will be heading up to the meeting this morning looking for a handout." They reached the intersection at the top of the hill and took a right that took them past the Brass Cannon.

Two young men dressed in black uniforms walked out into the middle of the street blocking the road. Both were wearing side arms and brandishing assault rifles. Carolyn grabbed Hawks' arm. "Baby, what do we do now?"

"Just keep quiet and don't panic; I'll handle it. They don't expect us to be armed or to put up any resistance. Don't pull out your gun; I don't want to let them know we're armed. I'll try and talk us through." Hawks stopped the car and rolled the window down and in his best southern country voice asked, "What can I help you boys with this morning?"

The one on the driver's side spoke, "I'm afraid you're going to have to exit the vehicle. We are commandeering every running vehicle and all food and medicine. It will be redistributed in the coming days from the high school."

Hawk meekly asked, "Do you want me to drive it over to the high school?"

The man answered, "No, sir, we'll have to drive it."

Hawks asked, "Have you ever driven a Model A Ford. Do you know how to double-clutch it?"

The man gave him a puzzled look. "I've never heard of that."

"Why don't you stand here on the running board while I make the block to the high school? We can be there by the time I explain it to you."

The man looked across to this partner. "Wait here; I'll be back in a few minutes."

Hawks nodded with his head. "Open the back door and roll down the window. You can hook your arm around the door post while you stand on the running board. I won't go fast, mainly because this thing doesn't go fast." Hawks looked over at Carolyn, who was petrified, and gave her a wink. The young man climbed aboard as Hawks gently pulled away from the intersection and took a left heading up the hill. When he was halfway up the hill, he double-clutched it, shifted to second gear, and increased his speed. As he approached the second turn, he reached into his jacket and pulled out the Schofield. He slowed to a stop as if he were going to make the turn, cocked the gun, turned in his seat and shoved the gun into the young man's midsection, while grasping the man by the gun belt, forcing him against the car.

"Son, what you do in the next five seconds will determine if you live or die. I have a cocked .45 caliber pistol buried in your belly. My finger is on the trigger, and I'm nervous as a cat. Keeping that assault rifle pointed in the air, I want you to put it in the back seat butt first. Then you're going to ever so carefully remove the pistol from your holster and drop it into the back seat as well. The slightest fast or wrong move by you will make me pull this trigger, and your guts will be scattered out all over this road; do you understand?"

The man stammered, "Y-Yes, s-sir."

"Now, the rifle first." The young man did as he was told. "Now the pistol. Remember, the slightest wrong move, and you're dead." Once again, he complied.

Hawks gave the man a shove, and he fell backward off the running board. He landed on his back on the pavement. Before the man could get up, Hawks punched the accelerator and headed up the hill. The man got up yelling obscenities. Hawks looked at Carolyn, who was now grinning. She said, "I would have just shot him."

"If I had been alone, I would have. I wasn't sure how you would handle it."

"Let me tell you how I would handle it—just shoot next time. Don't hold out on account of the way I might feel about something. Now that we are a couple, our job is to take care of each other. It's you and me against the world."

Hawks double-clutched the Model A, shifted it into third gear, and kept the speed under thirty-five miles per hour. The cold weather and slow speed kept the engine temperature under control even though the car was exceeding its towing capacity.

The heater on the Model A consisted of a metal shroud with the intake just behind the radiator. While underway, Carolyn got up on her knees on the front seat, reached into the back seat, and rolled up the rear window. The cabin of the car quickly warmed up. They slowly wormed their way through the country roads, driving around stalled cars and trucks as they went. Occasionally they would see people walking up and down the roads. People on horseback were encountered on numerous occasions, and they resisted the urge to stop and chat. The tough little Model A performed flawlessly as they made their way to the farm. On one particularly long uphill climb, the thermometer on the radiator cap started to climb. They pulled into a scenic overlook to give the engine a chance to cool and to stretch their legs.

Hawks pulled out their newly acquired assault rifle and examined it. It was a short Colt C7, which was the Colt M4 variant used by the Canadian army. It held one thirty-round magazine. The pistol was a Browning 9 mm with a thirteen-round magazine. He shortened the stock on the Colt for Carolyn and showed her how to fire it. "We only have one thirty-round magazine, so we won't shoot it unless we have to. The same with this 9 mm pistol. I wish

I had taken the man's gun belt so we'd have a holster and more ammo."

Carolyn adjusted the sling to fit her body. "At least we have some additional firepower or trade items." They went back to the camper where she broke out some bread and jam. She pulled out the gold pocket watch. "It's 11:00 a.m. island time. We've sure had a busy two days. How long should we let the car cool?"

"I think another forty minutes to an hour will be enough. I'll top off the water, and we'll finish the climb. The old timers would probably be laughing at me for giving the old gal a cool down. They would have probably just waited until she was blowing steam, but I can't take the chance."

Without a word, Carolyn gave him a wink, kicked off her shoes, and unbuttoned her shirt. She headed back to the bed. "All this is really turning me on. This is the first time I've been around a real man." Hawks quickly climbed out of the camper and stood on the rear bumper so he could get a good view of the road in both directions. There was no one in sight in any direction. He threw caution to the wind and climbed back into the camper.

CHAPTER 9

Dawson pressed the eject button on the Colt pistol and released the now-empty magazine. He pulled it from the magazine well, pushed it into his right pocket, and pulled a fresh one from the left pocket of his coat. He slammed it home and pressed the slide release on the left side of the pistol with his thumb. The spring thrust the slide forward and picked up the top cartridge, placing the gun back into battery. He watched as one of the men almost made it to the alleyway before he collapsed. The next one was on his knees, but that was as far as he got before falling over on his side clutching his abdomen. The nearest one lay where he fell with one leg involuntarily kicking. The bright red blood on the snow steamed in the freezing air. He lowered the hammer and shoved the pistol back into its holster. He grabbed the rope on the front of the sled and proceeded up the walkway. Henry looked back with her eyes wide with fear.

Dawson called out, "It's all over, Ms. Henry, keep moving. I don't want to stay out here in any longer than we have to."

Without a word, Henry continued in the direction of her home. Without stopping, they went straight up the drive and to their relief there were no tracks in the snow leading to the apartment or kitchen door. Olivia opened the door and asked, "I thought I heard shots; did you see anything?"

Dawson nodded. "We ran into a little trouble, but it's been handled."

Henry opened the door and called to Cathy, "Are you guys OK?"

Cathy came into view. "We're fine; what's happened?"

"Oh Cathy, we got out of the shop just in the nick of time. Dawson had to shoot at some men following us. It was terrible. I was so frightened."

They quickly unloaded the sleds and using one of them barricaded the remaining ground-floor windows inside Henry's house. He used the other one to barricade the front window in the garage. Dawson had barricaded the backdoor of the garage with a piece of plywood he could remove if they needed to make an escape out the back way.

After dinner Henry came over. "I want to thank you for taking me back to my shop and helping me today. I don't know what I would've done without you."

"You would have had your gun, and you would have used it."

"I don't know if I can do this."

Dawson looked her in the eyes. "I want you to think ahead. You're going to have to get those packs loaded with food and supplies. You also need to have water in your canteens ready to go. Let me show you what Olivia and I have on hand." He led her over to their gear laid out in the order it would be donned. "Look how I have everything laid out and ready to go. We can go from being naked and out the door in less than five minutes."

Henry asked, "Mr. Dawson, we aren't planning on going anywhere; why do you keep saying that we need to plan on leaving?"

"I can think of a million reasons why you couldn't stay in your home and would have to leave in a hurry. What if all the bad guys were beating down your front door, and you are out of bullets? How long would you, Cathy, and the twins survive out here in this weather? What if you had to walk pulling them in the sleds for ten miles with only a minute's notice? You guys would die in a matter of hours just from the exposure.

"If the lights don't come back on right away, you're going to see this city turn into hell on earth. Every house will be attacked and ransacked; I will be taking Olivia and leaving if I see we are running out of ammo. You need to have a plan and be fully prepared to move out if you have to. Even if you have a plan, that's no guarantee you're going to survive. The most difficult thing you've got to overcome is the idea that your world will not change. Three days ago, you couldn't conceive of a day when there would be no electricity. You couldn't imagine that every vehicle and electronic device would be dead."

"You're right Mr. Dawson; I'll get ready to go just in case. My sister lives ten miles north of the city. We'll try for her house. You can come with us."

"Thanks, Henry, but I can't make you any promises. I'm thinking of heading west into British Columbia and maybe as far as Vancouver Island. The weather on the island is survivable. If we travel south, we will have to contend with these temperatures for hundreds of miles. We'll have to eventually travel south, but we can expect months of these below-freezing temperatures. Another thing you must remember is that the gas that is keeping us warm may quit flowing at any time. It's a miracle that it hasn't run out already."

Olivia looked concerned. "You're serious, aren't you?"

"Of course. It's only been three days, and I've already had to shoot people, not to mention hitting the bum at the camping store."

Henry turned to leave. "I will have us ready to go before I go to bed tonight."

Dawson handed her one of the now-empty duffel bags. "This is an extra bag we aren't going to need if we have to leave."

She smiled. "Thanks."

After bolting the door, he looked over at Olivia. "It's going to get exciting around here pretty quick. I broke my leg back in college. I think I feel a Chinook coming. It always starts to ache when one is blowing in."

Olivia commented, "We're due for one. It will warm up pretty quick, and the snow may even melt."

"If it warms up, people will start scrounging for supplies. Remember people will be knocking on doors looking for food. Always ask them for something to eat before they can ask you. I know it seems cruel, but if we want to be alive in ninety days, that's what it's going to take. I want you to sit here at the table with me while I show you how to load the magazine for the Colt 1911 .45."

He pulled out the empty magazine and the box of .45 ammo. He took seven rounds of ammo and laid them on the table. "I'm going to insert the first one, and you can finish."

She watched as he inserted the first round into the magazine. With difficulty she got the first one in. The others came easy. He unloaded it and let her reload it from scratch a couple of times. He then un-holstered the gun and showed her how to operate it. She could operate the mechanism as her hands were a little larger than Henry's, but it was still cumbersome. He dug out his extra leather belt from his rolling suitcase. He positioned it around Olivia's waist and punched some holes so she could cinch it tight. He put the .22 pistol in the holster and let her try it on. "Anytime you are up and about, I want you to be wearing your pistol. The sooner we get in the habit of staying armed at all times the safer we'll be."

Olivia gave him a squeeze. "Why did you convince me to leave with you on our last day at work?"

"I was afraid you'd get hurt and wouldn't know what to do. I was also planning to ask you out once this project came to an end. I didn't want to take the chance of being accused of sexual harassment beforehand. When I realized what was taking place, I wasn't going to take the chance of losing you. If you had decided to stay and work, I would have hung around and made sure you made it home, if I couldn't convince you to come with me. Why did you come with me?"

She gave him a loving look. "I knew you were in love with me. I've caught you looking at me several times and pretended not to notice. You didn't pay any of the other ladies any attention. You timed your lunches at the same time as mine so we could make small talk in the employee break room. So if we can keep from getting killed or starve to death, everything will work out perfectly." He gave her a long kiss. When their lips parted, she took his hand and led him back to the bed.

That afternoon they melted snow until they had enough to bathe. They took turns pouring warm water over one another as showers and then laundered their soiled clothes with more melted snow in the bathtub. Dawson strung a clothesline using the paracord from Henry's shop. The dry Calgary climate had the clothes dry, ready to fold, and packed away in just a couple of hours.

They made sure all their containers were full of water just in case the snow melted. As expected, the Chinook blew in and brought the temperature up to near freezing. It did not warm up enough to melt the snow, but it allowed the people out of food and supplies to wander the streets. Every door on every store would be checked and, if not open, would be busted down. In another day the doors on every house would be checked to see if they were locked. One day after that, those same doors would be kicked in and the unarmed inhabitants subdued and, at worst, raped and murdered. The most dangerous warm-blooded creature on the planet would have no constraints.

The sound of an engine running caught their attention;

Dawson hopped up and looked out the window. An old farm trac-tor pulled a large cargo trailer. A policeman drove the tractor. He was in full swat gear. A half a dozen or so men in swat gear were going door to door. They carried bags of food out to the trailer. Henry came out the back door heading toward the garage. Dawson met her halfway.

"Don't panic, Henry. When they get here, let me do the talking." The man who walked up the driveway looked like a storm trooper. Dawson met him halfway up the drive. "Thank God you're here. I'm so glad that you guys are bringing us something to eat. We have four adults and two children; can I help you carry our supply? We need some bottled water as well."

The storm trooper gave him a stern look. "We are looking for hoarders and collecting their extra food to be distributed."

Dawson nodded. "I hope you find them. Can I come with you to help? Let me tell my girlfriend the good news. I'll be right back to help."

The storm trooper want-to-be waved him off. "I'll make note that you are willing to volunteer. We'll come back and get you as soon as we locate some supplies."

Henry caught on to what Dawson was doing and joined the act. "Thank you, thank you, thank you. We were afraid that we were going to starve. When are you coming back with our share?"

The man answered, "You'll be notified."

Henry and Dawson watched as the group proceeded down the street. Henry looked at Dawson. "How did I do?"

"You did great. If you had offered to give them any food, they would be emptying out your basement right now. The government officials will make certain that they are fed first. I want you to remember something; no matter who shows up, do not give them any food. If you feel you need to do something, we can take some down to the nearest church or we can set it out on the sidewalk down the street. Once this crisis accelerates, this will become more critical. Don't let anyone see you eating through one of your windows. Keep Cathy and the twins inside and out of sight. You, Cathy, and Olivia are now targets to those who will be using this as an opportunity to rape and rob."

"I understand. I will have dinner for you and Olivia tonight."

He grinned. "Little Tiger?"

She laughed. "You bring me a little tiger, and I'll find my father's recipe. Chicken and rice tonight. I'll have tea cakes for desert with tea made from snow water."

Olivia opened the door to admit Dawson. "What would you have done if he insisted on searching the houses?"

"I would have had to try and kill them. If they had confiscated our food, we would die, it's as simple as that."

Dawson pulled out his atlas and his maps of Calgary, Alberta, and British Columbia. "If we head out, we need to plan a route that most other people will not attempt to take. Masses of humanity will be our enemy. Once we cross the mountains and get into British Columbia, it'll be easier. There'll be wild game and lots of small farms and villages. The people over there will be more self-sufficient than those here. There are lots of farms and ranches on this side of the mountains, but the problem is the extremely low temperatures over here. The most important thing we are going to need is transportation."

Olivia wondered, "That tractor the police were driving was running. Why was it working when nothing else runs?"

"Most old vehicles such as classic cars and older diesel tractors should run just fine. Any vehicle with a computer or an integrated circuit will be disabled. If and when we leave, that will be one of the things we'll have to look for. We could even use a lawn tractor if it could pull a small trailer. There should be plenty of gasoline and diesel in all the abandoned vehicles along the way."

Olivia looked worried. "There's something bothering me that I want to talk to you about. I don't think Henry, Cathy, and the twins will last a day without you if they have to leave this house."

"I know it. I've been thinking about them. I think we'll have to at least get them to her sister's house. We can plan our escape from there. I'll take my maps when I go over to pick up our dinner. We can't stay and eat there because I don't want to leave our food and gear unguarded. We have to be more vigilant than ever; the streets are getting very busy, and I'm seeing people looking up and down the driveways and walks."

That evening at dinner, Dawson walked over to Henry's kitchen where she helped two plates of food for him and Olivia. He carried them back to the garage where they enjoyed the hot meal. Once they were finished and the plates washed, he walked back over to Henry's with his Alberta and Calgary map. Henry showed him the location of her sister's home and the location of her brother's home, which was twenty miles farther west. With transportation they could get into British Columbia without much difficulty. To get to the north part of Vancouver Island would be more difficult. Most of the roads on his map would take them down toward the city of Vancouver, which was a place they would need to avoid. The short-term goal was to stay alive and then get to the warmer climate of British Columbia.

That evening he took some fishing line from Uncle's ancient tackle box. He went to Henry's recycle bin and fished out all the aluminum cans and glass bottles. He set up trip wires tied to the cans and bottles so they would fall and give them an early warning system should intruders find their way up the driveway or into the backyard and patio. He ran a paracord line from a small hole he cut in the corner of Henry's kitchen window to the knocker on the front door of the garage. If she needed him, all she would need to do was pull on the cord, making the knocker hit the door.

He and Olivia sat around the light from one of the candles from Henry's shop munching on the sweet tea cakes. Olivia said, "You've had a very busy day, I bet you never thought that trying to stay hidden and surviving would be so strenuous."

"You're not kidding; at least we aren't sitting around bored."

She kissed his ear. "At least I know of one sure way to relieve the boredom."

He pulled her across his lap. "You know I believe I'm getting a little bored right this minute." A sudden sound of breaking glass brought them to their feet.

CHAPTER 10

Hawks tied his boots while sitting on the side of the bed. Carolyn kissed him on the neck. "We're going to have to get one of those signs that says 'If this trailer's a rockin', don't come a knockin'.'"

Hawks laughed. "I bet your dad never thought this kind of stuff would be taking place in his camper."

"I could just hear the lecture he'd be giving me."

The road was clear in both directions as they climbed out of the camper and went back to the car. The radiator had cooled, so he cranked it and slowly headed back up the road. They paused at a bridge where they could look out over the bay. One of the log ships sat swamped in the water and leaned almost all the way over. The log ships would flood a compartment and tip over sideways until the logs rolled off the deck. Once the logs were in the water, the ships were pumped out before returning for an additional load. This ship never got to dump its load and was now mired in the sand and mud flat. The tide was out, and there were a dozen or so people digging in the sand for clams. Hawks lamented, "I thought about doing that back in Crofton, but I would've had to

leave my food and gear unguarded. I didn't like leaving my stuff long enough to even get water."

When they neared the town of Lady Smith, they once again encountered a road block. Lady Smith was a larger town than

Crofton, and their city leaders obviously had the same idea. Carolyn squeezed his arm. "Oh hell, here we go again."

"Keep your gun hidden. I want you to use your greatest asset. I want you to distract them with your smile when they look in at us." When they got to the road block the men came from both sides. Carolyn gave them her killer smile. The man wasn't in uniform but wore a gun belt with a drop holster. The pistol was still secured in the holster so it would be easy for Hawks to get the jump on him if necessary. Hawks reached into his shirt pocket and pulled out a roll of $20.00 bills and rolled down his window. "I hope you guys are selling groceries or you have a store open up here. There's nothing left in Crofton."

The man answered, "We are working for the Royal Canadian Mounted Police, and we're going to have to ask you to surrender your vehicle. There is shortage of emergency vehicles. I can give you a receipt for it, and you will be reimbursed by the government."

Hawks asked, "Do you have anyone who knows how to drive a Model A Ford?"

The man looked puzzled. "I can drive a standard transmission, if that's what you're asking?"

"No, that's not what I asked. I asked if there is someone up here who can drive a Model A? It doesn't crank, or shift, like a modern auto, but I can show you. Where are you taking it?"

"We'll be taking it up to the police station at city hall."

Hawks looked over at Carolyn. "Sweetheart, will you get in the back so this gentleman can ride up here in the front? I want to show him how to shift the car."

She once again flashed her killer smile. "Sure thing, baby."

She was out and in the back seat before he could raise an objection. He walked around to the passenger side and got in. He called out to the other man, "Stay put, I'll be back in a few minutes."

The man slammed the door, and Hawks gave it the gas and let out the clutch. When he had gained enough speed, he double-clutched and shifted to second gear. Carolyn pointed out, "Baby, the road heading out to the farm is ahead on the left."

"Thanks, I'll remember that." When they neared the intersection, he applied the brakes, pulled the Schofield, and punched the barrel deep into the man's side. Carolyn placed her pistol behind the man's ear and cocked the hammer.

The man could only stammer. "You're going to get in trouble for this."

"Maybe so, but we're not giving you the car and our stuff. You and I both know that when you guys finish, we will both be sitting on a bench somewhere wondering if we can eat the receipt you give us. I assume you want to live, so here is what you're going to do: take your left hand, unsnap your gun belt, and slip it over into the back seat."

The man stammered, "Now you're really in trouble."

"No, sir, you're the one in trouble because I'm fixing to squeeze this trigger if you don't comply with my request." The man unsnapped the belt and passed it over into the back seat. Hawks instructed him, "Now, pull up your pants legs and let me see those pretty ankles." The man pulled up his pants leg to reveal an ankle holster. Hawks grinned. "With just the mere tips of your fingers, I want you to pull that pistol out and let it fall to the floorboard. Remember, I will blow a hole in you big enough to drive through if you so much as fart; do you understand me, boy?"

The man was starting to sweat profusely. "I understand."

The man gently pulled the gun out and dropped it on the floor. Hawks nodded to the door. "Now slowly get out; remember there are two guns on you. Once you are out, start walking up the street in the direction we were driving."

The man got out and started walking away. Once the man was

a hundred or so feet away, he gave the car some gas, let out the clutch, and made the turn toward the farm. Carolyn climbed back over the front seat and gave Hawks a big kiss on the cheek. "Darn, you're good. You keep your head better than anyone I know."

"I was nervous as a cat; I sure didn't want to blow him half in two."

"I thought you were going to shoot the next one."

"I didn't want to get blood and guts all over the front seat."

They took a road west snaking toward the center of the island. This road took them past farms and through forest lands. They had to stop when a small herd of the local black-tailed deer crossed in front of them. The weight of the trailer almost jack knifed them because the trailer didn't have brakes. Hawks shook his head. "We've got to keep it slow out here in the country. You never know what's around the next bend in the road. And something else we need to be mindful of is the fact that there will be more people that'll want a running vehicle. We will be in danger of getting hijacked. I hope your friend's farm has a barn where we can hide the car. Do you think your friend will mind us joining them at the farm?"

"I'm certain they won't say a word to us about it. When I talked to them early Saturday morning, they were on their way to Nova Scotia in their RV and had just left Toronto heading east. We'll probably have the place to ourselves forever. She and I grew up together, and this was her family's farm. She has no relatives on the island. I get to use it as a weekend retreat anytime I want, and I have the run of the place when they are out of town. There are hiking trails, tons of game, and there should be plenty of canned goods in the pantry. They always have a big garden and are big into canning their own vegetables. They are far enough off the beaten path that no one would think to go there."

"I'm looking forward to seeing the place. I'm already feeling guilty about using other people's stuff. To tell you the truth, I feel like a thief."

"You can get over feeling like that. My friend would want me here looking after her home and property. We are very close, and I would expect her to look after my place if I needed the help."

"Then all we have to do is get there in one piece and hope we don't have to evict anyone." They snaked their way through the quiet back roads, only occasionally having to drive around stranded vehicles. They came to a small, one-lane bridge crossing a rushing stream. A black bear on the sandbar stood on its hind legs before loping off up the bank and out of sight in the woods.

Hawks asked, "How much further?"

"Probably another twenty or thirty miles. I told you it was kind of remote."

"The more remote the better as far as I'm concerned. I feel better about this place the closer we get. There are a lot of starving people who don't have but one way to go and that's north, and every one of them will think they are Daniel Boone and can live off the land. This is far enough away that most of them won't make it."

After a couple of hours, they neared the road that led to the farm. As they approached the long drive, they came upon a man walking down the road. Carolyn recognized him as the owner of a small family inn further up the valley. She told Hawks, "Stop, this is Jim Banks. He owns a country inn four or five miles up the road from the farm." Hawks pulled to a stop, and Jim immediately recognized Carolyn.

"Carolyn, I can't believe it. I haven't seen anyone since we lost our electricity, my satellite internet is out, and I can't crank my van. I am going to hike down to the intersection and see if I can catch a ride."

Carolyn told Jim, "You won't be catching a ride. The electricity is out everywhere; along with every cell phone, vehicle, and electronic equipment. This is the only vehicle we've seen running since Saturday morning; even the ferries have died."

Jim gave her a bewildered look. "That's impossible; how are people going to get around? My wife went over to Vancouver to visit her sister Friday. I guess she'll have to fly back."

Hawks realized that what they had told Jim had not sunk in. "Jim, I don't think you understand what we're trying to tell you. It appears as though everything that runs on electricity and has a computer or integrated circuit in it has burnt out. All the planes are grounded if the airports are shut down."

Jim gave them an incredulous look. "That's preposterous. You must think I'm an imbecile. I've never heard such bull hockey in all my life. You sound like a couple of those right-wing conspiracy nuts; the government would never let that happen. Even if it did, they would be sending out rescue teams with food and supplies."

Hawks smiled. "Jim, let me know if I can ever help you."

Carolyn waved. "I'll be at the farm. Be careful out here by yourself. It's going to be dark soon. Do you have a flashlight or a lighter?"

"Don't be silly. I'm not going to need anything of the sort."

Hawks called out as he eased out on the clutch and gave the car some gas. "Good luck, Jim; stay safe."

Carolyn looked at Hawks. "I feel so bad. What if he gets hurt or dies?"

"If what he believes is true, then we've got an arrest warrant out for us, and the government is on the way to his rescue. If what we believe is true, this will probably be the last time we ever see the poor devil."

"This isn't going to be easy, is it? We can't save everyone."

"This will be survival of the fittest. We always laughed at the Darwin awards; Darwinism will have a whole new meaning now."

They turned off the road and were stopped by a gate. Carolyn said, "I'll unlock it and open it. Stop when you get through, and I'll lock it behind us. That way it will appear that no one has been here."

The driveway was a quarter of a mile or so long and went up to a farmhouse that was at least a hundred years old. Hawks stopped the car and camper at the front door. Carolyn got out and went up the stairs and found the front door key in its hiding place where it hung behind a porch light. She had the house open and soon had the drapes pulled open to let the late-afternoon sun into the living room. She came to the top of the front steps and called down, "Set the brake, come on in and see." Hawks killed the engine, set the brake, and walked up the steps. He was a bit stiff from all the riding. The old Model A rode good for an eighty-plus-year-old, car but it was built before anyone thought about orthopedic seats.

She quickly took him around the house, started a fire in the parlor wood heater and in the woodstove in the kitchen. She pointed to the propane range on the opposite wall. "They have a five-hundred-gallon propane tank out back."

On the porch just outside the backdoor was an old sink with an old-fashioned pitcher pump. He pointed to it and asked, "Does that thing still work?"

"All we have to do is prime it. There's an electric well, but I doubt we can ever get it going again. We can use the gas cooktop for a long time on what's in the tank. Tammy always made sure it was at least 50 percent full. Come look in the pantry; we can look at what she has in the basement in the morning." She opened the pantry door and showed Hawks it was stocked with canned goods. The refrigerator and freezer were empty. Carolyn explained that Tammy and her partner Roosevelt were on a year-long camping trip across Canada and the US. She looked over at Hawks. "I'm so glad we found each other, and I'm so glad I'm not working in that stinky old paper mill anymore. I know I should be worried, but I feel as free as a bird, and it's the first time I can honestly say I am happy with my life."

Hawks hugged her neck. "You know, I'm happy too. I've just been wandering through life waiting to get too old and decrepit to work. I guess I was just waiting for the end to come. My kids have their own lives, and the last thing they need is an old fart like me to complicate their lives. I do regret not being able to rescue them from what is taking place, but they both know where my old cabin is in the Ozarks. We can't even think about crossing the Northern Rockies in the dead of winter on foot. For now, I'm in control of everything I can control, and this is as fine a place as any I've ever seen. This is where I want to be, and you're who I want to be with. That's more than I deserve and more than I could ever dream of. I'm glad I've got back to living instead of waiting to die."

After a long embrace, Carolyn said, "OK partner, let's get our stuff moved in and the Model A and the camper stowed in the barn."

It was dark by the time they finished moving into the house. A stew on the woodstove provided a good dinner, and it was cozy sitting by the wood heater in the parlor. The old fireplace sat empty, and Hawks asked, "Does the fireplace work?"

"Sure, they had it reworked two years ago when Roosevelt moved in. I'm not sure how much firewood's on hand though."

Hawks grinned. "I thought my firewood cutting days were behind me. We better get some sleep if I'm going to be a farmhand tomorrow."

The next morning, they were up with the dawn. From the upstairs window, Hawks could look down across the meadows where deer fed along the wood line. He felt as though he had stepped back in time a hundred years. After breakfast, they went down to the basement to see what was stored. This was a walkout basement with a large double door opening to a driveway leading out to the barn. The same drive continued around to the front of the house and connected to the drive leading back out to the road-way. The basement also had a regular door to one side. Tammy and Roosevelt were evidently back-to-the-earth-type people. There was an abundance of canned vegetables, dry seeds in jars, canning supplies, and barrels of unground wheat. In plastic storage totes were hand grinders for the wheat. Hanging over a large table was an assortment of meat saws and knives for butchering animals. It didn't appear any of them had been used in recent history. Hawks looked at Carolyn. "The only thing this farm needs is animals. I half expect to hear a rooster crowing."

"When they decided to go on their trip, they sold all the animals and took their cat and dogs with them. We can check with some of the neighbors to see if they would be willing to sell some stock. They may be willing to take the remaining cash off our hands. I have a couple of thousand dollars, so that will give us $2,250.00 with what you've got."

"You know it's sort of like stealing, you know?"

"I like eating eggs, and besides we can always give them back vegetables and such."

The old barn was once a dairy barn with hay storage in the loft and large barn doors on each end. He backed the camper into a stall on one side and unhooked from it. There was an old Kubota diesel tractor with a battery maintainer to one side. Although the electricity was out, the battery should still be holding a charge as it had only been a few days since the event started. Hawks bumped the transmission into neutral and hit the key, allowing the glow plugs to heat the combustion chamber. He turned it to the start position, and the diesel sprung to life. He could now keep batteries charged and work the farm; their situation was improving by the hour.

"Grab your money and let's take the Model A around to the neighbors to see who's still around and what we can scrounge in the way of chickens, dogs, and cats. If we're going to be farmers, we need to have some animals, and we need to know who's around here."

He opened the big doors as she headed up to the house. She was a beautiful woman and his heart still jumped at the sight of her; it was still unsettling to have the feelings he was having. He loaded his backpack with the water bottles, his everyday emergency items, checked the oil, radiator water, and cranked the engine. He pulled around to the front where he met Carolyn, who came bounding down the steps wearing her pistol. She was smiling as she climbed in. "What are you gawking at?"

"I'm sorry; I can't help but stare."

She slid across the seat to sit next to him and gave him a smack on the cheek. "Let's go meet the neighbors."

They pulled out on the road after they closed and locked the gate and headed toward the next farm driveway, which was about a mile up the road. They came upon Jim walking back in the direction of his country inn. They pulled up alongside, and Carolyn slid back to her side and rolled down her window. Henry looked like he had been through hell and back. His hair was a mess; he was missing a lens and one leg from his glasses. He was missing a shoe, had numerous scratches, and his nylon jogging jacket was ripped. She looked at him and asked, "Jim, could you use a lift?"

Jim climbed in the back seat and simply said, "I would appreciate it."

Hawks couldn't help but ask, "Jim, were you able to catch a ride to town?"

"No, I stood out on the main road until it got too cold. I could see the road, so I decided to walk towards town since I had gone that far. Sometime in the night a pack of dogs got after me and chased me through the woods and off into a ravine. I climbed a tree and stayed up in it until they gave up and left. I found what's left of my glasses while I was climbing out. I went back to the road, decided to come back, and then you guys came along."

Carolyn handed him a bottle of water from the backpack. "We'll get you back home. Do you still have the chickens and farm animals down at the inn?"

"Yes, they are more of a problem than they're worth. I brought them in to attract families with children. Most of my guests are old retired people or yuppie couples. I'm tired of feeding them and picking up after them."

Carolyn asked, "Why don't you butcher them?"

Jim said, "Oh no, we would never do that; we're strict vegetarians. I need to pay someone to just come get them."

Carolyn quickly piped up, "We've just rented Tammy's farm since they are traveling for the next year. I might be interested in getting them. Can we start picking them up when we drop you off?"

Jim polished off the bottle of water. "Sure, as long as I don't have to help. I'm getting a bath and going to bed when I get home."

Carolyn glanced over at Hawks and winked. "Thanks, Jim, we'll take them off your hands for you."

The country inn was a picturesque building in a beautiful country setting. A big porch ran across the front of a large stone building. It was at one time the weekend home of the owner of one of the coal mining companies. Jim had done a wonderful job of maintaining the flavor and atmosphere of the old home. Hawks thought, Under normal times this would have probably been a relaxing place to spend a couple of weeks.

They pulled around to the back entrance and stopped where Jim slid out of the backdoor and limped up the back steps. He turned and pointed. "Carolyn, you know where the animals are; thanks for the ride."

Carolyn pointed to the drive heading around the back toward the riding stables. "There are pens and cages behind the stables." They quickly located the six goats, seventeen chickens, one donkey, and one cow with a bull calf. Hawks looked over at Carolyn and asked, "Are there pens, a chicken yard, and goat-proof fences at our farm? If not, we have a problem."

"We don't have a problem. Everything is waiting, and in fact, I recognize the milk cow. All we need to do is go back to the farm and get the stock trailer and come back. Two trips should take care of it. The hard part will be catching all the chickens. We can probably just lead the stock into the trailer."

"Poor old Jim still doesn't have a clue; do he and his wife have any children?"

"No, they've chosen to go childless in order to save the planet."

"That's probably a very wise decision on their part. Speaking of children, why none for you?"

She shrugged her shoulders. "I tried many years ago; it just never happened. By the time I thought about adopting, my husband decided that he was God's gift to women. After that, time got away while I wasted my time with some Scotch drinkers."

"I'm sorry. I lucked up; I had a good wife and good kids. I wish I could have been home more; that's why my kids and I aren't as close as I'd like to be. But on the whole, I lucked out."

"I can't relive my life, but as you can see, things work out. I found you."

She lovingly squeezed his arm. "Do you think our car will pull a stock trailer?"

"We may be pushing our luck with the Model A, but I bet I can rig up the tractor to pull it with no trouble."

Hawks stood in the window of the bedroom and looked down toward the highway. It had been three full days since they had settled the animals. All had been quiet and they had managed to meet all the neighbors who were still around. A cat showed up at the barn, and there were two Australian Shepard puppies from the neighbor down the road. Everything was peaceful and quiet. He knew it would just be a matter of time before people from the cities would make it this far, so he was never far from his rifle, and he always wore the Schofield pistol.

Carolyn brought him a cup of coffee and joined him at the window when they spotted the motorcycles on the highway. The sound of the exhaust pipes disturbed the peace of the little valley. He counted seven motorcycles and four old trucks. The last of the four trucks stopped at their gate. Carolyn clinched her fist, "Well, baby, it looks like it's show time."

CHAPTER 11

The sound of the crashing bottle brought him to his feet. Olivia blew out the candle and he peered out through the window into the darkness. It would take a while for his eyes to adjust after sitting next to the candle. There was no sign of anyone using a flashlight and none of the other trip alarms had been triggered. He had to be patient and let his eyes adjust to the moonlight. The snow reflected the moonlight, and he could soon see down the drive and beside the house. He located the bottle that had crashed to the ground. This particular glass bottle sat on top of the trash can and was now lay in the snow on the sidewalk in front of it. There was no sign of a human being in the area. He sat for a minute and watched as a raccoon proceeded to break into the trashcan.

He whispered back to Olivia, "Come see, this Chinook has warmed up the critters enough for them to come out and forage. I wonder what the Asians call raccoon when they're put on the menu?"

Olivia giggled. "If a cat is called Little Tiger, I bet the raccoon would be called Little Bear."

"I've got to tell Henry that we have to haul our garbage off. If someone were to go through our garbage, they'd figure out really quick that there's food here."

Dawson went out and wound the fishing line around the bottle and stowed it until he could reset it the next morning. Henry had raked out the dinner plates into the garbage. Under normal times this wouldn't raise a second thought, but this was a new world.

Olivia let him in and closed the door behind him. They left the curtain open a bit so that the moonlight could illuminate the room. Dawson pointed out, "We've got to limit our lights after dark. For one, we can't afford to lose our night vision, and two, we don't want to let anyone know we're back here."

Olivia squeezed his arm. "I have a question. Do you think we are moving too fast?"

Dawson held her hand. "Under normal times, I would say yes. I've thought about it a lot. We've known each other for almost a year. I can't remember how many lunches and breaks we have spent together. I pretty much know everything there is to know about you. It's not like we just met in a bar. In fact, the only reason I stuck around on this job was because you were there. I know you've heard my cell phone ring all during the day; most of those calls were from folks wanting to know if I am available for work."

She smiled, "I wondered why you were always getting calls. I was afraid they were calls from your girlfriends."

Dawson shook his head. "No, I have never been that popular with the ladies. I don't think we are moving too fast."

She entwined her fingers in his. "I think we would have wound up in each other's arms no matter what."

The next morning was spent sitting at the window and staying alert. There was a tremendous amount of foot activity. It was obvious the population was getting desperate. The gas was still working, so they were still warm. Each time someone came up the drive, Dawson would meet them with money in his hand asking if they had any food to sell. Gun fire was erupting across the city. At all hours, directions, and distances the sound of single and multiple gun shots could be heard.

Olivia said, "I can't believe that we are hearing so much gunfire. The government has tried to disarm us for many years, this is surprising."

"You can never get rid of weapons, whether its guns, knives, or rocks. There will always be people who are predators, and there will always be people willing to defend themselves. A lot of that gunfire could be the police and military. In all of history, governments have killed more of their citizens than anything else."

Olivia asked, "How long before we have to bolt and run?"

"I wish I knew, but I'm not feeling good about staying here. If it hadn't been so dramatically cold, we could have walked out on the second day. The one thing you need to remember is that there are fewer mouths to feed with each passing day, but the ones remaining are getting desperate and aggressive."

Henry came knocking on their door. Olivia answered the door. "Henry, come on in. What can we do for you?"

Henry smiled. "Mr. Dawson, you have been spot-on about what is taking place. I'm starting to worry. We've had a dozen people stop by already this morning looking for food. What are we going to do?"

Dawson sat at the window with the 12-gauge coach gun in his lap. "The only thing we can do at this point is to try and stay out of sight and keep begging them for food. Our neighbors will soon figure out our secret. Once they realize that we aren't out foraging as they are, we'll have some trouble. Even if we give them food, they'll tell their friends and family, and we'll be overrun or burned out. We're going to have to be prepared to move out in the middle of the night when the time comes. It's been less than a week, and you're already seeing what's taking place. Imagine what's going to be taking place in another week. Even if we found transportation, most of the roads in the city are going to be impassable from the abandoned vehicles."

Henry looked concerned. "I showed you where my sister lives. How long you think it would take us to walk that far?"

"Olivia and I could walk it in a day. Most of the people in Calgary can also make it that far in a day. What does your sister have that you don't have here?"

"She probably doesn't have as much as we do. This is my father and uncle's home. We moved in to take care of them when they got old. We have all the food and supplies they kept on hand."

Dawson pulled out his maps. "Tell me about your brother's place, which is twenty miles west of your sister's?"

"He has a bigger place with five acres of land. He has his place set up as a plant nursery. He'll have fresh vegetables. I don't know if he'll have any food stored. He will welcome us if we can get there. He is very secretive about his life and business, but we take care of our family."

Dawson sat and studied the map. "If we have to leave, that would be the preferred destination. If we made it to your sister's place in one piece, we wouldn't be any better off than we are here and maybe even worse. I think we need to shelter in place as long as possible. If we can survive for eight weeks, most of the people will have starved or froze to death. What kind of food do you have stored?"

"We have tons of rice, noodles, powdered eggs, canned chicken, canned fish, salt, pepper, sugar, wheat flour, rice flour, cooking oil, and canned vegetables. You need to come look."

Dawson thought for a moment, "This is what I want you to do, I want you to take the wheat flour and make hard, sweet, thin cookies. Be sure to put a small amount of salt in the mix as well. I'm talking as many as you can make, not a batch. I've never used rice flour, but if you can do the same thing using rice flour, do that as well. You can even add a little oil to the batter. Experiment with a couple of batches to see what works. I want you to put the most calories you can in the smallest package. It has to be lightweight so you can carry as many calories as possible with us. We can help cook in the oven over here too."

Olivia spoke up, "I'll help. I have a recipe for sugar cookies. Do you have any oatmeal stored; it also makes great cookies."

Henry thought. "Yes, there's some oatmeal, but not a lot. Can you use peanut butter?"

Olivia grinned. "Peanut butter cookies are easy to make; let's get started."

Dawson told them, "OK, ladies, start cooking."

Dawson kept an eye on the front walk and shooed away the people who stopped. He had to steel his emotions, especially when there were children involved. It was impossible to feed an entire city of children, and he kept telling himself the only thing that would be accomplished would be the death of himself, Olivia, Henry, Cathy, and the twins.

The cookie baking went well, and by late evening, there were a hundred pounds of cookies stored in canvas bags. The next morning, they took all the canned fruit and dried the contents for easy transport as well. They drank the juice from the cans as their beverages. Dawson insisted they not waste a single calorie. He knew that their bodies would store the excess calories, and if they were forced to flee, that could make the difference between life and death. Once they had all the food, they could conceivably carry ready to go, they went back to what for them was a normal routine.

Dawson sat in the front room of Henry's where he could cover the driveway and he could see the garage apartment door. As he sat watching, he noticed a group of five men going house to house. They kicked the door in on the house across the street, and he heard screams. He took the 12 gauge and went out the back door and down the driveway. The closer he got to the bottom of the driveway, the louder the screams became. He heard a gunshot, and the man of the house staggered out the door and collapsed. The screams of the man's wife and daughter were interrupted by the cursing of a man. Dawson drew the Colt 1911 and cocked the hammer. Without slowing, he walked through the front door and shot the first man he saw center mass. The man fell backward onto the floor. Dawson kept going and spotted the next man who only had time to say, "Oh shit."

The heavy .45 bullet entered the man's head just above his left eye and left a spray of blood and brains on the wall and door behind him. The screaming had stopped by the time he kicked open the blood-spattered door. A short, stout man was trying to get his pants up with one hand and attempting to shoot Dawson with a revolver in his other hand. The young lady cowered in the corner clinging to her torn clothes. The man's shot missed and hit the doorframe next to Dawson's head.

Dawson didn't miss; he was intent on killing the bastard. He shot the man center mass and dropped him in his tracks. Dawson kicked the gun aside and listened as he heard men running down the hall and out the back door. The men came running around the house and down the driveway heading back toward the street. He holstered the .45, ran to the front door, and using the coach gun cut loose on them. He fired both barrels of buckshot and put both on the ground rolling in the street. The other neighbors who had been watching ran out.

Several of the local men came out with baseball bats and golf clubs. One of them who recognized Dawson said, "We'll take it from here."

Dawson pointed to the house. "Someone needs to check on the ladies. There's a pistol on the floor next to a dead one."

The man answered, "We'll check on them and clean up the mess, thanks again."

Dawson was still angry as he broke open the shotgun and replaced the spent shells. He proceeded up the drive and was met by Olivia. "You've got to be careful. You could've been hurt or killed."

"I let my anger get the best of me. That's the caliber of people that are going to be left before too long. I just wanted to kill those sorry animals. I won't be losing any sleep over them."

He went back to the apartment and replaced the ammo while he kept his eyes open for more trouble. Henry asked, "Mr. Dawson, where did you learn to do what you do?"

"Henry, most of what I know is common sense. I came to understand human nature after Katrina hit. As far as the shooting is concerned, I have been a shooter my entire life. I never shot at a man until all this started. I imagine I'll be shooting more people before this is over. There's no 911 to call, even if we find a phone that works. There simply isn't enough functioning police and military to control a million starving people."

Henry took over his spot at the window so he could retire to the garage for rest. Olivia brought him some tea and asked, "Is this how it's going to be from now on?"

He put his arm around her waist as she stood next to him. "I'm afraid so. Things are going to deteriorate from this point on. There will be no food produced until the middle of next summer at the earliest. If we're going to live, we're going to have to get out of here. I'm going to inventory Henry's basement and try to figure out how long we can stay here with the food that's on hand. We can't wait until it's all gone before leaving. If we do that, we'll be dead within three weeks unless we turn into cannibals."

Olivia put her hand over her mouth. "What if we can't find food where we're going?"

"Then we'd better hope there's plenty of game and fish."

She asked, "Do you think you could eat somebody?"

"I guess that's a bridge I'll have to cross if the time comes. I have no intention of doing so, but hunger will dictate what we do. For the record, you have my permission to eat me after I die."

Olivia punched him. "Don't think I won't. I bet you'll be tough and have a gamey wild taste though."

"We have to look at the good side of all of this. We could be spending our life sitting in a cubicle dealing with unhappy people."

Olivia lamented, "We're still dealing with unhappy people; at least we don't have to kiss their rear ends like we did at the office."

Dawson laughed. "The arguments are being settled in a different manner now."

Dawson looked out down the driveway and watched as the neighbors drug the bodies he had just shot down the sidewalk. He didn't know or care where they took them.

Olivia hugged his neck. "I'm proud that you stepped up and did what you did. Somebody has to be civilized."

"Let's get over to Henry's and go through her basement. We need to determine exactly what she has and figure out how we are going to move everyone to her brother's place. Once we get moved, we're going to have to figure out how and where you and I are going. Her brother's place will be overrun just like everyone else's. His place may be more defensible, but we won't know until we get there."

Cathy relieved Henry from the watch so that Henry could take Dawson and Olivia down into the basement. Once they were in the basement, they found the two old men had installed wide shelving units down the center and had canned goods and plastic five-gallon buckets of wheat and rice. Dawson looked at Henry. "Those two old men must have been very hungry at one time."

Henry pulled out her notebook with the inventory she had

created. "They almost starved to death. They told me that they survived by eating rats and insects. Hunger was their constant fear. They also feared the government because the government stole all their family's food and property. My father and his brother were the only ones in their family to survive."

"What did they do for a living?"

"They owned a restaurant and a snow blowing business. They would remove snow in the early morning hours and then run the restaurant the rest of the day. Their snowblowers are in the shed out back. My brother was supposed to come get them but hasn't come to get them yet."

Dawson asked, "Do you mind if I look at them? There may be a way for us to use them for something."

Henry led them back up the stairs and into the warm kitchen where she handed him a key from a hook next to the back door. "Here's the key. You may need to use the propane torch to heat the lock in case it's frozen."

Dawson walked out to the shed with Olivia and quickly had the lock thawed and open. He scraped snow from the front of the door and pulled the doors back so the sun could shine inside. There sitting inside were two commercial snowblowers. One was a small, rubber-tracked skid steer with a snow blowing attachment on the front. It had an enclosed cab. The other was a smaller sidewalk sized unit on tracks. A trailer sat on the side of the shed that was used to haul the two snowblowers to the job locations. He went in and sat down in the cab of the skid steer. It was an old unit and was devoid of the electronic displays. He got out and popped the engine cover. It was a diesel-fueled unit with a Kubota diesel engine. He checked the oil in the engine and in the hydraulic reservoir before returning to the cockpit seat. Olivia stood outside the door with her fingers crossed. Dawson turned the key; the glow plug light glowed for a few seconds and went out. He turned it to the start position, and the engine slowly spun. The exhaust chugged puffs of black smoke, and he was about to give up when one of the cylinders hit. It gave the engine the much-needed spin allowing the other two cylinders to start firing. Finally, all three cylinders were firing. He let it run at a fast idle and climbed out.

Olivia smiled. "Finally we can get the driveway and sidewalks cleaned up. Our worries are over."

Dawson just shook his head as he walked around behind the skid steer. "If it has a trailer hitch that I can put a ball on, we can use it to travel on. It has a diesel engine, so it should be fairly fuel efficient. We can scavenge fuel from trucks if we see we're running low. We can load all our stuff in the trailer and make a run for it."

He came back around to the front with a grin on his face. Olivia asked, "Does it have it?"

"Yes, we just have to get everything in containers we can load on the trailer."

Henry heard the engine and came out. "Mr. Dawson, how did you get it cranked?"

"It's a miracle; how long has it been since it last cranked?"

"My husband cranked it to clean off the driveway just before he left for Toronto last week. He cranks it every week to keep the battery charged."

Dawson looked at her and asked, "Are there any other things you haven't told me about? We can load our stuff in the trailer and ride to your brother's house."

"I'm sorry, Mr. Dawson; it never crossed my mind that we could pull the trailer with it and use it for transportation. I assumed it wouldn't crank like all the other engines."

"Henry, this thing has an old diesel engine. There are no electronics on the machine to get damaged. We have to gather up all the food and load it in the trailer. Does your brother have enough beds to sleep everyone?"

"I don't think so."

"Henry, we're going to need to take some mattresses and bedding with us."

Olivia touched his arm. "I smell smoke."

CHAPTER 12

Hawks grabbed the Winchester and headed toward the door. "I don't want you to get hurt. Head out the back door with your pistol and that assault rifle we took off the cop. Don't let them see you, but get in a position where you can see. If I start firing, empty the rifle into the truck."

Carolyn headed out the back door as directed, and Hawks came out on the porch with the rifle at the ready. There were two men in the truck, and they slowed their run up the driveway when they realized Hawks had them covered. They rolled down their windows as they turned in the circle at the top of the drive where it stopped at the front door. Both were in uniform. Hawks recognized the driver as the cop back in Lady Smith. "Aren't you a little out of your jurisdiction?"

The cop smirked. "The RCMP doesn't have a jurisdiction, and I told you that you were in trouble."

Hawks grinned. "I guess you got me; now are you going to tell me what you want?"

"First I'm going to arrest you, then we're going to confiscate all your supplies and working vehicles."

Hawks never quit grinning. "I let you live before because I figured you didn't know what was taking place. You are now running around stealing everything you can get your hands on so you can feed yourselves and your families."

At that moment the passenger fired his pistol through the truck door window, and bullets splintered the post next to Hawks. Hawks didn't hesitate and started pumping rounds through the two men. Carolyn fired from the side of the house. The driver was dead, but in his death throws he punched the accelerator and ran head on into a large cedar tree beside the driveway. The engine died on impact, and the truck sat smoking with its dead driver and passenger. Hawks walked down the steps and put a round through each of their heads. He walked around to the driver's door and opened it and let the cop's body fall to the ground. He switched off the ignition key and looked over in the back of the truck. As expected, it was full of food and supplies they had confiscated in the name of the law.

The Australian pups were barking from inside the house, and the cat was nowhere to be seen. Hawks looked over to Carolyn walking around the corner of the house. "Be sure to put on the safety; this fight is over. Let's get this truck out of sight and get the gate closed and locked." She embraced him and gave him a fast kiss on the lips.

He opened the passenger door and let the passenger's body fall to the ground. He grabbed him by the collar and pulled him clear of the truck. Walking around to the driver's side, he stepped over the dead man, got behind the wheel, and cranked the old Ford truck. It looked to be an early seventies model.

He shifted it into reverse and gritted his teeth at the sound of the fan blade hitting the radiator. It rattled as he drove it around behind the barn where he shut it off. Going into the barn through the back door, he cranked the tractor to let it warm up. Rummaging around in the barn, he located an old padlock and key, then hopped on the tractor. He quickly drove down the drive to the gate and secured it with the lock. Driving back up to the house he rolled the dead men into the front bucket, then drove back to the barn.

Carolyn had already started emptying the truck of its stolen supplies and had the first man's guns and gear lying on the workbench. The two men were armed with government issued C7s and Browning 9 mm pistols. He now had three Browning army issue pistols with seven thirteen-round magazines and three C7 rifles with fourteen loaded thirty-round mags with holsters and belts. The C7s all had the standard optical sights. He was accumulating quite a firearms collection.

He raised the bucket, tilting it back so the bodies wouldn't roll out. Hawks drove down the farm lane past the farm's apple orchard and deep into the woods. The frontend loader on the tractor, normally used to spread gravel and mulch, did a good job of removing the topsoil from atop the underlying bedrock near the surface. The bodies were soon covered with the soil, and Hawks buried them in his mind. They started it; he had simply ended it. He doubted they would have given him the courtesy of a burial.

When he got back to the barn, he returned the tractor to its stall. He checked the weapons, choosing the one that looked the newest. He was familiar with them because they were variants of his sporting guns back home. He was also proficient with their use and operation. These guns were able to be switched to run fully automatic, whereas his rifles back home were regular semi-automatic AR 15s. He adjusted the stock and sling for Carolyn's small frame. He turned to her and said, "I know you know how to fire it."

She pointed to the left side of the rifle. "I just flipped it up to the fire position and started pulling the trigger as fast as I could while aiming at the front half of the truck."

"That worked great this time, but I'm not anxious for my new girl to get hurt."

Carolyn smiled. "Like I said, we make a great team."

Walking around to the front of the house, they watched as the motorcycles and old trucks roared back in the direction of town. Hawks looked over at Carolyn. "I bet poor old Jim is sitting in his country inn wishing he had his chickens back."

"I don't imagine he put up much of a fight."

As the sound of the vehicles faded into the distance, they turned and walked up the steps. Carolyn took a deep breath. "That was intense. I've never imagined what it would be like to shoot someone. I feel sick."

"Let's go inside and chill by the fire. I'll mix us a drink, and you relax."

Hawks mixed her a bourbon and coke and carried it to her. She looked up. "Aren't you going to have one?"

"No, I'm going to stay up tonight and keep an eye out in case they come back looking for their compadres."

"I can stay up with you; I don't think I will ever be able to sleep again."

Hawks touched her cheek. "I want to ask you a question. Did you fire the first shot?"

"No, the one in the passenger seat did."

"Exactly, we didn't start this; they did. We just defended ourselves. I was lucky that the idiot missed me and hit the porch post. It may not go this way the next time around. Arrogance killed those two men. They couldn't back down, especially not in front of one another."

Carolyn took a sip of her drink and sat back in her chair. "Do you think we need to check on Jim? I'd hate to imagine him lying wounded and helpless."

"He was pretty helpless before all this took place. If the posse doesn't show back up, we'll head over in the morning."

That evening they cooked some soup, canned ham, and some biscuits, all courtesy of the dead cops. With only the light from the fireplace, they sat and talked. Carolyn dozed off in the recliner.

The two puppies, Sally and Sydney, lay together on their dog bed. The old cat sat in an unoccupied chair. Hawks was careful to not disturb Carolyn when he slipped on his jacket and picked up the Winchester rifle. He walked out onto the front porch in the darkness. The wood floor creaked and popped under his weight and again when he sat back in an old rocker. The moon shined down bright on the farm. An occasional cloud drifted by, casting shadows across the pasture. From where he sat, he could see the dim outline of deer feeding in the pasture, but he was completely hidden under the porch in the shadows. The light wind was cold, so he turned up his collar and sat quietly. The rifle sat leaning on the rail, and he had his hands buried in his pockets. The deer would be alert for any sound or activity that was out of the ordinary. He went back in and stoked the fire and warmed up every couple of hours. The rifle was never more than an arm's length away at any time.

Hawks gently lay a comforter over Carolyn, being careful not to wake her. The puppies followed him out the door and disappeared around the corner of the house. His eyes adjusted to the night, and he settled back in the chair. He woke with a start when the puppies came back up the steps, their nails clicking on the wood floor, breaking the silence of the night. The deer still milled about down in the pasture but not so far from the woods that they couldn't run for safety in a moment.

Carolyn came to the door. "I can watch a while if you want to get some rest. I'll wake you at dawn."

"No, I want you to keep an eye out tomorrow when I grab a nap. If any of those guys have tactical training, they'll be more than likely to show up around 4 a.m. Supposedly, that is when humans are the soundest asleep. I'm not sure if they realize which farm they hit, but they know that somewhere between here and where they wound up, their friends disappeared."

Carolyn opened the door and let the puppies back in the house. "That means they'll be back as soon as they get hungry again."

"That's the way I see it."

"I feel like we're a bunch of sitting ducks."

"Not quite, it will probably be a couple of weeks before they run out of food. The puppies will be bigger and more alert, and with a little luck, some of them might be killed off by some of the other country people who realize what they are doing." The quiet of the night was interrupted by the abrupt snort of a deer. They looked up to see the small herd bounding toward the woods.

CHAPTER 13

They both looked in the direction from which the wind blew. This smoke was not from just wood. It had the smell of plastic, asphalt, and other noxious fumes. The Chinook winds blew hard from the west. There were no longer responding fire departments or water pressure to fight the fires. There was nothing on Earth that would stop the ensuing conflagration. The fire would roar across the city unabated, leaving the survivors in worse shape than they were already in.

Olivia asked, "What do we do?"

Dawson looked at Olivia and Henry. "Get packed to go now. I want everyone dressed and the backpacks loaded into the sleds. Get everyone a damp cloth to hold over their mouth to filter out some of the ash. I want everyone ready to leave in ten minutes."

Glowing embers were already flying through the sky above them. Fine ash had already started to stain the snow. Dawson and Olivia quickly had their travel clothes on and their packs loaded. He carried the SKS, and Olivia held the coach gun. Henry, her daughter, and the twins were packed up in their sleds. Dawson took the third sled and placed his toolbox in it and the one hundred pounds of cookies.

Henry looked at him. "Where do we go, Mr. Dawson?"

"The first place we are going is the little park next to the

Lougheed House. We can use the old stone house with the tile roof as a shield. It will resist burning until embers accumulate under the eaves. With a little luck, it will give us the time we need for the firestorm to blow past us, I just hope that we're the only ones with that idea. Let's roll."

Without a word, they followed Dawson down the driveway and up the street. The firestorm behind them created a huge column of smoke that blocked the sun. They covered their mouths with the damp cloths, but the smoke was still choking. The fire wasn't just one house catching the one next to it on fire. The forty-mile-per-hour winds caused the downwind structures to catch fire. The dozens became hundreds, and the hundreds became thousands. The intense heat melted the snow on the roofs, and soon even the largest apartment buildings were ablaze. The heat from the inferno pulled the surrounding air into itself.

They made it into the small park and shielded themselves against the embankment below the wide sidewalk lying between the little park and the old mansion. The Chinook winds changed direction as the cold air mass it fought won for a moment and caused the fire to proceed in yet another direction for an hour or so before the winds once again returned with a vengeance. The great old mansion was soon ablaze, along with the huge apartment buildings in every direction. They spent the rest of the day and evening surrounded by the burning and smoldering buildings. Scores of residents had taken shelter with them. The horizon glowed in every direction from the fire that continued unabated. They had been miraculously spared. Their clothes were gray from the ash. The snow had melted, so it wouldn't be easy dragging the sleds, but it could be done.

He told them, "We aren't going to wait. We have several hours before daylight so let's start out towards your brother's house."

Olivia hugged his neck. "You saved me again. Thank you for picking me."

He smiled. "We picked each other."

In single file they followed Dawson down the street as they passed burned-out buildings and vehicles still smoldering. They never paused to the pleas of bystanders as there was absolutely nothing they could do that would do anything but endanger themselves. They had several weeks of food, and it was at least a full day's walk to Henry's brother's home.

Henry asked, "Mr. Dawson, we are exhausted. Can we stop?"

"Sure, let me find a safe spot." He led them around a small wall surrounding a garden. Here they would be out of sight and out of the wind. They could hear people shouting; although, they couldn't see them. The sun was coming up, so they sat with their backs against the wall out of sight. The Chinook was coming to an end, just as quickly as it had begun. The temperature was starting to plummet, and Dawson recognized the snow cold. He was sad to see the return of the intense cold, but the snow would be welcome. The twins were bundled up good and warm.

Dawson, told them and the ladies, "Make sure your hands and feet don't freeze. If you even think you have freezing digits, let me know, and I'll build a fire. We have no way of treating frostbite, and it could prove fatal. Check the twins every time we stop."

Henry nodded. "Don't worry, Mr. Dawson. We'll let you know."

Dawson looked around. "While it's clear, let's get to moving. The exercise will keep us warm, and once it starts snowing, the going will get easier."

As he predicted, the snow came, immediately followed by the normal Alberta winter temperatures. Once the snow had accumulated a couple of inches, they were able to make good time. They made their way out into the suburbs' miles to the west where the fire had not burned. There were people everywhere going through the garbage; several begged them for food. When they saw Dawson was packing a rifle, they shied away.

Olivia asked, "How far have we left to go?"

"Let's see." He stopped and unfolded the map and studied it. He looked up at the nearest intersection. "We're only about halfway there, and we have about two more hours until dark. We need to start looking for someplace we can spend the night out of the cold where we can hide. Look for an empty building or an old house, preferably with a fireplace."

They glanced down the streets as they passed.

Every community has many abandoned or repossessed dwellings and buildings; they were soon rewarded when they spotted an overgrown, unkempt yard. The old house had roofing missing on the front slope and the eaves were rotting and unpainted. Dawson gingerly stepped up onto the porch and peered through the door that sat half open. He quickly checked out the house and basement; it was uninhabited. He helped get everyone into a room with an old brick fireplace. He broke up an old nightstand and, using some old magazines, he started a small fire.

He pulled the old shade down to cover the window and saw the door leading into the room could be barricaded. There were only two ways into the room, the window and the door. He pulled in a good supply of old decrepit wood furniture and the wooden door frames he could pull loose. He was able to break up the old wood furniture by stomping on it with his heavy boots. Olivia found some ancient glass-mixing bowls in one of the kitchen cabinets. They were filled with debris and dust from years of sitting on the shelf in the long-abandoned kitchen. All the metal pots and anything made from metal in the old house had been long stripped out and sold as scrap by the homeless. These were soon scrubbed out in the snow and then refilled and placed by the fire to melt.

All the canteens were filled while they all sat on the floor in front of the fire. The cookies they had made were the perfect meal after the very long day. The small fire was cozy, and once the bricks around the hearth were warm, the room became quite tolerable.

Henry sat crying. "I can't believe that my home and everything I've owned is gone. What's going to happen if my husband makes it back and finds us missing?"

Cathy tried to comfort her. "At least we are alive, and Papa will know that we have gone to your brother's place."

"I sure hope so. Mr. Dawson, do you think we'll make it?"

"If I have anything to do with it, we'll make it. We aren't giving up. You've got to remember that the only thing that we've got going for us is we left in the middle of the chaos, and we lucked up that the snow and cold came back. There will be people scrounging at all hours because they are starting to starve. We'll leave just as soon as it's light enough to see. Let's top off the canteens and drink our fill from the glass bowls in the morning."

Olivia took a bite out of a cookie. "Dawson, you get some sleep, and I'll set up and keep guard the first half of the night."

"I'm surely tired; wake me at midnight. We'll be most vulnerable in the early morning hours. Everyone, get in your sleeping bags. Put the twins in a bag together or each of them in bag with someone else. We can't take a chance of them freezing." He walked over to the corner in the shadows away from the fireplace.

Olivia said, "Why don't you get in a bag next to the fire?"

"My winter clothes are enough to keep me warm. If someone tries to get in, I need to be able to respond in a spit second, and I can't do that if I'm snug in a sleeping bag."

Henry said, "We'll put the twins in a bag together. The rest of us can lay on top of ours near the fire. You're right; we can't let down our guard for a minute." The fatigue from the long day soon took its toll, and soon they were all asleep.

Outside and down the street three men were poking around in the garbage. The largest of the three was a youngish man in his mid-thirties. When the lights went out, he was six-feet-four-inches tall and weighed three hundred pounds. The other two were in their early forties and were just shy of six feet and weighed about 210 pounds apiece. The three were all divorced men who shared a house, and all three missed their first meal three days earlier. They kept little or no food in their kitchen and ate virtually every meal out. Tim Horton's was no longer open for business, nor were any of the other places to grab a quick meal.

The big one named Jim said, "I've never been so hungry in my life. They say you can't go but two weeks without food before you starve to death."

The one nearest him was named Toby. "I've heard the same thing, but surely we have enough fat on us to help see us through."

The third one was named Leonard. Disgustedly, he threw the lid of a trash can on the ground. "Nothing, everything has been picked clean. I say we start taking what we need; you know there are people around who have plenty. Do you smell that wood smoke? There's someone sitting around a cozy fire probably roasting meat."

They all looked up in the direction of the old house. Toby said, "Let go and see if we can peak inside. They may have extra. I could sure use a good piece of roasted chicken."

Big Jim said, "What if it's roasted cat or dog?"

They soon located the smoke coming in little wisps from the old chimney.

Big Jim, "Do you think we should knock on the door?"

Toby grinned. "The chimney is on the right side of the house, and there should be a window. Since you're the tallest, slip around there and see if you can see anything through the window. Leonard, you go around the left side to the rear to see what it looks like back there."

Without a word, Big Jim and Leonard disappeared around each side of the house. Big Jim slipped up to the window and spotted a little spot of light coming through a hole in the old window shade. It was just above his level of eyesight, and no matter how high he tiptoed, he couldn't see in. In the moonlight he spotted some old concrete blocks from some long-forgot project and silently carried one over to window where he could stand and look through the little hole. He could see the three women, two were sleeping by the fire, and what appeared to be a sleeping bag with kids near them. There was also an attractive young woman adding some wood to the fire; she was munching a cookie. He could see the door was barred, but it was nothing so sturdy he couldn't burst through. What he couldn't see was Dawson leaning up against the wall in the corner nearest the window or the coach gun lying on the floor in front of Olivia, hidden by the sleeping bag she sat on in front of the fire.

Leonard and Big Jim came back to the front where Toby waited with his hands shoved into his pockets from the cold. "What did you find out?"

Leonard shook his head no, Big Jim grinned. "Three women are in front of the fire, two are asleep, one's snacking on a cookie. Looks like maybe a couple of kids sharing a sleeping bag. The door is barricaded, but I can go through it with one kick."

Jim pondered, "I don't know if we should bother them. What if they are like my mother and sisters?"

Toby said, "You need to get that thought out of your head. The world is coming unraveled. If we don't take what we need, someone else will. Let's do it; I'm hungry, and I could use some loving."

They tiptoed up the steps in single file trying not to make a sound. One board creaked under the weight of Big Jim, and they all paused and listened. They could see the light from the fire shining out from under the door in the near pitch-black darkness. They could almost taste the cookies and feel the women in their arms. When they reached the door, they hesitated for a moment and listened.

Toby whispered to big Jim, "Bust it open."

Big Jim leaned back and kicked the door with all his might. It gave way under his heavy boot but did not completely allow entrance, but before he could kick it again, he was met with a load of buckshot from the coach gun held by Olivia. Dawson opened up with the SKS from his corner of the room. Olivia was shaking as Dawson grabbed the barrel and eased the shotgun from her shaking hands. "It's OK; you did exactly the right thing."

"Did I kill him?"

"I'll tell you in a second."

The twins were crying. Henry and Cathy cradled them looking wild eyed. Dawson motioned for them to stay down. He drew the 1911 pistol from its holster and with one hand held the small flashlight from his coat pocket. With the pistol cocked and the safety off, he opened the door and shined the light out into the hall. A big man gasped his last three breaths and died with his eyes staring into oblivion; the second was dead with only an involuntary twitching of one foot. He stepped over the bodies and walked to the front door where he found the last one crumpled on the side of the steps. His head was cocked at an odd angle.

Dawson made his way back into the room and re-barricaded the door. "Maybe we can get some rest. They're all dead. I don't expect anyone else will come calling with all the bodies lying around."

Olive was looking up with questioning eyes. "Did I?"

"We both did; good job, baby. Before you start beating yourself up over killing a man, I want you to remember one thing, they didn't knock."

Henry asked, "How many, Mr. Dawson?"

"There were three. We killed two and the third one broke his neck running down the front steps. Now everyone, get back to bed and don't give them a second thought. This is a new world. Our old world went out with the lights, and I want you to remind yourselves, they could have politely knocked."

He reloaded the SKS and replaced the spent shells in the coach gun and handed it back to Olivia. She looked up. "I love you."

"I love you too."

Although Dawson had told them not to give the dead a second thought, he couldn't sleep. He thought back over the last few days and was somewhat shaken when he realized how many lives he had taken. One part of him wanted to just warn the men off. That hadn't worked with the first group of men following him and Henry after leaving her shop. The next group was armed and shooting at him, and if anybody deserved killing, it was them. No, he would bury his feelings and just do what he knew he would have to do.

CHAPTER 14

The deer bounded into the woods. Hawks turned to Carolyn. "Get the puppies in the house, keep quiet, and no lights."

Somewhere near the pasture and on the highway, something or someone moved. The pasture was out of sight of the highway but was within earshot. The deer could have just picked up a scent from something or the sound of movement. Carolyn came back out with her rifle and wearing one of the Browning 9 mm pistols.

Hawks touched her arm. "Stay back in the shadows of the porch; this may only be a coyote or a dog."

As they sat, they heard the chain rattling on the gate. Hawks picked up his rifle. "Whoever it is just climbed over the gate, I don't imagine that it's someone with training."

They sat quietly and waited as they detected a lone figure walking up the drive. The bright moonlight cast shadows from the trees. The lone figure approached, staggered, and fell, and struggled to his feet and plodded on in uncertain steps. He fell once again at the foot of the steps and called out, "Carolyn, this is Jim Banks; help me."

Hawks popped on his flashlight and shined it down on the pitiful figure lying before them. Jim looked up and squinted at the light. His eyes started quivering. He tilted his head back and passed out.

Carolyn knelt beside him. "Look, they beat him almost to death. Look at his hand and face."

"That hand has been stomped on while he was on the ground and the jury is still out on whether he's going to live or not. I think his skull has been cracked; look at the blood vessel on his temple beating. Let's get him inside." Hawks pulled him up into a sitting position and walked behind him so he could reach under his arms and across his chest. He leaned back so that he held Jim's weight with his legs dragging. He took one step at a time until he had him on the porch, got him into the parlor, and laid him next to the fireplace. The only positive thing was his breathing was slow and regular.

Carolyn cleaned his wounds and they turned him on one side with his injured hand and arm on the top side. Hawks pointed out, "This wasn't done with a fist; he was kicked while he was down, and he probably took a lick to the head from a baton or baseball bat. If they show up here, we won't give them the opportunity to get off or out of their vehicles. There's nothing to do but wait and see if he wakes up."

They dozed by the fire for a couple of hours when Jim regained consciousness. His mouth was busted and there were teeth broken and missing. He could barely sip water, and the pupil of one eye was completely dilated. The other eye was bloodied and almost swollen shut. With every breath, he would suddenly catch it. "I think my ribs are broke, and my chest hurts all the way up into my jaw."

Hawks asked, "Was it a bunch of men posing as law officers?"

"Yes, how did you know?" Before Hawks could answer, Jim started turning blue and collapsed, dead.

Carolyn cried out, "Do you know CPR?"

Without a word, Hawks rolled him onto his back and proceeded with the chest compressions followed by breaths to inflate his lungs. After fifteen minutes, he stopped from exhaustion. "It's no use; I believe he had a stroke from the licks to his head. He should have stayed home instead of trying to walk down here in the middle of the night."

Carolyn cried, "I guess we should have run down there to check on him."

Hawks shook his head. "We can't save the world. We could have left and come back to find the house and barn plundered, and then where would we be?"

Carolyn said, "Let's get him out on the porch, and we will bury him in the morning. There's an old cemetery about a half mile down the road by an old chapel."

Once they had Jim's body out on the porch, they cleaned up the floor and sat back down in front of the fire and dozed in their chairs.

The rooster had them up with the sun. Hawks smiled across at Carolyn. "I'll get the tractor cranked and a shovel and get Jim loaded in the bucket, if you'll fix us a bite of breakfast. I'll get started."

"I hate to say it, but it may be for the best that he died. He would never have adapted, and we would have had an invalid on our hands for weeks or months."

She cooked up a pan of biscuits and opened some canned sausage. A puddle of syrup topped with a bit of condensed milk made a hearty breakfast. Hawks came in and washed up at the kitchen sink. "I love this old country food. Just think, we don't have to worry about what we eat, and we don't have to feel guilty about not exercising, sleeping late, or anything that made our former lives miserable."

Carolyn gave him a grin. "Other than having to shoot people, I couldn't be happier. I find all the killing and dying a bit unsettling."

"When we get back, I want to put together a barrel or some way we can hide some food, guns, and medicine away from here in case we have to abandon the house or if someone slips in here trying to steal our stuff and catches us off guard."

Carolyn thought a moment. "I know just the spot. There was at one time a root cellar near an old cabin out in the woods. The old cabin was supposedly here before this house was built. Tammy showed it to me. It was sunk into the ground and has stone walls that rise above ground level and the roof is old shale shingles. Roosevelt overlaid it with corrugated metal and wanted to turn it into a wine cellar of sorts. He had an ambition of planting some grape vines and making a small winery."

Hawks ran his biscuit through the syrup and milk and took a bite. "As soon as we finish laying old Jim to rest, we'll run down and check it out."

Hawks had wrapped the body in an old canvas tarp. Carolyn asked, "Can we spare the tarp?"

"We can spare this one. It's so rotten it almost fell apart when I was wrapping him." Hawks climbed onto the tractor seat, and Carolyn sat on the fender next to him.

They drove down the driveway and up the road to the old chapel. The chapel was picturesque surrounded by old cedars. It had been many years since it had served as a functioning church but was used for the occasional wedding or funeral. The cemetery lay off to the right of the parking lot and was full of old headstones. The remains of a wooden fence surrounded the old cemetery. Hawks stopped the tractor and gently rolled the body from the bucket. He then went over to the remains of one section of the fence and crushed it with the tractor. At the edge of the cemetery, he used the bucket to excavate a rough grave opening. He then took the shovel and finished cleaning out the hole so it could accommodate the body.

Carolyn asked, "Do you want me to help?"

"No, I want you to watch the road. If those bikers make another run out this way, I want to hear about it before they get here."

They soon had the grave closed and the 23rd Psalms recited. They then took the tractor and filled the bucket with rocks from the hillside behind the chapel. These were used to cap the grave as it would go unmarked unless one of his relatives ever showed up to find out where he went.

Once they were back at the farm with the gate locked and the tractor put away, they proceeded to look at the old root cellar. Just as described, it was located up a little lane several hundred yards across a meadow behind the main house. The area was wooded, and all that remained of the old cabin was the rock chimney. Immediately behind the old cabin site sat the root cellar. The metal roof was covered with leaves and fronds from the cedar trees around it. The door had been replaced with one made of treated wood, and the hinge was secured into the rock door opening with fresh mortar. He opened the door and peered in. It took a moment for his eyes to adjust to the dim light coming in through the open door. Roosevelt and Tammy had built in shelves and had started building wine racks. One side was left clear.

Carolyn piped up, "Why can't we put a bed in here and some supplies? It's watertight, and I doubt it gets very hot or cold in here."

Hawks nodded his approval. "Why don't we go over to Jim's place and see if he has a bed we can use and get whatever else we can find that we might need. Otherwise, it will all go to waste and ruin. I doubt his wife will make it back if she is anything like him."

"She wore the pants of the house. She was a women's libber who hated men. I guess that's why she chose old Jim. He fell short of being a man in many ways."

"Let's hook up the stock trailer to the Model A and head over to Jim's. If we see we're going to have to haul a lot of stuff, we can go back and get the tractor or I can get to work on the Ford truck. I'd like to keep it out of sight for a while just in case."

The drive over to the inn was uneventful. The thought foremost in their mind was the gang of motorcycles and the old trucks making another run out to their part of the country. Hawks knew the gang realized that their friends had disappeared somewhere down this road. They pulled up to the country inn and found the front door standing wide open.

They drove around back to be out of sight of the main road. They were both armed. Hawks still carried the Winchester lever action and wore the Scofield pistol in its chest rig. Carolyn wore one of the Browning pistols in one of the holsters taken from the bad guys as well as one of the C7 rifles with some extra magazines in a pouch attached to a vest taken from one of the men. They walked up the steps and found the back door open.

When they walked in, they discovered the disarray in the home from it being ransacked. As expected, there was no food in the kitchen and the pantry was empty. They made a quick run down into the basement and found some old kerosene lamps and a couple of five-gallon cans of kerosene. They found a suitable bed for the root cellar, along with some linens upstairs. They also gathered up all the soap and other toiletries throughout the inn. These they put into pillow cases and in some of the reusable bags. They found no weapons of any kind.

Jim did have a small den where his office was located. In it they found some ornate gentlemen's walking canes and some vintage fly rods and a case full of flies that accompanied them. There was also a small cardboard box on his desk containing a gold pocket watch. It obviously held some sentimental value, probably an inheritance from a father or grandfather. This was removed and added to their loot. Everything was gathered and added to the contents of the stock trailer. In his desk drawer they found an unopened bottle of Jameson Irish whiskey.

Hawks grinned. "This works in a pinch if there isn't any good bourbon around."

All the candles and a few of the candle holders in the house were also added to their supplies. Next, they turned to the tool shed and barn where chainsaws, oil, and other tools were collected. They even located, stored in the loft, some old hand tools used prior to the invention of electric power tools. They wasted no time heading back to the farm to unload and organize their new acquisitions.

Hawks looked at Carolyn's old pocket watch. "It seems like it should be later, but it's only noon."

Carolyn glanced back, "It's been a long night and day, and I'm not surprised. We started before daylight."

"We've got to get some rest. Why don't you lay down, and I'll stir around for a few hours and wake you later."

Carolyn ran her fingers through his hair. "I had several hours of sleep in my chair, and you haven't slept at all. I want to get cleaned up. You grab a nap, and I'll wake you later. Go get in bed and sleep."

"I won't argue with you." He smacked her on the lips and headed upstairs.

He didn't remember getting in bed but woke sometime in the night with Carolyn snuggled up beside him. He lay quiet and didn't hear any sound other than her steady, rhythmic breathing. The 40 degree weather had the house cold everywhere but next to the fireplace, woodstoves, or in the bed. A large down comforter kept them warm. He dozed off and didn't wake until their faithful rooster started crowing from the chicken coop. Carolyn stirred. "I hope you don't mind me coming to bed and not waking you. I set up some empty cans around the downstairs windows and doors. If anyone were to try and get in, they would trip the empty cans and jars I set up to fall and make noise. That would in turn scare the pups, who would also start barking."

He pulled her close. "You're right. We can't stay up all the time. After we get the root cellar set up, I want to give some thought into creating a hidden room somewhere in this house where we can seek refuge."

Carolyn grinned. "Why not this bedroom. The sitting area at the top of the stairs has two doors, one for the next bedroom and this one. The other rooms are down the hall. What if we put a bookcase over it on rollers? All we would have to do is pull it closed behind us when we come in. No one would be the wiser."

"That's a great idea. I think I can do that. We can move the bookcases from the den downstairs, but first let's get the root cellar stocked with the bed, food, and weapons."

After breakfast they walked down the back porch and headed to the barn where the Model A was parked with the stock trailer still attached. They pulled out a .22 rifle and pistol stored in the barn. He also took one of the Browning pistols and one of the C7 rifles and a couple of loaded magazines. To this they added enough food for two weeks, some jugs of water, and clothes. They drove to the edge of the woods where the root cellar waited. When they got to the root cellar, they opened the door and peered in. Roosevelt's door was tight enough to keep out the mice and rats. They soon had a bedroom set up and the cellar well provisioned. They could easily retreat here and no one would be the wiser.

Hawks dusted his hands. "Now we can get that bookcase upstairs and set up to hide the door opening."

They went back to the barn and were greeted by the two pups. The old cat had a big rat in her jaws and disappeared behind some old hay bales. Hawks rummaged around in the barn looking for anything he could use to help him mount the bookcase to the wall. As in all old barns with old workshops, this one was full of used hardware such as screws, plumbing, electrical stuff, paint brushes, etc. He dug around and found a good-sized piano hinge. It had obviously been scrounged from some long-ago project or junked piece of equipment. He took the bookcase up to the bedroom door. It was a sturdy old bookcase made from oak. He fastened the piano hinge down one side and blocked up the bookcase about an eighth of an inch off the floor, then screwed the other side of the piano hinge to the door frame. When he finished, he knocked out the small blocks. The book case hung unsupported and swinging free. They further camouflaged the hinge side by placing a matching bookcase next to the bookcase on that side. On the back, he installed a screen door spring he found on an old door stored in the barn loft. The addition of a slide lock would allow them to secure it from inside the room. Carolyn soon had the bookshelf loaded with books and what-nots, and if someone didn't know any better, there wasn't any way it would be recognized as a doorway.

It had been a long, hurried day. They went downstairs and stoked the fire and added some wood. The sun was setting, and it was going to be a cold winter night. Carolyn said, "Did you notice the clouds building? It's going to snow."

Hawks rubbed his hands in front of the fire. "What's the date? I seem to have lost track."

"It's December 1st; Christmas is right around the corner."

"We'll have to get ready. I'm not going to let a little thing like the end of life as we know it get in the way of Christmas."

"Tammy was a big decorator at Christmas. I'm sure the attic has boxes just waiting to be retrieved." Hawks gazed off into the fire and remembered being a small boy at his childhood home. He looked over at Carolyn. "I wish I could travel back in time and spend one more Christmas in my childhood home."

Carolyn walked over to the fire and hugged his neck. "Me too."

Dalton and his fellow Mountie, Garrett, sat on the hillside across the road from the farm. Dalton peered through his binoculars from the seclusion of the woods. "This is where I saw Sonny and Jake stop when I looked in my rearview mirror."

Garrett complained, "I know Sonny was your brother, but I don't think we need to do anything until we need to get some more supplies. When we take them, we'll get a fight. I've seen the old man with the rifle. You can tell when someone is comfortable carrying a gun. He won't be easy like that stupid imbecile at the inn. We can shoot him from a hundred yards out. He'll never know what hit him."

Dalton lowered the binoculars. "If we do that, we won't know what happened to Sonny. There's smoke drifting from the fireplace. I think we need to conduct a safety check in the morning."

"Don't you think it would be better if we slipped down there tonight and looked around first?"

"Let's open some of those beans and get some sleep. We can sneak down there after midnight once we're sure they're asleep."

Garrett spoke, "What has become of us? I remember when we used to be good cops. We should be locking up bad guys, and now we are the bad guys."

Dalton agreed. "Everyone is a bad guy now. Remember when we gathered up all the food, supplies, and vehicles and dutifully delivered them to the city confiscated warehouse in Lady Smith."

"Yes, I remember, and I also remember the mayor, alderman, some of the judges, and the chief loading up their vehicles outside the back door. All we were doing was stealing for them and locking up and shooting the poor bastards we were cleaning out. And yes, I feel guilty about it, but I have a wife and children. They are foremost in my mind."

Under the light of the moon, they walked over the hill and

down into a rocky draw. Their fire was low, and they soon had it blazing and a couple of cans of beans heating up on a rock next to it. Dalton asked Garrett, "How much food do you think you have accumulated for your family?"

"I figure I have a year or more. We moved out of town to my grandfather's old place in the country."

Dalton gave him a questioning look. "I thought you guys sold that place."

Garrett grinned. "We did, those people decided to give it back after I had a talk with them."

"This might make a good country farm to move to. It's far enough from Victoria that it is out of walking range for almost everyone."

They lay their bedrolls near the fire and dozed. In the early morning hours, they rose, climbed up out of the draw, and back to their vantage point where they could see the farm. It was starting to snow, and there was no moonlight peeking through the clouds. They couldn't see the farm, and they could only see to walk with their small flashlight.

Hawks couldn't sleep. Nightmares that his children were hurt made him wake frequently, toss and turn. He eased out of the bed so as not disturb Carolyn and walked to the window. It was pitch black in the room and outside. He knew the cloud cover would block the moon, but he glanced out of the window out of habit. It was then he saw the flash of light on the hillside. It was faint, but light can be seen from a great distance when there is no other light.

He gently woke Carol. "We have company."

CHAPTER 15

Olivia gently touched Dawson on the cheek. "It's getting light, baby."

Dawson looked up at her. "I don't think I'll ever tire of seeing your face when I wake up."

She smiled, bent down, and gave him a kiss.

Dawson got to his feet, checked the rifle and pistol, and turned to the ladies. "You ladies get packed up while I clear the doorway."

Without a word they went to work getting packed up. Dawson cleared the door and went out into the hall. He grabbed each of the dead men in turn and dragged them back down the hall. The bodies had frozen in the hours since they had died. He went to the front door and down the steps where he rolled the last one off to the ground onto the side of the steps.

He thought to himself, It will only get worse from here.

Soon they had the sleds loaded and were on their way. The snow had the consistency of dry powder, and it squeaked under their footsteps; the sleds pulled easily. The cold was so oppressive that at one point Dawson was tempted to turn back to the old house where he knew there was warmth.

Onward they trudged until they came to a parking garage to get out of the wind. It was full of abandoned vehicles. He took the butt of his hunting knife and knocked out the window of someone's work van. He soon had the spare tire off and with a flick of his wrist cut off the air stem. The air quickly blew out with a whistle. Little BC grinned in amazement at the sound. Once it was empty, Dawson rolled it into a corner where they were out of the wind and lit it with the propane torch from Henry's shop. It was soon burning hot, and the thick black smoke rose to the concrete ceiling and toward the doors. It quickly warmed them up, and soon they had to back away from it.

Henry said, "Mr. Dawson, how do you know how to do all of this? I would have never thought to set a tire on fire."

Dawson looked up at her and said, "You need to start thinking outside of what you are accustomed to. Most people are at a loss for what to do if something happens that they can't imagine happening. I think the term is the normalcy bias. Many people have died during hurricanes and other natural disasters because they couldn't imagine their house being blown away or flooded. You will have to be absolutely ruthless before all of this is over. There may come a time when you may have to kill someone to feed BC and Lucy. If they were my children, I wouldn't hesitate. It's one thing to let yourself starve; it's entirely different when you have little ones."

Olivia spoke up, "I wonder how many people waited until their house was on fire before they tried to get out?"

Cathy added to what Olivia said, "I would have probably waited to see what happened. You are so right about what is taking place."

Dawson looked at the ladies. "Everyone, eat some cookies and drink some water. We'll need all the energy we can get to make the push to your brother's place."

A couple with two small children approached them. The man spoke up. "Do you mind if we warm up next to your fire?"

Dawson said, "Help yourself. That tire should burn another

couple of hours, and there are more tires in these abandoned cars if you need another. Just cut off the valve stem so they don't explode if you add one to the fire." He could see the hungry look on their faces.

The young lady asked, "Can you spare anything for my kids?"

Dawson started to say no, any food they gave up now would be food they couldn't eat later. Instead, he reached into his coat pocket and retrieved four of the trail bars and handed them over to the lady. Tears poured out of her eyes as she opened them and gave one to each of the little kids. She put the other two in her pocket.

Dawson looked at Olivia, Henry, and Cathy. "We need to get going."

He looked around at the couple. "Good luck, I wish you well."

He knew that in all probability they would be dead inside a week. The man nodded. "Thanks, I will. We're trying to make it to my father's ranch about thirty miles from here. We lost everything in the fire. I hope you guys have safe travels as well."

Dawson dreaded heading back into the cold Alberta winds. They checked their equipment and made sure the twins were bundled up warm. They put them, wearing their winter clothes, into a sleeping bag together down in the sled where they would be out of the wind. Dawson led the way with the heaviest of the sleds; Henry and Cathy brought up the rear and took turns pulling the sled with the twins. They walked for several hours before stopping again at a shopping center.

Olivia asked, "How come you gave them some food?"

He replied, "I did it because I'm stupid."

The shopping center had a large Walmart and a line of stores laid out like a strip mall. It wasn't abandoned but had the station for one of the C trains where there was an overhead walkway crossing over the tracks. The building was enclosed, and he could see there were homeless camping inside. A trail of smoke trailed out of the top from campfires within.

Dawson said, "Let's keep moving. No good can come from us slowing up here. I know we're cold and tired, but we need to get out of sight of these people."

They were perhaps a hundred yards past the building when Olivia called out, "Dawson, they're coming out."

Dawson looked over his shoulder at a half dozen men heading their way. "I feel like I'm in a zombie movie. Y'all keep moving." He wasn't going to wait until they got close to warn them away. He pulled up the SKS and put a round in the snow in front of them. The bullet's impact sprayed snow all over them, and they abruptly stopped. Another round had them running in the opposite direction. Dawson made sure they were back in the building before he grabbed the rope on his sled, slung it across his body, and caught up to them.

Olivia asked, "Did you have to kill any of them?"

"Not this time, but I had to waste two bullets to scare them."

Cathy asked, "Do you think they were going to harm us?"

"Let's put it this way; they weren't coming to invite us to a barbeque." They walked another two hours, and when they reached the next intersection, they stopped long enough to check the map. Dawson grinned. "Finally, one mile to go. I sure hope your brother is happy to see us."

The houses and neighborhoods had started to thin out as a lot of the property in this section of the province was light commercial, small farms, and even some ranches. When they reached Henry's brother's driveway, they found a locked gate.

Henry looked puzzled. "I'll go down and get him to come open it."

Dawson stopped her. "What if he isn't there, and the house is occupied by strangers?"

"I never thought of that."

"I can get us in, and we can all go in together." The gate was a typical farm gate with the hinges being simple flanges with a loop on the end hanging over large metal studs screwed into the heavy creosote post. Dawson simply lifted the gate off its hinges, and when they passed, re-hung it on the protruding pegs.

Olivia gave him a thumbs-up. "You know so much. I'm so glad I'm not trying to figure out how to eat my roommate's cat."

The driveway was several hundred yards long and turned to go around a half dozen greenhouses before turning back to the house in the rear. The sun was setting, and there was no light in the house. There was a small column of wood smoke coming from a chimney. Someone was home or had been home recently. As they approached the house a man stepped out onto the porch with a shotgun in his hand.

Henry called out, "Charlie, is that you? It's me, Angie."

Charlie came down the porch and called, "Thank God, it's you; I've been worried. Come get in out of the cold." They all hurried to the house where Charlie quickly herded them in and helped Dawson unload the sleds.

Charlie pointed to the parlor. "Get in there next to the heater and warm up. I'll stow the sleds in the carport."

"Thanks, Charlie, I'm about walked out." He shook Charlie's hand and went into the parlor where all the ladies were stripping off their cold weather gear.

Charlie came in. "Angie, what happened?"

"A huge wildfire ran through the city. All I have is what we have with us. Our house is gone, along with thousands of other homes and buildings. If Dawson hadn't showed up, we would be surely dead by now. By the way, this is Dawson Stewart and his girlfriend, Olivia Watson."

"I'm glad to meet you guys, and thank you for taking care of my family. I could see the glow and the smoke from here."

Henry looked concerned. "Where is Mary?"

"She went to Vancouver to visit the kids. I haven't heard a thing since the lights went out, and I don't believe they are coming back anytime soon or if at all."

Dawson nodded in agreement. "I haven't found any electronic devices that will work. Only things like old-fashioned flashlights will work. Olivia and I don't want to be a drain on your food and resources. If you'll let us warm up and rest a couple of days, we'll be on our way."

"You saved my family. My father made sure we were as well stocked as Angie. We've got a lot in storage. Our worry is all the starving people starting to show up. I've had to shoot three people so far."

Dawson looked over at Olivia and she nodded and he looked back at Charlie. "The problem you have here is that if we can walk this in little more than a day, there's thousands of other people who can also make it here. We made it here with full bellies. They will be desperate and more so with each passing hour. You'll have to survive here for several months; it'll take that long for most of the people to starve or die. They'll quit coming two or three at a time. It'll be dozens once they figure out that's what it takes to take over a house."

"I've thought about that, but if my wife and kids make it, I've got to be here. This is the only place they would come. I would love to have you here to back me up."

"We'll stay a couple of days and get rested up and give it some thought, but as of right now, I'm thinking about crossing the mountains."

Henry interrupted, "Mr. Dawson, we don't want to see you go. You saved us."

"Henry, you saved us too. If it weren't for your uncle's apartment and weapons, we would have been in a fix."

Charlie added, "I can't ask you to do any more than you've done, but I want you to realize that the mountains are full of snow and the snowplows aren't running. What you're thinking of doing is tantamount to suicide. If you insist, we'll see to it that you are well provisioned for your journey, but I ask that you reconsider."

Olivia squeezed Dawson's arm. "We appreciate you helping us."

Charlie pointed to the kitchen. "There's hot water on the stove, and there's beans and rice there too. You and Olivia get cleaned up. I made an outhouse just outside the back door. I'll have to move it once it starts getting warm, but for now it's all I've got. After you eat and get cleaned up, you folks can get to sleep. If you don't mind, I'll wake you up sometime after midnight so you can stand watch while I get some sleep."

"That's a good idea. Somebody has to stand guard." Dawson and Olivia freshened up in the kitchen, and when they returned Charlie pointed to the bedroom down the hall.

"You can sleep in my bedroom. I've changed the linen. I usually sleep on the couch so I can hear if anyone is trying to get in."

Dawson and Olivia climbed into the cold bed; this part of the house was almost as cold as the outside as it was farthest away from the woodstove in the den. They remained fully clothed as they had to always be ready at a moment's notice. Olivia was curled up with her back to him, and he had the pistol in his hand under the pillow.

Charlie called from the door, "Dawson, it's me Charlie. Its 2:00 a.m. Do you think you can spell me for a while?"

"Sure thing, I'll be right there."

Olivia kissed his hand. "I'll get up and help."

"No, I want you to get all the rest you can. We've got to decide if and when we're going to make our move, and rest is the most important thing right now." Dawson put on his boots and walked into the den carrying the SKS and wearing his pistol.

Charlie was reloading the woodstove. "Dawson, I have heated with wood for many years, and I have a 2,500 gallon propane tank that is almost full that I use for my greenhouses. I have a good business for fresh vegetables for several large restaurants. I don't start heating them until March, so my tank is full. It runs the stove in my kitchen and some space heaters. I'm holding off using the space heaters and will use them only if I can't reach the woodpile. The tank and its lines are all underground because of the intense cold we get around here in the winter."

"I was curious about how the cold affected it. I know you need to keep the little butane lighters next to your body to keep them warm if you expect them to work when it's this cold. I have a quick question. From which direction did the people you had to shoot come from?"

"I'm not sure. First two woke me up breaking into the house, and they chose to rush me instead of running. The third one caught me in the outhouse. I dropped the toilet paper and was bent over to pick it up when he fired. I killed him when he opened the door to see if I was dead."

Dawson grinned. "I hope you don't mind me sharing that story one day. What sort of weapon was he shooting?"

"I have it here." He reached behind his belt and pulled out an old Colt .38 revolver.

"I haven't seen many of those. Is that pistol and your shotgun the only weapons you have?"

"Yes, and I only have twenty rounds of buckshot for this old double barrel and the three bullets left in this revolver. My dad and uncle had the extra stored over at Angie's house. My wife and our other sister were afraid we'd get in trouble, so we told Angie to throw them away. I hid this shotgun from my wife. My dad and his uncle liked these coach gun shotguns."

"It's a good thing you kept it. You'd probably be dead now if you hadn't."

"I can't help but wonder if my other sister is alive."

"I don't want you to give up hope, but they were in the line of the fire. If she waited until her house was on fire to leave, I'd be doubtful if they made it."

"That's what I was thinking. I'll just have to hope she did and can make it here. I wouldn't know where to start looking for her and her family."

Dawson lay his hand on his shoulder. "You need to put that burden aside for a while and get some rest. Sleep as long as you can. I'll stay on guard, friend."

The only light was from the gentle glow coming from the little glass window in the door of the heater. The glass was stained dark amber from the fire residue that had built up on it. An entire wall of the room was stacked high with dry wood. Charlie went into the next room, where he had made a bed on the couch. Henry, Cathy, and the twins were obviously in other rooms. Locating the door to the basement in the short hall leading back to the kitchen, he looked to a comfortable chair sitting to the side of the woodstove. Anyone walking into the room would focus on the light coming from the woodstove window, which would give him the split second he would need to react. He walked to the front window and looked up the driveway toward the highway. The gate was obscured by the six greenhouses. The moonlight lit up the area and was helped by the reflection of the snow cover. All was quiet, and would probably stay quiet so long as there was a stiff breeze and the temperature was hovering somewhere below a negative 10 degrees Fahrenheit. It was a beautiful scene. Having been raised in the south where there was seldom any frozen precipitation, he always marveled at the snow. Although the snow was a terrible nuisance, he looked forward to seeing it.

He looked out of all the windows and thought of how to defend the home from every direction. The problem was they only had one high-powered rifle that had range and penetration. The coach guns were fantastic out to fifty or seventy-five feet with buckshot. Beyond that they would keep someone's head down and could kill, but they quickly lost lethality as the range increased.

Once he was satisfied there was no threat, he returned to the chair and proceeded to daydream and ponder the turn of events that had led to him sitting in a room standing guard.

He went over the reasons in his mind to stay and the reasons to leave. No matter how he ran the numbers, the problem was they were at ground zero for hundreds of thousands of refugees and an unknown number of well-armed police and military. Once the people on the outside realized they had something to fight for, nothing would stop them from trying to get it. It would just be a matter of time before someone got a lucky shot, and they would be history. If they were even a hundred miles away, it might make a difference, but they were sitting almost in the middle of the Calgary metropolitan area.

Olivia was the first one up, and she came in looking prettier than he had ever seen her. He rose to meet her giving her a deep, meaningful kiss. She smiled. "Have you made a decision?"

"I think the weather has made the decision for us. We're not going to make it unless we can cross the mountains. The snow-plows aren't running, and the snow is only piling up. Unless we have snow machines, we won't be moving very fast. We won't be able to carry enough food to see us through."

Olivia took a deep breath. "What if we planned to hold out here until we are forced out? Can we explore some escape routes?"

"We're going to have to. I'll find out from Charlie what's

around here and see what kind of machines and equipment he might have."

As soon as it was light enough to see, Dawson put on his cold weather gear and went outside to look around the property. There was a large barn out back where Charlie kept all the tools and equipment necessary to run a small plant nursery. It was mostly hand tools and a couple of lawn mowers, a rotary tiller, and a small garden tractor. The property was bounded on the rear by a ravine leading down to a creek that in turn emptied into the Bow River. A large group would be unlikely to encroach from the rear, but a fit individual or a small group could slip in from the rear.

The left side of the property was where the greenhouses sat. A road ran between them and a large hedgerow with a ten-foot chain-link fence was immediately behind them. It would be highly unlikely attack would come from this side. It would also trap them if they had to flee. The right side of the property was where the rows of plants were placed in various-sized pots to sell to the public. A small office with an area in the front was where they sold seed packets, fertilizer, and garden ornaments. This building had barn doors opening to the public and had a rolled-up fabric awning extended in the spring and summer to shelter small tables holding delicate plantings. Behind this building was another drive and another hedgerow with a matching chain-link fence.

Following the road to the rear led down the side of the house to the back where there was a huge wood shed that was almost full of stove wood. The wood was primarily the cut-off ends of wood from a sawmill that was cut down in size to fit the stove.

The front of the property was the most likely source of danger. The wood rail fence was decorative and allowed the public to view the nursery easily from the road. The only advantage to the property was the fact the house was in the back, and unless someone knew it was back there, they would think it was a plant nursery closed for the season. A closed nursery had no food written all over it. He walked back to the road, and one of the first things he noticed and smelled was the smoke from the wood heater. If he noticed it, so would anyone walking by.

He went back down to the house and met Charlie coming out. "I expected you to sleep longer."

Charlie reached and picked up a snow shovel. "With all this snow, I have to shovel the drive and walks. My snowblower was in the shop when all this started."

Dawson shook his head. "No, no, no! No more shoveling the snow. It needs to look like no one is here, and we have to do something about the wood heater. Do you think your twenty-five-hundred-gallon tank of propane will heat your house for several months?"

"Yes, it will easily heat the house for a year if we just use the stove and one of the space heaters in the den. I use the wood because I get it free from a friend of mine who owns a furniture factory an hour or so drive from here."

"Good, don't shovel the walk or steps. We'll use the back and side door only from here on. This is an abandoned business as far as anyone knows. We can handle the occasional prowler. We need to make sure the windows are covered so that no light can be seen from outside during the evening hours."

Charlie nodded his understanding. "I'm glad you've decided to stay. Your suggestions are invaluable."

"I think we need to move as much of that firewood into the house and around the exterior walls. If the house takes gunfire, we need something to stop or slow up the projectiles. You have enough wood to really fortify the house. I suggest we get started right away. We also need to make sure no one can enter the basement windows as well. Once we do that, I want to try my hand at making snowshoes."

Charlie pointed to the barn in the back, "I'm not sure what kind of shape they're in, but there are several stored in the loft of the barn. There are also some cross-country skis. When I was in college, I tried to take it up, but I never really mastered it. I was always working when I wasn't in class."

They spent the rest of the day ferrying in the firewood and stacking it along the outer walls, starting in the front. Everyone pitched in, even BC and Lucy.

The sun was setting by the time they finished. Henry had dinner ready, and they all gathered in the kitchen at the table and the bar. Henry amazed with Dawson asked, "Mr. Dawson, how do you think of all of this? You know how to do things."

"I don't know. I put myself in the shoes of other people. I don't hesitate. I've always been able to make split-action decisions and respond without hesitation. The Lord gave me gut feelings I always try to follow. My dad had it, and so do my brothers."

Charlie spoke up, "You have a warrior's mind; my father told me about men like you. You know how to use stealth, and you know how to create a defense."

Dawson looked up from his plate. "I know everything but how to keep us all from getting killed. I'm afraid we're only postponing the inevitable."

Olivia touched his arm. "Henry, Cathy, the twins, and I would all be dead if it weren't for him knowing what was going to take place. He was the first to recognize that the lights weren't coming back on. We all assumed it was just going to be an inconvenience, but not Dawson. He sized up the situation in just a few minutes and acted."

Dawson shook his head. "The one thing I'm sure of is we're going to be fighting for our lives very soon. As soon as someone figures out that we're not starving to death, they will be coming. Every day we can go undetected, the population dwindles. If we can survive two or three months, most of the people will be dead. If we can make it a year, 90 percent will have perished. There is another question on my mind. Was the southern half of the planet affected by the blackout? I don't expect them to come to the rescue. There may be some military assets that are EMP proof, but they won't be able to restore the infrastructure that is left or feed the masses. The local police and military will do whatever it takes to feed themselves."

Charlie agreed. "That is what my father and uncle were afraid of and what they warned me about. The Calgary winter is our friend right now. Another blizzard will keep us safe for at least a few days. I noticed the clouds building from the east when we were carrying in the wood."

CHAPTER 16

Carolyn spoke from the bed, "How many?"

"I can't tell, there's only one light, so however many there are, they've got to follow closely. It can't be many. I want you to stay here. I can't operate in the dark and fight unless I know your exact location. If I see movement, I may need to shoot without knowing for sure what my target is. Absolutely no lights."

She hugged his neck. "I understand. I'll stay put until I hear from you."

They quietly got dressed in the dark, and Hawks slipped out of the room with one of the C7 rifles and a Browning high power on his hip. He also carried two extra magazines for each. On his belt he wore the large hunting knife in its leather scabbard. Once he was certain the bedroom door was safely hidden behind the bookcase, he proceeded down the steps in the dark. When he reached the bottom of the steps, he went to the front door and got another glimpse of the light as it slowly progressed up the driveway. The puppies were locked in their kennel, and he was careful not to disturb them. The days of living in the house without electricity enabled him to negotiate inside without the aid of lights.

He tiptoed down the basement stairs and outside through the walkout door. With his eyes accustomed to the dark, he could negotiate the walkway and driveway in the ambient light. He went and stood next to a large tree where he could occasionally see the flicker of the light. The clouds had thinned a bit, allowing the moonlight to filter through. The light soon went out. He knew it would take their eyes a few minutes to adjust to the faint moon-light, so he patiently waited.

In low-light conditions, the human eye is limited in what it can see. Anything that isn't moving or silhouetted is practically invisible. Hawks knew that so long as he stood motionless against the big tree the men could walk within a few feet and he wouldn't be noticed.

Dalton spoke to Garrett in a low voice. "Let's stand here for a few minutes to let our eyes adjust. We need to be careful. That old man may have seen our light. Don't drag your feet when you walk. Try to roll your steps instead of stepping down, we'll have to sep-arate. I want you to take the right side of the house. I'll follow the drive around the side. We'll meet at the rear and look around the outbuildings. Then we'll slip in the house through the back door."

After a good thirty minutes they proceeded, each heading in their respective directions. Dalton snuck toward the front of the house, stopping every few steps to wait and listen. Despite his warning, he heard Garrett crunching the gravel as he headed across the drive and onto the lawn. At that moment, the sound of dogs barking erupted from inside the house.

"Dammit," he whispered under his breath. He took another few steps and paused as he neared a large tree across the driveway from the house.

Hawks now knew there were two. The dilemma was how to kill one without alerting the other. He had a large knife on his belt, but he wasn't a commando, and these were young men. He was certain he could get his knife into the man and make a fatal wound, but there would be noise, and he could get shot as well. The guy was within two feet of him when he made his move. He slammed his pistol onto the side of the man's head. Dalton never knew what hit him, and he collapsed where he stood.

The man lay with his lips moving as though he were speaking, but no sound came forth. Hawks put his fingers over the carotid artery on the man's neck. There was no pulse, so he checked his wrist as well, still nothing. The man's hand quivered in his death throws. Hawks removed the man's Browning from its holster and replaced his with it. It wasn't likely the gun he used to hit the man was damaged, but he hit him so hard the slide could have been bent. He took the new gun and quietly cycled the action; as expected, it had a round in the barrel. He replaced the magazine with the one from his gun, which was fully loaded. The new magazine went into his pocket as a backup. As a precaution, he plunged his knife into the dead man's throat, withdrew it, and wiped it on the man's chest. Without looking back, he headed around the right side of the house following the path the other man took. He had to be careful walking in the twilight so as not to injure himself or alert his quarry. What he did in the next thirty minutes would decide if he and Carolyn lived or died.

Garrett continued his trek around the right side of the house. He could hear the dogs barking and half expected to see someone come out the back door. The moonlight was filtered one minute and nonexistent the next. He paused when the clouds passed over and proceeded only when he could see. He kept glancing up at the back door and windows. The snow across the ground behind the house appeared to be flat and smooth. What he didn't see was the rainwater catch basin filled with snow. The lid had been removed and never replaced. He stepping off into it with his right leg and pitched forward on his face in the snow. The pain was intense, and he feared he had broken his knee. He crawled on his hands and knees until he reached a garden bench and pulled himself up to where he could sit for a moment. He shook the snow from his rifle and looked around. What he didn't and couldn't see was Hawks standing by the corner of the house.

Hawks almost felt sorry for the man until he remembered what they did to poor old Jim. He hit the man with a short burst from the C7 and watched him collapse in the snow. In his death throes, the man's hand squeezed the trigger on his rifle, and it fired wild until the thirty-round magazine was empty. Hawks fired one last shot into the man's head.

He called up to Carolyn, "It's over, honey; you can come on down."

When he didn't get a response, his heart jumped into his throat. He remembered the uncontrolled fire from the dead man's rifle. He knew the back door was locked, so he ran around to the walkout basement door, ran up the steps into the kitchen, and then up the stairs to the bedroom. He flung open the door and switched on his flashlight.

Carolyn lay motionless on the floor. He gathered her up in his arms and carried her to the bed so he could see her better. He lit a kerosene lamp and couldn't find a scratch on her, but when he ran his fingers through her hair, he felt a goose egg bump on her head. He dampened a cloth and wiped her face. She was breathing OK; all he could do was wait.

He looked across the room and realized she had tripped over a waste basket hitting her head on a nightstand as she fell. He stayed by her side the rest of the night. He lay next to her with his arm across her chest so he could feel her breath. He was awakened by a soft kiss on his cheek. Startled awake he looked up into her beautiful eyes.

"Well, handsome, it looks like you had a busy night. I got so excited when all those bullets were flying through the house that I tripped and fell. My head is very tender."

"You scared me to death; I thought I had lost you. I didn't anticipate that guy emptying the magazine on his rifle."

"Were they with the ones who killed Jim?"

"I'm not sure, but they were armed with the same rifles and pistols. I can only assume that they saw the ones in the pickup truck stop at our gate. Once I dispose of them, I want to go find where they were camped. I should be able to backtrack them in the snow unless it starts to snow again."

She gave him her killer smile and snuggled up next to him. "Let's get to work, and we'll rest up a few days. We've had an awful lot of excitement lately."

Hawks sat up and swung his legs to the floor. "I thought this was going to be like a vacation. Maybe it will be if we can live long enough."

"How long do you think it's going to be like this?"

"It's going to take a full three months for those who are starving to die. We're weeding out the crooks pretty fast. It didn't take them long to clean out all the food in Lady Smith. You know the routine; I want to haul them off and check out where they came from. Then I'm going to wipe out any trace of them. I want you to take it easy. You were knocked out cold. The last thing we need for you to do is overdo it until we know you are OK."

He helped her down the stairs and into a chair by the fire. He loaded the woodstove and the parlor heater and added a log to the fireplace hearth. He left her sitting warm near the fire with a cup of coffee. The puppies beat him down the steps and ran to the body of the man lying in the snow. They immediately started barking and circling the body. First one, then the other crept up and smelled and jumped back as though they sensed movement.

Hawks rolled him over and peered at the dead open eyes gazing into oblivion. What was once a living, breathing man was now only a lifeless thing. Hawks bent over and went through the man's pockets and retrieved his wallet and keys to a Honda motorcycle. The man was still wearing his police officer's badge. Hawks retrieved the man's government issued rifle, holster, and gear. He looked at the pistol he had struck the man with. Dried blood and hair were frozen to the end of the slide where it busted the man's skull and cracked his skull open. When he had time, he would disassemble the pistol, inspect, and test fire it, but for now, he had others.

He walked around back and relieved the other man of his belongings and found the key to a Harley Davidson in his pocket. Hawks went to the barn and fired up the Kubota tractor and drove it to the house, where he loaded both bodies in the bucket and drove it back to the barn. He walked down the driveway and climbed the gate and crossed the road.

He could see their tracks in the snow and backtracked them up the hill and over into the ravine. Their campsite was there, along with their backpacks with food, and so were the two motorcycles. He secured one of the backpacks to the Honda and cranked it using the foot crank lever. He carefully rode it back down the hill, being careful not to wreck on the frozen snow and ground. He rode it up to the gate, where he opened it and drove through. He stopped and closed it before continuing to the house and around to the barn. He then returned to their campsite and retrieved the Harley Davidson. He was surprised he hadn't heard them when they originally drove up to the campsite. They probably came back while they were stocking the root cellar.

Once he had the gear stowed, he took the Kubota with the bodies down the lane where he placed them adjacent to the other two dead from the initial confrontation. It was a grim business, but it ceased to bother him at this point. He was looking forward to the puppies becoming full-time guard dogs. It wouldn't be long before the people who were walking out of Victoria would be arriving. The storm clouds were starting to dump more snow, and soon all trace of the motorcycle tire tracks and the footsteps would disappear, and along with it any evidence of human activity.

He walked up the front steps and found Carolyn sitting in the chair with the two puppies in her lap. "I see our guard dogs are hard at work."

"You know it. They are sticking close to Mama."

Hawks laughed. "I'm getting cleaned up, then I want to get some rest. I'm going to heat a big pot of water on the woodstove, pour it in the bathtub, and I'm going to wash off my night's activities."

Carolyn gave him a wink, "Why don't you put on two pots, and I'll join you."

"That's the best offer I've had in a while."

"It won't be the last."

They woke up after lunch and went downstairs where the puppies waited by the fire. It was an unusually heavy snow for the island, and it would make the roads impassable as there would be no plowing taking place ever again. They were completely safe. Unless someone had snowshoes or cross county skis, there would be no trespassers for days or weeks. Hawks bundled up and headed out to the barn and animal pens to make sure the animals were fed, watered, and sheltered. The snow across the fields and in the trees was breathtakingly beautiful. It was reminiscent of a Currier and Ives postcard. They were doing fantastic even though they had to kill men. They were now armed beyond his wildest imagination, with enough guns and ammo to last them a long time. If he had to go to war, he had enough to get started.

He walked back to the house scooping up an armload of firewood and dropped it in the wood box as he walked past the woodstove in the kitchen. The snow was piling up, and there was a strong wind. The weather would grant them safety for a few days, so now was the time to relax and rest. Both and he and Carolyn had reached the point where taking a life was of no consequence. This psychological threshold increased their odds of survival by tenfold.

CHAPTER 17

Dawson stood outside in the cold night and thought back to the night on his balcony when he was looking up at the aurora streaming by above. He felt around in his pocket, and for the first time since that night, he pulled out his flask with the Jameson whiskey. He shook it and felt a satisfying slosh, indicating it still had a couple of pulls left in it. He took off the cap and took a long pull from it and felt the warmth of the liquor as it filled his body. He felt good; in fact, he felt better than he had in years. He had a beautiful girlfriend and actually felt like he had something to live for. Up until now, his life consisted of dealing with unhappy people and holding his tongue. He felt more alive than he ever had felt in his life.

He had been fearful when all this had started. In fact, he almost panicked when he shot the men in the alleyway behind Henry's secondhand store. He had killed the men attacking the family across the street with pure hatred. They had represented everything that was wrong, and the same with the men busting into the room at the old abandoned home. He knew he would kill again, and he would have no remorse.

He tightened the cap on his flask so the remaining shot of Jameson would be safe in his pocket. He stood on the back porch and watched as the snow slowly drifted down. Olivia walked out and pushed her bare hand down into his pocket to join his. Their fingers intertwined in the warm pocket. Dawson pulled her close and asked, "If we happen to find a pastor or a priest, would you become my bride?"

She tiptoed and kissed him. "As far as I'm concerned, I'm your wife right now."

"I feel the same way." They kissed and walked back into the warmth of the house, went to bed, and awoke refreshed the next morning.

Dawson went into the kitchen and found breakfast cooking on the stove. Charlie looked up from his chair at the window where he stood guard. Dawson asked, "Charlie, do you think it would be OK if I went out and had a look at those old snowshoes this morning?"

"Sure, in fact I can tell you where you can find them. When you go into the front of the shop out back, just go to the back wall, and you will see a ladder on the wall that goes up into the loft. If you go up there, they are stacked in the corner. You can't miss them. The skis are leaning in the corner behind them."

"Thanks, I'll take a look." He put on all his cold weather gear and put the belt containing the 1911 pistol over the pants. The days of being unarmed were over. He went out the back door and into the powdery snow. The wind was still blowing and the snow had piled up against the porch steps and onto the porch. He only moved enough snow so he could make it down the steps without falling. No chances could be taken. A minor injury could prove fatal with no medical care available.

He waded through the snow and stopped to clear away enough snow to open the man door on the side. Windows let filtered light into the space of the shop. He lit one of his candle lanterns and found the ladder leading up into the loft. The floor of the loft was dusty and cluttered with boxes and unused tools. He quickly located the snowshoes and skies. He carried them down the ladder and laid them on a workbench so he could examine them.

The snowshoe frames were sound but the bindings and straps were largely dry rotted. The same was true of the cross-country skis. He was glad he had recovered the roll of paracord from Henry's secondhand shop. He could re-lace and repair the bindings and straps with the paracord. It took him several hours to replace and adjust the bindings. He used some scrap wood and epoxy to repair the snowshoe frames and the skis. Once he had a pair of the snowshoes and skis adjusted for his boots, he called out Olivia and did the same. They could at least move out on foot if necessary.

The dilemma in his mind was whether to fight it out with this small family or start the journey over the mountain or south toward the US border. Staying here to help this family would be fatal. He knew that when he and Olivia disappeared down the road, it would be the last time he would see Henry's family. It reminded him of his last visit with his great uncle. His uncle was ninety years old and in very frail condition. When he told him goodbye, he knew in his heart it was the last time. He received the bad news a couple of months later.

He took one of the sleds and started making a list of everything he would need to start the journey with Olivia across the frozen mountains. The idea of traversing the mountains in the dead of winter was almost unimaginable. The other alternative was to travel back through Calgary and go south until they reached the Milk River. It would be frozen this time of year, but it may be possible to drag a canoe or flat bottom boat south until they eventually found running water. All they would have to do was float down into the Missouri River and then down to the Mississippi River and from there to south Louisiana.

Olivia called from the house, "Dinner's ready. You've worried enough today. Come eat and let Charlie take a break from guard duty." He walked up the path and up the steps to a warm hug from Olivia.

Once in the kitchen, he ate his fill of rice and stir fry. He and Olivia were alone at the table for a moment, and she touched his arm. "I know you are making plans for us to leave. I'm having misgivings; what if we are making a mistake?"

Dawson tipped the cup of hot tea up and drank the last few sips.

He said, "I'm really partial to this family. They would all be dead if I hadn't led them. But there's no way anyone of us will survive much longer here, and there's virtually no chance that we will survive taking them with us. Let's walk out to the front porch, and I want you to listen."

They walked into the living room to where Charlie was sitting, who looked up at Dawson. "Can you take over; I need to get some rest."

"Sure thing, I'll take it from here."

Charlie disappeared down the hall, and Dawson led Olivia over to the front door. He cracked it a bit and said, "Listen." The sound of gunfire echoed across the city. Some of it was alarmingly close. "It's going to come down that driveway at any time; we'll probably take care of the first few incursions and then will come the ones who are organized. There will be former military and police, or current military and police, and they will be armed to the teeth, and we won't have a prayer. If we are allowed to live, they will take everything, and we will all die over the next three or four weeks. I can't stop what is going to take place. I can only postpone the inevitable a few days or weeks."

A tear rolled down her check as they closed and barred the door. "How many people do you think have died out there?"

"I don't know. The city has between 1.5 and 2 million people.

Everyone on oxygen or requiring hospitalization is dead. The nursing homes are almost devoid of life by now. In another week or so, the insulin dependent diabetics will be gone. Then you have the people robbing and killing each other. I would venture to say 15 to 20 percent of the population is already dead. At least 75 percent of the remaining population have exhausted every bite of food they had on hand and any they could easily find. They are turning over every rock right now and cleaning out anyone they can overcome. In twelve months over 90 percent of the people here will be dead. I don't want me and you to be with them."

They sat quietly as the stark realism of what was taking place settled in. Charlie came in and sat down. "I apologize for eaves-dropping, but I must agree with everything you've said. I can't leave if there is even the slightest possibility that my wife and children make it here. We all know that Henry and her family wouldn't last a week on any trail you take getting out of here. He's right, Olivia. If you stay here, you're probably going to just sacrifice your lives." Before Dawson could say anything, a shotgun blast blew out the window on the front door and splintered the sheet of plywood behind it. The question of running or fighting was answered for the moment.

CHAPTER 18

Carolyn had the woodstove fired up and had breakfast cooking when Hawks stiffly came down the stairs. He backed up to the woodstove and rubbed his hands together and up and down the seat of his pants. It took some getting used to a house being cold and the only warm places being next to a fire or in the bed. His dad had described living on a farm back in the Louisiana delta. A fireplace and a woodstove were the only sources of heat. The old house had newspapers tacked to the walls to keep the wind from leaking through. The old windows rattled in the wind, and the cracks in the floorboards allowed cold air to filter into the old house from below. This old house had once been insulated and caulked, but it hadn't been upgraded in over sixty years. The windows leaked a bit, but at least there was a full basement with an insulated floor under it. The attic was also insulated, but there was no stopping the cold from seeping into the old house.

For the first time since he got to the house, he was starting to feel his age. Up until now, it had almost been like a vacation, but he couldn't help wonder what his children were going through. He was sure they would be making their way toward the cabin in the Ozarks. He sat down at the old farm table as Carolyn sat down a plate of homemade biscuits. A puddle of syrup was poured on the plate with condensed milk from a can poured on top of it. Once the cow or one of the goats could be milked, real cream would replace the condensed milk. Canned sausage topped off the meal. Soon the hens would start producing some eggs, and some fresh meat would come from local deer and other game. The game would disappear quickly once the hordes made it into the countryside.

One of the outbuildings behind the home and just out from the walkout basement door was an old smokehouse. It now housed old garden tools, empty clay pots, old water hoses, and a host of items that needed to be taken to the rubbish heap. It took him the better part of the morning to clean it out and set up the poles to hang the meat from. There was a small brick hearth where it was fed from the outside. All it needed was a stack of hardwood to feed it with.

He went back into the basement and pulled out the British Enfield. They had forty rounds of 150 grain soft point ammo. The question he had was if the old rifle had been sighted in. He hated to waste ammo sighting it in, but he would be wasting his time hunting unless he knew he could hit a deer with it.

He called up to Carolyn, "I'm going to check the sights on your father's rifle. Don't be alarmed if you hear a couple of shots."

He tapped a nail into a wood block and sat it on a rock about thirty yards away. A picnic table that had been stowed on its side against the house out of the weather made a great rifle rest. He sat a bucket on the table with a rolled-up burlap bag to rest the gun on. He chambered a round and took careful aim and carefully squeezed the trigger. The rifle bounced and the wood block went flying. The trigger wasn't as smooth as he would have liked, but this was a mass-produced military-grade rifle. He laid the rifle down on the table with the bolt retracted so the bore would cool while he checked the target.

To his delight, the bullet had hit just below the nail, so he took the block out to approximately one hundred yards and set it up again. He walked back to the table and cycled the action chambering a second round. He repeated the process of aiming and squeezing the trigger. Once again, the block went flying. This time the block was splintered in two, but he could tell the bullet had hit about an inch above the nail. He was confident he could bring down a deer with it. He reset up the remains of the block and went back to the house and retrieved the Winchester 1873 lever action. He felt certain the sights were set as it had been obviously used by his friend. He always kept this rifle in battery, so when he sat down and aimed, all he had to do was cock the hammer. He took careful aim, and as expected the block went flying when he fired. He had a backup deer rifle once he exhausted the ammo for the Enfield.

Carolyn came down the steps and out of the cellar door with the pups leading the way. "What are the plans?"

"After lunch, I'm going to take a walk down the tree line to where the deer have been coming out late in the afternoon. I've got a smokehouse that is ready to be loaded."

"I can't wait. We'll be eating high off the hog in no time at all."

Hawks cradled the Enfield across his arms as he made his way along the tree line. Deer tracks were plentiful, as were rubs on the small trees and bushes. He spotted a crossing in the fence line and was careful to stay well away from it. There was no need to spoil it with human scent, so he moved back into the woods to where he could sit on a rock outcropping putting him ten or so feet above and thirty yards downwind of it. He thought about the hunting trips he had taken with his son in years past. It saddened him to not have his son along for this hunt. The old memories made him worry about his son's well-being. It was likely the EMP event was continent or hemisphere wide as no assistance from the states had taken place.

He heard a stick crack and the sound of footsteps in the leaves on the forest floor. He sat motionless and watched in the direction of the sound. A squirrel bounded from the underbrush to his amusement. As was typical of every deer hunt he had ever been on, there were always birds and small animals making noise in the woods once the woods quieted after he sat still waiting. From where he sat, he could see the open field and the pawed-out scrape.

He was beginning to think the hunt was a bust when a doe came bounding from the thicket and hopped over the fence. He started to take her but waited a moment. He soon discovered the reason she was moving. A young buck followed behind her and jumped the fence following her. The young buck sported a set of pronghorns. He raised his head and turned toward Hawks and paused a moment. That was one moment too long.

Hawks had the rifle shouldered and the safety off. He squeezed the trigger and was surprised when the rifle bounced. The heavy bullet hit the buck just behind shoulder. The buck made a dying leap and landed dead about ten feet away from where he had stood. Hawks patiently waited as the buck made his final kicks, in case he had to make a second shot. Soon all was still, so he shouldered the rifle and headed into the field where the dead deer lay still. Steam rose from the pool of blood that had formed under its body. The blood was in sharp contrast to the white snow. He wasn't sure how other hunters felt about killing animals. There was the excitement of watching and waiting with the rush of adrenaline. Then there was the regret of ending the animal's life. Most people were so removed from the killing process that it never crossed their mind they were responsible for the death of an animal. They are, or were, concerned with the cut of the meat or the animal they had chosen to consume. The thought of the animal being killed and processed never entered their mind. They were as responsible for the death of the animal as the butcher who put down the animal.

He walked back to the house where Carolyn waited with her dynamite smile. "I take it from the gunshot that we have meat for the smokehouse?"

"Yes, we do, and you're going to have a real treat tonight. I bet you have never eaten chicken fried venison backstrap. You wait here, and I'll take the tractor down into the field and retrieve the buck."

He walked around to the barn and opened the big doors. The reliable diesel Kubota cranked as usual. He drove across the field retracing his footsteps in the snow. He lowered the bucket to the ground and rolled the buck into it. He soon had the buck pulled up in the barn where he skinned and dismembered it. He hung the meat on hooks in the smokehouse. One of the backstraps he cut into steaks for the kitchen. Once he had the meat hanging, he started a fire in the firebox, and soon smoke seeped from every crack in the old building. All he had to do now was keep a low fire until the meat was cured. It would have to be a matter of trial and error as he was learning as he went.

He took the backstrap up the steps, and while Carolyn watched, he cut them up into thin steaks and using a meat tenderizer hammered them even thinner. These he dipped in some canned milk and coated with flour. After dusting with salt and pepper, he chicken fried them in an old black skillet. The steaks, with canned peas and hot biscuits, made a great meal.

Carolyn pushed back from the table. "I don't think I've ever had a better meal."

Hawks grinned. "I grew up eating like this. Every year my father, grandfather, and uncles all went to the deer camp, and we kept our freezers well stocked with venison and other game. Hunting was a way of life; in the spring we hunted turkey, and in the summer we fished. Life was so much simpler in those days. Everyone had a big garden, and we shared the surplus with one another. We all lived within twenty miles of each other and had family gatherings every Sunday, usually at one set of grandparents or the other. It's sad to realize they are all gone now except for my cousins, and many of them may have already perished."

Carolyn walked around and put her arms around him from behind. "At least we've found one another; being alone is a terrible way to exist."

"I agree with you. We've got to remain alert, or one of us may be alone again."

They cleared off the table and washed the dishes before retiring to the big fireplace. The job at hand was to fill the smokehouse and further secure the farm. They walked out on the front porch for a bit of fresh air. The moon lit up the big field with its blanket of snow. The silence of the night was broken by gunfire. The sound came from the direction of the farm where they had obtained the pups. There were several different weapons firing. At first it was sporadic, then a single shot after about a thirty-second pause. Hawks visualized someone making a killing final shot.

Carolyn squeezed his arm, "What do you think?"

"I think we've got to keep our eyes open. There will be people from the coastal areas heading out into the country, and it won't be just former police and military. There may even be people from Vancouver making it this far by now. Tomorrow, I want to make sure that no light can be seen from our windows at night. I don't want to be sitting by the fireplace and someone being able to walk up and peer in the window and see us."

They went back in and sat by the fire with the puppies at their feet. Carolyn reached down and scratched the ear of the nearest one. "The only way to see into this room is from the front porch.

I don't believe someone can walk across the porch without it popping or creaking, and even if we missed it, the pups won't."

"I'm going to run out and top off the wood in the fire box on the smokehouse, and then we need to get some rest." It was starting to snow again, and a light breeze made it feel much colder than it actually was. An almost imperceptible column of smoke rose from the smokestack. He topped off the wood box and dialed the air intake down so that it would limit the amount of air coming into the box. He turned back to the house and looked up at the large central chimney of the old house. A very light trail of smoke disappeared into the night. There would be no way of hiding the fact the farm was inhabited to someone observing it from a distance. The rich smell of the smoke would travel for miles.

CHAPTER 19

The front door splintered and was torn from its frame. The first man through stopped a .45 slug from the Colt 1911 in Dawson's hand. The man wore a ballistic helmet and vest. The first round only stunned him as it impacted his vest. The second one hit him just below his chin and blew out through his neck, severing his spinal column and killing him almost instantly. Dawson never made it to the door. Everything went black.

He woke to an extreme headache, and he was looking up at Henry's daughter Cathy. Her eyes were almost black and her short brown hair was tucked behind her ears. Her face and clothes were spattered with blood. She touched his head with a damp cloth. "I'm not sure how bad you are hurt. You have a wound to your head over your right ear."

"What happened?"

"Everyone is dead except you, me, BC, and Lucy. The men outside are still loading all our stuff up in their truck and trailer. I need to get you down into the basement. Me and the kids hid in a large steamer trunk in the back of the basement." Dawson's adrenaline surged as he sat up and looked around. The man he shot lay on the floor with his gun under his body.

He looked around at Cathy. "Get back in the basement with the kids and keep them quiet. I've got some killing to do."

Cathy tried to pull his arm, "There are seven more of them outside; come with me."

"Get down in the basement with the kids." Dawson rolled the dead man off the Colt C7 rifle and checked the magazine; the thirty-round magazine was full. As he checked the chamber, he looked back at Cathy. "If I don't recover our supplies, we will have to eat the bodies of your mother, uncle, and Olivia. Are you ready to do that?" Cathy could only shake her head no. "For the last time, get back down in the basement with the kids."

He wiped the blood running down the side of his face with his sleeve as he donned the ballistic helmet of the dead man and stripped off his body armor. Cathy helped him put on the armor and disappeared toward the basement. Dawson knew the men outside may delay shooting him if they thought he were one of them. He stepped through the front door opening and sized up the situation.

Two guys stood in the open trailer while the other five handed supplies up to them. Three of them wore their rifles slung on their backs, using the rifle slings. Dawson knew the only way to take them out would be to cut their legs out from under them. He shot the nearest one just below his vest. The bullet tore through his pelvic girdle, instantly dropping him. The next one he shot just below his buttocks, shattering the bone in his left leg. Before he hit the ground, he shot the next one, and then the two in the trailer. He didn't wait to see if his shots hit home but moved immediately to the next target. The two on the opposite side dove to the ground.

Dawson dropped to the ground so that he could see through under the trailer. He could not place his shots as he could only see their prone bodies. He emptied the magazine on the two men hoping more than one bullet hit their mark. When he reached the first man who was writhing on the ground and screaming, Dawson grabbed the Glock pistol in his belt and shot him through the neck and proceeded to dispatch all the wounded men as fast as he could get to them. It was all over in less than forty-five seconds.

He wiped the blood from his face on his sleeve once again and proceeded to go through the pockets of the men. They all had rolls of money; only one had a government-issued ID. He dragged their carcasses off to the side and gathered up their weapons and magazines. Next, he dragged the body at the front door out to join his compadres. He found several of them had Glock 19 pistols and extra magazines.

Dawson put on a chest rig that held six thirty-round magazines for the C7 rifles. He commandeered a holster and soon had one of the Glocks holstered, along with four seventeen-round magazines of 9 mm ammo. The trailer and truck were still out of sight of the gate. He jogged up to the gate and secured it to make it appear it had never been opened. The Alberta weather obliged as a light snow filled in the tire tracks and footprints.

The truck was an old Dodge Power Wagon. It was so old it had a six-cylinder Plymouth engine. But what was most important about the truck was it had a large snowplow mounted on the front. This was obviously one of the old trucks he had seen in a museum outside of the city. He cranked the engine and backed the trailer down the side of the house and stopped near the side door. He trotted back around to the remnants of the front door and went through. The first thing he spotted was Olivia crumpled in the corner.

"Oh, Olivia." He gently pulled her lifeless body to him and started crying. She had been shot through her heart. He carefully carried her out to the front porch, then pulled Charlie and Henry's lifeless bodies out to join her. He walked to the basement door and called down to Cathy, "It's over; you can come up now."

Without waiting he stood the front door back up and used a

chair to hold it in place. For now, the house could warm back up. He sat at the kitchen table and once again wiped the blood from his face. He took off the ballistic vest and helmet and checked his weapons. All were loaded and in battery and ready for the next fight.

Cathy came up the steps and came over to him. "I need to clean your wound and face before I get the kids. You look like you should be dying."

"My head is killing me; I can count my heartbeats with every throb." Cathy's hands shook as she gently wiped away the blood and trimmed the hair around the gash created where the bullet had torn through his scalp. "I'm going to stitch it closed." She found a sewing kit from her aunt's sewing room. She came out with the needle and thread.

Dawson reached into his back pocket and produced a flask with his last remaining Jameson whiskey. Cathy poured some into a bowl and soaked her needle and thread. When she bathed the wound with the remaining whiskey he winced, clinching his teeth. The wound had the skin opened to the bone. In effect, the bullet slapped the side of his head, knocking him out and giving the impression he was dead from being shot through the head. The throbbing headache, the open wound, and the closing of the wound merged into just one constant pain seeming to penetrate his entire body.

Once the wound was closed, she filled a Ziploc bag with snow and wrapped it with a cloth. He went into the living room and sat in the recliner with the cold pack held to his head. In a few moments, BC and Lucy quietly came to his side. They crawled into his lap and rested their heads on each of his shoulders. He sat the cold pack down and embraced their diminutive forms. Cathy brought him some aspirin and some tea.

"What do we do now?"

"It's starting to get dark, and it feels like it's getting colder.

We're going to stay buttoned up here tonight and let me recuperate for a bit. I don't feel like I'm up to going through the trailer, and I don't want to have a flashlight flashing outside to attract attention. We're going to leave here tomorrow and put some distance between us and the city. You are going to get a crash course in the operation of weapons."

She nodded in agreement. "I'm ready, and I'm thankful you are taking care of us."

Dawson looked up at her. "I'm curious, what is your last name and where is your husband?"

"I am Cathy Wong. My husband divorced me about six months ago. He was away from home most of the time. He sent child support, but he was not a family man. Mother said that we were better off without him, she was right as usual."

"That's a shame, I can't imagine a man treating his family like that."

"He was angry because I refused to have an abortion."

"I need some rest, and I don't want to eat with this head injury. I want you and the kids to get a good supper and some rest. Tomorrow is not going to be an easy day. If I dose off, check on me to make sure that I am still alive. I probably have a concussion, let me sleep, just make sure I don't stop breathing."

"You're starting to scare me."

"I'm feeling a little woozy still. I'll be better by morning."

While the twins watched Dawson sleep, Cathy retrieved some food from the trailer and cooked their supper. She also brought in all the weapons and holsters and laid them out on the kitchen table so she could adjust them to her small body. She put on her winter gear and adjusted a holster to fit over them. She did not try to adjust the rifle slings as she wanted Dawson to show her how to operate the one she would carry. BC and Lucy took turns coming to her to tell her that Mr. Dawson was still breathing.

Dawson woke up in the night, and his thoughts immediately turned to Olivia. A rage was building in him. He considered what had taken place and what he had to do. He couldn't have imagined in his wildest dreams he would wind up with a young woman and two little kids whose only hope in this world now rested on his shoulders. He thought, I'm sure God has a hand in all this. I wish he could give me a hint on how I'm going to pull off saving myself, Cathy, and the two kids.

Cathy walked around the corner from the kitchen. "You slept peacefully all night. Are you ready for some breakfast? I've been keeping an eye out for danger. The twins are still asleep on a pallet in the corner where I can watch them and stand guard at the window. Let me check your head, and then I want to get you fed. After that you are going to show me how to shoot the weapons. Everything has changed. I'm not going to let anything happen to the twins or to you. I know you hadn't planned on any of this, but we need you, and I hope you need us."

"I guess God puts us where we need to be; I could use some breakfast."

She touched his cheek. "I just cooked up some eggs and canned pork. I'll bring you a plate. I've got stuff on the kitchen table."

Dawson squeezed her hand. "Thanks for patching me up. Once I eat, we've got to go through the truck and trailer and get ready to run."

"What are we going to do about Mother, Uncle Charlie, and Olivia?"

"I've thought about it. We can't dig graves in the frozen ground, and the basement has a concrete floor. I noticed that there are five or six large bundles of landscaping boulders sitting near the garden center office. We can lay them out near the home, and we can cover them deep enough that animals can't get to them. I want to put first things first. We've got to get ready to go first; we can't help the dead no matter how much we love them. Once we are packed up and ready, we'll say our goodbyes and lay them to rest."

Tears were running down her cheeks. "You're right. Mother told me to listen to you. You make good sense."

Dawson looked up from his breakfast plate. "I'm not so sure I've made a single right decision since all this started. Everyone may be still alive if I had just gone back to my condo when the lights went out."

"You and I both know that you did a great job of keeping everyone alive until now. I know without a doubt the twins and I would have died in the fire; you saved us. Don't second guess yourself; you keep us alive, and I'll take care of feeding and nursing you. Just try not to get shot again. Let's face it; we're stuck with each other, and I can't think of a better person in this world to be stuck with."

Dawson wiped his lips and stood up. He reached over and dried her tears with the clean side of his napkin and pulled her close. "You're right; I'm fond of you guys too." He picked up one of the Glocks. "We'll start with this one; it is the easiest one to master."

After teaching her how to operate the gun, he took her out to the back porch and let her empty a magazine at a chunk of wood. She was amazingly accurate considering it was the first time she had ever fired a pistol. He gathered up all the Glock magazines. They had apparently cleaned out a police or military armory; they all carried the C7 rifles. He had seven rifles and seventy loaded thirty-round magazines. There were also several cans of 5.56 ammo. He adjusted the slings on two of the rifles to fit him and two rifles for Cathy. She mastered the use of the rifles and their red dot optical sights. There were backup mechanical sights on each of them as well.

Cathy asked, "Why are we setting up two rifles for each of us?"

"We have to have backup for everything. We can't get on the internet and order replacement parts. We'll stow the extra weapons in the back of the truck. We'll keep our main rifle and pistols close to us so they can be grabbed in a moment. We will wear our pistols at all times. I know it can be uncomfortable, but you can't use it if you can't put your hand on it. I'm surprised the red dot scopes work. I guess their metal construction and miniature electronics aren't affected."

They spent the rest of the day unloading the trailer and Power Wagon. The attackers had haphazardly thrown in all the food and supplies they had stolen from them and other people. It would have to be inventoried to see what they would take and what they would leave behind. Dawson went down to the barn and used lumber stored there along with lumber he pulled from the barn itself to build a camper shell on the bed of the Power Wagon and onto the trailer. That way they could camp in the back of the Power Wagon and stow additional gear on top of the camper shell and the cab of the truck. The shell built over the trailer would allow them also store items in the trailer and on the top as well. They lost their daylight, so they decided to stay one more night before leaving.

Cathy came up to him. "That looks great. I think I know where we can lay everyone to rest. We can put them near the Garden Center near the piles of rocks."

"I think that is a good idea. I'll carry their bodies over there, and I'll let you know before I cover them."

"I want to help."

"You can help me by standing guard and watching the kids."

Cathy agreed, "You're right; do you feel up to it with your head?"

"My head is going to hurt whether I am working or not. It will take a few days before I get over that hit."

Dawson used one of Charlie's large garden carts to carry the bodies to where they could be placed. He covered them with some burlap sacks stored in the garden center. He waved to Cathy, who came out with the twins.

Dawson asked, "I am Christian. What religion are you?"

"We are Christians too. I can recite the 23 Psalms."

"That would be great." She recited the 23 Psalms, and they said a brief prayer. Dawson pointed to the house. "Take the kids back and get warmed up. I'll be finished here in a couple of hours."

"I'll have your supper ready when you finish."

Dawson took his time and placed the rocks over the bodies. When he finished, there were three rectangular piles of rocks. He was certain that they would be safe from any large animals. He stood for a moment, reflecting on what had taken place. He could not feel any worse. His head was killing him, he was depressed, and he was thoroughly exhausted.

As he turned to walk back to house, he looked up to see a man standing on the porch with a gun to Cathy's head.

CHAPTER 20

Hawks and Carolyn sat quietly in the chairs near the fireplace. The only light came from the fire. Hawks looked over at Carolyn. "I know we are comfortable and well fed for now, but this is only temporary. There are four hundred thousand people in Victoria, and that doesn't include all the other coastal towns within one hundred miles of here. There are now thousands and thousands of people robbing, stealing, and killing each other. It's all coming this way. There will be people who have figured out a way to use old vehicles, and many more will be walking out of the city. The officials will probably clean them out just like they tried to clean us out. We are about a week or ten-day walk from Victoria, three to five days from most of the coastal towns and villages. I'm surprised we haven't seen some already. The smokehouse will summon them from miles with its aroma. The wind is taking the smoke north and east; hopefully, it will dissipate before it reaches anyone who is traveling in this direction."

Carolyn shook her head in disbelief. "What else can we do?"

"I'm thinking we need to prep the Model A and the trailer with supplies so we can make a run to the coast. If we make it to the coast, we can steal an old sailboat and head south to the American border. Once we get there, we can travel east until we can steal another boat and float down the Missouri River. We will have to paddle across a number of reservoirs, but we would be in relative safety in the river. The problem will be food; I don't believe we can carry enough to sustain us. We can hunt and fish, but there will be multitudes of people trying to do the same thing."

"Do you think we need to check on our neighbors after we heard the gunshots?"

"I'm afraid we're on our own. I'd like to take the night watch while you get some sleep."

Carolyn grinned. "Do I have to sleep alone at first?"

Hawks woke sometime after midnight and slipped out of the bed. As he had done on many nights, he stood at the window. He expected to see a moonlit landscape. In the direction of their neighbor's house was a glow. The house or one of the buildings was ablaze. His first impulse was to rush over, but he paused a minute before waking Carolyn. He thought about staying, but he figured they would be hit next if he didn't go and help.

He gently shook her. "Carolyn, wake up."

"What's up, hon?"

"It looks like the neighbor's house or barn is on fire. There is a glow through the woods and in the sky. I'm going over there to see what is going on."

"I'm coming with you."

Hawks touched her arm. "You can follow me, but I insist that you hang back. If I have to fight, I need to know exactly where you are. I can't chance accidentally shooting you."

"Understood," Carolyn agreed, "but I'm packing guns too."

They got dressed and geared up. They both had the C7 rifles and the Browning high power pistols on their belts. They also had belt knives and a canteen. Hawks fired up one of the motorcycles, and with Carolyn behind him, they idled down the driveway. They opened the gate and locked it behind themselves. He kept it slow and quiet and relied on the light from the moon to illuminate the way. When they approached the driveway leading up to the home, he stopped and ran the motorcycle off the road and up into the brush out of sight.

He told Carolyn, "We have to be quiet and move slow; line up behind me."

"No worries, I'll stop when you tell me." They crept up the driveway, hearing the sound of the fire as they approached.

The fire roared and embers rose high in the sky. It sounded as though some stored ammo was cooking off somewhere inside the house as it was popping like fireworks. A large explosion sent a cascade of debris thrown from the conflagration. They came upon a body lying alongside the driveway. Hawks took a chance to use his flashlight but did not recognize him. The man was shot clean through the head. They continued moving toward the fire.

Hawks made Carolyn stay behind a large cedar tree. "Don't forget; stay here."

She gave him the thumbs-up and disappeared in the shadow behind the tree. Hawks stayed in the shadows and moved closer to the burning house. It was completely enveloped in flames. He could feel the heat on his face. The front doors of the barn were open, and the group of people there were busy loading up what they had stolen. The sound of his footsteps was masked by the noise from the fire. He walked up behind the large open door completely hidden in the shadows. He could hear them now.

The woman in charge said, "I hate we lost Tate, but it couldn't be avoided. We lost the element of surprise when that damned dog started barking. But we got even with them."

The three women and two men didn't seem to be bothered about losing Tate. One of the men pointed back at the house. "That man was a good shot; he almost got me after he killed Tate. If Sadie hadn't picked him off, he would have gotten me with his next shot."

Sadie piped up, "His wife and kids put up a good fight. It's a shame a bullet hit that kerosene lamp. We barely had enough time to clean out the kitchen, pantry, and basement." The group was driving an old Mercedes diesel station wagon with an open trailer behind it. Both were loaded with all the food and supplies from the house.

The woman in charge said, "Let's hit that farm up the road with the locked gate. We can stow all this stuff there until we finish working this road."

Hawks watched through a knot hole until they were all in a group breaking out some food. The rifle was already switched to auto. He clicked the safety off as he rounded the corner. He emptied the magazine on them and left them bloody on the floor of the barn. He flipped the switch on the side of the rifle to single fire before popping each of them through the head for good measure. Looking around the barn, he found the mother of his puppies dead in the back.

He called down to Carolyn, "It's over, come on up."

She came up and looked at the dead people on the floor. "I wish we could have gotten here sooner."

"It wouldn't have done any good. The family was dead after we heard the shooting. Their bodies are being consumed in the fire; the dog is dead in the back. We'll take the car and trailer back with us and come back tomorrow to see what we can find. Maybe we can round up some of the animals."

"What about the dead bodies?"

"We'll drag them off in the morning, I overheard them talking; they were planning to hit us tonight. We've got to really be on our toes. Let's gather up their weapons and stow them in the trailer."

They loaded up the weapons and climbed into the car. Hawks turned the key and let the glow plugs heat up. He then turned the key further, and the engine came to life. They pulled out of the barn and down the driveway. They drove around the dead body and down the highway to their locked gate. Carolyn got out and opened the gate and closed it behind them. They parked the car in front of the barn and went into the house.

Hawks plopped down in a chair by the fire. "I'm tired, and we still have a lot of things to do. I'm going to make up some trip alarms that will set off some shotgun shells around the property. The trick is putting them where the deer can't set them off."

Carolyn rubbed his shoulders. "What can I do to help?"

"I need you to stand guard while I build what I need in the barn. I've also been thinking about what happened to our neighbors. They were fighting from the house. The killers concentrated their attention on the house. I think we need to figure out how to slip out of the house and fight from outside. I can barricade the basement doors and set up a way to crawl out from under the house through some of the basement windows. We can camouflage the windows from the outside so we can slip out with no one being the wiser. We can't have a fortress mentality. We have to do the opposite of what they expect. In fact, I may set up a blind where I can watch the house hidden from cover. I also want to create several barriers that I can jump behind and shoot from."

Carolyn asked, "Do you think we are OK for tonight?"

"With all the shooting we've been doing, I think we are OK. After we gather what we can from our neighbors, I'll get started. I'm going to leave the bodies where they lay." They went to bed depending on the puppies to alert them to any danger.

They woke midmorning, and as usual, Hawks went to the window and looked down the drive and across the meadow. All was quiet. He went around to windows on all four corners of the house. He was careful not to disturb the curtains or blinds when he looked out. Everything was quiet for the moment.

After breakfast, they went out and unloaded the station wagon and trailer. Food was stored in the basement; other items were stowed in the barn. They cranked the old diesel station wagon and traveled back to their neighbor's house. They went through the pockets of the dead and found very little they could use. They stripped off their pistol belts and holsters. They did not have any military weapons, only shotguns and deer rifles. Only two of them had pistols; both were antiquated Smith and Wesson .38 revolvers. They couldn't catch the chickens, and the cow and calf were on the far side of the pasture.

Hawks peered out into the pasture. "Until we can get the trailer set up, I'm not going to try and catch the cow; in fact, it may be dangerous since she may think we are going to hurt her calf."

He walked back to the equipment shed in the back and discovered an International Cub tractor and all its implements. The Cub was what a small farmer would have bought back in the late '40s or '50s to use on a small ten- or twenty-acre farm. He reached over and pulled out the choke and hit the key. It cranked right up. There was a utility trailer next to it. As expected, there was a trailer ball on the draw bar of the tractor. He backed the Cub up to the trailer and pulled it out into the drive. He unhooked the trailer and looked around for some chain and found some hanging from the back wall of the shed.

The Cub tractors were equipped with a hydraulic lift; this one had the arm that would raise a plow or disc attached to the draw bar. He backed the tractor up to each piece of equipment and used the chain to lift each piece so he could move them over to the side of the trailer. The lift was unable to pick them up high enough to drop them into the trailer, but it allowed him to get them high enough for him to muscle them over the side. Once he had the trailer loaded, he searched and loaded up all the other tools and equipment he thought he could use. He found some cans of diesel and gasoline.

Carolyn drove the station wagon, and Hawks followed, driving the Cub tractor with the trailer behind it. They would come back and retrieve the motorcycle hidden in the bushes later. They stopped back at the barn where Hawks surveyed all the vehicles they had been accumulating. "If this keeps up, we can open up a used car lot."

Carolyn said, "I'm glad we picked up this old diesel station wagon."

"Me too, these old Mercedes diesel engines will run on diesel, liquid vegetable oil, transmission fluid, and motor oil if we dilute it with a little gasoline. They're practically bullet-proof engines."

While Carolyn stood guard, Hawks fashioned some early warning devices using blocks of wood and nails that would hit the percussion cap on 12-gauge shotgun shells. He fashioned triggers using nails and fishing line so that, when the wire was tripped, a brick would fall and land on the device firing the shotgun shell. He installed the devices on the front gates, around the barn, smokehouse, and all the first-floor and basement windows. He put out two dozen alarms, placing them around the fence lines and around every concealable hiding spot he could find where he could see the house unobserved. If he were planning on assaulting the house, he would approach and observe from a hidden position. It was impossible to build and install enough of them to cover every single spot on the property, but at least he had the most obvious ones secured. They could sleep a bit easier, but it would be a very long time before anyone had a peaceful nap or night's rest.

They soon had the motorcycle stashed up the road parked in one of the horse stalls in the barn. The Cub tractor was parked under a lean-to shed off the side of the barn. The Mercedes station wagon was left outside for daily use. They also stored much more food and other supplies in the old cabin intended to be Roosevelt's wine cellar. Hawks knew the house could not be thought of as a fortress. Fighting would have to take place on the outside while all the attackers were focusing their attention on the house. If necessary, they could abandon the house, hide in the old cabin, and come back to fight another day.

The next day was quiet as he created a barrier in the basement to hide the passage; they would crawl down to reach the exterior. The window was hidden by some large bushes, so when they exited the window, they could not be seen from anywhere on the grounds. Afterward they rested up for what they knew would be coming. That evening as they sat in the dark next to a low fire in the fireplace, they heard a distant pop and the pups came up barking.

CHAPTER 21

The rage boiled up inside him. The pain started throbbing in his head wound once again. Time seemed to start going in slow motion. His first instinct was to run forward. The gun in the man's hand was a cocked revolver. Even if he made a good, clean headshot, the man's hand could involuntarily squeeze off a shot. The other question was if there were other people in the house or if there were others waiting in ambush. Why hadn't they just shot him while he was covering the graves?

Cathy's eyes were closed, and he could see a trickle of blood running from her nose and off her chin. He glanced around and didn't see anyone lurking around. No one could be seen peering out of the windows. For some reason the man chose not to kill Cathy. He pulled his rifle around into position.

"What are your plans. If you're going to kill her, go ahead and shoot so I can blow your ass away." The man was unkempt, but didn't look like he was starving.

The man answered, "What did you say?"

"I said go ahead and shoot her so I can blow your ass away."

"I'll really do it." Dawson had flipped the safety to fire when he transitioned the rifle from his back to the front. Dawson grinned. "I guess it's a Mexican standoff."

Cathy opened her eyes and gave Dawson a wink. In one move,

Cathy squatted, making the man pitch forward just enough for the gun to leave her head and the pistol to harmlessly discharge behind her head. Dawson brought the rifle to his shoulder, and as soon as the red dot centered on the man's head, he squeezed the trigger. The rifle bounced, and when he got back on target, the man was falling. The bullet entered through the man's left eye and exited from the back of his skull. Blood and brains covered the window and wall behind him.

Dawson broke into a trot and scooped Cathy up. "Where's BC and Lucy?"

Cathy said, "I screamed for them to hide, and they took off. He slipped in the back door and punched me. He said that I was just what he had been looking for."

"Let's get in and check on the kids."

They went through the front door, and Cathy called to the kids, "Come on out; everything is OK." They came running back up from the basement crying and clinging to their mother. Cathy slipped her hand into Dawson's. "How did you know he wouldn't shoot me?"

"He was trying to disarm me. He figured I would put the weapons down and put my hands up. He would then shoot me, and he would have you and all our supplies. Never ever give up your weapon unless you have another within reach."

Dawson cleaned the blood from her face and filled a Ziploc bag with snow for her to use on her face. Her eyes were already starting to blacken from the blow. Her nose did not seem broken, and her front teeth were not hurt. He barred the doors and warmed up some food for her and the kids.

Cathy started to stand and said, "Let's get packing; the sooner we get on the road the better."

"No, it's your turn to take it easy. You took a hard lick to your face. We'll fort up here for the night, and we'll finish packing up in the morning. We've been through a lot. We can't see what we're doing, and I don't want to be firing up flashlights or lanterns and attracting any attention."

Cathy shook her head. "You are right. Mama told me to listen to you."

He went outside and grabbed the dead man's feet and drug him off the porch and placed his body with the others.

The night was quiet. They both needed time for recuperation. The next morning, they rose before the sun and ate an early breakfast. They neatly packed the trailer and the bed of the truck. He took a mattress out of the house with bedding and placed it on top of the supplies in the truck. He took all the extra weapons and hid them in the barn. The snow sleds they had used to evacuate the city were secured to the top of the trailer in case they had to abandon the old truck. He placed all the cans of fuel in the rear of the trailer for easy access. In addition, he had some water hose cut to use as a siphon hose to scrounge fuel from abandoned vehicles. He also found some small tubing in the greenhouse in case he encountered filler necks that were too small for the water hose.

The old Power Wagon had a heater, so they bundled up the kids and put them between them on the bench seat. The extra rifles and extra magazines were stowed under the seats. They each leaned their rifles on the dash next to the doors. They also wore their pistol belts and magazine carriers in case they got involved in another firefight.

He cranked the truck and flipped the switch, raising the snowplow off the ground. He had pulled out the map from the night before and mentally prepared himself for the drive. He pulled up to the gate and set the hand brake. He flipped on the headlights to verify they worked. If he managed to get further from the city and on the open highway, he wanted to run at night when most everyone alive would be seeking shelter from the cold. He didn't bother to close the gate behind them as he pulled out onto the roadway. His heart was heavy knowing he was leaving Olivia under a pile of rocks in her makeshift grave.

He ran slow as he didn't want to overtax the old truck and its running gear. He was able to maneuver around stalled cars, and he used the snowplow to push cars blocking the road to the side. He lowered the plow and plowed snow out of the way as they proceeded. Remarkably, there were few people out and about.

He made it out to Hwy One heading west toward Banff and the Banff National Park. The lakes would be frozen over; although beautiful, the intense cold would be deadly. The roads would not be maintained, and anyone left alive would be desperate. The further they went the worse the roads became. The snow was deeper than the old truck and snowplow could move. He realized his attempt to cross the mountains was futile. With snowshoes and the sleds, they could continue on foot, but there was no way for them to carry the food and supplies that would see them through the winter.

They had travelled almost to Banff after driving all night. The going was slow, but the old truck soldiered on. "Cathy, hand me my map, we've got to rethink our plans. I was hoping this truck and plow could handle it. At least it got us away from the city and all those starving people. This old truck is tough as they come. They were used in the military, but anything this old has its weaknesses."

"There doesn't seem to be many people or buildings we can see. Do you think we can camp here for a while?"

Dawson looked around and could see nothing but abandoned vehicles mostly buried in the snow. "We have the bed made up in the back; you and the kids can bundle up back there, and I'll hang out up here." He went to the back of the trailer and pulled out a fuel can and topped off the fuel tank. Cathy and the twins climbed up into the back of the truck and disappeared under the cover. Dawson pulled the canvas flap down to keep the cold Alberta wind out. He climbed back into the cab of the truck and closed the door to keep out the wind.

He could see down the snow-covered highway through the windshield and by using the rear-view mirrors cover the rear. He sat lost in thought as he was once again almost overcome with anguish when his thoughts turned to Olivia. Exhaustion and cold had taken its toll, and he found himself nodding off. He was startled awake when he bumped his head on the steering wheel and jerked awake. He cranked the engine and let the heater knock back the penetrating cold. In the distance he could see movement on the highway in his rearview mirror. He checked his weapons, sat, and waited.

He could only watch as the large vehicle approached. As it got closer, he realized it was a huge bulldozer pulling several enclosed trailers. There was only one man driving, and his first impulse was to simply shoot the man, turn the Power Wagon, around and head south. The front blade was canted to the right, and it easily threw snow and abandoned vehicles to the side. Dawson slid across the seat of the Power Wagon and exited the passenger door.

He called out to Cathy, "Keep quiet and your weapons ready. We have company, and I don't know if this is going to be good or bad."

"Please be careful; don't take any chances."

"We can't have a firefight with the kids. I'm not going to fight unless I have no choice."

He positioned himself so that the engine of the Power Wagon could possibly stop incoming rifle rounds. His heart raced as the big dozer grew closer. He changed his mind and walked around the truck and opened the driver's door and flashed the headlights on and off. He then walked around the door and laid his rifle on the hood and waited. He did not take off his pistol but left it holstered. The dozer rumbled up and throttled down. A large mountain of a man stood up. He laid his rifle on the seat behind him, opened the cab door, and stepped onto the tracks and hopped down.

"Glad you put your rifle on the hood of your truck; my son would have shot you from a shooting position in the trailer. It looks like you have a plan."

Dawson reached out and shook the man's hand. "I have been fighting for days. I'm Dawson Stewart, and I have a young lady and two little kids bundled up in the back. Where on earth are you heading?"

"I'm Scott McGregor. I have my family inside the trailers. This is an old dozer I had on my gold mine property way back up a trail in the mountains. I was up there checking on things when the lights went out. I was able to get this old monster cranked, so I hooked up two of my work trailers with tools and equipment and all the freeze-dried food I had on hand. A friend of mine convinced me that we needed to get ready for WWIII or an economic collapse with everything that has been taking place around the world. So I bought enough freeze-dried food for our entire family for two years. The back trailer has a 500 gallon diesel fuel tank. We have a hunting lodge just outside of the park south of here. This is probably the only vehicle made that could push through to it. We have most of our provisions stored there. I thought we would have a nuclear EMP, not a natural one."

Dawson motioned to the trailer behind the Power Wagon. "We have enough food for the four of us for maybe a year. I don't have a lot of fuel, but I can get fuel from abandoned vehicles and even engine oil if necessary."

McGregor waved his arm and his two sons came out of the trailer to meet Dawson. "Boys, meet Dawson Stewart; this is Greg and Charles. I think we need to invite him to join us. He has his family with him and he has food and supplies. He is obviously proficient with his weapons, or he wouldn't be still alive. We are going to need all the firepower we can muster just in case."

The boys agreed. Greg said, "Follow us, and be ready to fight. We're going to have to go through Banff and cross the bridge there."

Dawson raised the canvas flap on the trailer. Cathy was sitting up with her rifle across her lap. The kids were sitting next to her.

"Dawson what do we do now?"

"You and the kids stay back here bundled up and warm. We're going to follow them to their hunting lodge, just outside of the park in the mountains. We may have some trouble when we drive through Banff. I'll have my rifle handy, but I want to avoid a firefight with the kids in the back. I can't take a chance of them getting hurt, and I'm not going to get into a firefight unless I have no choice."

McGregor kicked up the throttle on the big dozer and pulled around the Power Wagon. Dawson put the Power Wagon in gear and followed behind. It was slow going, but at least they were going, and there was a plan. As they approached Banff, McGregor stopped the dozer long enough for his son Charles to get out and join Dawson in the old truck.

He had a 12 gauge shotgun and a bandolier of buckshot across his body. "Greg is set up in the front trailer with shooting ports on all four sides. If he starts shooting, we'll be the backup. His job is to cover Dad so we can keep moving. We can't stop, because if we do, they will be able to summon reinforcements."

Dawson, leaned out of the window and looked down the road toward the downtown area; all he could see was just a cold silent landscape. It was unlikely anyone would be manning a checkpoint in this weather. It was more than likely someone would be in one of the buildings with more than one story where the roadway could be monitored from shelter. The big dozer was not a silent vehicle. It was loud and the tracks clanked as they made contact with ice and the roadway below. Black smoke belched from the smokestack and was quickly carried away in the wind. There was no hiding the fact something big was coming through town.

They rumbled down the street, leaving the windows down so they could readily see any approaching danger. As expected, trouble walked out into the middle of the road. They looked up to see two uniformed officers trying to block the road. The one to the right raised his rifle and a shot rang out.

CHAPTER 22

Hawks looked over at Carolyn. She was instinctively clutching her throat. "What do we do?"

"We're going to bundle up, arm up, and slip out the basement window and see who or what set off the trip alarm." Carolyn slipped on her jacket and tuque before strapping on her pistol and shouldering her rifle. A small backpack topped off her gear. Hawks geared up just like Carolyn, except for a large hunting knife added to his belt. They quickly headed down into the basement; the puppies were left upstairs in the house. The puppies would only alert strangers to their location.

They quickly disappeared behind the barrier and crawled down the passage and silently exited the window behind the bush. They crawled under the large bush and waited until their eyes became accustomed to the darkness. There was a bit of moon peeking out between the clouds, and they could soon make out shapes of trees, the fence line, and the gate down by the highway. The tripped alarm seemed to have come from the direction of the corner post located at the end of front fence line.

Hawks whispered, "I don't expect them to come from the direction of the corner post where I set the trip alarm. It is likely that they will retreat into the woods and come back from another direction."

In her lowest voice she asked, "What do we do?"

"Simple, we make ourselves comfortable and wait. Anyone out there will be concentrating on the house; we'll listen and watch from here. If the pups start barking, we can expect they have crept in very close."

They held each other close to stave off the cold. They dozed and were jolted awake by the puppies barking at the back door. Hawks whispered, "They're making their move. Can you promise to sit tight so I can slip around in the shadows? If I have to start shooting, I can't worry about what is behind my target."

She touched his arm. "I'll sit tight, but you know the time is going to come when I am going to have to start fighting as well."

"You're right; you're never going to learn by staying in the shadows. You will back me up. Just follow me about twelve feet back. When I move forward, you come up to where I stopped. Remember that there is a difference between cover and concealment. Just because they can't see you, doesn't mean that they can't shoot and kill you. Cover is a very big tree, an engine block in a truck, a brick wall; understand?"

"I understand, and I will stay back and back you up."

Hawks hugged her neck and gave her a kiss. "We go slow and quiet. Watch your every step; the only light we have is from the moonlight and the reflection off the snow."

Hawks eased around until he reached the corner of the house and slowly peered around and saw only undisturbed snow. He slowly made his way to the nearest large bush and waited while Carolyn made it to the corner he had just left. He crossed exposed until he reached a large cedar tree and stayed in its shadow as he made his way up onto a small ridge running parallel to the side of the house. He made his way halfway up the ridge and paused, giving Carolyn time to start up the ridge as well. He waved for Carolyn to join him.

From this vantage point he could see the side of the house and the length of the entire back porch. The dogs were barking and a figure walked out from inside the back door and shouted into the woods, "There is no one home; come on up."

Two more obviously armed figures crossed from the woods. As soon as they started up the stairs, Hawks placed the red dot on his rifle's sight on the figure on the porch and pulled the trigger. Not waiting to see if his shot connected, he moved his sight to the next one and pulled the trigger. The third one turned and started running, but it was too late. Carolyn's gun fired, and he spun and watched as she shot another one he hadn't seen. This one was further up on the ridge. He came rolling down the ridge in their direction. Hawks cut loose on him, and he sprawled dead about twenty feet away.

Hawks told Carolyn, "Stay here. I'm heading up the ridge to see if there are anymore. If any of them move, shoot them again."

"Don't worry; I'm tempted to shoot them again just because."

Hawks stepped around the body and cautiously headed up the ridge. From his position he could see the sprawled bodies of the dead on the back porch, steps, and walkway. There was no indication there were any other people involved. He walked back down the ridge where Carolyn dutifully sat covering the porch and looking for movement.

Carolyn looked up. "I think they are finished; you were sure right about them expecting us to be in the house."

Hawks checked the body of the dead man. There was no need to use a killing shot. One bullet had traveled through his head. They went down the ridge and walked around to the back porch. A quick shot to each of their heads made certain no one would wake up wounded and start fighting. He dragged them out into the yard to where he could load them up in the tractor's front bucket. All the men had hunting rifles, but one also had an old revolver.

Hawks checked the backdoor and saw where one of the small window panes next to the lock had been broken. He would have to devise a way to block the doors and ground floor windows so entry would be drastically impeded from someone trying to get in. He patched the broken window pane with some scrap plywood and some caulk. The puppies were unharmed, and their value as an early warning system proved invaluable.

They retired to the den and stoked up the fire in the fireplace and dozed in their recliners. They slept from exhaustion and didn't wake until daylight. Hawks headed out the front door, but not before walking around the house and peering out through the windows without disturbing the drapes and blinds. Once he felt it was clear, he grabbed his rifle, tool belt, and a shotgun shell to replace the one set off in the tripped alarm. He stayed close to the fence line so as not to be exposed in the open pasture. He quickly reached the tripped alarm and rearmed it. He scrutinized the area and quickly found the men's trail and was able to backtrack them out to the road. Although he was expecting an antiquated vehicle, he was surprised to see eight horses. Four were saddled; the others were loaded with packs. Using the line they were picketed to, he led them down the road to the gate, unlocked it, and led them up to the house.

Carolyn came out. "What are we going to do with them?"

"I guess we now have alternative transportation and a lot of meat to put in the smokehouse."

He led them around to the barn where he unloaded the pack horses to give the poor beasts some relief from their loads. One by one he led them to the pasture where he turned them loose. There was plenty of grass poking through the snow. Once he had them all in the pasture, he carried water from the house and filled up the old stock tank that sat just over the fence. The horses were soon settled in, and his back ached from all the exertion.

He went up the front steps and into the house and was met by Carolyn's beautiful smile. She was cooking up some breakfast on the old woodstove. "I know you've worked up an appetite. I'm sorry I didn't help. I'm afraid of horses. I got thrown off one when I was a teenager."

"No worries, I've ridden horses my whole life. Once they've had a chance to settle down, I'll figure out which one is the gentlest and that will be yours to start. I can also use one of them to round up the cow and calf down the road." He went down the back steps, being careful not to step in any of the blood on the porch and steps. He rifled through the pockets of the men. They all had wads of useless cash and some jewelry. The cash he chucked in the burn barrel and the jewelry was thrown in an old coffee can. He rolled the bodies two at a time into the bucket on the Kubota tractor and hauled them away. He made no effort to bury them but found a spot where he could simply dump them over a rock ledge down into a ravine.

He felt absolutely no remorse or regret in killing them, because he knew exactly what would have happened to him and Carolyn had they made it into the house undetected. He next gathered up some old hay from the barn and used it to cover up the now frozen blood on the porch and steps. When the weather warmed up a bit, he would sweep up the blood-soaked straw. He kept thinking, We can't keep fighting at this rate. It would be just a matter of time before one of more thieves would overcome them. In fact, a lone gunman with a deer rifle could take their time and snipe them from anywhere along the wood line. Going forward, he would let the pups run loose. They would at least catch a scent of someone if the wind were blowing in the right direction. The cat finally showed up none the worse for wear after disappearing during all the commotion.

His mind wandered back to when he was on the sinking ferry.

Life was so simple; all he had to do was do his work, write his reports, and relax. There was no one or nothing that worried him. He was quite content to just wind down in his final years, relax, and spoil his grandson. Now he felt like he did when he was a young man, up to ears in debt with a young family and only a hundred dollars to his name. Having the weight of the world on your shoulders was hard when you are a young man just learning how to cope.

Now it was worse than ever. He was now looking over his shoulder every minute, worrying about a girlfriend, and worried about his children and grandson. He could only imagine the hell they were going through. Atlanta and Houston would be like war zones. The population would be going absolutely berserk. Both cities had extremely high crime rates. There was also a huge percentage of the population depending on the government for all their food, housing, and medical. Now that the food cards no longer worked and the grocery stores were out of food, a blood bath had and was taking place. He hoped his children were smart enough to get out in some way. Surely, they could think of ways to survive; after all, they were raised by him, and both were very smart.

He had to figure out a way to keep him and Carolyn from getting killed, and he had to figure a way to travel south and travel toward his camp in the Ozarks. That would mean carrying lots of food. If he had someone to help, they could stay forted up here. But there was no one he knew still alive who could help. Winter was raging in the North Country. British Columbia winters could be bad, but they were largely tempered by the Pacific Ocean currents. However, on the other side of the mountains, the winter was in full force. Twenty-below temperatures were the norm through the northern third of the continent. Then the problem was getting off the island with all the supplies they would need to travel across half the country. If they loaded up backpacks, they would be dead inside of two weeks, and that was only if they could avoid getting killed or robbed.

Carolyn walked out. "That's a good idea to put the hay out on the blood. You seem to be lost in thought."

"I am. I can usually plan things out, and I know exactly what to do. I just don't know how I'm going to solve this problem that is facing us down. The last thing I want to do is give up this house, land, and the comfort it affords. But we are sitting ducks here any way you look at it. Even with all the food we have, it will not last us ninety days. We lucked up with the horses. There are a lot of calories in one of them. They'll overeat the field in a few weeks, so we've got to figure out which ones we'll put in the smokehouse and which ones we'll ride and use."

Carolyn grinned. "I ate some horse when I was on vacation in France. It was pretty good. I'm sure I can cook it."

"Maybe we can make horse jerky and even kill and jerk the cow and calf from the neighbor's farm." He shooed the puppies away from sniffing at the frozen blood under the hay. They ran down the steps and around the house. In the coming days, he had some decisions to make. For one they needed to set up at least one other stocked offsite camp. Nothing was going to stop the golden hoard, and it was imperative they survive. The third option was to get prepared to run with enough supplies to see them through what was unfolding.

CHAPTER 23

Greg dropped the one on the left from his position in the trailer. The one on the right bolted across in front of the dozer to get on the side to take a shot at McGregor. Charles blasted him with three rounds of buckshot and put him down, rolling in the snow. All the blood against the snow outlined his still writhing body as he died. The dozer never slowed as they proceeded across the dead body in the road. They soon crossed the bridge and proceeded south toward the hunting lodge. There was no one pursuing them, but the tracks they left would be easy to follow. Only another snowstorm would hide the tracks, which was likely at this time of year. A column of black smoke bellowed from the dozer's exhaust stack routed so that it ended above the cab of the dozer. Dawson kept an eye on the rear-view mirrors just in case anyone was foolish enough to pursue them.

Charles was quiet. Dawson looked over at him. "Is this your first kill?"

"No, I was in the Middle East when I was in the army. I was in a firefight when the convoy I was in was hit. We fought for about three hours. I know I killed four, and I'm sure I hit at least a dozen more. I've had to kill three since all this started. I'm just waiting for the adrenaline rush to run down. How about you?"

"I haven't been counting, but I'm sure I've killed close to twenty."

"Did it bother you?"

"Sadly, no; in fact, it was somewhat satisfying. Everyone was asking for it I just wish I could have killed some of them a lot slower."

Charles nodded in agreement. "I'm glad to hear you say that because that's exactly the way I feel. Do you mind if I take a nap?"

"Of course not, get some rest while you can." Charles dozed off, and the only sound was the engine running and the sound of the truck rolling through the snow- and ice-covered road. After they had traveled about ten miles, they pulled over for a rest stop. He walked back to the rear of the old truck and raised the tarp, peering in. Three sets of eyes peered out above their cover.

Cathy asked, "We need a rest break?"

"That is why we're stopping. Have y'all been warm enough?"

"Yes, we are warm and scared. What happened back there?"

"A couple of men tried to stop us; they lived to regret the attempt." Dawson helped Cathy out of the back and lifted each of the twins out onto the road. While they were stretching their legs, he checked the engine fluids and the tires on the truck.

McGregor and his family also stretched their legs. The old dozer sat idling. In another time they would be enjoying the beautiful trees, mountain, and snow. But now they were in a flight for their lives. There was danger behind them and, in all probability, danger in front of them. They dug out the leftover cookies they had cooked while they were still at Henry's. The cookies sated their hunger. An ice chest held some water and apple juice. They were placed in the chest to keep them thawed rather than to keep them frozen. After their quick meal, they sent the twins back in to the warmth of the bed.

Cathy said, "We've been telling stories to keep ourselves occupied."

"Great idea, I don't have a clue about taking care of kids. All I know is that you have to keep them fed and unfrozen."

McGregor walked back to where they were and said, "We have about thirty or so miles to go. We'll try to make it today, but if not, we'll have to overnight on the road."

Dawson looked back up the road. "I don't think anyone is going to follow us, and it feels like it is going to snow."

McGregor gave him a skeptical look. "You could get a job as a weather forecaster one day."

Dawson grinned. "I'm just a snow forecaster. It just seems like it is colder somehow. Every time I get this sense of cold, it snows within the day. I just call it snow cold."

McGregor smiled. "Let me know every time you get that feeling. That sounds like a handy talent to have."

Charles went up to the first trailer and came back munching on a sandwich. He assumed his position on the passenger side. "Do you want me to spell you at the wheel?"

Dawson said, "Thanks, but I'm wide awake. I'm not tired enough to sleep yet."

Dawson cranked up while the engine was still warm and loaded up. Thirty miles by bulldozer was going to take hours. The dozer was moving about as fast as a man walks. It was certain they would be camping tonight. They had warm bedding, firewood, and food; with the coming snow, they should be safe.

The column of black smoke rose to the sky as McGregor throttled up the dozer. They moved out, and Dawson fought the thoughts of losing Olivia. As desperate as he was to relive the past and fix it, it was impossible. No amount of prayer would change a thing. There was no doubt his nights would be haunted by nightmares. He could only imagine the hell regular people went through when they realized there was no hope of survival or the people who were now resorting to cannibalism who would also die as soon as they ran out of their fellow humans. Every dog, cat, bird, rabbit, and anything that moved would soon be consumed if there were any left at this point. They slowly continued their trek down through the mountains. To the left of the road was the frozen river; the mountains rose to the right. Occasionally they would pass a valley heading up between sections of the mountains. Some had roads; others just trails.

The days were short this far north, and they were soon traveling in the dark. The dozer plowed the snow as it slowly made its way south. About three hours after dark, McGregor stopped the dozer but left it idling as before. Dawson stopped and went up to the dozer as McGregor stepped down. It was starting to snow just as Dawson had predicted.

McGregor smiled at Dawson. "Looks like the snow caster was right."

"What can I say? When you have it, you have it," grinned Dawson. "What are the plans?"

McGregor pointed to the engine. "This old bird burns a little oil, so I need to give it a gallon every day or so when it is heavily used. I'm not going to turn off the engine until we get there. I can't take a chance on this old diesel engine getting cold. We wouldn't get it started until spring. I had to put a torch to the engine block to get it hot enough to fire off the diesel when I started it a few days ago. I'm really tired, and the lights on the dozer aren't strong enough for me to see the outline of the road."

"Sounds good to me. We need to take turns standing guard. We'll eat a cold supper, and I can take the first watch."

Charles walked up in time to hear him. "No, I've slept for the past four hours. I'll take the first watch. You need to sleep until you are rested or until daylight. I can sleep in the morning when we are back rolling."

"I won't argue with you. I'm exhausted and my head is still aching from getting shot." He walked back to the rear of the truck and lifted the canvas flat and called out to Cathy, "We've stopped for the night; I'm going to try and get some sleep."

She answered from the darkness, "The kids are getting sleepy. Help us out for a rest break, and then you can join us in this warm bed. There's plenty of space. The kids don't take up much room." He was too tired to argue, so he helped them out so they could take a bathroom break. He helped them back out of the cold and into the bed. He slid off his coat and loosened the laces on his boots so he could slip them on and off quickly. He slipped in next to Cathy and pulled the cover over them. One of the kids promptly crawled over and lay on his belly with their head on his shoulder. He was too tired to complain and was soon asleep. He slept soundly with Cathy laying against him on his left side and one of the twins on his stomach.

He was awakened when the flap of canvas was opened and Greg McGregor called, "Its daylight. Are y'all ready to rise and shine?"

Dawson blinked. "I can't believe it's morning already. I just closed my eyes."

Cathy reached up and checked the bandage on his head. "How does your head feel this morning?"

"I think it feels better; I just needed some rest." They crawled out into the cold. The McGregor's had some biscuits and sliced ham. McGregor's wife, daughters-in-law, and five grandkids were busy warming up the ham and passing out the biscuits with the ham and jelly. McGregor's wife was named Ellen, and the daughters-in-law were Linda and Monica. He couldn't keep track of the kids' names. Maybe in the coming days he could figure out who was who.

McGregor throttled up the old dozer after topping off the fuel. The black smoke disappeared into the wind coming off the mountain. The air had warmed a bit before the snow started, but now the bitter cold was settling back in. The old truck ran flawlessly as it idled in line behind the McGregor caravan. The cold and the snow would keep them safe from attack for now.

Charles was still awake. "I hope no one has moved into our hunting lodge."

"What do we do if we find it occupied?"

"We will have no choice but to oust them. It's either us or them."

"I agree. I suggest we stop before we get there and walk in so we can observe."

"That's the plan."

For the next four hours they methodically continued their journey. Charles stirred and rolled his window down and leaned out. "We are nearing the turnoff to the road which will take us to our lodge. Once we turn, we'll only have about fifteen miles to go. It would be difficult but not impossible for someone to get to the lodge. The lodge road is not maintained by the snowplows, and we always used snow mobiles to get in and out. The dozer should be able to plow it. Once we get there and check it out, we can use the snow mobiles in the barn."

Dawson shivered as Charles rolled up the window. "I hope it is abandoned when we get there. I sure don't want to have to take the lodge."

They made the turn onto the lodge road. There would be no turning around from this point forward. The road was narrow, but the huge dozer made short work of shoving the snow and the occasional boulder that had fallen from up on the mountain out of the way. The road followed what was now a frozen stream on the left side of the road. McGregor stopped the dozer and came back to where Dawson, Charles, and Greg had gathered. "We walk from here. Dawson do you have some snowshoes?"

Dawson pointed to the trailer. "I have a pair ready to go."

Dawson dug out the snowshoes from the trailer and uncovered the stash of rifles. He called out to Charles, "Come see what I've got."

Charles came over and grinned when he saw the cache of rifles and called over to McGregor and his brother, "We've struck gold. Dawson is going to up our game." He held up one of the C7 rifles while grinning from ear to ear.

CHAPTER 24

The exertion of the evening before and the hard work of the morning had taken their toll on him. Hawks climbed the front porch stairs and walked into the living room and sat in the chair closest to the fireplace. His rifle sat across his lap; his pistol was in his holster. There he slept for the better part of the day. He awoke from the sound of Carolyn placing some more wood on the fire. A cloud of sparks rose through the smoke and disappeared up the flue. She smiled. "Wake up, sleepy head. I let you rest. I know you needed it."

"Thanks, I'm not a spring chicken anymore. I'm ready to grab a bath and some chow. I sure hope we have a quieter night than last."

"Don't worry; I've got water heating on the stove for your bath, and I just set off a pot of soup to cool a bit. I've had my bath, and I'm ready to scrub your back."

Hawks heartily ate his soup with some homemade bread and coffee with a shot of bourbon. The warm bath soothed his sore muscles. As he dressed, he looked at Carolyn. "Tomorrow we're going to start sleeping in Roosevelt's old wine cellar. No one will be looking to storm it, and where it's located, no one will think to look. We can come back to the house during the day; we just can't take a chance on being surprised."

Carolyn asked, "What if we built a hidden room in the basement? If someone comes in, the pups will warn us."

"I just don't want to get caught in here if it gets torched. I want to make certain that we have complete supplies away from here, so if we must leave here naked, we can get re-outfitted with clothes and supplies and can come back and fight another day."

"For now, let's forget the day."

They broke out some bourbon and retired to the large fireplace. Hawks finished his drink and said, "One is plenty for me, and I've decided what we need to do."

Carolyn had her elbows resting on the armrest and was looking over the glass she held with two hands. "What's the plan?"

"I remember what the killers at our neighbor's house were saying just before I took them out. They said they were going to hit the place with the locked gate. We need to make this place look like no one is here. It's going to be hard considering we have a chimney and a working smokehouse. The smokehouse is around the side and doesn't produce a column of smoke. During the day, we'll have to make sure that we are only burning seasoned wood on the fireplace and stove to reduce the smoke from the chimney. I'm going to open the gate and lift one side off the hinge to make it appear it had been broken through. I'll move the bodies from up at our burned-out neighbors out to the end of the driveway, and we'll throw our garbage out down the drive along with any other refuse we can find like old tires and trash barrels.

Carolyn pointed out, "What about all the horses?"

"They can't see the pasture from the road and once someone comes up the road, the dogs will be barking. We're also going to set up another camp across the highway up in the woods where the first two who tried to sneak in here at night set up with their motorcycles."

Carolyn grinned. "I like it when we have a plan, and I like the idea of spending one more night in in our bed. Do you think we can get the Model A trailer up that trail across the road?"

"I think I can, and I can drop a couple of trees across the road so that no will try to go up there."

They slept peacefully that night and rose to the crowing of the rooster. The first order of business was to crank the Kubota and drive down to the neighbors to retrieve the four dead bodies. The old Kubota had reliably cranked once again. He drove down the driveway and stopped long enough to take the gate off its hinges and drag it to the side as if it had been broken through. He turned to see Carolyn wave from the porch, and with his rifle on his shoulder and his pistol on his belt, he ran the tractor at a fast clip down the road and up the drive of his neighbor's farm.

He stopped at the body of the first man. Fortunately, the temperatures were hovering below freezing, and the body showed no sign of decay. One eye was bulging its socket from the pressure created in the brain cavity when the bullet had passed through his skull. The other stared blankly at nothing. He rolled the body into the bucket of the tractor and proceeded to the barn where the other bodies lay where they had died. He rolled them into the bucket and used some bailing wire from the barn to secure them in place. He picked up the dead mother dog in the back of the barn and secured it on the front as well.

The trip back was uneventful. The tractor bounced more from the weight of the dead in the bucket. The extra weight in the bucket of a tractor had the effect of a seesaw as it tried to lift the back of the tractor. When he got back to the farm, he wheeled in and laid the mother dog next to the road. He went several yards up the driveway where he dumped the bodies out. He placed a couple of them so they partially blocked the drive. The other two he left lying in a haphazard fashion to the side. He made sure their pants pockets were left wrong side out to make them appear as though they had been robbed.

Next, he ran back to the house to be greeted by Carolyn, who came down the side steps and followed him to the barn. "I'm glad you're back; what next?"

"We're going to hook up the camper behind the Cub tractor and take it up the trail across the road. First, I'll have to take a hike up there with a machete to see if the trail is wide enough to let the camper past."

Carolyn pointed to the barn. "I can help clear brush. I'm turning into a farm girl."

They proceeded to the barn and loaded their tools in the Kubota tractor's bucket. Armed as usual, they drove down the driveway. Carolyn rode sitting on the fender next to Hawks. Cold chills ran up her back as they drove around the corpses lying in the driveway. The tractor easily negotiated the trail heading up the hill. Near the top of the ridge the trail narrowed. They stopped, and Hawks retrieved an axe from the bucket.

Carolyn asked, "Why didn't you get one of the chainsaws?"

"Simple, the sound of a chainsaw would travel a mile or so from this height. We don't need to alert anyone to our presence. I can trim these bushes and saplings with the axe. I want you to stand guard and keep your eyes on the farmhouse in case anyone decides to stop and gets curious."

She smiled. "I'll stand guard and bring you the canteen when needed."

"Thanks, I'm sweating even though it's a cold day. In fact, I could use a swig from that canteen now." They sat on a rock outcropping and looked across the road at the farm. From this vantage point, they could observe the farm and fields. From this commanding height, they could see the horses in the field, and other than the bodies lying in the driveway, it was an ideal pastural setting. It was hard to believe they were at the center of what would probably become hell on earth. They had only received a taste thus far of what was coming, it was a miracle they had survived up until now.

The hours passed as they finished opening the trail and creating a spot to park the camper out of sight of the farm. Hawks pointed at the sun. "We have just enough time to go back and get the camper."

"Great, let's go hook it up and get it up here." The trip back was short, and they were soon putting the Kubota back in its spot in the barn. Hawks checked the oil and made sure there was adequate gas in the tank of the Cub tractor. He cranked and backed up the Cub tractor to the old camper and lowered the hitch onto the ball on the drawbar. Before he climbed back into the driver's seat, he used a screwdriver and hammer to knock up and over the steel bar that connected the two brake pedals. The brake pedals on most tractors were separate, so that if one wheel lost traction and started to spin, it could be stopped by stepping on the corresponding brake pedal. This pushed the power to the opposite wheel that still had traction. Once he had the hitch latched and the safety chains secured, he put the tractor in low gear and proceeded out of the barn and onto the drive.

Carolyn stood on the draw bar straddling the hitch. "Am I OK to ride back here?"

"Sure thing, just don't get tangled up in the hitch and chains. If you decide to get off, let me know so I can stop and let you off." Hawks let the clutch up, and they proceeded down the drive. He left the tractor in low and let the engine compression slow the descent down the hill. They drove around the bodies and crossed the road and proceeded up the trail. The little tractor had more than enough power to pull the camper up the hill. Although it was a small tractor, it had a lot of power in low gear. The engine's governor increased the fuel to the engine as it maintained its speed. He only had to touch the brake once to stop the spinning when it got into some loose soil and rocks. Once at the top, he stopped so Carolyn could hop off. He spun the camper around and, with Carolyn guiding, backed into the opening they had cleared. They leveled the camper by backing it up on some flat rocks. They cranked down the jacks on each corner to stabilize it after chocking the wheels to prevent it from rolling away. They unhitched it from the tractor as the sun was going down.

From the crest of the hill, they could see the farmhouse on the hill in the fading light. They rode the tractor down the hill and paused halfway down when they spotted vehicle lights coming down the road from the direction of town. Hawks put the tractor in high gear and hurried down the hill and across the road. They ran at top speed until they got around to the side of the house. They left the tractor and ran back around to the front of the house where they watched as an old sedan sped by, not slowing at their drive, and proceeded past the farm, disappearing down the road. They evidently had purpose in their travel and took no mind of the farm.

Hawks, looked around at Carolyn. "Let's get buttoned up for the night and get some chow. Tomorrow we'll get to work on a hidden room in the basement where we can sleep and where we can escape down our hidden passage to leave the house."

Carolyn slung her rifle on her shoulder and turned toward the house. "The pups will easily warn us of anything going on around here." At that moment they heard the car that just passed coming back. They turned to see the headlights coming back down the road.

CHAPTER 25

Charles McGregor quickly showed his brother and father how to operate the C7 rifles. Dawson handed them the sidearms he had accumulated as well. They instructed the ladies to stay put and stand guard. Donning their snowshoes, they headed out in single file with McGregor leading the way. Once he was about thirty feet ahead, Greg started out. They headed down the road with each about thirty feet apart from one another. The going was slow as McGregor was breaking trail in the snow. Once he tired, the second in line overtook him and lead the way.

They were soon out of hearing of the idling dozer and eagerly looking forward. There was no indication man or machine had been down the road recently. The road wound as it followed the contours of the stream and the mountain on their right. The evergreen trees were still intact in this little valley. Many areas of Alberta had lost a lot of their forest to the forest fires plaguing the area over the past few years.

After traveling a couple of miles, McGregor called out, "We're getting near. I want to take the lead, and we're going to go slow. I don't want to be spotted if there is anyone there. We are within a half mile of the lodge, so keep your heads on a swivel." They all nodded in agreement and followed McGregor.

It took them another twenty minutes to get within sight of

the lodge. They all stopped and waited. There was no sign of life in the lodge. There was no smoke coming from the chimneys or the stove pipes. Snow was piled up on the steps and spilled over onto the porch.

McGregor told Dawson, "You set up here. The boys and I will circle the house and check out the barn and sheds. Once we are sure it's OK, we'll let you know."

McGregor and the boys made short work of exploring the property and grounds. Dawson watched as McGregor came out the front door and waved to him to come on down. Dawson came down the road and up the drive and took off his snowshoes so he could climb the steps.

McGregor told Greg, "Stay here and get some fire started in the stoves to get the house heated up. We'll go back and get the families."

They double timed it back; the going was faster as the trail had already been broken by their snowshoes on the trip in. As they approached the idling dozer, shots rang out. McGregor went down, and without hesitation, Charles grabbed him by his belt and pulled him down the hill toward the creek so that they were out of line of sight of the dozer.

Dawson dove to the opposite side where a boulder and a huge fir tree provided cover and concealment. He called down to Charles, "How's McGregor?"

Charles called back up, "He's taken one through the shoulder, just a lot of blood, but nothing from an artery that would kill him."

"Tell him to stay put and let us work." Dawson moved so that he could see between the boulder and the tree. He slipped off his snow shows so he could move freely. He got a glimpse of a man standing on the dozer treads to get a better look down the hill where McGregor and Charles took shelter. Dawson put the red dot on his tuque-covered head and squeezed the trigger. The man collapsed back on the tread and rolled off dead into the snow.

Dawson didn't hesitate and bolted to the front of the dozer and glanced around to the left side. If he changed his position, he would have no cover if he moved around the side. He thought about Cathy and the twins and threw caution to the wind. He couldn't just open fire without endangering everyone in the trailer and in the Power Wagon. He stomped through the snow, and when he reached the back of the dozer, another man appeared and threw down on him with a rifle. Before Dawson could fire, the man collapsed. Charles's shot from the opposite side of the road had put him down. Dawson popped him through the head for good measure.

Gunfire erupted from behind the Power Wagon. Dawson ran full tilt, and when he reached the rear of the Power Wagon, two more men lay dying in the snow. Cathy had emptied her Glock on them when they were distracted by the gunfire from Dawson and Charles. Charles ran to the trailer behind the dozer where his family was trapped. He unlocked the door and flung it open; everyone was safe.

Cathy came out of the back and threw her arms around Dawson's neck. "Thank God, you are OK."

Dawson called to the twins, "Stay in your bed and don't come out. We've got some stuff to do before we get moving. Don't come out no matter what." He didn't want them to see the dead men.

He and Charles helped McGregor up out of the ravine and into the back of the trailer so the ladies could tend to his wound. They drug the dead bodies off into the ravine out of sight. Bears would make short work of the bodies in the spring. The problem would be the people who knew the men who were following them and would know where they were heading.

Dawson backtracked down the road and found the vehicle the

men had used to follow them. It was an old Ford tractor with a small trailer behind it. He would have to come back and retrieve it once they got everyone safely to the lodge. Charles drove the dozer, and he followed in the Power Wagon. They were soon back at the lodge where they dropped the trailers near the back and side doors. They parked the dozer next to the barn and killed the engine. Dawson parked the Power Wagon next to the trailers so he could unload it later.

Once they had McGregor in the house along with the families, Dawson put on his snowshoes and double timed it back to the old Ford tractor. He cranked it and headed back to the lodge and dropped it out behind the barn. He walked up the back steps and into the lodge kitchen. It was markedly warmer in the house as they had the stoves stoked up. Cathy and the kids sat near the stove.

Cathy smiled as he came in. "They have a bedroom for us. They are going to start melting snow on the stove so we can get washed up."

McGregor sat in a big chair with his shirt off to let his wife clean and bandage the wound. He looked up at Dawson. "Well, it looks like we lucked out; it could have been a lot worse. We're going to leave my wound open so it can drain; we have antibiotics I bought to go with our food storage."

"I hope you have some pain killer."

"Indeed, I do. I'm going to start with aspirin and a double shot of Irish whisky."

"I would have thought you to be a scotch drinker."

"I never developed a taste for it. I make a poor Scotsman."

Dawson pointed toward the road. "We are going to have to set up a schedule for keeping watch." McGregor winced as he repositioned himself in his chair. "We need an Alberta blizzard to completely hide our trail. Let me know when you have that snow cold feeling again."

Greg volunteered, "I'll take the first watch."

Dawson said, "Thanks, I'm exhausted from all this action." Without saying a word, Cathy handed him a sandwich and some tea. She summoned the twins. "Come, children, we're going to bed." She motioned to Dawson. "Let me show you to our room."

They walked down the hall after he finished his sandwich, where Cathy led him into a spacious room with a wood heater in the corner. A fire was burning and had the room warming nicely. There was a queen-sized bed and a large overstuffed chair. Dawson pointed to the chair. "I'll take the chair."

Cathy shook her head no. "You can't get the rest you need sitting up in a chair all night. We'll do it exactly like we did in the back of the Power Wagon last night." She rolled back the covers and told him, "Strip down to your long underwear and get in."

Dawson was too tired to argue and rolled in after leaning his rifle against the wall on his side of the bed. He placed his pistol on the nightstand in its holster. Cathy and the twins stripped down to their long underwear and Cathy backed up to his side with the kids next to her.

Charles dutifully stood guard. The house was lit by candles and several gas lamps mounted on the wall fed by a propane tank. He suited up in his cold weather gear and went outside to where he could cover the lodge. Anyone trying to sneak up would be concentrating on the house with the light showing through the windows. His breath fogged through the wool scarf he had wrapped around his neck and face below his eyes. Ice from his breath was building up on the outside of his scarf. The wool tuque was doing its job, but the cold was starting to penetrate his coat. He gathered up some rocks and made a wall of stones so he could build a small fire. By placing the rock wall between him and the lodge, it would reflect the heat toward him, but more important, it would block some of the light until it burned down to a bed of coals.

The woods on the hill where he sat was littered by fallen limbs. He gathered up an armful of limbs and placed them in a carefully stacked pile. He took dried fronds from the cedar trees and created a bundle that would easily light and start the larger wood burning. The bundle readily flared when he directed the flame from his butane lighter. He was temporarily blinded by the flame, but it soon died down and started heating up the stack of wood. The small unburned embers quickly burned out and the logs soon settled down to a good, slow burn. The warmth radiating from the fire felt good. Once he was warm, he moved away from the fire so his eyes could become accustomed to the low light. The faint moonlight filtering through the trees was magnified by the snow cover so that it was possible to clearly see the entire area.

Until a good snowstorm could bury the vehicle tracks leading to the lodge, they would be vulnerable. In the quietness of the night, the dangers of the world seemed miles away. From his vantage point on the hill, he could see the lodge, the vehicles parked to the side, and the barns. To his left he could see up the road and drive leading out to the main highway from which they had come. In the stillness he could easily hear any vehicles and could see anyone trekking down the road. Several deer came running out of the creek bottom and down the road toward the lodge. He was surprised they were active in this cold. They bounded by and disappeared into the forest behind the barn. Something or someone had spooked them from where they were taking shelter. A pack of five wolves suddenly came up from the creek bottom and, with their nose to the ground, followed the deer at a dead run. He thought about killing them but chose to remain silent so as not to alert anyone within earshot. The rest of the night was quiet.

Dawson had slept soundly. When he awoke, he discovered Cathy was snuggly sleeping next to him. His arms cradled her, and she clung to him as well. The twins were still asleep, and for the moment he felt contentment. He stirred and pulled away from Cathy. It had only been a few days since Olivia had been murdered. He felt sorrow and guilt for sleeping with Cathy and briefly forgetting about Olivia.

Cathy stirred and looked at Dawson. "Thank you for saving us and keeping us safe. I won't force myself on you, and I will understand if you don't want us."

Dawson touched her cheek. "Don't worry; I'm not going anywhere, and I promise to protect you and the twins."

Tears filled her eyes. "Thank you, and I hope you don't mind me taking care of you."

Dawson nodded. "It's obvious we need each other." The twins woke and quickly piled on them and were soon giggling and lightened the mood as only small children can. A knock on the door brought Dawson to his feet. He called out, "Come in."

Greg poked his head in. "It's breakfast time. We need to spell Charles and get to unloading the trailers and truck." Dawson gave him the thumbs-up.

CHAPTER 26

The sedan came roaring back and once again did not slow. It had either dropped off a passenger or verified the existence of a structure or a landmark. Either conclusion would lead to a sleepless night. Hawks once again had the nagging thought they needed to make a run for the United States border and head south to the cabin in the Ozarks. It would take riding horses and pack horses to make the trip, at least until they could make it to the Missouri River and find an appropriate boat.

Carolyn saw the concerned look on his face as they walked into the living room. "What are you thinking?"

"I think our world is going to get even more treacherous. That car probably dropped one or more people off up the road. In the short time it took them to come back down the highway, it means there is someone within three miles of here."

Carolyn pointed out, "If we're lucky, it was someone who lives out here that they dropped off."

Hawks added a log to the fire. "I guess time will tell."

The puppies were anxious to go out. He walked down the stairs and listened as each step had a separate and distinct squeak. He let the pups out the back door and watched as they disappeared into the dim morning light. He stoked up the kitchen woodstove to knock the chill off and to make a pot of coffee. The stove would be good and hot so biscuits could be baked when Carolyn got up. He didn't light any lights and depended on his knowledge of the house to navigate to the basement stairs.

The early morning light filtered through the windows in the walkout door heading out to the driveway leading to the barn. He rummaged around in the toolbox and found a twenty-five-foot tape measure. His plan for the fake wall soon came into focus as he measured the room and his plan came into mind. He would build a wall with a workbench in front of it. The door would be partially obscured by the workbench and would have some shelves built on it. Using another one of the piano hinges would allow him to walk around the bench and shove the door open. Unless someone had the time or inclination to carefully examine the wall, no one would ever notice the door.

He could hear Carolyn stirring around up in the kitchen. The old wood floors creaked as she moved around the kitchen. No one would be able to quietly slip around the house unnoticed.

She called down the stairs, "I know you're down there working. Come on up and eat."

Hawks climbed up the stairs with his empty cup. He smacked Carolyn on the lips and pointed down the stairs.

"I've got it figured out how we're going to build a hidden room."

They spent the next three days building the fake wall and installing the hidden door. They soon had it outfitted with bedroom furniture. The room was small but cozy. The bed and nightstands took up most of the room. A ladder on the back wall led up to the crawlspace leading to the basement window they used to escape the house unnoticed.

Carolyn lamented, "I'm going to miss my big bedroom."

"I understand, but think how good we can sleep now that we are completely hidden and there is no danger of us getting trapped upstairs if we are attacked and the house gets torched. The next thing we are going to do is set up some trip alarms, and I'm going to prepack the horse packs so that all we have to do is put them on the horses and go."

Carolyn asked, "I think we need to practice riding and leading the pack horses."

Hawks scratched his chin. "That's a great idea. We need to figure out which of the horses are best to ride and which ones are difficult to work with. Horses are like dogs and people. Some are good; some are bad."

Carolyn grinned. "We can eat the bad ones."

"I guess if we don't have room in the smokehouse, we can always make horse jerky. I can also try my hand at tanning horse hide."

Carolyn had made a bag of sugar cookies, which made it easy to call the horses up. Fortunately, the horses were well mannered, and they soon had the best two riding horses saddled and ready to go. The saddles had rifle scabbards. Two of the rifles had single point slings allowing them to carry the rifles hanging by their sides or passed around behind them. This type of sling made it almost impossible to be separated from the rifle in the event of a fall or while running. They would always carry these, and backup rifles would be placed in the scabbards.

Carolyn asked, "Why the backup rifles?"

"We need to have functioning firearms. The spare rifles will be a source of parts for the other two. If one of our carry rifles get damaged or a critical part wears out, we've got to have backups. It will be the same with all our critical gear. When we pack up the packs, I'll make sure we have extra machetes, axes, and basic supplies. They will be in separate packs on separate horses. If we lose a horse with its packs, we won't be stuck with no supplies."

Carolyn nodded her head in agreement. "I'm glad you can see all the possibilities."

"You can't foresee everything. There are so many variables that you can only look for the probabilities. Horses are like vehicles; you never know when one will break down."

Carolyn asked, "When we pack up the horses to go, we must assume we are never coming back. So we have to pack accordingly. That means as much food as possible."

They rode the two horses down the lane past their hidden cabin near the future vineyard. They made it back after a couple of hours and unsaddled the horses and led them back to the pasture. Hawks ran his hand down one of the horse's back. "These are large horses, each probably in the thousand-pound range. They should be able to handle up to two hundred pounds including the weight of the packs. We'll keep the packs around one hundred and sixty pounds, that way we have a margin for error. If we have to escape on them, we have to be mindful that we can't wear them out."

Fortunately, the weather warmed and the melting snow exposed vast amounts of grass in the large pasture with the horses. The horses were well fed and the decaying corpses were attracting birds. A number of crows, ravens, and magpies were busy pecking away and jockeying for position on the dead. They put the horses back in the pasture and retreated to the rocking chairs on the front porch. From there they could see the front gate and the roadway beyond. Suddenly the birds scattered as a coyote came bounding up to share the bounty. They watched for a few minutes in disgust at the coyote feasted on a corpse. A sudden yelp from the coyote surprised them as it jumped and collapsed kicking. An arrow was protruding from its side.

CHAPTER 27

Dawson and Cathy dressed and joined the family at the long table in the kitchen. McGregor had taken his place at the front of the table. It was obvious he was in pain but assumed the leadership position. The ladies had dug into the dehydrated food and had a generous pot of oatmeal, scrambled eggs, and sausage in the middle of the table. McGregor bowed his head. "Let us pray. Thank you, Father, for delivering us safely to our lodge, and thank you for our new friends who without their help we may have not made it. Please be mindful of our needs and bless this food and everyone here. In Christ name we pray, amen."

McGregor looked around at everyone in the room. "I know you think that we have been through the roughest part, but I'm afraid the worst is yet to come. Our bellies are full; we are warm and safe for the moment. We only have about two years of food on hand. That seems like a lot of food, but two years is not a long time. If we can survive that long, we will be in a world of hurt."

Greg spoke up, "I think we need to start taking any deer or animals that come through. That will stretch our food supply. I saw some deer and wolves last night. I could have easily taken the deer. I thought it would be a good idea to stay quiet."

Dawson pointed out, "We might as well take anything that comes through. Anyone still alive in Calgary will be killing and eating everything that moves. I don't like the idea of eating wolves, dogs, or cats, but I'm sure we can figure out a way to make it palatable."

Cathy pointed out, "My grandfather and uncle came over from China at the end of World War II. They told us that dog and cat were quite delicious." The McGregor women were all making faces at the prospect.

Charles grinned. "I bet I can cook them in the smoker out back."

His wife punched him. "Just don't tell us what we're eating."

Dawson pointed out, "We need to get all our supplies squared away and always need someone on guard. We can't enjoy a time together with all of us inside. We can't let our guard down."

Charles agreed. "When I was deployed in the army, we always had one or more people on guard duty."

Mrs. McGregor spoke up, "Going forward, the girls and I will stand guard from the upstairs windows, one in the front and one in the back. We can keep an eye out and take turns wrangling the kids."

McGregor pointed at the food on the table. "Everyone eat your fill, and let's get to it."

Dawson asked, "Is there any other road or way to get in here that we need to monitor?"

McGregor said, "We are the end of the road. There are trails leading back in the mountains that you can travel by snow machine or on ATVs after the thaw. All the trails dead end in remote wilderness. We don't have electricity back here unless we run the generator. That's why we have propane gas lights and stove. We also have the wood heaters. This old log house was built as a hunting lodge back in the 1920s. I installed five one-thousand-gallon propane tanks, and they are all full. We have running water because there is a hot spring back up the main trail. They buried a water line from it into the house. We opened the valves when we got in last night after we got the heat on. It is gravity fed, so we have working toilets, baths, and showers. If I can crank the propane generator, we can run the washing machine and charge batteries."

McGregor nodded to Charles, "You take the next watch; find a place down the road where you can see down the road and still see the lodge. You may want to make a camp so you can build a wind break and maybe have a fire ring to keep from freezing. Greg will sleep until he gets some rest, and Dawson and the ladies will start unloading the trailers and getting stuff stowed away. We'll put some food in the barn so that if something happens to the lodge, we'll have some options."

They helped McGregor to his feet and headed to the bathroom to get cleaned up. Cathy and Dawson went back to their room where they put on their heavy clothes. The twins were happily playing with the McGregor children.

Cathy asked, "Do you think we will be safe here?"

Dawson pulled a sweater over his head and looked over at her. "There's no way of knowing; it all depends on how many people have survived and how many that will try and walk out of the city. We are good until the next Chinook. We have a couple of months of hard, cold weather and then it's anyone's guess."

"How many people do you think are left?"

"They are dying off pretty fast by now. We are several weeks out, so the skinny people will be already dead. The fat ones will still be hanging on, but they will be killing each other looking for food. They are probably feasting on the dead now."

"That's a horrible thought; what are we going to do if they find us?"

"We'll fight like dogs and do whatever it takes. Let's help get the trailers unloaded and get settled in; at least we have a defensible location. One way in and one way out makes this place defendable. One man up on the side of the mountain can stop any number of people coming in."

"What if the army shows up? I'm sure there are thousands of men with military experience. What if they gang up and come?"

"If that happens, we are in trouble."

It took them three days to get everything unloaded and squared away. McGregor was healing a bit and getting around. The next order of business was to set up some defenses up and down the road. They spotted a half dozen trees they could drop facing the road so anyone trying to come down the road would have felled trees facing them. The trees could be pushed aside with the dozer should the need arise to clear the road. For now, they were marked and ready to be dropped. One of the men would always be on guard covering the road twenty-four hours a day. The ladies all had guns, and the children had orders to hide in the basement if trouble started. The kids all took gun safety lessons so they would not be tempted to touch any that were unattended.

At the end of the week, Cathy took out the stitches on Dawson's head. She stood back and admired her work. "I think I like that new part in your hair; it gives you character."

Dawson looked in the dresser mirror. "If I live long enough, I'll have a story to tell when I'm sitting around with all the other old codgers at the rest home."

The next three weeks were quiet, and everyone fell into a routine. Dawson, Greg, and Charles each took turns guarding the road from several stands with hidden fire pits and rock walls to provide cover and concealment. They managed to take several deer and a wolf. The wolf they skinned and buried the carcass in snow, just in case they would ever need to retrieve it for food. The deer were cleaned and butchered and eaten right away. Dawson built a smokehouse on his off shift and explored the trails that threaded back up into the mountains. He wanted to know the back country in case the need to run arose. He also located game trails and a couple of natural caves that probably housed a bear or two at this time of year.

On short trips, he took BC with him after fashioning a pint-sized pair of snowshoes for him and Lucy. He figured if the boy was going to survive, he would need to start learning now. There's only one way to turn a boy into a man, and that is for him to follow one. BC didn't say much but was well behaved and obedient. He dutifully followed and didn't ask questions. Dawson took him back into the mountains and stopped at a good spot to set up a blind. He looked down at BC. "BC, are you ready to help me build a fort?"

BC answered, "Yes, sir."

"Have you ever built a fort before?"

BC finally loosened up. "Me and Lucy made one using the couch, cushions, and some blankets. What are we going to use?"

Dawson grinned. He had quit being the big scary man to being his friend. "We are going to climb up on the side of the mountain to that ledge. Behind it is a cave that can give us shelter if the weather gets bad." BC pulled down his scarf and grinned through the fog from his breath. Dawson pointed further down the trail. "We will walk further down the trail, and then we'll climb up from there and come back to the ledge. We can't leave any evidence that there is a blind up there. If we go up from here, anyone walking down this trail will see the path we take and will look directly up from the path and see where we are sitting. If we walk past before we go up, we'll see them first. That gives us a big advantage if the bad guys are following us." BC took it all in without question.

"We have to keep it secret, right?"

"That's exactly right, son. We have to think two steps ahead of the bad guys. You've seen a great deal for a little guy, but the more you learn now the stronger man you will become. I want you to be strong so you can help me take care of your mother and sister."

Looking back with his child eyes, he answered, "Mr. Dawson, I'm stronger than my sister already."

Dawson pulled him over and gave him a bear hug and smiled for the first time in weeks. They walked about two hundred yards up the trail where he came to a spot where they could negotiate the rocks and make it to the ledge. Once on the ledge they had a commanding view of the trail below. They built a rock wall on the edge of the ledge. Dawson carried the big rocks while BC supplied the small ones. The rocks came from the collapsed ceiling of the cave. The little cave was about twenty feet deep and about twelve feet wide. The ceiling was about ten feet tall. There was a fire pit from some long-ago fire. Hunters, trappers, or even Indians could have used this cave and perch as a blind. Since there was no rock wall on the ledge, the cave was probably used for shelter or a place of refuge. They did not expect return fire from the trail below.

They built a fire in the old pit and warmed themselves. Dawson watched as BC poked at the fire and watched as sparks and smoke rose to the ceiling and disappeared through a crack in the ceiling. Dawson opened his pack and pulled out some of the cookies made by Henry, Cathy, and Olivia from what seemed like a year ago now. After their snack, they cut boughs from the fur trees and created several beds and cut some others to block the entrance to keep out the wind.

Dawson asked him, "Why do they call you BC; is that short for something?"

"Yes, my name is Bruce Charles. I'm named after an uncle that was called BC."

Dawson could tell BC was getting tired. "Are you ready to go home and tell your mother and sister about our fort?"

"Yes, sir, when can we come up here and camp out?"

"We'll try and come back in a few days. Do you want to build a couple more forts up some of the other trails?"

BC grinned. "Yes, sir, I can't wait."

Dawson made sure the going was slow for BC, and they stopped frequently to look at stuff. When they got back to the lodge, they were greeted at the side door by Cathy and Lucy. BC pulled off his winter gear and couldn't stop talking about the fort. Cathy quizzed, "What fort is he talking about?"

Dawson grinned. "We built a fort; it'll also work as a campsite or deer blind. As soon as the weather warms a little, we'll take you and Lucy to see it."

McGregor called out to Dawson, "Come tell me what you've been up to."

Dawson dropped down next to him and smiled. "I thought it would be a good idea to set up a few sites to escape to in the event we are overrun. I found a ledge overlooking the north trail and built a rock wall for shelter. We then set up in the little cave behind it in case we need to use it for shelter. From up there we can cover the trail just like we cover the roadway."

McGregor agreed. "That's a great idea. You're sure a great asset to our family."

"I'm glad to help. I appreciate you taking us in. I'm afraid we would have perished stuck on the road."

McGregor pointed to a backpack in the corner. "We are making up backpacks and duffels for everyone. I want everyone to have a bag with food, clothes, and basic supplies should we have to evacuate."

Dawson agreed. "Bug-out bags can be the difference between life and death. I'm going to grab a bite and head out. It's my turn to stand guard." Cathy already had him a plate of food warming on the stove. Dawson grinned as BC joined him at the table. Cathy fixed him a plate as well. The two men, young and old, ate in silence like a couple of old men.

Dawson headed out down the road with his rifle and gear. He got to within sight of Charles up on the hill. Just as Charles waved to him, a shot rang out.

CHAPTER 28

Hawks tightened his grip on his rifle, and to his dismay the two pups started barking and had to be called back to keep them from charging down the hill. He looked over at Carolyn.

"Our secret is out, get around the side of the house where you are hidden and can shoot." He watched as a man with a crossbow walked over to the dead coyote and casually pulled out the arrow from the crossbow. He replaced the arrow in his quiver, and he slowly proceeded up the driveway toward the house.

The man had on hunting clothes, and he walked right up to the porch and looked at Hawks. "The dogs gave you away." Hawks noticed the man had the crossbow cocked and his hand was on the trigger grip. Hawks was ready. The rifle resting across his lap was aimed directly at the midsection of the man. The man appeared to be in his late forties or early fifties as grey hair filled his temples and spilled out from under his felt hat.

"I was afraid they would do that, but I like having them around because they are also an early warning system." The man nodded to Hawks' gun as he lay his bow on the ground and opened his coat and pulled out a pistol by the grip and lay it next to the bow.

"If you'll take your finger of your rifle's trigger, I'll feel a little better."

Hawks relaxed knowing Carolyn had a bead on him from the bushes from the side. "What brings you up to my door?"

"I'm out hunting. I live about five miles down the road. Every farm I've stopped at has been raided and the families killed. I was trapped in Victoria; my wife and kids were at her sister's house in Orlando. I bought a ride from a man in Lady Smith. It cost me my cash, the supplies in my truck, wedding band, watch, rifle, and what little food was in my bug-out bag. He also received three ounces of gold and a hundred one-ounce silver dollars I had buried in the yard."

Hawk asked him, "How long since you've eaten?"

"I ate a rabbit a couple of days ago; I was planning on eating the coyote tonight."

Hawks said, "Leave your bow and pistol and follow me." He went around to the smokehouse and called to Carolyn, "Can you fix this gentleman something to eat? I'm giving him a piece of venison to take with him." Carolyn poked her head out from behind the bushes.

She shouldered her rifle and said, "I know you. Weren't you at a Christmas party here three or four years ago?"

"Yes, I remember you. My name is Chuck Fisher. I live about five miles up the road."

She smiled. "You have the wife with the red hair, and you had the two red-headed little boys with all the freckles. I'm Carolyn Bishop, and this is Bill Hawks, just call him Hawks."

Chuck asked, "How have you two survived?"

Hawks answered, "Immediate and accurate gunfire."

Carolyn pointed upstairs. "Let's go eat." She headed through the basement doors.

Hawks told Chuck, "Follow me, we'll go through the front door and into the kitchen. You can wash up there, and we'll eat at the kitchen table." Hawks pointed to the steps and followed him.

He didn't trust him as of yet; starving men and animals can be unpredictable and dangerous. Carolyn opened a jar of soup put up in the pantry from some time before her friends Tammy and Roosevelt had left. Once it was heated, she served up a bowl.

Chuck looked at it and said, "Thanks, you have no idea how good this looks."

Hawks told him, "Eat slow until you get used to it. You don't want to puke it up."

Carolyn asked, "What were you doing in Vancouver?"

"I was down there to pick up farm supplies and a trip by the sporting goods store. Then the lights went out, and everything went to hell pretty quick. It was getting crazy, so I went down to the harbor and worked my way around by the water heading south. I found an ancient powered barge that was tied up to an old wharf. I stole aboard and discovered that it was abandoned. I looked for food, but there were just a couple of cans of beans and some stale crackers. I checked the four fuel tanks and discovered that they were full. It had about a thousand gallons onboard. There was no cargo, but the batteries were hot. I jumped the starter solenoid and cranked the Perkins diesel. Once it was started, I was able to move it out into the harbor. From there I just followed the coast until I got to Lady Smith."

This peaked Hawk's attention. "Where is it now?"

"I left it anchored up in a little cove just south of Lady Smith."

"If it's still there, do you think we could get eight horses on it?"

"I think so. It has a ramp that lets down in the front."

"What do you think of our chances of surviving here?"

Chuck looked at Carolyn and back at Hawks. "Your odds of surviving what's coming are exactly zero. If you are like me and eating coyotes, they'll leave you alone. It's not the poor starving masses. Most of them are already dead or will be soon. The military and police are using martial law to clean out all the food and accumulate anything of value. The problem is they will just be the last ones to die. No one is producing anything. Unless there are people growing food and animals, they are all going to die. People can't fish because they can't run the boats. They will soon be scouring the countryside killing anything that moves or flies."

Hawks pushed his chair back. "Will you excuse Carolyn and me for a few minutes?" He looked at Carolyn and nodded his head toward the living room. Once they were in the room, he looked at her. "It is just as I feared. I think now is our chance to pack up the horses and with Chuck's help escape the island before we are taken out."

Carolyn sighed. "I'm afraid you're right; let's ask Chuck if he's willing to help. I bet he would like the opportunity to try and find his family."

"Agreed."

They walked back into the kitchen and refilled Chuck's soup bowl. Hawks looked at him and spoke, "I have a proposition for you. I assume you are anxious about your wife and children. We have eight horses. Four have saddles and the other four packs. We have a substantial amount of food and supplies. I can also arm you up. Do you think we could make it to the barge on horseback?"

Chuck wiped his chin. "We can only make it if we travel at night. We'll probably have to kill some people, and I hope the work barge is still there. I doubt anyone has messed with it because very few people are left that can figure out how to run it. I also pulled the battery and hid it behind a bulkhead, along with the starter solenoid. There was a small skiff on the back that I rowed over to the bank. I hid it in some brush. If it's not there, I'll have to swim out and get it cranked."

Hawks asked, "Do you think it will handle the seas to carry us over to the US?"

"Sure, it has tall sides and it has four bilge pumps that work. I tested them before I put to sea with it."

Hawks asked, "How soon before we can leave?"

"I can leave right away; I just need to get my backpack and some extra clothes."

Hawks asked, "If you've had enough to eat, I can loan you a vehicle to go get your stuff. It'll take us a couple of days to collect up enough food, and I want to jerk as much meat as we can to carry with us."

Carolyn served up some coffee and said, "Sounds like a plan; do you want to stay here tonight?"

Chuck said, "Yes, it'll take me a couple of hours to get my stuff together."

Carolyn asked, "Has your home been ransacked?"

"Yes, they broke into my gun safe and stole all my guns, ammo, and my wife's jewelry. They also took some silver silverware. I'm surprised they didn't take my crossbow, and they didn't find my pistol that was hidden in a book on my bookshelf where I could get my hands on it in an emergency."

They escorted Chuck out the front door where he stopped to retrieve his crossbow and pistol. Hawks handed him a rifle and then led him out to the barn. He let him take the Mercedes wagon to go to his farm. Hawks started cutting up the venison from the smokehouse into thin strips and soaking them in buckets of salt water with black pepper and maple syrup for a couple of hours.

Carolyn turned the propane oven on and set it on a low setting to get ready for the meat to be jerked. They also used the oven in the woodstove. They placed the strips on the oven racks to start drying. Once he had all the venison processed, he took his rifle and shot the bull calf through the head and drug his carcass to the barn with the Cub tractor. He pulled it up by the hind legs to a beam where he could skin, gut, and debone it. Steam rose from the carcass as he pulled off the skin and opened the body cavity. The entrails fell into a large, galvanized wash tub Hawks had positioned underneath the carcass. The strong smell of the blood had the puppies' hair on end as their primal instincts reacted to it. He soon had the buckets full of beef strips so they could make jerky from the young bull as well. He boiled the liver, lungs, and kidneys for the puppies. The heart was cut into strips to join the meat being jerked.

While the meat dried in the oven, they took turns hand grinding the wheat berries into flour they could carry and cook on the journey. They put the flour into pillow cases for placing on the pack horses. When Chuck arrived, he helped kill and butcher the cow, and she too was processed into jerky. To speed things up, they ran lines inside the smokehouse to hang strips on. They built a larger fire in the smokehouse, and it soon cooked and dried the meat as well. In the back of the Mercedes, he had four-hundred pounds of sweet feed for the horses.

He pointed to the bags of feed. "My animals were all gone when I got home, but they left the horse feed in my barn. I suggest we feed them up really good. We may need to postpone heading out until we get as much of the feed in them as possible. The more fat we can put on them, the longer they can go between feedings."

Hawks agreed. "This is both the best and worst time of year to travel. The cold and snow will be a horrible hindrance for us traveling through the mountains this time of year. It will also be the best time, because anyone who can will be holed up trying to keep warm." When they brought out the feed and started dumping it in the trough, the horses, donkey, and goats came running.

Hawks said, "I think we need to process the donkey and the goats into jerky as well. We can't waste food on them, and we can't waste their protein."

Chuck said, "I agree; let's put them down and get started.

They lured them into a small corral and quickly dispatched them. It took them two days to butcher the goats and donkey. It took another three days to turn them all into jerky. The horses eagerly consumed all the feed. They had to be careful not to over feed them so they wouldn't founder from overeating. They also ate as much food as possible to fortify their own bodies to also store food. In addition to the jerky, Carolyn baked bread and cookies and sacked up dried beans and rice.

The next afternoon they saddled the four riding horses and had packs on the four pack horses. Each packed pistols and rifles. The fourth saddle horse had a makeshift pack slung across the saddle. They wanted the fourth horse saddled in case they lost one of the other saddle horses along with their saddle. They headed down the driveway with the pups running alongside.

Chuck pointed out, "It may be a big mistake letting the dogs join us. If we are hiding somewhere, they may give us away."

Hawks agreed. "I thought about that, but they can also warn us early, and if it comes down to it, we can eat them."

Carolyn screwed up her face. "I hope it doesn't come to that."

Hawks reminded them, "We'll also hunt as we go. If we can kill some game, we won't have to eat our reserves. Chuck can use that crossbow to silently kill."

The horses headed out in single file with Hawks in the lead. He kept the horses on the shoulder of the road as he didn't want the pavement grinding on their hooves and steel shoes. Once the horses lost their shoes, there would be no replacements as there were no longer any farriers or vets. As they rode, he kept a mental note of all the driveways and lanes leading off the main road. If they had to turn and run, he would have to remember possible escape routes. Soon the sun was down and their eyes slowly adjusted to the night. The horses' night vision was vastly superior to theirs, and they quickly learned to let them take their little detours as they could see washouts and culverts the riders couldn't see until they were almost on top of them.

The horses came to an abrupt stop, and the puppies ran ahead. A young girl sat hugging the two pups who returned the love. Carolyn dismounted and handed Chuck the reins. She walked over to the little girl, and in the darkness, she could see a dirty face and matted hair. She handed the little girl her canteen and let her drink a good swig and stopped her before she had taken too much. She wet her handkerchief from the canteen and wiped her face off. "What's your name, sweetheart?"

In the semi darkness, she could see that she had dark-brown eyes. "I'm Emma Jane Rice."

"My name is Carolyn; where's your mommy and daddy?"

Big tears rolled down her face, and she pointed back up the road. "The bad men shot them and kicked me down the hill. I was scared and stayed quiet a long time. I couldn't climb up, so I started walking until I came to this road, and the puppies found me."

Carolyn hugged the little girl's neck. "Have you had anything to eat?"

"No, it's been a long time since we had any food." Hawks and Chuck dismounted, and while Chuck held the lead, Hawks walked over to where Carolyn stood next to the little girl.

"What do we have here?"

"Hawks, this is Emma; she is coming with us."

"Hello, Emma, are you hungry?" She nodded her head.

Carolyn helped her up. "I've got some cookies I think you'll like."

Chuck pointed out, "We may be faced with this dilemma again. We may get to a point where all hope of survival is lost."

Hawks nodded his head in agreement. "I know; that's the price for being honorable men."

"What makes you think I'm an honorable man?"

"Easy, you've had at least a dozen opportunities to kill me and Carolyn. However, the main reason is I have a gut feeling that is never wrong. They say it's God's way of talking to you."

Once Emma was fed, Hawks lifted her up behind Carolyn on the saddle. "I want you to hang on to Carolyn, and if you start getting sleepy, call out, and I will let you ride with me so I can hang on to you. I don't want you falling off the horse in the middle of the night. If you start getting cold, let her know so we can get you wrapped up better."

"Yes, sir, Mr. Hawks."

"Just call me Hawks, Sweetie."

They rode for another two hours when they heard a vehicle coming in their direction. Hawks pointed over his shoulder. "Let's head up that lane we just passed and set up camp when we find a quiet spot until tomorrow evening." Without a word they quickly headed up the lane and into a pasture which had a pond they could camp next to. There was plenty of water and grass for the horses. They created a picket line and tied up all the horses, hobbling two at a time and letting them drink and graze until they were all watered and fed. They ate bread and jerky and took turns sleeping, then built a small fire and heated a pot of pond water. Carolyn and Emma washed up first. Emma even got a shampoo and felt better.

Carolyn asked her, "How old are you, Emma?"

"I'm seven years old; my birthday was last week, but I didn't have a party. What's going to happen to me?"

Carolyn put her arms around her. "Would it be OK with you if you were my little girl now? I never had a little girl." Big tears rolled down both of their faces and they hugged.

Hawks overheard them and agreed. "It's settled; you're our little girl now." Emma came and threw her arms around his neck.

CHAPTER 29

Dawson quickly ducked around a tree just as a wounded deer collapsed in the roadway ten yards away. He pulled out his knife and quickly put the young buck out of his misery. Steam poured from the hot blood and the open wound from the rifle bullet that had hit him.

Greg came walking up the road. "Fresh meat tonight, boys, fresh meat tonight."

Charles came down from the blind and passed Dawson on the way up.

Dawson grinned. "Perfect timing, if it wasn't my turn for guard duty, I'd help y'all drag it out. Gut him in the road. It will make him lighter to drag and the gut pile will attract the wolves. I may be able to kill a couple."

Dawson climbed up the trail to the blind where he could stand guard. He added some wood to the fire and warmed his hands before he put on his gloves. He could see a column of steam rising from the body of the deer as they disemboweled it. They each grabbed an antler and started dragging it through the snow to the lodge. He watched until they disappeared behind the lodge. The barn had a place for them to pull the carcass up into the air so they could skin and butcher it.

He could feel the cold that usually meant more snow. As

predicted, it started snowing, a wet snow sticking to the tree boughs and soon had them sagging. The snow, when it is intensely cold, is like powder and blows around like sand. This snow built up on the peaks. This was the sort of snow that made excellent snowmen and snowballs. It snowed all afternoon and into the night. Greg relieved him around 11 p.m. The trek down the side of the mountain was treacherous as the many foot and handholds were now covered in snow. He walked past the now-frozen gut pile and carefully climbed the snow-covered steps, then stomped his feet and stepped onto the grate just inside of the back door. He stomped once again to loosen the remaining snow and untied the strings and kicked his boots off.

Cathy quickly met him and said, "I've got your dinner ready."

"You didn't have to do that. I could have just had a snack."

"Nonsense, I told you; we take care of each other. You don't even have to be here looking out for us. You just spent eight hours sitting out there in the snow. We've been in here safe and warm. Now sit and eat while I draw you a hot bath. You look half frozen." He couldn't argue and went to the table where he found chicken fried venison tenderloin, mash potatoes with gravy, and hot biscuits. A teapot was on the table, and a steaming cup sat next to his plate.

Cathy disappeared through the door and in the direction of the bathroom. The meal was more delicious than it looked. He didn't realize how much the cold had penetrated his body as the warm tea felt hot going down. She came back in, and before he said anything, his dishes were quickly cleared and a couple of homemade sugar cookies replaced them.

She squeezed his arm. "Your bath is ready as soon as you finish." She disappeared again down the hall.

When he ate his last bite and finished the tea, he sat his cup in the sink full of soapy water along with the other dishes waiting to be washed. Normally he would have washed the dishes and put them in the draining rack, but he knew Cathy would admonish him, so he resisted. He walked down the hall and into the large bath. Cathy had fresh clothes laid out for him. She had thought of everything.

He took his bath and thought about shaving, but the beard kept his face warm in the cold wind. He dressed in the clean clothes and folded up his dirty ones. When he opened the bathroom door, Cathy was there and took them to the hamper in his room. When he walked in, he was surprised to see the twins weren't asleep in bed. They were nowhere in the room.

He turned to Cathy. "Where are the kids?"

"They are pretending to camp with some of the younger McGregor kids. I just checked on them, and they are all fast asleep." He stripped down to his long johns and headed to the bed. Cathy stripped down as well, but she didn't stop at her long johns. She tiptoed across the room and slid the bolt on the door, locking it. She crawled in beside him and snuggled close.

Dawson held her close. "Are you sure we're ready for this?"

"Yes, you are ten times the man, a better father and husband, than my ex-husband ever was."

Dawson pulled her close. "I don't want to take a chance on getting you pregnant."

She smiled. "No worries, just before my husband left me last year, I had a Norplant implanted. I'm safe for another four years."

"It looks like you've thought of everything."

"That's why we make such a great team. All we have are each other, and by the time my Norplant wears off, we'll be ready for children."

He awoke sometime before dawn. Cathy stirred as he slid out of the bed and gathered up his long johns. She asked, "Are you ready for breakfast, or do you want to start with desert from last night?"

Dawson thought for a moment and said, "I've never been one to pass up desert."

An hour or so later, she gave him a big kiss and said, "I know I've made the right decision, how 'bout you?"

He held her close. "I must agree. I want to get something to eat, and I want to go stomp down the snow on the trail heading up to where BC and me made the camp. We can't escape in that direction unless we can negotiate the trail. I want to be prepared."

She said, "Do you think me and the kids can help?"

"I don't see why not. We've all got snowshoes, and we have the sleds on top of the trailer. We can put our packs on one of the sleds, and the kids can even ride if they get too tired to follow."

The house was a buzz as the sun came up. All the kids were up and the ladies already had a stack of pancakes on the table. It was Charles's turn to relieve Greg. When Dawson looked out, he saw the snow hadn't let up and at least a foot had accumulated on the steps and drive. He bundled up and went to the barn where he retrieved a snow shovel and proceeded to clear the steps, porch, and the trail between the house and barn.

McGregor was at the table when he made it back into the house. "Dawson. What are your plans for today?"

"I thought I might head back up the trail with Cathy and the kids to make sure it is stomped down in case we need to use it."

"That's not a bad idea. Take some of the canned food with you, and store it in the cave you found. The bears and raccoons won't bother it in the cans."

"How's the shoulder healing up?"

"It gets better every day; I have a feeling it will bother me for many years to come."

Dawson poured a cup of black coffee and called out to Cathy, "You and the kids get bundled up. We're going to see if we can make it to the camp up the trail."

245

They took two of the sleds they had previously used to escape the Calgary fire. Once they were loaded with their backpacks and a good supply of canned food, they proceeded up the trail. The snow was steadily falling, making the going slow. The wet snow gave way to their snowshoes. BC and Lucy didn't last long but were soon enjoying a ride on the sleds as Dawson broke trail with Cathy right behind him. It took a couple of hours of steady trudging for them to get to the base of the ridge where their camp was located.

Dawson pointed up to the rock wall. "If you look close, you can see the rock wall BC and I built."

BC beamed with pride. "You won't believe our fort when you see it."

Cathy grinned. "Lucy and I can't wait to see it."

They proceeded down the trail to where they could make their way up to the ridge. The going was steep, so Dawson took Cathy and the kids up to the cave and had a fire going. Once he had them squared away, he went back and attached rope to the first sled and climbed back to the camp. Once there, he pulled it up hand over hand until he had it and its cargo at the camp. He repeated the process with the other one and joined them at the campfire. They soon had the food stored away and a pot of canned stew cooking over the fire.

After eating the warm stew, BC and Lucy pretended to take naps on the beds as Cathy and Dawson sat by the fire. Dawson squeezed her hand. "I'm glad I have a family. I never realized how empty my life has been."

They walked out onto the ridge and watched as the snow continued to fall. From where they stood, they could see the top of the mountain standing over the lodge. A large overhang of snow that had accumulated all winter was perched over the lodge. His heart was in his throat when he realized what was going to take place.

He told Cathy, "That wave of snow protruding over the lodge

is on the verge of collapse. You stay here with the kids, and I am going to book it back and warn them. I hope Charles doesn't shoot a deer; the sound of a gunshot could be all it takes to make it give way."

Cathy clung to him. "I don't want to lose you."

"If for some reason I don't make it, there is at least two months of food for the three of you. You've got your rifle and pistol. All the food will still be at the lodge just buried in the debris. You'll have to be careful, but there will be enough to last y'all for years if you can recover it."

"Don't say that. You will make it back."

Dawson went back into the cave and gave the kids a hug. Cathy gave him a big kiss, and he headed back down from the ridge with his snowshoes across his back. He was halfway down when he heard and then felt the avalanche. His heart sank as he realized what was taking place at the lodge. Once he was back on the trail, he put on his snowshoes and headed toward the lodge. A quarter of a mile before he got to the lodge, the trail was blocked by snow. He clawed his way to the top and continued. He soon made it to where the lodge used to be.

The barn was collapsed, but the Power Wagon and the bulldozer were only partially buried. He called out, but no one responded. He continued past in the direction of the road leading in. He wanted to see if Charles had survived. He came to the blind and found it was vacant. The coals were still warm. Charles must have left when the avalanche started to get back to his family. There was no sign of life.

His heart beat in his ears as he tried to listen for anyone calling or crying from under the snow. The water line from the hot springs was steaming from the pipe where it was ruptured near the barn. A plan was forming in his mind. There was plenty of food still stowed in the remains of the barn. The dozer was partially

247

buried. The warm water from the spring could be used to heat the engine block on the dozer. Once the dozer was cranked, it could be used to move the snow and debris and open the road out. He knew the Power Wagon would crank because he made a point to crank it at least once a week to make sure the battery stayed hot.

He spent the next three hours carefully looking and probing, trying to find anyone. It was starting to get dark, so he went back to the Power Wagon and looked in the back. The bed he had made for Cathy and the kids was still there along with the blankets and pillows. He folded the blankets with the pillows in the middle. He pulled out the roll of paracord he had found in Henry's second-hand shop. Using the paracord, he lashed it into a tight bundle and made a sling. He was soon plodding down the trail toward their camp.

The shadows were long and the snow was still coming down. He buried the thoughts of the McGregors in their icy tomb; just like when he lost Olivia and the others, he would bury the thoughts and fight on. Once the snow stopped, they would have to return and try to dig out the dozer, Power Wagon, the barn with supplies, and if possible, down into the rubble of the lodge. They would need extra clothes and supplies that were now buried. The dozer could help with the excavation.

It was almost dark when he got back to the camp. He climbed up and found Cathy and the twins sitting by the fire. Cathy looked up as he came into the cave. She had added some additional boughs from the fir trees across the cave opening, which helped keep the cold at bay. He looked at her and shook his head no. "There were no survivors. We are on our own."

Tears rolled down her face. "What are we to do?"

"We do what we started out to do. We will fight and survive." He looked at the kids taking turns tending the fire. Their childhood innocence was about to be shattered.

Cathy asked, "What do we tell the kids?"

He looked back at Cathy. "We will tell them the truth. Death has been a big part of their lives, and it will continue to be so."

"Can it wait until morning? I think they need to get a good night's sleep."

"I agree; let's let them be kids tonight." The cave was warm enough from the fire as it had heated the rocks, and the boughs from the fir tree blocked out the wind. The snow piled up against the boughs, further sealing out the cold. Cathy made up two beds while Dawson gathered a good supply of limbs to make sure the fire could be fed all night and into tomorrow. They ate a good supper and told stories, and the kids were soon asleep in their cozy bed.

Cathy stripped off her clothes and crawled under the covers. Dawson looked at her. "I feel funny about doing this with the kids in the room."

Cathy gave him a knowing look. "You are their father and my husband; we are a family. Daddies sleep with their mommies. And we have been sleeping together for a couple of weeks now."

"I see your point; I've just got to go with it."

She said, "They haven't seen or talked to their father in over a year. They barely remember him and never ask about him anymore. You are their father as far as they are concerned. Their father sent child support and that was it, and he only paid that because it was court ordered."

Dawson slipped under the cover. "Y'all are Stewarts now."

She smiled and gave him a kiss. "Agreed."

The next morning Dawson rose early and got dressed. The snow was still coming down, so they had to stay put. Once they left the safety and security of the cave, they would be living in the back of the Power Wagon until they could find or make shelter. Once he had gathered some more wood, he came back into the cave to find Cathy tending to two sleepy kids who had just woken up.

Dawson looked down. "How do you guys like camping in the mountains?"

Lucy beamed up. "Yes, do we have to go back yet?"

Dawson touched her cheek. "We get to stay until the snow lets up."

BC chimed in, "Oh boy."

Cathy got busy cooking breakfast and melting snow for water. Dawson took a deep breath and prepared himself to be the man of the family. He looked at the two little faces and said, "I have some sad news this morning. Do you remember when I had to leave in a hurry yesterday?"

Lucy answered for both of them, "Yes, sir."

"There was a terrible accident. A huge amount of snow fell off the top of the mountain and landed on the lodge and destroyed it and killed all our friends. No one survived, and now it's our job to survive. The good news is we are a family. I'm now your father. You have a mommy and daddy who are going to take care of you. We are going to keep working and traveling until we find a safe place to live."

BC asked, "Are our friends buried under the snow?"

Dawson answered, "They were all buried, and it was sudden. No one was afraid, and it was over very quick." They were quiet and ate their breakfast in silence. He didn't want them to get back into their little shells as they were when he first met them. When he met them, they only interacted with their mother and each other. He figured they would perk up once they got over the shock of losing the McGregors.

After breakfast, Cathy bundled up the kids and they went outside to build snowmen. Dawson knew they were on the mend when they built a snowman family and named them Dawson,

Cathy, BC, and Lucy. The snow was starting to let up, but Dawson decided to spend one more night in the cave before they headed back. They would need to pack up all the food and gear before heading back. They had a good day and went to bed that night, safe warm and fed. Tomorrow would be a new day.

CHAPTER 30

Hawks looked down at Emma. "Sweetie Pop, are you ready to start riding some more?"

"Yes, sir, I like riding on horses."

Carolyn bundled her up. "You are going to be a regular cowgirl in the next few days."

Emma smiled. "Do you think I could ride a horse by myself one day?"

Hawks gave her a big grin. "If everything goes as planned, you'll be riding your own horse before the end of our journey."

They soon had the picket rope coiled and attached to the saddle of the spare horse. They headed out as the sun went down with Hawks in the lead. Chuck brought up the rear. Hawks led the riderless horse with one of the pack horses tied to the horn on the saddle. Carolyn had one pack horse tied to a loop on her saddle. Chuck had the other three horses tied in line. If they were spooked, it would be hard to hang on to them, but they had no other options. Fortunately, that night's travel was uneventful.

As the sun came up, they found a drive heading up to a burned-out farm. Even though the house was gone, it would be a safe place to take refuge. No one would be coming up to search a burned-out and looted farm. But a farm had pastures and hopefully a pond, stream, or some source of water. They rode past the burned-out home and followed a grass-covered road winding its way back to a large pasture. They rode past the butchered remains of a horse and a cow to the back of the pasture near the wood line. A small stream crossed the back corner of the pasture, which made it perfect for the night. There were trees to set the picket line and plenty of grass peeking out from the snow.

Today's camp setup went smoother than the night before. They would soon get into a routine, and each day would get easier. Carolyn took some of her clothes and with the use of a rope for a belt soon had Emma a new change of clothes. They rinsed out her clothes in the stream and hung them on a line to dry. Since it wasn't raining or snowing, they slept in the open with blanket rolls, using the blankets from the farm.

Carolyn checked to make sure her clothes were dry. She helped Emma change into her own clothes. "We'll get you some new clothes as soon as we can."

Emma smiled. "I have a question. What can I call you? Are you my new mommy?"

Carolyn gave her a hug. "I can never take the place of your real mother. You can call me Mommy, and I will do my best to be your mommy. I have never been a mommy before, so if you see me doing anything wrong, will you let me know?"

Emma clung to her. "You're doing a great job so far."

"And you're doing a great job of being my little girl."

They were soon saddled up and moving toward Lady Smith once again. Tonight, they would cross a bridge on the road leading to the town. Hawks hated the idea of crossing a bridge. Bridges were choke points, especially for vehicles. If he remembered correctly, it was a fairly shallow river. A bear had waded across it when they originally crossed it in the Model A many weeks earlier.

As they approached the descent into the river bottom, Hawks told Carolyn and Chuck to wait while he quietly rode to within sight of the bridge. He tied his two pack horses to a limb and climbed back on his mount. Chuck tied up the puppies so they wouldn't run ahead and warn anyone under the bridge they were here. Hawks urged his horse forward, and they proceeded toward the bridge at a slow walk. His eyesight had become most acute at night with only the moonlight. When he got close enough to the bridge, he stopped to watch and listen. The night was still. There was no wind. It was a cold, clear night. The sky was full of stars and the moon was shining somewhere behind the trees, making them cast long shadows. It was almost imperceptible, but he heard a cough down the hill in the direction of the bridge. The faint smell of smoke met his nose, and his horse's ears perked up. He quietly turned back and went back to where Carolyn, Chuck, and Emma waited.

Chuck asked, "What did you see?"

"I didn't see anything, but I heard a cough and smelled wood smoke. I think someone is camping under the bridge. We have a choice; I can slip down there and take care of them or hold a gun on them until y'all can cross."

Carolyn spoke up, "Once we cross, what are you going to do? As soon as you turn your back to join us, you're a dead man."

Hawks thought a minute. "There's only one reason they are camping under the bridge, and that's to ambush and rob anyone crossing. Y'all wait here. If you hear gunfire, stay put. I'll come get you when it's over."

Hawks took his horse over to a tree and securely tied it to a low limb. He took his C7 rifle and checked to make sure it was in battery. He carried a six pack of thirty-round loaded magazines in a pouch over his shoulder. In addition, he had a Browning 9 mm and three spare magazines for it on his belt. His hunting knife was in a sheath behind his Browning. Chuck and Carolyn dismounted.

Chuck asked, "Don't you think I need to come with you?"

"No, I've got this. If something happens to me, the girls will need you to take them to safety."

Carolyn pulled him close. "Please, be careful. After all, you're a new daddy." Emma still sat on the horse. He lifted her down and gave her a hug on the way down.

Emma asked, "Are you coming back?"

"That's the plan, Sweetie Pop."

He slowly walked down the hill toward the bridge, taking great care to watch his footing. He had already made sure none of his gear rattled or squeaked. As he got closer, he could see where a trail led down the embankment to the water. He could hear the man cough again and could smell smoke from the fire. He concentrated on the trail as he started down, taking special care to not make a sound. He soon reached the bottom of the trail and could see under the bridge. The light from the fire cast its dancing light on the bottom of the bridge and onto the pilings. He could see the man sitting, staring into the fire, and he started to just speak out when he saw them.

Next to the pier were a number of bodies neatly lined up. The man threw a couple of pieces of wood on the fire, causing a cascade of sparks. The flames jumped up, and he could see that the body of a young woman lay nude at the end. From somewhere behind the man someone stirred.

Another man came walking to the fire and rubbed his hands to warm up. "I'm ready for some more people coming through. We are getting low on supplies."

The man sitting by the fire answered, "Supplies are getting few and far between, but our collection of jewelry is adding up."

The man standing by the fire pondered, "I wonder what happened to that little girl I kicked down that gully?"

"She probably froze to death; she is out of her misery now." Hawks felt the rage building up and had to force himself not to go charging in and trying to kill them with his bare hands. Instead, he quietly flipped the safety to full auto. In one motion, he riddled them with a single, long burst. The one standing by the fire fell into it, and the last moments of his life were further agonized by the flames burning his flesh. Hawks grabbed him by his pants cuffs and dragged him out of the flame. He didn't want the smell of burning flesh to permeate the air. He didn't want little Emma having that odor in her psyche.

Hawks made his way back to where the others waited. Chuck asked, "I assume our problem has been resolved."

Hawks nodded. "Yes, and with great prejudice."

Carolyn asked, "What do you mean?"

He held her close and told her what he had overheard before he killed them. He then whispered to Chuck what he had overheard. He handed them a bag full of jewelry and expensive watches. The Rolex watches were all mechanical versions and would work for many years to come. Most of the others were already worthless as time pieces.

He looked at Carolyn and Chuck. "I know what you're thinking. You think I'm no better than them. We're going to need whatever we can gather that can be used for barter or bribes." They both nodded in agreement. He replaced the spent magazine in his rifle with a fresh, fully loaded, thirty-round magazine, released the puppies, and mounted his horse.

That night, they made at least another twenty-five miles. One more day of travel would get them to Lady Smith. Hawks felt a great deal of satisfaction having killed the two men. He felt like an avenging angel for Emma. One day he would tell her the men who killed her parents had been caught and executed. She would not have to spend the rest of her life wondering, but for now, she would be a little girl feeling safe and loved.

Once again, they found an abandoned home with some land

behind it with a swimming pool full of water. There was a barn with paddocks for horses, and the barn still had a supply of hay and horse feed. The horses were long gone, but they had a good place to stay for the day. Hawks went into the open house and discovered the skeletal remains of the family in the living room. He explored the house and discovered the house had been ransacked. All the food and anything of value such as jewelry was long gone. There was a gun safe left open and empty. Personal papers were left on the top shelf, and any weapons were gone. There was a girl's room with clothes and toys. He returned to the living room, closed and barricaded the door. He didn't want Emma to see the remains of the family.

He called out to Carolyn, "You and Emma come on in." Once they came in, he told Carolyn, "There is a bedroom down the hall that looks like it may have some clothes that will fit Emma. Don't take down the barricade and look in the living room."

"I take it there is something in there we don't need to see."

"Correct, I'm going to look around and see if there is anything else we can use." Carolyn and Emma disappeared down the hall and into the bedroom.

Looking in the kitchen, he turned on the gas cooktop and was happy to see the burners still were fed by a gas source. He found a large pot and filled it with water from the pool. Steam was soon drifting from the pot. If the gas held out, they would all have a good bath today and maybe some clean clothes.

He looked out into the garage and located a large storage room containing the usual junk families store away. He located some camping gear that included sleeping bags and backpacks. Chuck was busy feeding and watering the horses. Hawks carried the sleeping bags out to the barn, along with a tarp and a tent.

Chuck said, "Those will come in handy. At least we can get out of the wind and weather when we try to sleep."

Hawks pointed to the barn. "Why don't you get some rest on some hay out in the barn? I'll stay up and boil water. You can get cleaned up after you get some rest. We had a busy night last night."

Chuck nodded. "If someone had told me that I would look forward to sleeping in a horse barn on a pile of hay, I would have called them crazy. Do you think we are crazy trying to take to the wild country to survive?"

"I think only people who are willing to do the unthinkable are going to survive. We will have to kill without hesitation or remorse."

"After what I've seen thus far, I am starting to relish the thought."

Hawks asked, "Have you had any combat experience?"

"Yes, I was in Iraq. I've had a number of kills under my belt; you can count on me in a fight."

Hawks paused and looked at him, "What did you do for a living?"

Chuck grinned. "I was a chaplain."

Hawks gave him a perplexed look. "You don't come across as a chaplain."

"Yes, but all that changed when some Islamist beheaded four of our men who were wounded. I heard that we had some gravely injured men, so I went along for the extraction. We arrived too late, and the Islamist had set up a trap. I was so enraged I drew my pistol and started fighting back. I killed two and retreated into a building. Once I made it through the door, I ran out of ammo and had to beat one of them to death with my empty pistol. I took his AK47 and magazines and fought until it was over.

"I'm not sure how many I killed. I just kept fighting until the sergeant told me it was over. I never felt any remorse, and I gave up my position and volunteered for regular duty. I couldn't bring myself to pray for the bastards I killed."

Hawks pointed out, "My understanding is that the command-ment means do not commit murder; it does not apply to killing in self-defense. Don't feel bad. I have no remorse over the ones I've taken out so far."

Chuck lamented, "This reminds me of a prayer I heard in a John Wayne movie. One of the characters said in his prayer: please forgive me for the men I have killed and for those I am about to."

Hawks agreed. "That prayer surely applies to us. I think we need to be forgiven for those that we have to execute."

Chuck nodded in agreement. "I'll be in the barn. Wake me up when you're ready to rest."

"Sleep well, my friend." The puppies followed him into the barn. Chuck would have two bunk mates for a while. Hawks turned and grabbed an empty big-box-store bucket and headed to the pool. He glanced around the property and down the drive toward the road. He took the bucket and scooped up a bucket of water from the pool, and when he stood up, he saw an elderly man slowly walking up the drive. The man had an old army pack and used a walking stick. There was no obvious weapon, and he didn't slow up when he saw Hawks standing there with the bucket of water.

Hawks shifted the bucket to his left hand so he could readily reach the pistol on his right side should the need arise. The man walked up to Hawks. "I mean no trouble. I'm not armed, and I don't have any food or anything of value. My name is Hiram Ketchum. This is my son and his family's home. I've been walking from the north part of the island for the past couple of weeks. I ran out of food three days ago, and I could use a good drink from that bucket you're holding."

Hawks said, "Follow me."

He led him over to the barn, handed him a canteen, and dug out a big handful of jerky for him. The old man drank most of the canteen before he put it down. "I don't mean to be ungrateful, but I want to find my family."

Hawks put his hand on the old man's shoulder. "I think your family is dead. I found some bodies in the living room; they've been dead for some time. We just got here a couple of hours ago."

The old man sobbed. "Can you take me to them?" "

Sure, let's go. I've got my family in there getting cleaned up and dressed. I don't want my little girl to be afraid."

Between sobs, he answered, "I will do my best to contain my emotions."

Hawks pointed to the house. "Are you ready?" The old man could only nod. They went through the back door and Hawks said, "Wait here in the kitchen. I want to make sure my family stays in the back of the house. I don't want them to see."

The old man stood with tears dripping off his chin. "I'll wait."

Hawks went back to the bedroom where Carolyn and Emma tried on clothes. "Stay here in the room with the door closed. This family's father is waiting in the kitchen. I've got to show him."

Carolyn nodded. "Call us when you're finished."

Hawks went down to the hall and took the old man to the living room door and took down his makeshift barricade. He opened the door and went in with the old man. The old man trembled. He dropped to his knees and ran his hands over the clothes still covering the semi skeletons.

Hawks asked, "Is this your family?"

The old man composed himself. "That's my granddaughter; see the rainbow braces." He pulled up the pants leg of his son. "See that exposed metal plate on his ankle? He broke his leg in high school. I bought my grandson those fancy tennis shoes at Christmas. My daughter in law had a head full of red hair."

Hawks asked him, "Do you want us to help you lay them to rest?"

The old man started crying again. "I would appreciate it."

With Hawks' help, he got to his feet, and they headed back to the kitchen. Hawks took a handful of the jerky and put it in pot of water to soften it up. He made the old man sit and eat. He was obviously suffering physically and mentally. He sat quietly while he ate his meal and drank some more water.

He closed the living room door and called Carolyn and Emma. "Y'all can come out now." They came into the kitchen and Hawks introduced them to the old man. They were very sad.

Emma told him, "Bad guys killed my mommy and daddy and kicked me. I know how you feel."

The old man patted her head. "I'm so sorry that you had to see that."

Once they finished, Hawks and the old man went outside and looked around. The old man pointed to his daughter in law's flower garden. "I think that section of yard next to her flowers will be good. My son's tool room is in the barn. There should be a shovel out there." Hawks quietly slipped into the barn and found the room and retrieved a couple of shovels.

Chuck was not disturbed, but the puppies woke and followed him out. The old man took his shovel out and made the outline of a grave on the ground and through the wet snow. "I want them all together in the same grave. There should be a tarp or something in the barn we can line it with."

Hawks sunk his shovel into the ground and dumped the first shovel full to the side. "Don't worry; we'll find something to line the grave with." The digging went easy as this area of the yard was good top soil and cut easy with the shovel.

The old man tried to help, but Hawks told him, "You've been through enough. I can handle this."

The old man, using the shovel like a cane, went over to a garden bench and sat watching. "I have absolutely nothing left.

My wife died three years ago, and this is all the family I had. They kept asking me to move in with them, but I didn't want to be in the way. Maybe if I did, I could have helped my son fight them off."

"Mr. Ketchum, how old are you?"

"I'll be eighty-eight in a couple of weeks. My days on earth are about wrapped up. I have a bad heart, and I don't have any more medicine. I'll just hang around here until the end."

Hawks threw the last shovel full of dirt up out of the hole and climbed out. "We'll be leaving as soon as it gets dark. We're traveling at night when the chances of running across people is less."

The old man pointed to the barn. "Who's that coming out of the barn?"

"That's Chuck. He's traveling with us, we're heading to Lady Smith where we hope to find a boat to cross over to the States side of the border and head south. I have a place in the Ozarks, and I hope my children have made it there. Chuck's family was in Florida. He is going to head in that direction, but as you know we have little hope."

The old man reached out and shook Chuck's hand. "Chuck, I'm Hiram Ketchum. I guess you know what we're doing."

Chuck pointed to the grave. "Y'all should have woken me so I could help."

Hawks pointed to the barn. "You can help us move them out here to the grave. There should be a tarp in the barn."

Chuck turned back to the barn, saying, "I saw several stacked on a shelf in the tack room. I'll be right back."

With the old man watching, Hawks and Chuck rolled out the tarp in the living room and gently moved the remains onto it. They folded the tarp over them, and with each on an end, they slid them out of the house and to the grave. They lowered them into the grave. Mr. Ketchum didn't know what to say or do. Carolyn and

Emma joined them at the grave. He looked at them and opened his mouth but couldn't speak; he only wept. Carolyn put her arm around him, and Emma held his hand.

Chuck said, "I can take it from here." As he had done on many previous occasions over the years, he preached a nice sermon and ended it with the 23 Psalms and a prayer.

Mr. Ketchum, using his cane, went over to the bench and sat. He slowly slid to his side. Chuck caught him and held him as he took his last breath. They all wept at the old man's death. Hawks slipped into the grave and unwrapped the tarp, and they gently passed Mr. Ketchum in with his family and folded the tarp over him. Chuck said another prayer and ended it with, "Lord, please take Mr. Ketchum to his family and keep them all in your loving arms, amen."

Emma asked, "What do we do now?"

Carolyn took her hand. "First, we've got to get cleaned up and go to bed. We're going to have another busy night." They left for the house while Hawks and Chuck closed the grave.

Chuck said, "I'll finish up here. You get cleaned up and go get some rest. I'll get cleaned up after the girls, and we'll head out tonight."

"Thanks, I'm about tuckered out. That was the first grave I ever dug." Hawks and the puppies went back to the barn and found a spot in the hay and covered up with one of the sleeping bags. They fell asleep right away.

CHAPTER 31

The next morning Cathy awoke before Dawson and gently shook him awake. "We've got a busy day today. What are you thinking?" Dawson rubbed his eyes and walked out to check the snow. He took a double handful and rubbed his face and beard and instantly woke up from the cold on his face.

He turned and walked back in. "Let's get packed up and head back. We'll need to set up a safe camp and proceed with getting ready to hit the road."

"Where are we going?"

"I studied the maps and I think we need to head south and cross into the US. The cold will keep most people in. If we can make it to one of the tributaries of the Missouri River, we can take a boat all the way to the Mississippi and from there to my camp in South Louisiana. We can live off the marsh, if we can stay alive that long. We can live there forever."

Cathy put her arm around him. "Tell me about your camp."

Dawson hugged her back. "Our camp is a big cypress camp house sitting on ancient piers to put it above any storm flood water. It has a wood heater in the living room and a deep, screened-in porch on all sides. It even has the original wood-stove in the kitchen. The windows are from the floor almost to the ceiling. It has a big bedroom on the first floor with two bedrooms upstairs. It has a water tower fed by gutters that provide rainwater to the kitchen and bathroom."

Cathy grinned. "It sounds like heaven."

"If it's still there, it will be."

They woke the kids and ate a good breakfast. It took them a couple of hours to pack up their camp in the cave. Dawson lowered the loaded sleds with the rope, and they were soon on the trail where they put on their snowshoes and slowly made their way back. The heavy snow made for slow going, but the kids liked riding on the sled. Dawson stopped frequently for them to rest. When they stopped, he noticed a change in the weather. There was a steady wind coming from the west, and it was noticeably warm. He unwrapped the wool scarf from around his neck and pulled off his coat. He was plenty warm with just his bib overalls and canvas shirt. Cathy and the kids were soon shucking off their outer wear. The snow was trying to melt.

Dawson asked Cathy, "Are your boots waterproof?"

She replied, "Yes, I bought them for walking in the wet snow."

"Great, let's make sure the kids don't get wet. Even though it's warming up, they can still get too cold in this wet snow." As they made their way down the trail, he was glad it was warming up. He also dreaded what the melting snow would uncover. They would have to take great care to not let the twins see any of the McGregor's remains exposed with the melted snow. The Chinook winds could sometimes last for days with temperatures as high as 60 degrees Fahrenheit. At their next rest stop, Cathy pointed out, "If this snow melts, it will make it easy for us to escape south, and it will make it easier to get our supplies. I'll keep the kids away if you uncover any of their bodies."

They made it back to the lodge and soon had a makeshift camp behind the Power Wagon. The first order of business was to locate food and supplies in what was left of the barn. The melting snow helped with the search as much of the food was exposed and most of it was still secure in their containers. The trailer they previously used was still intact, so all they had to do was reload it with supplies. They needed additional clothes, first-aid supplies, water filters, and fuel. Fortunately, the warm weather was warming up the engine block on the dozer so it could be cranked. They would need it to open the road heading out to the highway.

The Chinook held for another four days and enabled them to gather up supplies for the trip south. They found all the McGregors and placed them together and covered them with rocks as the ground was still frozen solid. They found everything they needed; the extra gas was still intact under the remains of one of the other sheds. Dawson pulled a claw foot tub from the remains of the lodge and used the water line from the hot springs to fill it up.

Dawson pointed to the tub of warm water. "Everyone gets a good hot bath before we leave."

Cathy told the twins, "You guys first." The kids dutifully stripped and hit the tub. Cathy used a cloth and a bar of soap and soon had them cleaned up, dried off, and dressed. She washed their dirty clothes and laid them out on the hood of the Power Wagon. Cathy bathed next while the hot water continued to flow into the tub.

Dawson looked at Cathy. "I feel kinda funny stripping down in front of the kids."

Cathy grinned. "You're the daddy now. They are very young and it's OK for families to see each other naked."

"It still feels weird." He stripped down; the kids giggled a little at first but soon forgot and went about playing. He bathed, dried, and changed into clean, dry clothes. He rigged a line from the remains of a tree to the Power Wagon, and they soon had the clothes hanging; the dry Chinook air quickly had them dry.

He climbed up into the cab of the dozer and surveyed the

controls. This was much like the one he had operated while on a construction crew when he was in college. The old man who ran the dozer showed him how to run the old Caterpillar, and he wound up running it when the old man missed a week of work while sick. This dozer was laid out very similarly, so he knew how to crank and run it.

The engine oil showed full, so he didn't add any. He went through the process of starting the pony engine used to start the old dozer. He pulled back the engagement clutch lever, pulled out the choke on it, and pushed the starter button. The little gasoline engine slowly started spinning and caught on. First one cylinder and then the other. Once he had the diesel engine controls in place, he checked to make sure the dozer was out of gear. He didn't have any starter fluid, so it would require a bit of cranking to get the engine firing. He set the throttle on the diesel engine and then returned to the pony engine, where he revved it up a bit. He engaged the clutch lever, and the big diesel started to spin. It started to hit, and a belch of black smoke left the exhaust stack. Soon the one puff became two, and it was soon chugging away.

He disengaged the pony engine and the old engine puffed and soon ran smoothly. It would take a few minutes to get the engine block hot. He took the opportunity to make sure it had coolant and the diesel tank topped off. From the cab he called down to Cathy, "Keep the kids away from the dozer while I get it moving."

He put the dozer in gear and raised the blade so that it was almost a foot off the ground. He made short work of pushing the avalanche debris to the side, along with the remnants of the lodge. The logs from the lodge were largely intact and as such rolled to the side without much effort from the big dozer. After several hours, he had the road opened. Cathy quickly gathered anything of use that turned up in the debris after he finished. Trees and rocks were pushed to the side.

Somewhere below the frozen stream lay buried. It would remain entombed in snow until spring. It was getting dark when he finished; he took the dozer back to the remains of the barn and parked it so the Power Wagon could be pulled up behind it. He would pull the Power Wagon up behind it and chain it to the dozer. His plan was to use the dozer to clear the way while conserving the gasoline in the Power Wagon. Once they were well down the highway and he was sure the road was clear enough for the Power Wagon to operate, they would abandon the dozer and head south. He left it idling in place. He put in a half gallon of oil in the crankcase as he had witnessed Old Man McGregor do. He topped off the diesel and went back to their temporary camp.

Cathy asked, "Why are you leaving it running?"

"I don't want to take a chance of it not cranking in the morning. A diesel can run for days or years idling. Diesel engines use very little fuel just idling. Let's get a good dinner in our stomachs and get a good night's rest."

Cathy quickly had a meal going in a skillet she salvaged from the lodge. After eating, she made a bed for her and Dawson from a salvaged mattress and quilts. The kids would sleep in the bed in the back of the Power Wagon.

Cathy pointed to the bed, "I want to have one more night with just of the two of us. I don't know what the future will bring. I don't want to pass up an opportunity for some personal time for us."

Dawson agreed. "Part of me wants to stay here and build a cabin from the remains of the lodge, but I'm afraid we will be overtaken, especially since the Chinook has warmed things up."

They sat around the fire until the kids got sleepy. After tucking the kids in, they retreated to the fire; a log from the cabin made a bench to sit on. Dawson put his arm around her. "Tomorrow is going to be the start of a big adventure. We're not unlike early explorers, only we have a map and a lot of ordnance."

Cathy looked in on the twins; they were both asleep. She reached out to him. "Come, let's get some rest." He took her hand as she led him to their bed. The idling dozer provided the background noise for a good night's sleep. Their lips met in the darkness.

The next morning, they awoke and woke up the twins.

BC asked, "Can I ride on the dozer?"

Cathy said, "If you ride on the dozer, you won't be able to help us steer the Power Wagon."

He answered, "Darn, I forgot about helping you and Lucy."

Lucy put her hands on her hips. "That's right; you have to help us. We can't steer it by ourselves."

Dawson grinned at them. "Once we get out on the highway and I see the way is clear, I'll let you ride in the cab with me for a bit."

BC beamed. "Thanks."

After breakfast, they finished packing everything away and got ready for the trip. Dawson cranked the Power Wagon and hooked up the trailer and then pulled it up behind the dozer with the snow blade well off the ground. He took a chain from the shed and tied it to the maintenance I-bolt on the top of the snow blade; the other end went to the hitch ball McGregor had mounted on the back of the dozer. Cathy, BC, and Lucy climbed into the cab of the Power Wagon. Dawson reached in and bumped the shifter into neutral.

He looked at Cathy. "All you have to do is steer it if it starts to veer off the road. It should pretty much steer itself and follow the dozer. We'll be going very slow, so just hang on. Are y'all ready?"

Cathy pulled him close and gave him a kiss. "We're ready."

Dawson climbed onto the track of the dozer and into the cab. He shoved the clutch lever and put the dozer in gear. He lowered the blade to within a foot of the ground and eased out the clutch and started the beast moving. He made sure it took up the slack on the chain slowly so as not to jerk the Power Wagon. He looked back over his shoulder and watched as the Power Wagon started to move.

The big dozer moved at about five miles per hour. It would take them at least an hour to make it out to the main road. He had his rifle leaning next to him in the cab. He prayed they wouldn't run into anyone coming down the road or when they turned to go south. The dozer drove along dutifully, never missing a beat. He looked back at Cathy behind the wheel of the Power Wagon. She gave him a smile and a thumbs-up.

Once they made the turn onto the highway, Dawson stopped and climbed up onto the top of the cab of the dozer. From there he could see a little farther down the highway in both directions. There was nothing but the frozen road. He would run the dozer until it was out of fuel, and then they would be running the Power Wagon. The Chinook had lowered the snow load on the road, so the blade on the Power Wagon could handle what was there. If another blizzard blew in, they could be stranded once again, but it was a risk they would have to take.

He walked back to the Power Wagon and opened the door. "Do you guys need a rest stop?"

Cathy nodded. "Out, kids, this is our last chance to make potty."

The kids followed her out, and they tended to business. BC was the first one back. "Can I ride in the dozer for a while?"

He looked down into his dark little eyes. "Sure thing, son, I can use some company."

With BC in the cab of the dozer with him, they proceeded down the highway. BC frequently looked back at his mother and sister riding in the Power Wagon. They exchanged waves and smiles; the going was smooth. The dozer didn't have a working fuel gauge, but he figured it would run for a day, maybe more. They proceeded without incident for a dozen miles or so before BC grew tired of riding on the dozer.

He stopped the dozer and looked at BC. "I bet the girls are tired of steering by themselves. I bet they could use some help."

BC agreed. "I've been worried about them. They need a man to help take care of them."

"I agree. Real men like us look after our family."

They went back to the Power Wagon, and the girls got out to stretch. Dawson made sure he had his rifle in hand any time he went out and about. Even here on a wilderness road, there could be human and animal predators. Cathy broke out some of the cookies still sacked up from when they made them back in Calgary.

Dawson snagged one. "One thing about this dry Alberta weather is the fact that the dry air keeps them dry and tasting fresh."

Cathy laughed. "I thought you were a nut making us cook all these cookies. Thank God we listened to you."

Dawson lamented, "I hope us making a run for the states is a good decision. I just feel that the sooner we get far away from any big city the safer we will be. The cold and snow have been a blessing and a curse."

Cathy smiled. "The cold keeps the bad guys indoors, but it makes it miserable for us to travel."

Once they finished with the rest stop, Cathy and the kids assumed their places in the Power Wagon, and Dawson climbed back aboard the dozer. As he walked across the track toward the door, he sensed a change in the weather. It looked like the Chinook was going to let up. He just hoped it was followed only by cold weather and the snow held off for a few more days or weeks.

He bumped up the throttle and eased out the clutch, and they started steadily moving. The tracks rattled along on the frozen snow and ice. Each time he looked back to check on Cathy and the kids, he was greeted by smiles and little waving hands. He had often pondered what his purpose in life was. He realized you never know until it is thrown in your lap. He had almost lost track of time since this disaster started unfolding. He felt as though he had lived a lifetime in the last few weeks. His life prior to this almost seemed like a blur now.

He thought about his brothers and their families. Both were as resourceful as he, and they at least had military training. They were as versed in firearms as himself. They all grew up hunting and fishing with their father, uncles, and grandfathers.

He traveled another three hours and came upon an eighteen-wheeler abandoned on the highway. He stopped and looked in the cab; it was empty. He went through it and only found a package of gum and a couple of butane lighters. He walked around to the trailer and looked at the backdoor. The metal tag sealing the doors was still intact. No one had opened these doors since it left the warehouse. He took his multi-tool and using the pliers easily broke the seal and flung open the doors. It was full of merchandise destined for a Canadian Tire store. It appeared to be a Christmas shipment.

He waved Cathy and the twins over. "I bet you guys didn't have much of a Christmas this year."

Cathy smiled. "No, I kept telling them that Christmas was late this year."

Dawson grinned. "You stand guard, and I'll start unloading the truck. I'm sure we'll find something for all of us." He found a soccer ball for BC and a Barbie Doll for Lucy right away. This was a good place to camp while they went through the truck. He wondered what had happened to the driver.

It would take at least a day to go through the truck and salvage the contents. But if it had anything that could help them survive, it was worth losing the day. He turned off the dozer and checked the oil; it was pretty low on the dip stick, so he poured his last gallon of motor oil in it. It was still pretty low, so he took some five-gallon plastic buckets he found in the trailer and, using tools from of the tool kits he found in the trailer, drained the oil from the truck. He next dug out his siphon hose and drew down the diesel fuel tanks on the truck. He topped off the diesel fuel tank on the dozer and topped off the oil as well. He cranked the dozer before the engine block began to cool. He kept a bucket of the oil to use later. The buckets had snap on lids, so he filled them with extra diesel and engine oil. He anticipated ditching the dozer later today, but the extra fuel gave them one, maybe two, more days of travel with the dozer, thus saving valuable gasoline for the Power Wagon.

The Alberta cold was coming back and probably more snow was on the way. Having the dozer to clear the road could be a life saver. He went back to the semi-trailer and discovered it was loaded with outdoor gear, popular items for Christmas gifts. There were a lot more toys, tool sets, and camping gear. He dug out some sleeping bags, a tent, cots, and backpacker sleeping pads. He soon had them set up off the road next to the mountain the road ran beside.

BC and Lucy were excited setting up the camp. BC showed Lucy how to gather rocks to make a fire. Dawson dug out some additional toys for them to play with.

Cathy told them, "You can play with them all you want, but you can only pick out a couple of toys each to carry with us when we leave. And remember they need to be small so we can stow them away."

He unloaded the truck and laid out the contents. Cathy and the kids were able to get some fresh new clothes and boots. Dawson found machetes, shovels, an axe, and was able to put together a good, serviceable tool kit in a toolbox. In a locked case he found some hunting knives and some multi-tools. There was a good supply of flashlights, lanterns, headlamps, and assorted batteries. He kept some small ones for the kids to use at some point in the future. Several cases of Christmas candy were soon packed away in the trailer. There was a supply of artificial Christmas trees.

That night after the kids went to sleep, he crept back into the truck and, with one of the headlamps, he dug out a Christmas tree and opened the box. He set up the tree and decorated it with candy canes and pulled out some prepackaged stockings loaded with candy and small toys. The chocolate gold bricks would be a welcome treat.

Cathy came out and grinned. "You're just an old softy."

"I guess so. They need to have something good to remember, not all the death and destruction."

The next morning, they stayed quiet and let the kids wake first. They stayed while the kids stirred. Dawson told BC, "Can you go out and throw some more wood on the fire so we can warm up."

BC grinned and told Lucy, "C'mon, let's go."

They quickly put on their boots and jackets and went out of the tent flap. Dawson and Cathy waited until they suddenly burst back in. "Santa came last night, and he left a bunch of candy and some toys."

Dawson laughed. "That's because y'all have been good all year."

They stayed for a couple of hours to finish going through the truck to make certain they didn't overlook anything of use. The kids selected a few toys each and a small sack full of candy each. They packed up the tent, sleeping bags, and other camping items. Dawson climbed into the cab of the dozer once he had Cathy and the kids squared away in the Power Wagon. He eased out the clutch, and the dozer started heading down the highway, leaving the Canadian Tire truck behind.

The fuel in the dozer along with the extra in the buckets lasted two days before the smoking beast died. The snow held off. He salvaged the battery out of the dozer in case the one in the Power Wagon gave out. The old Power Wagon dutifully made its way down the highway. They were making good, steady time. They passed an occasional car on the highway, so Dawson stopped each time and siphoned off the gas to use in the Power Wagon. It made for slow going, but they continued uninterrupted. On the sixth day of travel, they came to an abandoned travel center. One quick walk thru netted them some motor oil, hand soap, a road atlas, and some empty plastic gas cans. He filled these from abandoned cars at the location.

They found a half a dozen corpses in the empty drink cooler. This border crossing they were heading to was one of the more remote crossings. If they ran across anyone up here, they would have to be resourceful to have survived. The sun was starting to go down, and just as he reached for the headlight switch, he spotted in the distance what appeared to be a bonfire.

Cathy reached over and squeezed his arm. "What do we do?"

"It's dark enough that I can sneak down there unnoticed."

"Please, be careful. I'm not ready to be a widow." He kissed her, hugged the kids, and grabbed his gear. The cold wind hit his face as he concentrated on the blaze ahead.

CHAPTER 32

Hawks was lost in a dream when he awoke to Carolyn giving him a kiss on the cheek and snuggling up next to him. She said, "I've got a big pot of water hot and ready for you to get cleaned up. It's going to be dark soon."

Hawks stretched and winced. "I can sure tell that I dug a grave today. My muscles are stiff and sore already."

Carolyn rubbed his shoulders. "Do you want to spend another day here and rest up?"

"As tempting as that sounds, we have to keep moving. We are using up resources every day, so the sooner we get on the boat and across the border the safer we'll be." The pups took off and found Emma. She gave them a good loving, and they made sure she was well coated in dog slobber.

The hot water felt good on his sore muscles as he washed up. They found some aspirin, acetaminophen, ibuprofen and other first-aid items to add to their supplies. He took some of the ibuprofen and felt much better after a bit. Chuck and Carolyn had the horses saddled and the pack horses loaded. He had on clean clothes and was armed back up. He glanced over at the grave that would soon be overgrown and forgotten. This family had joined countless others as orphans of history. He put them out of his mind and helped Carolyn and Emma saddle up.

"Okay, girls, let's head out. I want to get through Lady Smith and on the boat by morning."

Chuck piped up, "We should be able to make it. We don't want to try and spend the night in Lady Smith. Hopefully, we can quietly make our way through without having to fight. I know some back streets we can take."

Carolyn stated the obvious. "Anyone who sees us will see the horses as food and probably the dogs as well."

They waited until after midnight to start riding through the city. Every house was dark. There were no dogs barking or any indication of life at all. Hawks let the pups trot alongside as they proceeded. The roads were still littered with dead cars. There was a smell of wood smoke in the air. They rode slow as they didn't want the clomping of horse hoofs on the road to alert anyone to their presence.

Miraculously they made it through the city and down a backroad heading to the cove where the boat hopefully sat anchored. They managed to avoid every major intersection that would have been manned. They made it to a dark lane leading down to the cove where the powered barge was anchored. The lane turned downhill as they descended to the water. It then turned to follow the shoreline. They could smell wood smoke that had to be coming from an encampment. There were no houses this close to the water.

They quietly proceeded until one of the pups growled. Hawks stopped and gathered them up and gazed in the direction they looked. In the distance he saw the flare of a cigarette as someone took a puff. In the darkness of night, a cigarette can be seen well over a mile. He was glad he never picked up the tobacco habit. Getting up in the middle of the night to smoke a cigarette was something he couldn't imagine doing.

He whispered to Chuck, "How much further to the barge?"

"Maybe five hundred yards or so. It's past where the person smoking that cigarette is and there's not another way around."

Hawks handed him the reins of the horse and got his rifle into position. "Hand me a small bag of jerky and a handful of the jewelry from our stash, if possible. I will buy our passage. If not, I'll just have to kill again." Emma hugged Carolyn tight as she watched Hawks disappear into the darkness.

The cigarette flared really big, and he could see the face of the man for an instant. The man was a chain smoker and had lit his new cigarette from the old one. Hawks stopped when he was about thirty feet away to watch and listen. The man moved over to his fire and dropped a couple of pieces of driftwood on top and poked it up. He soon had a flame going that lit up the entire area. He wore a pistol on his belt. Just as he squatted to sit in a folding chair, he saw Hawks in the light of the flame. He was taken aback and fell backward onto the ground. He rolled in the dirt, grabbing for his pistol.

Hawks called out, "It's OK; I'm not here to kill or rob you, and besides I've got you covered."

The man lifted his hands up and made it to his knees. "I don't have anything if you're here to rob me."

"Calm down, I'm not here to rob you. Are you all by yourself down here?"

"Yes, I'm running some crab traps and digging clams to take back to my family. We're a day from starving if I don't get back."

Hawks didn't lower his rifle. "I'm not going to hurt you unless I have to. My family and I are passing through. I have a man with a rifle behind me. I've got a bag of jerky I want to give you and a few pieces of jewelry I'll trade you for safe passage. I don't have any tobacco."

The man stood up. "I knew those damn cigarettes were bad for me, and smoking one in the middle of the night almost got me shot."

"Can we pass in peace?"

"I can sure use the jerky, and I can use the jewelry for trade, but the one thing I really need is ammo. I've only got two rounds left."

"What caliber is your pistol?"

"Nine millimeter, it's been a daily fight for the past couple of weeks."

Hawks reached around and pulled one of the full magazines from his belt and thumbed out thirteen rounds. "Here's thirteen rounds; will that help you out?"

"Yes, sir, I want to kill a couple of those former policemen who take half of what I catch, then I'll have their guns and ammo."

Hawks nodded in agreement. "I've encountered a few of them myself." He handed the man the ammo and said, "I'll be back in a minute with my family. I trust I won't have to kill you."

"No, sir, you are OK to pass. You could have easily killed me and didn't."

"I'm going to disappear up the road, and we'll be back in a minute. I'm glad I didn't have to kill you."

"I'm glad you didn't kill me too."

Hawks walked back to where he had left them waiting. "I think we are OK to pass. Chuck, hold back just a bit in case he changes his mind. He has a fully loaded 9 mm pistol that I didn't take away from him." Hawks remounted and proceeded down the lane to where the man stood by the fire. The man gazed in amazement as they passed. Chuck brought up the rear as Hawks waited with his rifle handy just in case. Once they were well out of sight, Hawks relaxed.

Chuck said, "There's a dead Jeep just ahead. We'll stop there, and I'll look for the skiff." They pulled up and dismounted. Hawks told Carolyn, "I want you and Emma to stay here. Keep your rifle in your hands. I don't want it slung on your shoulder should trouble erupt."

Chuck disappeared into the darkness. They could hear the aluminum hull of the skiff being dragged through the brush. Chuck came back to where they waited. "I found the skiff and drug it down to the water. As soon as it's light enough to see, I'll row across and get her cranked up. I should be able to drop the ramp somewhere close. In the meantime, I'm going to go back and make sure the man we just passed is still sitting by his fire. If he's gone, he's gone to get help, and we'll have a fight on our hands. This lane is one way. It ends about a quarter of a mile further."

Hawks asked, "What is at the end?"

"An old fisherman at one time sold crabs down there; he's been dead for years." Chuck went back to where the man had his camp. As expected, he was gone. He double timed it back.

Hawks asked, "Was he gone?"

"He's gone. Take the horses down to the end. There should be the remains of the old man's shack. It should provide us some cover."

Hawks said, "I'm not going to wait. I'm going to hide back up the lane past his camp where I can cover his camp and the lane. I want you to take Carolyn and Emma on the skiff with you if I haven't returned by morning."

Carolyn had been quiet up until now. "I'm not leaving you."

Hawks put his finger to her lip to quiet her. "Protecting Emma is our prime concern at this point. I don't want to have her in the middle of a firefight. The fewer folks I have to look out for, the better I can fight. If y'all aren't here, I don't have to worry about hitting y'all by accident."

She hugged his neck. "I understand; I'll take care of Emma."

He answered, "I'll take care of the bad guys."

Chuck said, "I can take them and some of the food over now. I could see the barge in the moonlight. I know it's still there. There's a ladder welded on the stern where we can climb up."

Hawks agreed. "It's a plan. I'm getting into position. It's up to y'all to load up some supplies. Make sure you take all the water and as much food as possible when you leave." He kissed Carolyn and Emma.

Emma started crying. "Please, come with us."

Hawks picked her up and gave her a hug. "I'll be right over as soon as I get rid of some bad people. We have to have our horses and supplies to get home. I want you to help Chuck and your mommy. Can you do that for me until I can come aboard with the horses?" He wiped her tears and she nodded yes. Chuck gave him a fist bump.

Hawks proceeded up the lane past the man's camp and set up behind a cluster of trees.

Chuck took the horses near the end of the trail and securely tied them up. Afterward they loaded up the skiff and rowed out to the barge. They tied up to the ladder, and Chuck climbed up. He whispered to the girls, "Not a sound until I check to make sure the barge is empty. If you hear shooting, don't come aboard. I'll come back and get you if everything is clear. If I don't come back, you'll need to row back to shore and wait for Hawks."

Carolyn whispered back, "You won't hear a peep out of us." She watched as Chuck disappeared up the ladder.

After what seemed an eternity, Chuck still speaking in a whisper said, "It's all clear; send up Emma."

Carolyn looked around and whispered to Emma, "We have to stay quiet because we don't want anyone on shore hearing us. Our voices will travel a long way at night, so we have to keep our voices low."

Emma whispered back, "Is it something like keeping a secret?"

"Yes, it is. Now you get to climb the ladder. Chuck will help you when you get to the top." She helped her get her foot on the bottom rung and told her, "Just take your time and go one step at a time. You are brave and strong, and this will be easy for you." Emma dutifully climbed to the top where Chuck waited.

He told her, "Stand here on the back deck while I help get the supplies and help your mommy onboard."

Hawks sat back in silence and watched as the fire burned down; an occasional ember drifted to the sky and a small flame would briefly flare from time to time. It was faint at first, but he heard a metallic sound from up the lane. It was the sort of sound that a belt buckle would make if it encountered a gun or a machete. Next, he heard some faint murmuring from people talking under their breath. Six men came up to the campsite; the man he gave the ammo to was leading them.

The man said, "They went down the lane, and it is a dead end."

Three of the men had pistols, another had a rifle. The other two had baseball bats. Hawks already had the selector switch on his rifle set to full auto. He waited a moment to make sure they weren't being followed. He aimed, squeezed the trigger, and made a sweep across them and then back across them. They fell in every direction. Once they were all down, he put in a fresh magazine and switched it to select fire. From his hidden position, he aimed at each of the men and put a bullet through each of their chests. Once he was sure none of them moved, he walked over to the camp and shot each one through the head. He gathered up their guns and emptied all the magazines from the weapons. They could use the extra ammo. He carried the other weapons down to the water where he chunked them.

Once the sun came up, he heard the engine of the barge crank. He could see Carolyn and Emma waving to him from the bow. He saw the anchor chain being retrieved, and the anchor came clanking up the side. He could see Chuck up in the pilot's house and waved him to come over. The exhaust stack on the barge belched smoke as the engine revved up. It made its way over to where he stood, and he lowered the ramp to the shore. Hawks motioned for them to stay put. He brought the horses aboard two at a time until he had all eight aboard. The puppies scrambled aboard and quickly found Emma. He motioned for Chuck to raise the ramp and back off into the small bay. Carolyn and Emma came down to greet him.

Emma asked, "We heard shooting; what happened?"

"Nothing for you to worry about, Sweetie Pop. I just had to scare them away."

"Did they run away like scared rabbits?"

"Yes, they took off running as fast as their legs could carry them."

Carolyn winked. "They knew when they were licked."

Chuck dropped the anchor so he and Hawks could bring up the skiff and settle the horses. There was a fresh water tank onboard to supply the bathroom and kitchen. It was at least two hundred and fifty gallons and almost full. They should have plenty of water for themselves and the horses until they could make it to the mainland.

Chuck asked, "How many did they send to take us?"

"There were only six; it didn't take much to put them down. I have an old map of the island that should show us the islands around here. We know where we're located; we just have to slowly make our way south."

Chuck agreed, "We'll have to travel during the day; this tub doesn't have radar."

"Where did you learn about boats?"

"I worked my way through college on the lumber boats, bringing logs to the paper mill. What I didn't actually do or work on, I watched, so I know how to operate in these waters. I didn't find any charts in the pilot house, so your map is going to come in handy."

The engine idled below, and you could feel the distant vibration throughout the vessel. Chuck cranked the onboard generator, giving them lights and running water. Carolyn and Emma poked their heads in.

Emma was carrying a bag of beans and said, "Guess what we're having for lunch?"

Hawks grinned. "I want to know what's for breakfast. I've had a long night."

Carolyn said, "If I can get the stove fired up, I can whip up some biscuits and boil some jerky."

Chuck said, "It's a propane stove, so you should be good to go. There are several full bottles of propane just outside the kitchen door under the roof overhang; one of them is already hooked up to the line leading inside."

Carolyn and Emma soon had a pot of beans cooking on the propane stove. Chuck looked at the map and told Hawks, "We might as well get started. All that shooting this morning is bound to draw attention. You stand guard, and I'll get us underway."

They pulled up the anchor, and Chuck kicked up the throttle a bit and turned the barge out into the sea between Salt Spring Island and the main island. The barge wasn't built for speed but to haul machinery and cargo. They proceeded dead slow down the shipping lane, taking care to stay in the middle and hopefully out of rifle range from the either shore. They proceeded south for most of the day without incident. The current flowed northward around the island, so the barge had to overcome the current to make some headway. Chuck had it throttled up, but they were only moving about as fast as a man could run.

The first day they made it down to Salt Spring Island, where they found an inlet below Mount Maxwell Provincial Park. They could see no structures or boats near the shore, so they dropped anchor and prepared to spend the night.

Hawks told Chuck, "You eat some supper and get some sleep. I'll take the first half of the night."

Carolyn piped in, "I've got beans with chipped beef from the jerky ready to eat. Emma was our taster."

Hawks went back to the stern of the barge where the boarding ladder was mounted. He found some aluminum cans in a recycling bin in the kitchen. He spread these out so that anyone climbing over the stern would overturn them and give them early warning.

After everyone had eaten and went to bed, Hawks proceeded to stand guard. His eyes quickly grew accustomed to the twilight. He looked up at the clear night sky; the northern lights were long gone. His thoughts turned to his children and then to his parents and grandparents. It's funny how memories come back to you in the stillness of the night. Small things he hadn't thought about in years would pop into his head. Fishing with his dad, helping his grandfather hoe cotton, and helping his grandmother milk the cow were a few of the long-buried memories. Life was simple, but it didn't seem so at the time. It seemed like just yesterday his children were small and they looked up to him. He was heartbroken thinking he couldn't take care of them now.

Carolyn came out sometime after midnight with Emma. "Us girls had to take a bathroom break."

Emma came up and leaned heavy against him. "Can I help you stand guard?"

"Sure, sweetie, we can spend some time together."

Carolyn gave him a kiss. "Y'all don't stay up too late. Tomorrow is going to be another long day." Carolyn went back to the bunk room, leaving Hawks and Emma sitting on a couple of five-gallon grease buckets. Emma was bundled up and leaned hard against his side. He put his arm around her and remembered how his dad held him when he was little. He remembered feeling safe and loved.

Emma asked him, "Do you have any other children?"

"Yes, I do. I have a son and a daughter. They are both grown, and I have a grandson your age. I hope they will be at my cabin when we get there so you can meet them."

"Do you think they'll like me?"

"Don't worry; I know they will like you, and you'll like them." He pointed up to the stars. "Have you ever sat and looked at all the stars before?"

"I've seen them, but I've never sat and watched them like this. Why are there so many?"

"I don't know, sweetie. I just know that there are more than you can count. If we gaze long enough, we'll see a falling star and maybe a satellite crossing the sky.

"I remember staying on my grandfather's farm during the summer. It was hot and we didn't have air conditioning, so we were sitting outside where it was cool. It was dark like tonight, and a meteor streaked across the sky. I was about your age, and it scared me. It was a bright blue-green color."

"Do you think we'll see one tonight?"

"I hope so, but if we don't, we'll have plenty of time to look for one in the coming weeks. But I do see a satellite crossing the sky." He pointed, and they watched the tiny star slowly cross the sky, going north to south.

Emma yawned really big, and Hawks held her close. "Let's get you back to bed." He carried her to bed, and he walked back through the cabin, and just as he reached the door, he heard the cans rattling. Luckily the pups were in the bunk room with Emma. His hands tightened on his rifle, and he peered into the darkness and waited.

CHAPTER 33

Dawson walked steadily down the road; he wasn't wearing his snowshoes but wore his snow-proof hiking boots. He unzipped his coat a bit as he was starting to sweat from the exertion. He stopped well short of the fire. He didn't want to be illuminated. He squatted in the darkness and waited. The fire was the small building that once served as the border guards' office. It was completely consumed, and there was no one around that he could see. He was tempted to walk on in, but in the abundance of caution, he waited. It was unlikely the building caught fire on its own. He made a broad circle, exploring the perimeter of the border crossing. He quickly found a gap in the fence and eased through it. He purposely didn't look at the fire as his eyes probed the darkness. Behind the border crossing were a few stores and a couple of small restaurants. Before progressing, he stopped to see if there were any lights in any of the stores.

There was only darkness. The flickering of the light from the fire made it impossible to know for sure. He made his way behind the stores and as quietly as possible tried the doors. They were all unlocked. If someone were staying in the buildings, the door would surely be locked. He walked around the last one and was getting ready to cross the road when a lady's voice called out from the darkness, "What are you looking for?"

Dawson flicked off the safety and turned toward the voice. "I'm looking for danger."

The voice answered, "You won't find it here. I just burned the danger alive in that building." A woman walked out of the darkness. He could make out her features from the fire. She was a little over five feet. She was packing a rifle like his. He assumed she had a pistol in one of her pockets or inside her coat.

She pointed to the fire, "Let's walk a little closer to the fire, its cold out here." They walked closer to the fire and could see each other quite well. She lowered her hood and revealed shoulder-length gray hair and looked to be close to sixty years old. She had hard, worried eyes and features. She asked, "What brings you here?"

"I wanted to see what was going on before I tried to cross. Are you here alone?"

She answered, "I am now. I'm all that's left. Those bastards I have barbecuing in there killed my husband, children, and grandchildren."

"How did you get away?"

"I was knocked out when they shot up the house. When my husband was hit, he fell back hard on me, and I hit my head on the kitchen table. I assume they thought they killed me. I woke up, and they didn't see me awake because they were busy going through our belongings. One of them was dumb enough to leave his rifle on the kitchen table. While they were picking out what they wanted, I picked up the rifle and looked at it, the little lever on the side showed safe, fire, and auto. I switched it to auto, and I emptied the rifle on them. All four went down in the living room. I got their weapons and put them where they couldn't get them. Three of them were still alive; one of them appeared to be paralyzed and tried to drag his way toward the door. Two of them were unconscious. That was when I got the idea."

Dawson knew what the idea was. "Sounds like a good idea to me. How did you get them out there by yourself?"

"I tied the arms behind the ones that were unconscious in case they woke up. I then grabbed the paralyzed one by his feet, and I drug him out to the building and into it. I tied him to a chair so he couldn't drag himself out. I dragged the other two out, and it was my good fortune that they woke up to know what I was doing. I dragged the dead one out last. Once I had them all inside, I set the building on fire and stayed long enough to watch their faces."

"I wish I could have been here to help; I just shoot them in the head. How did they get here?"

"They were driving an old Volkswagen bus. I already have it hidden down the driveway a bit."

"Why didn't you shoot me?"

"You weren't going into any of the buildings. You were looking for the person who started the fire."

"I have my family waiting down the road for me to come get them."

"Go get them. Don't leave them alone. We'll talk more when you get back."

Dawson made the walk back in short order and found Cathy and the kids safe in the Power Wagon. Cathy asked, "What did you find?"

"I found a grandmother who just lost her entire family. The bad guys didn't make it."

"You're kidding?"

"No, she did it. It's OK for us to proceed. I want to help her bury her family, then we can get on our way." They proceeded down the highway toward the burning building. The kids looked out in amazement. Lucy asked, "Can we roast marshmallows?"

He patted her leg. "We can't roast marshmallows over this

fire; it's much too hot. We'll have to wait on our marshmallow roast. I've got to help the lady who lives here."

They turned into the parking lot behind the burning building. He could see the lady in the window of her home. She had a lantern burning somewhere within. Once they were parked, he told Cathy and the kids, "We'll stay here tonight. Go ahead and dig out our camping gear, and don't let the kids come in the house or go near the fire." He bent close to Cathy. "The bad guys or what's left of them are in the burning building."

Dawson helped unload the tent, cots, and sleeping bags. Cathy pulled out a cooking pot and got ready to start a campfire. The kids were helping. Dawson then walked up to the house where the old woman was busily working on cleaning up her house. He knocked on the door. When she answered he asked, "We're setting up camp. What can I do to help?"

She looked at him without speaking. Tears ran down her face and dripped off her chin. The only thing he could do was reach out and pull her close. She sobbed and sobbed until he felt her weakening. He led her over to the couch and let her sit. "Where is your family?"

"I have them in the front bedroom. I've been cleaning my house."

"Do you want me to help you bury them?"

"No, the weather is cold, and I don't expect to live much longer."

"Are you ill?"

"Yes, I have nothing to live for. I'm going to stay here until my food runs out or somebody comes by here and kills me."

"Do you have any friends or relatives nearby?"

"I have nobody. Everyone we know around here are either dead or have left. I have nobody. Please, don't ask me go with y'all. I want to stay right here in my home. Since it's just me eating, I have enough food to last four or five months. I have enough guns and ammo to defend myself. I'm not leaving my family. I also have stage four breast cancer. I just want to ride it out here."

Dawson could only agree. "I agree with what you've decided. Is there anything I can help you with?"

"If you and your wife can help bandage up my head, that would be a help."

He brought the lantern over and looked at her head. "I think it needs stitches, but if we put them in, there won't be anyone around to take them out."

She looked up at him. "I have some butterfly bandages. If you can cut the hair back or shave around it, that should do the trick until it heals up."

Dawson walked over to the door. "Cathy, can you come give me a hand?"

She called back, "I'll gather up the kids and be right there."

Cathy and the kids came in, and he pointed to the old lady. "This young lady needs a little first aid. I'm afraid my big hands are going to be too clumsy."

Cathy put out her hand. "I'm Cathy Stewart. I'm glad to meet you."

The old lady grabbed her hand with both of hers. "I'm Helen Chavalier."

Dawson touched her shoulder. "I'm Dawson Stewart, and these two little critters running around are BC and Lucy. What happened to the border guards who worked here?"

"They stole my husband's old Mercedes diesel and some canned goods and left. They called it commandeering. I can show you the receipt they gave me."

"We understand. They were going door to door in Calgary confiscating food. Fortunately, they didn't try to clean us out, and I didn't have to shoot them."

Cathy took the lantern and looked at Helen's head. "Let's get you patched up."

Dawson headed for the door. "C'mon, kids, we don't need to be underfoot."

Dawson took the kids out to their campfire and put one of the dehydrated food dinners in the pot of water to rehydrate and warm up.

BC said, "Ever since Lucy mentioned that she wanted to toast marshmallows, I've been hungry for some."

Dawson answered, "I happen to know that we have a package of the chocolate Gold Bricks in the trailer. That will make a great desert." He filled up three bowls of the dinner and mixed up three cups of powdered milk. Once they finished eating, he broke out the chocolate Gold Bars. They spent the next hour watching the stars and making plans for their trip.

Cathy opened the door, and they watched as she hugged Helen's neck and came down to the fire. "I got her head wound dressed. I'm afraid the other wounds will never heal."

Dawson squeezed her hand. "I feel so sorry for her."

"She said that she wanted to get some rest, and she would see us off in the morning."

They spent the next couple of hours by the fire before giving in to the cold and going to bed. The tent stopped the wind, and the sleeping bags kept everyone toasty. The building gradually burned down to a pile of smoking rubble. When morning came, Dawson went out and punched up the fire so Cathy could start breakfast. He rolled up the sleeping bags and packed up the cots and tent.

Helen came out and looked at the Power Wagon. "Where did you find this contraption?"

"I commandeered it from the men who tried to kill us. They wound up dead like those bastards you got rid of. You know this country better than we do. Our goal is to head south and east so we can make it to my place in Louisiana."

Helen pointed out, "I believe you're going to find a lot of empty farms and hunting lodges. Sooner or later you're going to run out of gas or your machine is going to break. After all, it looks like it's over seventy years old. They don't sell parts for these any longer."

Dawson shook his head in agreement. "That is one of my biggest concerns, but we need to go somewhere where we can survive the winters, starving masses, and bandits."

Helen pointed to her garage. "My car is there. It has gas you can drain, and there are a couple of five-gallon cans full of gas."

"I don't know how to thank you; can I leave you some food or anything else you might need?"

She sighed. "You know my situation. This picture show is about to end, and there ain't gonna be no happy ending."

Cathy walked up. "You are helping us to hopefully have a happy ending."

Dawson emptied the two five-gallon cans into the Power Wagon and went back and drained the remaining gas from her car into the cans. One more five-gallon can topped off the tank in the Power Wagon.

Helen said, "There's some fuel in the border guard trucks and in the VW bus. I won't be needing any of it. It'll make me feel good knowing I helped you escape."

He spent the next couple of hours filling every spare container with gas for the Power Wagon. Once he was finished, he and Carolyn went up to Helen's house and knocked on the door. Helen came to the door and gave each of them a goodbye hug. "Good luck, there isn't much south of here, so you should be able to travel a couple of days before running into trouble. I have a feeling a winter storm is forming up."

Dawson agreed. "I can feel it in the air."

She pointed down the road. "About seventy miles from here, you're going to come to a little village. There's a big highway department barn that you can probably take shelter in until it passes. I don't know if you'll run into anyone unless they have plenty of food on hand. Just be careful."

Cathy hugged Dawson's arm and said, "Don't worry; my husband will take good care of us."

The snow started falling as they pulled out onto the road. Fortunately, the road was well outlined, so they could follow it without running off the road. The road also had abandoned vehicles they had to maneuver around. So long as the Power Wagon ran, there would be plenty of fuel to salvage from the dead vehicles. The going was slow, but the faithful old machine trudged on. They made it to the highway barn just before dark.

Snow was piled up around the few buildings that remained, and there was no smoke from any of the chimneys. The highway department barn had doors that slid sideways. He stopped and hopped out with his rifle and cautiously walked to the main door and tried it. It readily opened, and he investigated the cavernous building. He walked through the building and found no signs of life in the small office or in the supply and tool rooms. He came out and slid open the front barn door. There was a door in the back so they could drive their equipment all the way through. He drove the Power Wagon with the trailer attached and pulled all the way through and closed the door behind them. He found some wooden pallets that he broke up to make a small fire.

He told the kids, "Stay close and don't go exploring; there's a lot of stuff in here that can hurt you." The kids stayed really close to the trailer where Cathy unloaded the camping gear.

Dawson told them, "I'll start a fire when I finish barricading the doors. I don't want anyone surprising us in here." He found some chain and secured both large barn doors. He locked and barricaded the man doors with some planks, a hammer, and some nails from the tool room. He went back to where Cathy and the kids waited. He broke up more of the wooden pallets and added to the small fire.

Cathy asked him, "Where's the smoke going to go?"

Dawson pointed to the ceiling. "There is a cupola in the center of the roof. There won't be much smoke, but any that does rise will vent through it." They soon had the warm fire burning well. The snowstorm continued unabated. There was little wind, just a lot of snow. Dawson told Cathy, "We might as well get comfortable, this storm could last a while."

Cathy smiled. "We are safe and warm for the moment. We are protected by the storm, this building, and you."

Dawson smiled. "We can use a couple of days rest. We are in no hurry at this point. We will move when it's safe and fort up when we must." They had a great evening, and after a warm meal and some stories, they all went to bed.

Sometime late in the evening, Dawson woke with Cathy cradled in his arms. He gently moved her aside so as not to wake her. He climbed out of their bed and left the tent to check things out. Even in the safety of the building, he carried his weapons. They were as much a part of him as his hands. He stood silent and listened. The big building creaked as the snow accumulated on it. The roof was very steep, so there was no danger of the roof being overloaded as it was designed to shed the snow. He stoked the fire and added a few boards. He sat quiet, thinking about all the dead: Olivia, Henry, and then all the men he had eagerly killed.

They spent the next week holed up while the blizzard blew itself out. Dawson stood at the man door and pried the boards loose so he could open it. He gathered several buckets of snow to melt by the fire. The blizzard had piled snow up against the front of the building. He re-secured the front door and went to the back door. There was a lot of snow, but he could easily dig them out from here. The big barn sat parallel to the highway, so from the back door he could see down the highway.

There was a big accumulation of snow, but he felt the Power Wagon could handle it, so he spent the rest of the day shoveling snow to clear the main door so they could leave. The exercise made him feel invigorated. The inactivity of the past week was nice, but he felt useless just sitting around. Tonight would be the last night in the big barn. He pulled out a Road Atlas he had found in the barn office and studied the map.

Cathy looked over his shoulder. "Show me on the map. I'd like to see where we're going."

He pointed to a large reservoir. "That is the headwaters of the upper Missouri River. If we can make it that far, we will follow the river until we get past all the dams. Once we get past the dams, we should be able to find a boat, and with a little more luck, we can float down the Missouri and ultimately to the Mississippi. The Mississippi will take us near my camp in South Louisiana."

"Do you think we can make it that far?"

"I hope so. All the wild game that is assessable by foot will have been taken by now. I know the Louisiana marsh will provide all the fish, crabs, and shrimp we'll ever need. The population of New Orleans will have killed each other off and starved to death by the time we make it that far. So will most of the populations of the cities we'll be floating past."

Suddenly they were disturbed by a loud banging on the door. Someone was trying to break in. Dawson took his rifle and headed to the sound of the banging. Standing at the side, he discreetly looked out the window. A half dozen men with lanterns were trying to break down the door. It would take them a few minutes. Suddenly he heard a commotion at the back door.

He ran back to Cathy. "Let's get packed up. We won't keep them out much longer." Without saying a word, she gathered up the kids and deposited them on the front seat of the Power Wagon. Next, they broke down the tent and loaded all their gear back into the truck and trailer. Dawson cranked up the Power Wagon and turned on the lights. He raised the massive snow blade up off the ground a couple of feet.

Cathy looked at him. "The doors not open."

Dawson shifted to low gear. "That door won't keep standing when I hit it with the snow blade." Without another word, he revved it up and let off the clutch. In a flash they were barreling toward the big door and struck it with enough force to knock it from the rack supporting it. It fell flat in one piece, so he drove across it. In the glow of the headlights, they spotted two men with weapons to the side at the man door. Before the men could respond, they were out of the drive and heading down the highway. Cathy watched in the rear-view mirror to see if they were being followed. Dawson lowered the blade and proceeded to plow their way down the road. He kept going, being careful not to run off the road. He could see road signs on the shoulders, so he kept dead in the middle. If they got stranded out here, they could be stuck until another Chinook blew in or even until the spring thaw.

Cathy kept a sharp look in the side rear-view mirror. She shook Dawson's arm. "I see lights in the distance."

Dawson told her, "Do you think you can drive it?"

Without hesitation she said, "Yes, I learned how to drive a standard on my grandfather's truck. This one works the same way."

Dawson slowed to a stop and bumped it into neutral. "I'm suiting up, and you are going to continue slow for another two miles. Keep it in the middle of the road. I'm going to ambush them as they approach." Without another word, he stepped out, put on his heavy jacket, and donned his rifle and ammo pack. Cathy crawled across the kids and got into the driver's seat.

Dawson poked his head in and got a quick kiss from Cathy, and he looked at the kids, "Do everything your mother says with no argument." They looked at him with wide eyes, and both nodded yes.

Dawson stood in the road and watched them drive a way. He turned and concentrated his attention on the headlights following in the distance. He positioned himself to the side and checked his rifle. He spotted a large limb from a fallen tree and drug it out to partially block the road. He wanted to slow them just enough that he could massacre them in their vehicle. The thought occurred to him they were just following because he was clearing the road, but he could take no chances. The only reason they were following him at night instead of holing up in the barn was to rob them of what they had. Just as he anticipated, they slowed down for the limb. He raised his rifle and fired.

CHAPTER 34

Hawks remained frozen. Even in the low light he could see movement. It was almost impossible for a human to see anything in the dark that is motionless, but humans were sensitive to movement. As long as he remained motionless, he was basically invisible to whoever was on the back of the barge. He watched as the person carefully walked around the remaining cans. He heard someone else coming up the ladder, so he made his move. When the person turned around to look at the ladder, Hawks gave the person a good shove. The man yelled as he tumbled over the rail and into the boat that had brought him and his companion to the ladder.

Hawks called to the man on the ladder, "Get back on your boat, or I'm going to kill you, understand?"

The man on the ladder answered, "We aren't looking for trouble. We're just looking for food."

"Get in your boat, and don't look back. Your friend is probably hurt, so you need to hurry." He walked down the deck so that he could see the boat as they paddled it back toward shore. Once they were out of sight of the barge, he walked back and reset the cans. The cans worked once; maybe they would work again. He was thankful he hadn't had to kill them. The problem was now he had two men going back to shore to possibly get help. Instead of killing two, he may have to kill many more.

Chuck walked out. "What's all the commotion?"

"A couple of fellas tried to board us. I ran them off without killing them."

Chuck pointed out, "We need to stay out of sight. Walking around on the deck can get us killed. If someone has a deer rifle on the island, they may be able to pick us off."

Hawks pointed out, "The steel on the wheel house is only about a quarter of an inch thick. It won't stop a high-powered rifle round."

Chuck turned to go into the pilot's house when a loud ping rang out from high on the pilot house. It was followed by the distant boom from the island. Hawks started to fire, but chose not to. "Unless I can see a flash, I'm not wasting ammo."

Chuck pointed out, "They may think we are unarmed, which could be to our advantage."

Hawks lamented, "My hesitation to kill may wind up killing us yet. They are waiting for dawn to get better shots. We know the shots came from the island. Before daylight, I think we should move the barge further from shore. If they decide to chase us with a boat, I can handle them."

Chuck said, "Let's move Carolyn and Emma and the pups down lower in the boat near the horses. They will be somewhat below the water line and some protection from the bodies of the horses and gear."

"Let's get them heading down there now. I don't want to take the chance of a stray bullet."

Chuck unshouldered his rifle. "You get them. I'll stand guard. Once they're safe, I'll move the barge due west away from the island a half a mile or so. Unless they have a trained sniper to reach us from that far away, any bullet fired would also lose some of its lethality as their velocity decreases from the range."

Hawks went into the crew quarters and gently woke Carolyn. She smiled and asked, "Is it time to set sail?"

He gave her a smack on the lips. "We've got some people shooting at us. I want to get you and Emma down in the bottom of the barge behind the horses until we can move further away."

He woke Emma next. "Sweetie Pop, we've got to get you and Mommy to a safer spot. You don't mind hanging out with the horses, do you?"

She answered, "I like the horses."

Once he had them settled, he went back up to the upper deck. Chuck cranked the engine, and he assisted retrieving the anchor. He expected rifle fire once the sound of the engine and the rattling anchor chains reached the island. He and Chuck stayed as close to the thick steal bulkheads as possible while they powered away from the island.

Chuck said, "They're either out of ammo or they figure they can catch us."

Hawks looked back across the bay to the island. He concentrated on the shoreline of the island. There was enough light from the moon that he could make out the shore. He saw a flashlight come as three men climbed into a boat. He could see one of them pulling the starter cord on an outboard. He took his rifle and placed the red dot at the top of the men's heads. At that distance, the bullet would be dropping maybe as much as a foot. He started firing the rifle semi automatically and emptied the thirty-round mag on the men and boat. The flashlight went out and flames leaped up from the boat. Fortunately, a bullet had hit the fuel tank and started a fire. This group was either dead or wounded, but most assuredly disabled.

Chuck looked out of the bridge window. "I think they got the message."

Hawks called down to Carolyn and Emma, "No worries, girls, the danger is gone for now. We'll be getting underway in a bit."

Emma called up, "Once we get underway, can me and Mommy cook breakfast?"

Hawks could barely make her little smiling face out in the near twilight. "Yes, you can. I can't wait to eat and get a little rest."

It was soon light enough to see, so Chuck increased the throttle so that they were making good headway. Hawks stayed on guard to make sure no other boats left the island. Carolyn and Emma cooked up some breakfast as the barge plodded steadily south. The channel was much wider here, so the current wasn't nearly as strong. When the ocean current was funneled between the smaller Salt Spring Island and Vancouver Island, the velocity of the water increased, so they were lucky to make headway at all. Now they were making good headway as they rounded the Salt Spring Island.

Their destination was Blanchard, Washington. It was between Vancouver and Seattle, and according to the maps and charts should be an easy place to nose the barge in and drop the ramp so they could offload the horses and gear. The only problem they would have would be passing Victoria. There might be people with working boats that would surely try to take them, and they would probably be in uniform.

Hawks studied the charts with Chuck. "Do you think we could navigate these waters at night?"

Chuck pointed to the islands on the route. "If we have a bright enough moon, we can thread our way through the islands, but only if we go slow and careful."

Hawks put an X on the spot they were shooting for. "If we try anytime other than night, you and I both know that they'll be coming to board us."

Chuck pointed out, "It was a miracle I didn't get stopped

when I cranked it and headed up to Lady Smith. I figure the locals had already gone through it, and since I was heading north, the current helped me with the speed."

Hawks stated, "I think we ought to go nonstop. Carolyn can help keep lookout, and I can spell you at the helm so you can get some rest."

Chuck agreed. "I want to be at the helm at night. You're going to have to keep an eye out for obstacles. If we rip the bottom out on a rock, we won't survive the cold water."

Carolyn came in with Emma. "What's our plan?"

Hawks told her, "We aren't going to stop until we reach the US shore. Do you think you can stand watch back here, while I go to the front and watch where we're going? We'll be traveling slowly and at night. Anyone who spots us from shore and who has a working boat will probably try and take us. There will be about a 90 percent chance they will be wearing badges or uniforms."

Chuck shook his head in agreement. "We'll have to do what we have to do."

They traveled without incident most of the day. They tried to stay as far from each shore as possible. Only once did they see someone digging clams. The lady stood up and waved at them. She didn't yell for help or run toward the shore. They plowed through the waves whipped up by the wind on the open water. As they crossed the wide expanse between the islands, the wind was brisk, and so were the waves. Occasionally one would lap over the gunnel. The bilge pumps dutifully came on and kept the bilge pumped dry. They went behind a small, uninhabited island and waited until the sun started to set. They would make the trip past Victoria after dark. There was a three quarters moon and there was mixed cloud cover. The mixed cloud cover would break up their silhouette on the water. If they could avoid running aground, their odds of survival went up a bit.

Hawks and Carolyn kept their eyes peeled, and it was close to midnight when Carolyn spotted a flare of light across the water. She called to Hawks, "I'm sure I saw a flare of light. It was orange."

Hawks said, "Good catch, someone is smoking a cigarette or a cigar. How far away do you think it was?"

"I can't be sure; it was just a bright flare that lit up and dimmed." She pointed in the direction it came from. Just as expected, they took another puff.

Hawks pointed. "I'm going to let them get a lot closer before I light them up."

The cigarette light drifted behind them before going out. Hawks went to the stern and sat on a grease bucket so that he could aim across the rail. Once when the clouds parted, he finally got a glimpse of the craft. It was a large skiff; he counted at least a half a dozen occupants. They were still out about a hundred yards when he clicked his safety to select fire. He had two extra thirty-round magazines in each of his coat pockets.

He told Carolyn, "Take Emma and the pups and get down in the bottom of the boat. They may not go down easy. Take your weapons with you and try to stay on the other side of the horses. I don't want a stray bullet making it to y'all."

She kissed him on the cheek. "Good luck, I'll keep Emma safe."

Chuck called back, "I've got her wide open, good luck."

Hawks said, "With these waves I've got to let them get within fifty yards so I won't miss. The size of these waves will hurt their accuracy as their little boat is bouncing around pretty good. I just hope they aren't military with a machine gun or RPG."

Chuck laughed. "If you hit them hard and fast, they will be so busy dying they won't have a chance to shoot back."

As he watched the boat, someone on board called out with a bull horn. "This is the coast guard; prepare to be boarded."

Hawks could clearly see the man in the moonlight standing near the center console. Without waiting Hawks made him the first target and proceeded to evenly cover the entire vessel with thirty rounds. He rapidly reloaded and kept firing into the boat. One of the men got off a round that struck the bridge above Chuck's head. The boat soon started falling back and started making a circle. The torque of the engine made it shift so that it pivoted in its mount, and with no one to correct the steering, it went into never-ending circles. Hawks continued firing until he had emptied the second magazine. He slapped the third magazine in and waited as the boat fell out of sight behind them. It would continue to circle until it exhausted its fuel or ran aground with its dead and dying occupants.

He looked back at Chuck. "Are you OK?"

"Yeah, that slug bounced around the cabin a bit, but missed me and the equipment."

"I'm heading down to check on Carolyn and Emma." He disappeared down and called to Carolyn, "Are you girls OK?"

She called back, "We're OK. Are you ready for us to stand guard again?"

"Yes, we should be past the city in another hour, then we head to where we're going to land." The barge continued heading south toward the US shore without any more attempts to be stopped or boarded. The sun was starting to rise as they approached the shore.

Chuck said, "It's now or nothing. Get the horses saddled and ready to ride."

Hawks agreed. "They'll be ready when you're ready to drop the ramp." He went down to where the horses were and proceeded to get them saddled. He called up to Carolyn, "Keep an eye out for Chuck. I'll get the horses saddled and packed."

Emma came down to help. "Can I help?"

"You sure can, Sweetie Pop. I want you to fill up a bucket with water and carry it around to each of the horses, and let them get a drink. Don't walk around behind them. I don't one of them to get spooked and kick you. We'll get them fed the first chance we find some grass, and we'll let them graze."

Hawks had them ready as they approached the shore. Carolyn tossed down the sack of grub she had been cooking from. Chuck called down, "I'm going to leave the barge in gear and running so that it will remain firmly against the bank after I drop the ramp. I'll be down to help get them off on the ground." The barge slowed as it plowed into the shallows. The front ramp dropped and landed on the sandy bank. Chuck came down, and he and Hawks led the horses off the ramp and onto the bank. Carolyn was in the saddle.

Hawks picked up Emma and asked, "Are you ready for a horse ride?"

She grinned from ear to ear. "I like to ride." Hawks mounted up. They followed the shore until they came to a small trail leading up the bank, and they headed up it until it reached a grass-covered lane. Once they were on the lane, they followed it until it reached an open field with a commercial warehouse out on the main road.

Chuck said, "I'm going to walk up there on foot and make sure there is no one there. If it's empty, we can let the horses graze for a bit, and we can maybe hide in the building until dark."

Carolyn said, "Be careful."

Hawks told him, "I'll try to cover you from the wood line. If you get in trouble, book it back in this direction, and I'll start shooting."

Chuck shook his hand. "If I'm discovered, you'll just have to wait it out. I don't want to endanger Emma if we have a shootout."

Hawks agreed. "Good luck, buddy. I'll get the girls back down in the woods."

Emma called the pups as they disappeared down the hill into the woods. Chuck had a pistol tucked in his waistband behind his back under his coat. He walked across the field as if he had nothing to hide. He reached the back door of the building, tried it, and went in after pausing a moment and announcing himself. They waited for what seemed like an eternity. Chuck came out followed by a couple of men. None of them were apparently armed, so Hawks held his fire.

They walked straight up to Hawks. Chuck introduced them. "Believe it or not, these two bums were in my unit in the Army. There's water for the horses in a ditch by the building. They are trying to get back to the island to get to their families."

Hawks told them, "The barge should still be wedged against the bank. If you hurry, you can get the anchors down, and they can use it to cross back over. I hope you guys have guns." They opened their coats and showed that they carried pistols. Hawks told them, "You're going to need them."

Without another word, Chuck and the two men disappeared down the road. In about an hour, Chuck and one of the men came back. Chuck nodded over his shoulder. "It was still there. I helped them secure it. We left Larry to stand guard. Pete and I are going to get their gear to the barge. Let the horses get fed and watered. It's going to take a couple of hours to get all their gear moved."

Hawks said, "We'll move up to the building while y'all are moving the gear. We'll plan on moving out after you get back and travel as far as we can tonight. Once we get far enough away from the cities, we can move by day."

Pete piped up, "It's been pretty quiet around here for the last few days. Larry and me were truck drivers, and we were tag teaming a load to Utah. We geared up as we hiked our way back."

Chuck asked, "Can you show us on a map where you crossed the mountain?"

Pete answered, "Sure thing, it should still be open. We haven't had much snow, and we seem to be having an unusually warm winter this side of the divide." Being a trucker, he had torn maps from his atlas they carried in their truck of the states they would be crossing. He retrieved them from his pack and gave them the pages he didn't need. He pointed to the pass they had come across on the map. That information was more than worth the gift of the barge.

Hawks looked at Chuck. "As soon as you get back, we'll plan our run for the pass. It will probably take us a couple of days at least to cross it."

Pete agreed. "We crossed on foot. At least you have horses and supplies. We had a garden cart and some food from our truck. We took warm clothes off some dead men we ran across. Whoever killed them didn't need their clothes."

As they turned away, Carolyn walked up with Emma. "I've been listening. Good luck and be careful."

Pete smiled. "If it wasn't for luck, we would be dead in the snow right now."

Chuck and Pete disappeared down the road, while Hawks, Carolyn, and Emma took the horses out into the field with the grass poking through the snow. Hawks hobbled them and put long leads on their halters and let them eat. Carolyn went into the building and checked it out. It was an old moving and storage warehouse with separate storage units. Most of them had been broken into and ransacked. They found some packing blankets and made some sleeping pads. They were out of the wind, and it was comfortable for the time being.

Hawks let the horses feed until they reached their fill. He led them around to the ditch and busted the ice on top so they could drink. Chuck made it back and helped lead them into the building through a rollup door. Once the horses were secure, they locked the doors and ate a cold supper.

Carolyn asked, "What are the plans, guys?"

Chuck answered, "I think we need to get some rest, fill our bellies, and head out first thing in the morning."

Hawks said, "I concur. I'm worn out after the last couple of days."

They found some chairs from the open storage units. In one they found a kerosene heater and a can of kerosene. They soon had it lit and putting out heat. With water from the ditch boiling on top, they prepared a pot of coffee and made some hot cocoa for Emma. They soon were settled in for the night. The puppies were lying next to Emma. Hawks walked over to a corner of the warehouse where a couch from one of the storage units sat in the shadows. He leaned back on one of the cushions, and with his rifle across his lap, he rested. With the horses and dogs inside, they would stir and alert him to anyone trying to get in. He fell asleep and dreamed.

CHAPTER 35

He didn't stop firing into the vehicle's passenger compartment until he had exhausted the magazine. The car burst forward and ran into the snow bank created by the snowplow. He slapped a fresh magazine into his rifle and cautiously approached the car. The back door burst open, and a guy rolled out with a pistol in his hand. Dawson dropped him with a short burst from the rifle and proceeded to fire into the car to make sure no one else emerged. He just prayed he wouldn't find a family with children. He dropped in a fresh magazine and opened the driver's door. A man lay dead slumped over the wheel. There were four more dead men in the car. That accounted for five of the men who were breaking into the highway barn.

The old Mercedes they were riding in was still running with the rear wheels spinning. He reached in and killed the motor before dragging the men out and getting their weapons. This must have been the Mercedes commandeered from Helen back at the border crossing. They all had Glocks and M4 rifles and magazines. He gathered up the loaded magazines for the Glocks and M4 rifles. He tossed their guns out into the snow where they would remain buried until spring. There was no food in the car, so he knew what they were coming for. He placed all the loaded magazines in a backpack he found in the car trunk and headed back down the road to where Cathy had the Power Wagon waiting.

He found them patiently waiting. Cathy threw her arms around him. "What happened? I heard the gunfire."

"They were the men who commandeered Helen's husband's old Mercedes. We now have a good supply of magazines and ammo; hopefully, we can continue for some time. So long as this old machine does its job, we can make headway."

They drove through the night and stopped only to top off the fuel. The old truck was not designed for fuel economy but for low-end power. The six-cylinder Plymouth engine was a workhorse with untold thousands produced during and after the war. It trudged on through the snow unabated. The sun was rising, the skies were clear, and the sun was bright. They came to a driveway with a good road leading up to what appeared to be a log cabin up on a hill in the distance. It was almost a half a mile off the road, and it appeared to back up to the mountains. The drive was well marked with stakes that stuck out above the snow. There was a turnaround at the top.

He wheeled the Power Wagon up the hill, clearing the driveway as they went. Once at the top, he stopped and got out and went to the cabin. The door was unlocked, and it was vacant. There was absolutely no indication of recent occupation. This could have been one of many weekend getaways for rich people from the West Coast. He trudged around the back and found a barn with snow machines and another that was a stable. There were bales of hay stored in the loft and rodent-proof barrels with horse feed. The tack room had saddles, blankets, halters, bridles, and pack saddles. A large paddock was attached to the side of the barn. This was probably where a guide ran his service from. On the side of the barn was a room to butcher deer and elk. The walk-in freezer was empty.

There was plenty of room to hide the Power Wagon out of sight of the road and plenty of room to turn it around when they were ready to leave. He went back and pulled it around and turned it so that it was heading out in case they needed to leave in a hurry. Cathy and the twins went into the cabin; Dawson went to the wood shed and gathered an armload of wood. When he came around to the back door, he discovered why there were no occupants.

A note on the door said, "Brady, we've run out of food and are going to hike into town. Come find us if you read this note."

The note was well weathered as it had been on the door for quite a while. He walked in with the wood and built a fire in the wood heater located in the middle of the main room. The kitchen had a propane stove that still worked.

Cathy said, "There is clean bedding. The bathrooms appear to be winterized, so we should be able to have flush toilets and bathtubs that drain once the house warms up. How much wood do we have?"

"There are eight or ten cords of wood in the shed. We can easily stay here until spring if necessary. The only bad thing is that we have a plowed road leading right up to our door. If anyone has a working vehicle and tries to follow us, we will be sitting ducks."

Cathy said, "We'll have to be vigilant until there is enough snow to cover our tracks."

Dawson called to the kids, "Help me and your mother carry in some food so we can eat breakfast and rest a bit."

They soon had breakfast cooking and went through the kitchen, pantry, and basement. There was no food, only some salt, pepper, and odd seasonings. The fridge was empty, but the dishes were clean. Whoever had left the cabin had left it clean and orderly.

Dawson pointed out, "The fact that this place has not been

ransacked means that we are far enough away from a city for people to walk, especially in winter. I think we need to hold up here for a while. We have enough food to last us more than a year. We salvaged most of the food from the McGregors, plus the food we brought with us from your uncle's place. This is a well-insulated log cabin that should stop any pistol-caliber weapon and a lot of rifle calibers. I'll spend the next few days moving in the firewood. We'll place it around the walls, like we did at your uncle's house. I don't think anyone will be coming in here on foot."

Cathy said, "The way we can fight, most people wouldn't have a chance. Besides, one of us will always be awake and watching. I was able to sleep in the truck last night. Why don't you sack out on the couch next to the woodstove until the cabin warms up?"

Dawson told the kids, "I want y'all to stay in the house unless I am outside with you. We are in the wilderness here in the mountains. There are wild animals like wolves and coyotes around here. Let's get your toys and anything else you want out of the trailer you need."

BC said, "Are we going to build a fort?"

Lucy beamed. "Yeah, let's build a fort."

Dawson grinned. "We're going to build sort of a fort, follow me."

He carried them out to the wood shed. "Here's what we're going to build our fort out of." BC and Lucy each grabbed a stick of firewood while Dawson gathered an armful. He said, "Follow me; we're going to turn the big room into a fort." They enthusiastically helped him carry in wood as he lined the front wall up about four feet high. After they had the front covered and their toys brought in from the trailer, Dawson told them, "Help your mommy stand watch while I grab a nap next to the fire."

BC said, "Don't worry; I know what to do."

Dawson grinned. "I know you do." He loaded up the woodstove that already had the cabin somewhat warm. He unrolled one of the sleeping bags and used it as a comforter while he closed his eyes and stretched out on the couch. He slept soundly, even though the kids were playing and Cathy was organizing their food for the next few days.

Cathy let him sleep most of the day. He awoke to the smell of her cooking. The kids had found some copy paper and some pencils and were busy drawing pictures. If they weren't in constant danger, this would be a great place to live for a while. He reloaded the woodstove and then explored the cabin. There was a bunk room with its own bathroom, a master bedroom, and three smaller bedrooms. There was a bathroom in the hall and one in the master bedroom. He went outside and checked the 500 gallon propane tank; it was half full. It should last for quite a while if they used it just for cooking. They could always cook on the wood heater as well.

There was also a cistern full of water fed by gutters on the cabin's roof. They were all frozen now, but the water down in the cistern only had a thin layer of ice on top. It was deep enough the ground temperature kept it from freezing solid. It was also covered on top, which helped keep it thawed. He found some buckets in the stable that he could use to carry water to the house.

There was a small diesel generator near the barn in its own shed. There was a drum of diesel and one of kerosene next to it. It looked to be pretty old and would probably crank, but unless there were an emergency, he couldn't take the chance of it being heard running.

The electric water pump on a water well had been winterized. The house had kerosene lanterns in every room for lighting. It was set up as a true hunting lodge. For now, they would heat water on the wood heater and use the water from the cistern to flush toilets and bathe.

He went back in and told Cathy, "I think we need to fort

up here until the weather warms up. There are so few running vehicles I don't expect anyone coming our way. I feel certain no one will come walking in." He pulled out the map and estimated where they were at on the route. "We are at least sixty miles from any settlement or town. Unless there are some nearby cabins or ranches, we are very isolated. The longer we stay, there will be fewer people left to come after us. I think we should bring in several weeks of food in case we are trapped in the cabin. There are mountains behind the cabin, but they are far enough away we don't have to worry about an avalanche. I don't want to get pinned down with no food and water in here. I'll keep two of the bathtubs filled with water; we can melt snow on the wood heater and just use the propane for cooking."

The next few days were spent hauling in food, water, and firewood. The wood heater kept the cabin warm, and there were plenty of quilts for the beds. The twins shared a bed in one of the bedrooms; Dawson and Cathy took the master bedroom. Dawson spent most of the nights on the couch near the wood heater so he would be alert to any danger. The woodstove did a great job of heating the cabin and was very efficient. It only needed to be loaded several times a day. He could remember using an old homemade barrel stove at his hunting camp in south Louisiana. It used a lot more wood, there were holes rusted through on the sides so the light from the fire would shine out into the dark room. It also leaked a bit of smoke, so everything in the room always had a smoky aroma. There were always mice in the old camp, and they frequently tried to join you in the bunk, so nights were sometimes exciting when one of them scampered across the covers.

For now, they were warm, safe, and fed. As he sat in the dark next to the heater, his thoughts returned to Olivia, and he felt sad. The flames of the fire behind the glass window of the woodstove were mesmerizing. He thought of all the men he had killed; he was surprised at how easy killing men had become. He had absolutely no remorse or regret. He had even grown accustomed to wearing a pistol day and night. He even felt funny taking it off to bathe.

They quickly fell into a routine of hauling in snow to melt, playing games, telling stories, and enjoying the rest and safety afforded by the cabin and remote location. Soon any surviving elk and mule deer would be moving back into the safety of the mountains, and they would have fresh meat. Life was good for now.

CHAPTER 36

Emma woke up and immediately sought out Hawks. She ran over to where he was sleeping. Carolyn called out, "Don't surprise him. Gently call out to rouse him. Never startle a man with a gun."

She called back, "Don't worry; I'll be sweet." All the calling back and forth had woken him up, and he was grinning when she came up and plopped down on his lap. He remembered when his kids were small. He missed having a little one looking up to him. He gave her a big hug.

"What say we see if the horses will eat some more; I want them well fed before we head out. We may have trouble finding them food with all this snow. They can go a while without eating, but they won't be able to carry us and their packs very far or fast if they are starving." Chuck rolled out of his sleeping bag and poured a cup of coffee from the pot simmering on the kerosene heater for some time.

He grimaced, "Wow, I believe that's the strongest cup of coffee I have ever drunk."

Carolyn added some water and said, "That should help a little, but I'm afraid we're a little short of creamer to tone it down."

Chuck piped up, "Thanks, I'll take the horses out and see if they are up to eating some more. They should be able to handle another feeding and watering. We can head out midmorning. If what Pete and Larry said are true, we may not have much trouble since we will be heading up to the pass. We should make it in a few days if we don't run into any trouble."

Hawks peeped out the man doors and windows. The coast was clear, so they rolled up the door and led the horses out. They ate for a bit, but were still full from the afternoon before. Once they were watered, they saddled them up for the trip. The puppies bounded out and burned off some energy before returning to join them. After consulting the map, they saddled up and headed out to the road, slowly making their way toward the road leading to the pass.

Once over the pass the going would be easier, and according to the route they planned, they avoided any large cities and villages. It would be impossible to make the trip without going through the area, but most of the people would be dead by now. Skinny people would have starved to death, and the others would have probably killed each other off by now.

Keeping their weapons at the ready, they dutifully headed down the road as the first town came into sight. They rode around abandoned vehicles and looked to see if there was smoke coming from any of the chimneys. It was eerily quiet; not even a dog was barking. Nothing caught the attention of the pups or of the horses.

They passed a farm store with the front doors wide open. They rode the horses up to the door. Hawks dismounted and tied his horses to one of the bollards by the front door. He moved his rifle into position and walked into the vacant building. All the dog food was gone, but there were bags of horse feed still stacked in the back. With Chuck and Carolyn standing guard, he carried out fifty-pound sacks of the feed and placed one on each of the pack horses and three across the saddle of the horse that didn't have a rider. He also found a small galvanized tub he lashed on the riderless horse's saddle. He could feed the horses from the tub.

Carolyn said, "Is that too much weight to add to the pack horses?"

"We'll feed them from those sacks first. I think they can handle the extra weight. We've been lightening their load as we have been using supplies from their packs as we traveled."

Emma asked, "Can people eat horse food?"

Hawks said, "No, that's why it is still in the store. All the dog food is gone because people can eat dog and cat food." He went back in and found some farrier tools he could use in case he had to take a loose shoe off any of the horses. He also found a brush he could brush them down with when they were unsaddled. Spray on antiseptic and some liniment for the horses and his knees rounded out his quick walkthrough.

They proceeded on their trip and only once did they see some smoke from the chimney of a house down a side road. They continued uninterrupted. They didn't stop until they were well out of town before resecuring the packs and checking on the horses' feet. The trip was going well so far. The puppies were getting tired, so he sat one on the back of Chuck's horse and the other on his. He let them ride for a few miles until they got fidgety and wanted down to run. They quickly learned to follow in the tracks of the horses where the snow had been trampled down.

It was getting dark as they approached a roadside park. There were several abandoned semi-trucks, two motorhomes, and a number of passenger cars. There was no one alive here that they could see. They rode to the back and up an embankment so they could overlook the parking lot and building. Once they were stopped, Chuck took his rifle and the pups and checked out all the vehicles and the rest area building.

He found several dead bodies. All the vending machines were empty; only the guest register and some maps remained. Chuck came back up the embankment with the pups. "There are only the dead back there. All the vehicles are empty. There's no food or anything I could see we could use. There are some wooden pallets on one of the trucks that we can use for firewood."

Hawks told Carolyn and Emma, "I want y'all to stay up here and stand guard. Chuck and I will carry up some of those wooden pallets."

Emma piped up, "Don't worry; me and the puppies will keep guard." Everyone grinned at her, and they proceeded to bust the pallets loose from the truck's trailer and drag them to their camp.

Soon they had a fire going and snow melting so they could water the horses. They created a picket line and had the horses tied, fed, and watered. They gave each horse several pounds of feed for the day.

Once everyone was fed, Hawks slung his rifle on his shoulder. "I'll take the first watch from across the lot. We really lucked out when we found the horse feed."

Chuck agreed. "We would be eating them in a few more days if we hadn't lucked up on the feed. There's no way to find grass to feed them going over the pass until we are at least halfway down the other side."

Emma grimaced. "I hope we don't have to eat our horses."

Carolyn told her, "I don't want to eat them either, so we're going to take real good care of them."

Hawks smiled at the girls and disappeared across the lot and found a spot where he could see the campfire on the hill as well as the lot. The bright moonlit night enabled him to clearly see the lot once his eyes adjusted to the night. He sat quiet for several hours and was almost ready to nod off. A fox caught his attention trotting across the lot, pausing to look under each car. He quickly darted under one; a rabbit darted out from under the other side with the fox in hot pursuit. The fox suddenly stopped, turned, and retreated; something had spooked him.

Hawks sat quietly and watched to see what had spooked the fox. A man crept up behind a car; his eyes were glued on the campfire. Hawks could see movement around the campfire. Chuck was adding some wood to the fire. The man pulled out a rifle and proceeded to take aim across the hood of the car. Hawks shot him through the back of the head, and he collapsed where he stood. The rifle stayed on the car as he fell to the ground. Hawks turned his attention away from the man. If anyone were with him, they would think he had made the shot. He sat still and waited; he knew Chuck had already moved the girls back into the brush to conceal them. No one showed up to check on the dead man; hopefully, he had no one with him or anyone waiting for him.

He was getting ready to move when out of the corner of his eye there was movement. A figure moved forward crouching, going from vehicle to vehicle. When the figure reached the dead man, it bent down and muttered, "Crap." It was a woman's voice. She stood and looked in every direction. She did not see Hawks as he remain motionless next to a large tree.

Hawks had her covered and waited. He watched as she turned back to rifle through the man's pockets before gathering his guns and ammo. She muttered to herself, "I told the son of a bitch not to try it again; I told him."

Hawks started to speak but decided to remain hidden as she returned from the direction from which she had come. Hawks waited a couple of hours before returning to camp.

Chuck waited for him. "I had the girls bedded down away from the fire; I heard you shoot."

Hawks said, "Let's move away from the fire. I killed a man who was fixing to snipe you from across the lot. There is a woman out there with his weapons. I should have shot her, but I thought it better to not reveal my position again."

Chuck said, "I'll take the next watch. I'll see you in the morning."

Carolyn left Emma snug in her sleeping bag and came to Hawks. "Are you OK? All this fighting and killing has got to weigh heavy on you."

Hawks lamented, "Maybe one day it will impact me. The trouble always came to us, we didn't ask for it nor have we instigated it. There are evil men in this world, and I'm not giving them a chance to hurt us. It's every man for himself."

"I heard you tell Chuck that there was a woman back there. Why didn't you kill her?"

"I started to, but I couldn't help but wonder if she had children to care for. I may live to regret it. Every time I failed to just kill when I had the opportunity, it came back to bite us."

Carolyn sighed. "Well I guess that is what separates us from the killers. Let's get some rest."

Hawks put some wood on the fire; the horses were close enough to get some heat from it. The less energy they spent trying to stay warm, the less feed they would require. They had a good winter coat, and they were holding up well to the cold so far. He scooped up a tub of snow and put it next to the fire so they would have water in the morning. He finished and went back to where the girls were sleeping. He wrapped himself up in a sleeping bag and used a saddle as a pillow. The rest of the night was peaceful, and he slept until dawn.

Chuck came into camp just as the sun was coming up. Hawks asked, "Was there anything going on last night?"

Chuck tilted his head in the direction of the lot. "I followed the woman's tracks back across the lot and into the woods. She was alone and had a fire going, I watched her for an hour or so. She has food, because she heated something up, ate, and went to bed. She didn't seem too upset."

Carolyn and Emma joined them at the fire. "I hope we run out of bad guys soon. I feel like we are in a war."

Emma clung to Hawks. "Are we going to be OK?"

Hawks picked her up. "I don't want you to worry. We are going to do everything in our power to keep us safe and to get us to a place where we can be safe forever."

Emma buried her little face against his cheek. "I miss my mommy and daddy."

Hawks held her close. "I know you do, but I will keep you safe and loved as long as I can, and so will Carolyn and Chuck."

Carolyn took her from Hawks. "Let's get the boys fed so we can head out."

The next three days were spent traveling and camping without incident. They were soon heading up the pass. Fortunately, there had been foot and vehicle traffic across the pass in recent days and weeks. The vehicles appeared to have been tracked vehicles as well as snowmobiles. The well-packed snow made travel easy. They were going through a choke point as there was no other way to cross the mountains without going through the pass. They were constantly on alert for ambush.

They passed many disabled vehicles on the roadway, along with evidence of violence as frozen patches of bloody snow were found on occasion. Several were where elk and deer had been butchered. Others were dead people who had been killed and left.

Once down the east side of the pass, the going was a bit easier as the road tended to be downhill. On the descent they paused as little as possible. They needed to get back below the timber line so there was fuel for fire and they could give the horses a much-needed rest. If they could get to where there was some grass, it would stretch out their horse feed. They pushed the horses on until they came to the timber line. They could smell wood smoke from somewhere south and west of them. A side road led up a trail where they could get out of sight and get set up before dark. The puppies surveyed the area quite thoroughly, putting them at ease for the moment.

Morning found them once again in the saddle heading for their planned destination. According to the map, they should soon be on the road leading to the first large lake on the Missouri River. Once there, all they had to do was follow the river, and if the horses gave out, they could find a boat and let the current carry them south.

They were in mostly remote areas now. Occasionally they spotted smoke in the distance. A cabin on the side of a mountain had smoke coming from a stove pipe on the roof. Under normal times, they might have ridden up and introduced themselves, but in this new reality, they were the prey. They found a burned-out cabin with a large barn close by.

Hawks told them, "Y'all stay put with you guns ready, I'm going to see if there is any hay or feed in that barn." With the pups leading the way, he rode up to the barn. There were no tracks in the snow. No one had been around here in recent days. He dismounted and tied the horses to the paddock fence. He went through the man door with his rifle ready. It was empty, but as expected, it had hay and horse feed in barrels. He walked down and called for them to join him. Soon they had the horses inside and fed and watered from melted snow.

Chuck checked out the burned cabin. All he could see was the burned out remains that had collapsed into the basement. Anyone here was either dead or long gone.

They found some contractor garbage bags and sacked up another supply of horse feed to carry with them. After letting the horses rest unloaded for a couple of hours, they reloaded their packs and headed out.

In three more days, they came to a highway turning south and took it. It had been recently plowed, and it made the going easy for a change. The horses weren't having to push through the snow.

Carolyn asked Hawks, "What do we do if the snowplow comes back our way?"

"If they put up a fight, we'll just have to go off the road or stand and fight." The puppies turned and howled. In the distance behind them they could hear the whine of snowmobile engines.

Chuck called out, "We've got trouble. I'm sure they are heading our way."

Hawks told them, "Let's ride hard to see if we can get to a protected area that we can defend."

They put the horses into a gallop and headed down the plowed road. Hawks looked over his shoulder and could see the snowmobiles in the distance, and they were closing fast. The crack of a bullet passed near him as he neared where the plowed road turned up a driveway heading to a log cabin.

He yelled out, "Follow me and don't stop."

They were halfway up the hill when the snowmobiles reached the bottom of the drive. Bullets were flying, so he motioned for Carolyn and Emma to head to the log cabin. He pulled out his rifle and opened up on the snowmobiles and their riders. Chuck caught a bullet between his shoulder blades but hung on as his horses charged past Hawks. The pups were hot on his trail. He heard gunfire from behind him. He assumed Carolyn was firing but couldn't stop to turn and see.

Suddenly his horse leaped in the air, the two pack horses took off following the others up the drive. His horse turned and galloped up the road, oblivious to Hawks trying to turn it. The horse made it to the top before collapsing and sending Hawks flying. The horse had been shot and had made it to the top of the drive before dying. Hawks jumped behind the dead horse and starting firing across his saddle at the snowmobiles now halfway up the drive. There were at least a half a dozen snowmobiles. They turned and headed back down the drive and retreated in the direction from which they had come. The pups continued barking until they were out of hearing. Hawks looked around and saw that Chuck was dead where he had fallen from his horse.

Hawks called out, "Carolyn, Emma, are y'all OK?"

They both yelled, 'We're OK."

Carolyn came down the back steps of the house and told Emma, "Stay inside."

They both looked at Chuck, who was obviously dead. Hawks took his rifle and pistol belt and handed them to Carolyn. "I'll carry him back to the barn. Thanks for giving me cover while I was fighting down the drive."

She said, "It wasn't me; it was him," pointing to Dawson coming down the back steps.

Dawson came down with his rifle in his hands. He asked, "Are you hit?"

Hawks looked up, "No, just mad as hell and ready to follow them. Why didn't you shoot us?"

Dawson pointed to Carolyn. "I figure anyone trying to get away from trouble with a young child are not attacking. I've been expecting someone to follow the plowed road and driveway. That is the only way we made it this far is by using the snowplow."

Hawks turned to Chuck lying dead in the snow, "I need to get Chuck taken care of."

Dawson told Carolyn, "I'm Dawson Stewart, please introduce yourselves to Cathy and the kids inside."

Carolyn answered, "I'm Carolyn, this is Hawks, and our little girl is Emma. We rescued her sometime back; she is our little girl now."

While Carolyn went back into the cabin, Hawks and Dawson carried Chuck back into the barn and placed him on a table in the back.

Dawson told Hawks, "There is a stable with horse feed and a

cistern where we can get water for them. Let's get them out of the weather and safe from gunfire."

They rounded up the horses and had them unsaddled and in the stalls. Before unsaddling Chuck's mount, he rode him to the bottom of the drive to see if he could see any sign of the snowmobiles. There were several bloody patches in the snow. Some of their return fire had struck home. He rode back up and put the horse away, and once they were fed and watered, he turned to the task of dealing with the dead horse.

Dawson quietly stated, "We are short of fresh meat. I think we need to get this horse butchered up before it freezes."

"I agree."

Dawson motioned for him to follow. "First, let's go meet my family and get to know one another."

They went inside and formally introduced themselves. Hawks found Emma near the woodstove not saying anything. He held her close and said, "I have some terrible news. Chuck was killed by the bad guys. There was nothing I could do to save him. He didn't suffer because it happened so fast."

Emma started crying. "What do we do now?"

Carolyn was there, and she said, "Nothing has changed. You're still our little girl. We are safe and warm for now; we have some new friends that I'm sure will let us stay for a couple of days."

Cathy spoke up, "You can stay as long as you need. We couldn't have survived an attack like that by ourselves." BC and Lucy came out from hiding.

Cathy introduced them, "This is Emma. I want you to welcome her and show her around." They soon had Emma in tow and showed her the entire cabin.

Dawson turned to Cathy and Carolyn. "Hawks and I are going to butcher the dead horse. We'll bring in some meat to cook later."

CHAPTER 37

It didn't take them long to get the saddle and bridle off of the dead mare and stowed in the tack room. They saddled a couple of the horses and used them to drag the dead horse up to the room next to the barn where elk and deer were processed. They put the horses away and hooked the dead mare up to the winch in the room. The puppies had a keen interest in the dead horse. They hooked up the gambrel to the rear legs and winched the mare into the room. They pulled the carcass part of the way up and realized they were about to overload the winch and gambrel. They gutted the horse and drug the entrails out of the door where they removed the heart and liver. They put the rest in buckets outside to freeze to feed the puppies later.

They hoisted the carcass up and proceeded to skin it. Dawson pointed toward the driveway. "I expect those thugs will be coming back."

Hawks' face tightened. "I expect they'll be licking their wounds today and tonight. They'll have to work up their courage to come back. We'll be ready for them. They won't expect one of us to be set up away from the cabin. How far can you hit with your rifle?"

"Everyone I've killed so far has been pretty close. I under- stand that these rifles are good out to three hundred meters. I haven't had the opportunity to range it. I've been trying to stay low key."

Hawks said, "While we have the opportunity, let's set up some targets at one hundred, two hundred, and three hundred yards. The rifles with the red dot scopes should be sighted in. I believe all of them are military and police issued. We were making hits on them halfway down the drive. There was too much blood for them to be hit by stray bullets. There are stakes along the driveway so it can be navigated when the snow piles up. I suggest we pick out one about half way down the drive and see how close we can get to it."

"Great idea. Let's finishing cutting up this carcass and get this meat put away."

Carolyn sat by the window looking down the driveway. There was no one she could see down the drive or the road.

Cathy came over. "You can go get cleaned up. I have hot water on the wood heater."

"Thanks, it's been a few days since we had a chance to stop long enough to rest and clean up."

Cathy said, "Help me carry this to the tub. You can get a bath. I'll start melting a fresh bucket of water for Emma and then for Hawks."

Soon, everyone was bathed, had fresh clothes, and were fed. Carolyn asked, "What do we do now?"

Hawks said, "Running is out of the question now. We can't outrun snowmobiles on horses or with the Power Wagon."

Dawson agreed. "We've got to take the fight to them. I don't want them attacking or sniping the house with the kids in here."

Cathy said, "Why don't Carolyn and I take the kids back up into the mountains a couple of miles. We have tents and camping equipment, snowshoes, and the sleds. They like camping, and we'll be more trouble than its worth for them to come look for us."

Hawks agreed. "Great idea, I can fight a lot better knowing that you guys are out of harm's way. Let's get started. Those guys aren't going to wait forever. If one of them has a scoped deer rifle, we're in trouble." Dawson stood and grabbed his coat. "I'll get the sleds, snowshoes, and camping equipment out of the trailer so we can get started."

Emma, BC, and Lucy came into the room. Carolyn asked, "Are you kids ready to go camping in the mountains?"

Emma pointed out, "Do we have to? We've been camping for days."

Carolyn smiled. "I know, sweetie; we'll try to have fun this time. You can show BC and Lucy how we do it."

Emma asked, "Do we get to ride the horses?"

Hawks scooped her up. "Not this time, the horses are going to get a well-deserved rest."

It took them a couple of hours to get them packed and in their winter clothes. The temperature was in the twenties but not warm enough to start a melt. The cabin had a map of the trail with locations of hunting blinds and stands for the guides and hunters. Dawson brought it out and showed them where to go. The trails should be well marked and obvious, even with the snow. Dawson pointed to the map to a desired location.

Carolyn grinned. "I don't think we'll have any trouble." Without a word, she and Cathy armed up with their rifles, pistols, and packs of extra ammo mags. The kids each had a toy and their backpacks. The pups were getting older, and they followed the kids.

Hawks went with them to the first waypoint to make certain they could follow the trail. Hawks made sure the pups stayed with them. They would give them an added layer of security. They would bark if anything or anyone showed up.

He kissed Carolyn and Emma. "We're going to sight in a

couple of rifles as soon as I get back, so don't be alarmed. If you hear some shooting later, it will be us fighting."

He headed back down the trail to the cabin where he found Dawson coming down the hill from the north side of the cabin. Hawks asked him, "You're putting a lot of trust in someone you just met."

Dawson pointed down the hill at the wooden stake on the trail. "Sometimes you have to go with your gut. My grandfather called it his "Zizzy Witch." It's more than a gut feeling. It's like an inner voice that compels you to do or think something. Sometimes it is as simple as don't get on that bus or telling you to shoot first and ask questions later."

Hawks agreed. "I think I have a touch of it at times. That's why I didn't kill Chuck when I first met him. How long have you and Cathy been together?"

"I'm not sure. We were literally thrown together when all this started. I saved her and her family and we were attacked and everyone but the four of us were killed. I killed the bad guys, and we've been running for our lives ever since. To make a long story short, I'm a family man. How about you?"

"My story is much the same. We met when the lights went out. We hit it off and managed our escape. We realized that the place we were trying to live was a target. I have or had a cabin in the Ozarks where there are few people, and I can hunt and fish in the mountains and hopefully keep us safe and fed. What are your plans?"

"I have or rather had a camp down in South Louisiana. I fig-ure most everyone will be dead or have killed each other by the time we get back. I grew up in the marsh and bayous. I can feed us there. We ran across this abandoned log cabin and with our food we can hold out for a year if needed. I figure we have just lucked out so far running this old Power Wagon. I am thinking about staying until spring thaw, that way if the Power Wagon dies, we can continue on foot. If we can get below the manmade lakes on the Missouri, we can get a boat and float all the way to South Louisiana."

"That's what we had in mind as well. The horses are mortal; when one of them goes down, our only option is to eat them or leave them."

They took out several of the rifles and took turns firing at the wooden stake. They selected the two that were most accurate at that distance. They soon had them outfitted with the slings from the rifles they had been packing. They had accurate rifles with red-dot scopes and plenty of loaded mags.

Dawson turned to Hawks. "Do we go find them or wait for them to come back?"

"We know they came from up the road, but from how far we don't know. It all depends on how much fuel they have."

"Let's assume they have plenty. I found fuel my entire trip. There are so many dead vehicles that still have gas in their tanks, they should have plenty."

Hawks surveyed the terrain. "If you were them and wanted to take us, what would you do?"

"I'd come from the woods. They could stop a couple of miles down the road and work their way through the forest. They are expecting us to look for them coming back down the highway. They may even come roaring past the drive on some snowmobiles to divert our attention. While you were taking the families away, I found a couple of spots where we can cover the cabin and the woods up on that hill."

Hawks agreed. "Good tactical thinking. Don't start shooting until we have as many as possible exposed. I want to kill them all if possible. Chuck is lying in that barn dead because of them."

They loaded up and headed to the woods. Dawson showed

Hawks a rock outcropping where there was cover and conceal-ment. "From there you can see the cabin, the highway north of the driveway, and anyone sneaking through the woods. I'm heading west up that ridge where I can cover the woods, the cabin, and the trail the family took. I can also cover your position in case you are pinned down."

Hawks asked, "What do I do if you're overrun?"

"You better come running. If they try to take the cabin or come up through the woods, we'll have them in a crossfire."

Hawks gave him a nod. "Good luck, I'll take care of your fam-ily if something happens."

Dawson grinned. "My Zizzy Witch already told me that you would."

"Let's get into position. I hope it's not a long night."

Hawks pointed out, "Unless they have lights, they'll have to come when it's light enough to see."

Hawks found a spot where he could sit with plenty of rocks to cover him should he come under fire. It would be highly unlikely anyone would spot him from his perch. He watched as Dawson disappeared up the hill. He could see the top third of the driveway and the area in front of the cabin, as well as all the parking level, including the front of the barn and stables. He kept his ears peeled for any engine noise on the wind. The one thing that was hard to become accustomed to was the total absence of any equipment noise. You never realize how much noise all the machines make in modern society. There was only the wind, birds, water, and animals now.

Dawson reached his perch above Hawks. From this spot he could see the rear of the cabin and the rear of the barns and stable. The driveway was not visible, but most of the parking area was in sight. He could look down through the woods and canopy and see the forest floor between him and Hawks, as well as Hawks sitting in the rocks. Anyone walking between them would be committing suicide. He wished they would return soon; he wasn't looking forward to a cold night in the mountains, but a fire was out of the question. He remembered standing guard in the blind back at the McGregor lodge. That seemed like a long time ago, but it had only been a few weeks. He thought, By necessity, I have turned into a cold-blooded killer. Fortunately, they had enough food to last them quite a while. Against all odds he had found Henry, who unwittingly had food and the McGregors who had food. If he hadn't literally lucked up, he would probably be no better than the raiders coming after him now.

Hawks settled back and listened. There were some snowshoe rabbits starting to move. Now would be a good time to have a sling shot or bow and arrow. His homemade bow was back on the farm on Vancouver Island. The silence was broken by the distant sound of snowmobile engines. He wondered what Dawson's Zizzy Witch was telling him now.

CHAPTER 38

Cathy had a small, warm fire going with a pot of melted snow perched across several rocks to keep it above the flame and coals. Carolyn and the kids had the tent set up and the sleeping bags unrolled. The kids played well together and had already built a snowman; BC was working on a snow fort. They turned the sleds over to use as seating around the fire.

Carolyn asked Cathy, "How long have you known Dawson?"

"We met about three days after the lights went out. He was renting an apartment from my mother, and he saved us. His girlfriend, my mother, and uncle were killed. He was almost killed, but he killed all the men who attacked us. He took all their guns, gear, food, and vehicle and carried me and my kids to safety. One thing led to another, and we're together. I am his wife for all intents and purposes. We desperately need him, and I think he needs us. Love grows each day. I was divorced and my ex-husband was a terrible father. Dawson has been more of a husband in the last few weeks than my ex was the entire time we were married. How about you and Mr. Hawks?"

Carolyn smiled. "I've spent my entire life not having or knowing a decent man other than my father. We met the day the lights went out. He has known what to do and has saved us over and over. I never had kids until we found Emma on the side of the road. I have a man I love and respect and a little girl that needs me. My life consisted of going to work at the paper mill and coming home to eat by myself. My father died some time back, so it was just me. I hate to say it, but the lights going out have let me live again. I've made love, run for my life, killed bad guys, ridden horses, camped, and now I have a little girl. That's a lot of living in a short time."

Cathy agreed. "I feel like I've lived a lifetime in the last few weeks and I have so much more to live for. If we can make it south to Dawson's camp in the marsh, I think we can have a safe, happy life."

Emma came up and sat on Carolyn's lap. "I'm glad we came camping. I'm having fun."

She hugged her neck and Carolyn held her close. "Let's let our hearts talk."

Emma whispered in her ear, "What are they talking about?"

Carolyn whispered back, "I'm sure they are telling each other how much they like and love each other." After a minute she said, "Are you kids ready to eat?"

They all gathered and enjoyed their meal. Lucy pointed out, "This would really be good if we had some marshmallows to toast." They all agreed. The pups finished up the scraps, and they got ready for a quiet night. After a few more stories, Cathy added another log to the fire, and they zipped up the tent flap.

She told them, "I'll stand guard until later. I'll wake you later when I start getting drowsy."

Carolyn answered, "If I wake up later, I'll come out and get you."

Cathy and the pups sat by the fire for hours. The sky was clear and there was a bright, full moon. Wolves were howling in the distance. Cathy hoped they weren't following the scent of the horse meat they roasted on the fire. All was quiet for a while, and the thoughts of wolves faded. A shift in the wind brought the smoke toward her, so she moved to the other side of the fire. The pups' ears perked up, and they started to growl. Cathy knew the wolves would also look at the pups and themselves as food. The last thing she needed was them trying to take on the wolves.

Carolyn heard the commotion and came out, saying, "I hear the commotion."

"Get the puppies in the tent. There are wolves coming."

Carolyn pointed to the fire. "Let's build up the fire. I don't want to start shooting and distract our men. If the wolves get too brave, we can shoot; otherwise, we've got to just keep them at bay."

Cathy pointed in the direction of the howling she had heard earlier. "I hope they haven't lost their fear of man."

The wolves came and stayed just out of the light from the fire. The puppies were barking and the kids were awake.

Carolyn told them, "Stay in the tent with the puppies. Everything is OK out here; just stay in the tent."

They gathered some rocks for throwing and waited. Slowly the wolves got bolder and ventured closer, and they could clearly be seen. One tried to slip in behind the tent but was met with a rock the size of a tennis ball. It yelped, and they all retreated for a moment, but they soon got up their nerve again. They threw some more wood on the fire and soon had a good blaze; the battle was now if they could keep the fire going without having to venture too far away.

The fire was starting to dim but there was no shortage of rocks. They continued the fire for several more hours when they heard the echo of gunfire from in the direction of the log cabin. The sound of the gunfire cowered the wolves. They seemed to have regained their lost fear and disappeared into the darkness.

Cathy and Carolyn clung to each other as they listened in

terror as the gunfire continued for another thirty minutes. Cathy asked, "What do we do?"

Carolyn looked into the darkness and said, "We wait. We have three kids to protect. If they are fighting now like they've fought so far, one of them will be coming for us in the morning." One last gunshot rang out and then silence.

CHAPTER 39

Hawks looked down at the dead man, the contents of his skull in stark contrast to the white snow. His last shot had finished him off. They had come much as they had suspected. A group of seven had come up the side of the mountain through the forest directly between him and Dawson. Another group had fired up their snowmobiles and ran down the road below the driveway to the cabin. They had let the group get almost to the cabin before firing on them. Their gunfire from above them had been devastating. Once the shooting had started, the men on the snowmobiles had come charging up the driveway in anticipation of helping their comrades.

Hawks had the best view of the driveway. He had slapped in a fresh magazine and waited until they were almost to the top so that he could clearly see them in the bright moonlight. They had their headlights on, which made them easy to see and track. He had aimed at the rear one first and shot three rounds just across the handlebars and seat. Without slowing he had done the same thing on the other five machines. He had continued firing until his magazine was empty and slapped in a fresh thirty-round one. He had turned to head in their direction when gunfire erupted from down in the woods below. A round had hit the rocks around him, sending a rock fragment flying into his forehead. Dawson had opened on the two men in the woods they hadn't spotted. With blood pouring down his face, Hawks had gone down to the parking area, making kill shots on all the bodies in the woods. He had proceeded down the driveway to where the wrecked snowmobiles lay running and finished them off.

Dawson came down from his perch to where Hawks stood wiping the blood from his eyes. A moment later, one of the men who had made it to the top of the driveway moaned and looked up at Hawks. It was then that Hawks blew his brains out.

Dawson said, "We need to get you cleaned up."

Hawks said, "Not yet, there may be some more waiting down the road. I want to take one of these machines and run down the hill and down the road. If someone is there, they won't expect one of us to come riding up on one of these machines."

Dawson said, "I'll do it. I don't have blood in my eyes."

Hawks agreed. "I can't argue with you, good luck."

Dawson climbed onto one of the running machines and turned it down the driveway. His rifle was fully loaded and hung in front of him, resting across his lap. He ran down the road at full throttle and never found anyone. They had lucked out and gotten them all. He turned and headed back to the cabin where he found Hawks wrapping a bandana around his bloody head.

Hawks said, "We've got a mess to clean up. I don't want the kids seeing this."

Dawson pointed out, "I know they are small, but maybe they need to see us tending to them without emotion. My little ones watched me kill people, dispose of bodies, and bury our families."

Hawks nodded in agreement. "I guess they won't have the innocence of childhood that we enjoyed. I'll start dragging out the bodies if you'll go tell Carolyn and Cathy that we survived."

Dawson said, "Good idea. We need to get your head wound tended to. You don't want me trying to stitch you up."

The sun was starting to come up as Dawson headed out on foot; their path was easy to follow in the snow. When he arrived, he found the tent and the fire but the family was out of sight.

He walked up to the light of the fire and called out, "It's me, Dawson."

BC and Lucy came running out from behind some bushes and tackled him. Cathy was right behind them and hugged his neck. "How's Hawks? I assume y'all got the bad guys."

Carolyn asked, "What happened?"

Dawson said, "They came just like we expected, I think we got all of them. Hawks may need a few stitches, but otherwise we are good, just a mess to clean up and some equipment to store."

Hawks proceeded to gather the weapons, unload them, and stack them in the barn. Once he had the weapons safely stored, he began dragging out the dead and going through their pockets. Most had government-issued ID and carried Glock 19 pistols. There were five MP5 submachine guns, and the rest were M4 Colt rifles. The snowmobiles were mostly older ones of various makes. He wondered where they were encamped and who was waiting on them.

Once he had the contents of their pockets unloaded and put in a bucket, he stripped off any clothing items he thought they could use and put in a pile. He tied their legs together at the ankles with some string from around the bales of hay in the barn. He then tied three of them together behind one of the snowmobiles so he could drag them away.

The puppies were the first to arrive. The hair on their backs stood up as they smelled the blood and all the dead. Carolyn called out from the trail when she saw the bandana tied around his head, "Oh baby, let me see."

She and Emma ran up and almost toppled him hugging him. Cathy and the twins followed. The kids were busy ogling the dead;

Dawson didn't make a big deal if it. "Kids, this is what happens when you try to kill and steal from folks like us. We'll get them hauled off like the garbage they are."

Cathy said, "Let's get inside and get the heater stoked up. We'll pack away the camping gear once we get warmed up."

As they watched Cathy and the three kids head into the house, Carolyn asked, "How are we going to dispose of the bodies?"

Dawson said, "I plan to drag them back up the trail with one of the horses where there is a cliff we can throw them over. The only thing that will find them will be wolves, coyotes, and bears once they come out of hibernation. I can take it from here. Hawks, you get inside so the gals can get your head patched up."

Hawks agreed. "Good idea, I thought about taking the bodies down the road and piling them up in the middle, but having them simply disappear will have a more profound effect on anyone who comes to look for them. Let's stow the snowmobiles behind the barn out of sight."

Carolyn took Hawks into the kitchen and set up a kerosene lamp so she could get a good look at his wound. The rock shard had cut a gash across the middle of his forehead. Cathy came over and looked. "I found some super glue. I think this will be a good opportunity to try it."

Hawks' dry humor surfaced, "Do you think you can do it without gluing your thumbs to my head?"

Carolyn grinned as she swabbed it with alcohol before gluing the skin back together. She asked, "Does it hurt?"

Hawks answered, "Everything hurts. I've been sleeping on the ground, leaning against trees, climbing rocks, dragging deer, riding horses, and killing people. I think the only thing that doesn't hurt are my teeth."

Cathy came over with a shot glass filled with bourbon. "I found some liquor in a cabinet when we moved in. This will help you feel better. I've made up a bed in one of the bedrooms. I suggest you get some rest."

"I'll take your advice; I appreciate you taking care of us."

Cathy pointed out, "There is no way we could have survived if that gang had attacked with just me and Dawson." Hawks drank the bourbon and let Cathy lead him to the bedroom. He leaned his rifle on the wall between the bed and nightstand. He did not take off his pistol or take off his boots. He lay on top of the covers. Carolyn covered him with a quilt. Oblivious to his throbbing head, he soon fell sound asleep. Later in the day, he awoke to Carolyn gently stroking his hair.

"We got the yard cleaned up, the bodies hauled off, and the snowmobiles stowed behind the barn. Dawson is taking a nap, and the kids are playing quietly in their room. We also moved Chuck out to the other side of the cabin. The ground was frozen, so we covered him in a deep layer of rock and stones. If we are still here after the spring thaw, we can add some soil. We will have a service for him the first chance we get."

Hawks sat on the side of the bed. "I needed that rest. I guess Chuck is just going to be another orphan of history. His family is probably dead, and if they make it back, all they will find is an empty looted house. We sure could have used him to perform a wedding ceremony for us."

Carolyn smiled. "That was a beautiful proposal, and yes, I accept." They kissed and went into the main room.

Cathy had been standing watch at the window. Hawks slipped on his jacket and headed to the door. "I'll watch from outside for a while. I want to listen for anymore snowmobile engines in the distance. In this cold, clear air, we can hear from far away."

He went out into the late-afternoon sun and stood by Chuck's grave. He only had good thoughts of the man and he would never forget him. Dawson came out and stood by the grave with Hawks.

"I don't know about you, but I'm tired of fighting for our lives and running."

Hawks pointed to Chuck's grave. "What he said was true. Most of the everyday people will starve or get killed. He pointed out that the people in the military and law enforcement would be taking what they need for themselves and their kin. That is mostly who we've been fighting."

"Do you think there's more of them?"

"If I were to venture a guess, I'd say yes. They were well out-fitted, and none of them appeared to be on starvation. I bet there are survivors of the ones we shot up yesterday laid up somewhere, and I bet they have their families with them as well."

Dawson said, "I see where we only have two options, go find and kill them or pack up and run."

Hawks looked over at Carolyn and Cathy. "I'm done running. I'm tired. Every muscle in my body hurts along with my head. I think I'm going to take my rifle and finish it."

Carolyn looked at him. "I don't want you hurt or killed; we can't go on without you."

Hawks looked around at Dawson. "I know what you are think-ing. You can't come with me. You have to take care of them if I don't come back."

Carolyn asked, "Can you at least wait until morning?"

He took her hand. "There's a full moon. I can see the trail, and they won't be expecting a man by himself. Can you find me a white sheet and a white pillowcase? I want to make a white parka and cover my hat with a pillow case. If I move slow, once I get within sight of them, they won't spot me until it's too late."

Once dressed in his snow camo, he kissed them goodbye and headed down the drive toward the roadway. He looked back to see Emma waving, he waved back and wondered if he was making a good decision. The time had come to go to war.

CHAPTER 40

Alcied White sat next to the fire in the fireplace. His shoulder ached from where it had been dislocated. When the shooting started from the man on horseback, it hit his brother Fount, who was driving the snowmobile he was riding. In the confusion, Fount was hit through the shoulder, and the snowmobile turned over and rolled down the hill and landed sitting up. His shoulder was dislocated, and Fount was bleeding profusely. Fount managed to get back on the machine now pointing downhill, so they, along with their companions, ran for their lives. Two of the other men were hit; one of them died on the way back, the other one was lying in a bunk gut shot with no hope of surviving. The women tended to him while he lay in a coma gasping for breath. The one medic, now dead, in their group had put his shoulder back in its socket.

Fount sat at the table with his arm in a sling. "I wonder why they haven't come back?"

Alcied looked up and said, "I think we know why. They shouldn't have been greedy; our entire company is now gone. It's just us, the women, and kids. We have at least two years of food. I shouldn't have sent them out in the first place."

Fount said, "They wanted revenge, and it got them all killed."

Alcied pointed out, "If I were them, I'd come clean us out. They don't act like people who'd run."

Alcied's wife Mattie came out of the back room. "Eugene just died; what do we do?"

Alcied pointed to the kitchen and great room, "Go get the ladies. Y'all are going to have to take him out and make a grave next to George."

She looked puzzled. "Can we wait until the boys get back?"

Fount spoke up, "They aren't coming back."

She put her hand to her throat. "They are surely coming back, aren't they? Maybe they are being held prisoner."

Alcied shook his head. "They would have been back midmorning at the latest. It's only about five miles away. They could have walked back by now. How many prisoners have we ever taken?" Mattie called in all the ladies and gave them the bad news. They in turn told their children. The old lodge was filled with great sorrow and dread.

Mattie came back to Alcied. "Do we stay here and wait, or do we go looking for our boys?"

"All we are going to find is a pile of bodies or nothing at all. There's nothing we can do. I think you girls can put up a fight here if it comes to it. None of us are capable of mounting an offensive. Me and Fount can't even fire a rifle right now, and we can't attack with one arm and just pistols. Most of our rifles were carried by the boys."

Fount pointed out, "We are at their mercy. You girls need to keep your pistols handy. We don't know how many there are and if they will be coming for us."

Mattie asked, "Can we make peace with them?"

Alcied shrugged. "If they let us get within a half a mile, they might."

Mattie said, "I'll do it."

"No, you won't. You're the only thing that's going to hold our group together. If I were them, I'd drop you as soon as you were within range. We attacked them unprovoked."

They spent the rest of the day waiting. Alcied kept going to the door and looking down the snow-covered road. He pulled his old police badge from his pocket and rubbed it with his thumb before returning it to his pocket. Twenty years in the TSA had amounted to nothing now. He had commanded this group from the very start. Once the lights went out, they managed to gather their families and commandeer this old ski lodge along with all its equipment. They also confiscated all the food and equipment from every house, business, and lodge they had found. They had cleaned out the hunting lodge where the fight took place a month earlier. They killed the former occupants down the road and stole what little food they had.

Fount sat at the table drinking a cup of coffee. "I wish we hadn't seen those horses. We might have ignored them. I wish we could have some fresh meat right now, even if it is horse."

Alcied said, "I'm getting tired of eating MRE's from that FEMA warehouse we cleaned out too. But at least we have a couple of years' worth, and I'm glad the old school bus held up for the three trips it took to get it all here."

Fount asked, "Do you think they would suspect one man sneaking in with just a pistol?"

"I'm sure that no one is going to sneak up on them. Our best bet is to sit tight and hope for a snowstorm to hide our trail."

It took Hawks several hours following the snowmobile tracks to reach the sign pointing to the ski lodge. He stopped and waited to see if there was any activity he could see or hear. If they were smart, they would be laying in ambush, but would they expect someone to just quietly walk up to the door? He remembered how Chuck had just walked straight up to him back at the farm on the island. He thought, If we had Dawson back on the island, maybe we could have held out. He slowly made his way up the road, and when within sight of the lodge, he started moving slow, keeping to the side so that he was obscured from the windows. He was able to follow a snowmobile trail up to one side that gave him a commanding view of the lodge. He couldn't believe there was no one standing guard. It was at that moment he realized there was a good chance he and Dawson had killed most or all of the able-bodied men.

He sat on the ridge where he could see the front windows. As he sat, he occasionally saw a man come to one of the downstairs windows and look out. There were lights in some of the upstairs rooms; it was obviously occupied by a number of people. There was no wind, so he was able to tolerate the cold as he sat and waited. The sun came up, and he waited. He watched a half dozen women carry out a body and create a grave next to a previous one. The first grave was recent; it was not covered in snow yet. There were children helping gather stones. He had no intention of killing children.

Alcied and Fount watched as the ladies and kids buried Eugene. Alcied said, "We need to go out and say something."

Fount turned and looked at him. "Do you think it's wise for both of us to go out at the same time?"

"I think we can chance it; I doubt anyone would attack in broad daylight." They walked out to the grave and resisted the urge to look around. They wanted to appear confident for the families and to anyone watching them.

Hawks was watching when the two men came out; both had their arms in slings. They had obviously been injured in the attack yesterday. A couple of the women were holding rifles. He thought he spotted pistols in drop holsters on the men. Before they could say anything, Hawks put the red dot from his rifle sight between the shoulder blade of the first man and followed up with a shot to the torso of the second. Alcied and Fount both collapsed where they stood. One of the women started to raise her rifle but dropped it and ran. He then turned his attention back to the two men on the ground. He ran five more rounds into each of their thrashing bodies to make sure they were finished. The women and children ran for the lodge and quickly disappeared thru the side door. A few minutes later a woman walked out holding a white cloth over her head.

She called out, "Can we talk?" Hawks carefully looked at every window to make sure there wasn't an open one someone could shoot from. There was no indication of anyone even looking out, let alone trying to shoot.

He called down, "What do you want to talk about?"

She answered, "I'm Mattie, you just killed my husband and brother-in-law. We have no more living men here. It's just six women and our children, and we don't want to die."

Hawks called down, "Don't even think about coming to look for us. If we catch any of you anywhere south of here, we'll kill all of you. All your men are dead, and I will personally burn all of you alive in this lodge if I even think you are heading in our direction. Remember, you sorry animals started this; do you understand?"

She answered, "You'll never see or hear us again." She turned and disappeared back through the door she had come out.

Hawks quietly backed his way out of sight of the lodge and made his way back to the road. He waited to make certain none of the women or kids had tried to follow. He got back to the hunting lodge by midafternoon and was greeted by Dawson, who had been watching the road. "What happened?"

"I killed the two men who were there. There were two fresh graves from the ones we shot when they were trying to kill us when we got here. A lady came out with a white flag and begged me not to kill them. We've apparently killed all the men, only women and children remain. I explained that if we saw any of them again, we would burn them alive in the ski lodge. I think they got the message."

They walked back through the back door; Carolyn and Emma stormed him. Emma hung on to him as if she couldn't believe he was really back. "Don't die, Poppy; please, don't die."

He cradled her. "I'm OK, Sweetie Pop. I'm not going to die anytime soon if I can help it. There will be times when I have to protect you and your mommy. Please believe me; I have no intention of dying or getting hurt."

Carolyn kissed him on the cheek. "Just make sure you don't."

Cathy and the twins were watching from the kitchen. Cathy said, "That goes for all of us too."

Dawson came in the back door. "We've had a busy couple of days. I suggest we spend a few days resting up and praying for snow. A good snow would make sure those women back there stay put. If there was no return fire when you finished off the men, tells me they aren't trained or particularly upset."

"One of them dropped her gun and ran; the other one ran for cover into the house with the other women and children."

Hawks pointed out, "The puppies don't miss much, so we can let them run loose."

Cathy said, "We have to keep an eye out for wolves. We had to hold off a pack when we were camping. I'm sure the pups are on their menu."

Dawson added, "I'm sure they have horses on the menu as well. We need to shoot any that we see." Hawks went and sat down by the wood heater. "I am still chilled to the bone from sitting out all night. Tomorrow, after I'm rested, I want us to sit down so we can make plans."

Cathy and Carolyn disappeared back into the kitchen and Dawson went out to water and tend to the horses. The kids sat quietly playing a card game on the large wooden table serving as kitchen and dining room table. Before he knew it, he fell asleep by the fire and dreamed about laying in ambush for the men at the ski lodge. Carolyn came and woke him for supper.

Dawson sat at the window watching the road. The puppies were coming and going as they got cold and barked to come in. The house was alive with the kids and dogs. Rather than waste kerosene to light the house, everyone went to bed except for Dawson, who rested on the couch near the woodstove.

Carolyn led Hawks to the bedroom and told him, "I'll be right back."

She came back with Emma, who said, "Goodnight, Poppy, I have my own bed in the room with BC and Lucy."

Hawks squeezed her hand and told her, "Have sweet dreams; we're safe, warm, and fed. I'll see you in the morning."

Carolyn took her to bed and tucked her in. "Good night, if you need us, come knock on the door." Carolyn went back to the bedroom where Hawks was getting undressed. She closed and bolted the door behind her. Hawks was down to his long johns and was getting ready to climb into bed.

She quickly undressed but did not stop with her long johns. She climbed into bed and told him, "I think you need a poor man's sleeping pill."

Hawks smiled. "I've never heard it put that way." He blew out the lantern and climbed into the bed.

Cathy came up to the front room to sit with Dawson after she had BC and Lucy tucked in. She sat with her head leaning on his shoulder. She was freshly bathed, and Dawson could smell the remnants of the soap she had used to wash her hair.

Dawson asked her, "Do you want to travel with them when we take the trail south?"

She held his hand. "I think we are lucky to have them. If those men from the ski lodge knew we were here, they would have simply come here and killed us. I realize they wouldn't have found us right away if they hadn't chased Hawks and Carolyn up here. But let's face it; one man can't defend this place, especially since we have the kids to protect."

"It's been about six weeks. The only people left alive will be the ones who have food storage or those who have robbed and killed the ones who do. You would think the supply of bad guys should be starting to dwindle."

Cathy lamented, "If we don't get to a location where there is lots of game, we'll be going hungry and may have to take drastic measures. I'm not going to let my children starve."

Dawson said, "There may still be a good population of elk, bear, deer, and buffalo up here. We'll know once the snow starts to melt. The animals may start moving back up into the mountains. This hunting lodge is here for a reason."

Cathy left Dawson standing watch and disappeared down the hall to their room. The pups were curled up near the woodstove on a rug. Dawson stoked the stove and relaxed in a leather arm chair with his feet resting on a matching ottoman. From where he sat, he was not visible from any of the windows or door glass, so he allowed himself the luxury of dozing. His rifle rested in his lap and his pistol was in its holster on his belt.

The next morning, Hawks was the first to rise. As was his habit, he looked out the bedroom window to make sure all was quiet. It was starting to snow, which brought him a sense of security. They had all the snowmobiles stowed behind the barn; it would be highly unlikely any of the women would be venturing out on foot.

He told Dawson, "You go get some sleep. I'll take over."

Dawson answered, "I got plenty of sleep sitting here. The pups were here, so I knew nothing would surprise me. We want to sit with you and Carolyn and make some plans. Do you and Carolyn mind if we travel with you guys? We are heading in the same direction, and we need your help for security."

Hawks agreed. "We were thinking the same thing. I sure wish Chuck hadn't been killed. I just wish we could have helped him rescue his family."

Dawson pointed out, "Our goal is to now make sure our families are rescued. It's not going to be easy."

After the rest of the house woke up, they sent the kids to play. Carolyn and Cathy made a pot of coffee and brought it to the table. Carolyn told them, "Better enjoy it, we don't have a lot of it left, maybe a couple of weeks' worth."

Cathy said, "We have lots of tea. It should last us several months; after that, we'll have to start making pine needle tea."

Hawks grimaced. "I like my morning coffee. Maybe we can save it for special occasions or if the need arises for us to have to remain alert."

Dawson said, "I'm not a big coffee or tea drinker. I miss having milk."

Hawks grinned. "You may be in luck. One of our horses is a young stallion. He has hooked up with two of the mares that I know of. You'll just have to figure out how to milk a horse."

Dawson frowned. "This is going to be an adventure. When do you think we should start?"

Hawks stood and looked out the window. "I think we need to sit tight here until the weather starts to thaw. I haven't exactly kept up with the exact date, but I believe it's the first of February. We've probably got another six weeks of snow at this altitude. If we have an early thaw for some reason, we can head out earlier. If we aren't bucking the snow, we can make twice the time we would make if we left now."

Dawson agreed. "This is a defendable position for now, and we may get a chance to kill some game that will extend our food. That one poor horse will feed us several weeks; an elk or two would take all the pressure off what we're going to eat."

Carolyn asked, "What about those women?"

Hawks turned back to the window. "I think they're whipped. They aren't going to fight the snow, and I doubt we see anyone traveling the roads."

Cathy agreed. "If they have kids, they won't be trying to do anything but survive. I say we take the trail south."

CHAPTER 41

The weeks wore on without incident. They never once let down their guard while waiting for the spring thaw. From where the hunting lodge sat, it overlooked a broad valley below. Occasionally they saw small herds of elk in the distance. A small herd of mule deer crossed the road and headed into the woods on the north side of the cabin. Hawks retrieved the .303 Enfield rifle and took to the woods, making sure he stayed high on the ridge so he wouldn't spook the herd.

He soon spotted them making their way and feeding on shrubs sticking up from the melted snow. He selected a doe that didn't have a fawn following her and shot her through the chest. She dropped where she stood. The others scattered and disappeared down the mountain. He carefully made his way down the side of the rocky hill where he found the dead doe. He quickly gutted her and filled the body cavity with snow to rapidly cool it. He dragged the carcass down to the road where they could easily retrieve it.

He trudged back to the drive and walked up the drive to be greeted by Dawson. "I assume we have some meat on the ground."

Hawks grinned. "Yes, sir, let's saddle a couple of horses. I can ride one and tie a rope to the other one and get the deer back up here and processed."

Emma came out. "Can I go with you?"

Hawks smiled. "Sure thing, I can use the help."

They saddled up, and she rode behind Hawks. They led the other horse. He wasn't sure how the horses would react to the dead deer, so he made sure Emma hung on tight when they got to the carcass. Emma held their reins as Hawks looped a rope around the doe's neck and tied it off to the saddle horn of the second horse.

She wrinkled her nose when she saw the bloody carcass. "That looks yucky."

Hawks said, "Do you want to help me skin her out and process the meat?"

She beamed. "Can I?"

"You sure can, Sweetie Pop. You are also going to learn how to cook venison." Hawk climbed into the saddle, bent down, scooped her up, and swung her behind him. Once they were in the saddle, it was a short ride back to the cabin. BC and Lucy anxiously waited for Emma to return with the deer. Hawks handed the horse's reins to Dawson, who led it back to the skinning shack. He lowered Emma to the ground, where she proudly showed off the dead deer. Once they had the deer up on the gambrel, they let the kids watch as they skinned it out and quartered it for processing.

That evening they sat around the fire making plans for the trail south. The dogs were maturing, and there was nothing going on around the place they didn't know about or have their noses in. The plans were for the Power Wagon to lead the way. With it, they could transport all the food and supplies. The horses and riders would follow and would be used once and if the Power Wagon gave out. The goal was to reach the upper Missouri River.

Hawks spread out the maps. "I think we need to head to the upper Missouri, probably near Fort Benton. We are sure to find some suitable boats somewhere along the river."

Dawson agreed. "We need to be able to transport the boats

around the reservoir damns. Hopefully; we can successfully hunt and fish along the way. I drove up through there on my way. It's pretty desolate country, if I remember. There will be game along the river and, other than a few areas, lightly populated."

Cathy asked, "What are we going to do in the populated areas?"

Dawson answered, "We can float by those areas at night."

Carolyn asked, "I know we are going to have to concentrate our supplies into two or three boats. Have y'all thought about using a raft?"

Hawks said, "We will use whatever we can find. I'm certain there will be houseboats, party barges, and all sorts of watercraft. There may even be some outfitter boats like the ones they use on the Colorado River canyon tours." Hawks stood up. "It's settled. We start inventorying our supplies and get the Power Wagon and trailer set up to load. I'll also check the horses' hoofs. I imagine some of their shoes are coming off. I don't know how to shoe a horse, but I can take off any loose shoes and maybe trim up their hoofs. If the roads melt off, walking on the pavement will hopefully wear the hooves down."

They all retired for the night. Dawson elected to sleep in the recliner out of sight of the windows and doors. The pups sacked out next to the wood heater as usual. It was sometime in the middle of the night they were abruptly awakened by the dogs going crazy. They could hear the horses snorting and whinnying and the sound of ripping boards.

Dawson was first to the back door and could see a huge bear in the light of the moon trying to get into the barn. He took his rifle and emptied it into the beast. It reared up on its legs and towered a good eight feet high. Just as he fired his last round, he was joined by Hawks, who started firing. The beast dropped to its feet and charged. The last shot from Hawks' rifle entered the bear's open mouth and exiting through the base of its spine, collapsing it on the back steps. Dawson slapped a fresh magazine in the gun and chambered another round. He ran past the dying bear in time to keep the horses from running through the damaged barn door. Dawson came back as Carolyn brought out a kerosene lamp. The huge beast was dead and probably weighed six hundred pounds.

Dawson picked up one of the front paws to show its size and the length of its claws. "Who wants a bear claw necklace?"

Carolyn looked at them both. "Does this mean that spring time is here? Shouldn't he be hibernating?"

Cathy laughed. "He's hibernating now for sure."

Hawks looked down at the bruin. "I'd say we can expect the spring melt any day now. I've never eaten bear, but I imagine we can get a lot of meat off him."

Dawson speculated, "I bet we'll have to boil it quite a while to get this old boy tender enough to chew."

Carolyn said, "Let's cut him up into thin strips and smoke him over a fire. We should have him worked up in just a few days."

Hawks thought for a moment. "One thing we are going to need is a water filter or some way to disinfect the water when we get to the river. Is there any chlorine bleach in the cabin?"

Cathy said, "Yes, there are several unopened gallons in the laundry."

Hawks grinned. "That's fantastic. That will let us disinfect hundreds of gallons of water and save us the time and energy to boil the water. If the water is reasonably clear, all we have to do is add eight drops of chlorine to a gallon. See if you can find an eye dropper or a bottle of nose spray we can clean out so we can count the drops as we dispense it."

Dawson said, "I want to let the horses calm down before we get one out to drag this rascal up to the skinning room. It'll be daylight in a couple of hours, and it is still freezing. I think we can wait until its light to get him processed."

The kids slept through the battle with the bear. They would be excited to see it in the morning. They all went back to bed, but it was not easy sleeping after the excitement. The next morning, they saddled two horses, tied two ropes around the bear and dragged it to the room where they could work. The horses were a bit skittish at first but calmed down right away when they were given a couple of the sugar cookies. The bear was too big to winch up in the room, so they gutted him on the ground and skinned him where he lay. They were able to separate his back legs and pelvic area from the torso and pulled it up on the Gambrel where they could start deboning the meat. It took several hours to completely debone all the meat and start cutting it up into thin strips. They took the bones, hide, and entrails and dumped them off the cliff to join the dead men they had discarded weeks ago. The hide had too many bullet holes for them to use as a tarp. BC wanted the claws and teeth, but his mother quickly squashed the idea.

"We aren't hauling bear parts across the country. We'll be carrying bear jerky." Once they had a frame and some poultry wire strewn across it, they built a fire. While the coals were forming, they broke up a salt block from the barn and coated all the meat. It then took the rest of the day to get a large portion of it smoked into hard strips. It was terribly gamey but was passable if you didn't think about it. By the end of the next day, they had it sacked up in some feed sacks and hung in the skinning shed awaiting their journey.

CHAPTER 42

They stood at the top of the long drive and looked down to see portions of it peeking out of the snow. The roadway below was starting to break through as well. Hawks looked around. "I wish Chuck were here. He would know the prayer we need to say before we start."

Cathy had her arms around her the twins; Carolyn hugged Emma. "Does anyone want to give it a try?"

Emma said, "I can, my daddy used to say prayers with me every night. I still do. I just say them to myself."

Hawks said, "Go ahead, Sweetie Pop."

She cleared her throat, "Dear Jesus, thank you for letting us have each other and bless everyone we love here and in heaven. Please let us travel safe, amen."

Dawson said, "That was real good Emmy; let's hit the road."

The Power Wagon cranked right up. He left it in low range because they had it and the trailer loaded with as much as they dared put in them. Hawks, Carolyn, and Emma each rode a horse and the pack horses were loaded but not as heavy as they had been loaded. Hawks had taught Emma to ride in the past few weeks, and she was on the gentlest old mare in the group. Evidently, she had been ridden by kids sometime in her past.

They left the snow blade on the Power Wagon in case they

encountered a late snow or if they went through some areas that had not quite melted. They stopped every two hours to let the horses rest and to check the oil and tires. They had a hand pump and some tire plug kits salvaged from the Canadian Tire truck many weeks ago.

It took two weeks of steady travel to reach the upper reaches of the river. They weren't sure if they had found the actual Missouri River, but if not, it had to be a tributary. It flowed east, which meant this water had to make it to the Missouri and ultimately the Mississippi River. Luckily, they found no human life, and there was scattered game. They did not stop as they went through small towns. When they found farm stores, they stopped for horse feed. Occasionally they saw smoke from faraway chimneys, and once while resting, they heard the boom of a rifle. Hopefully, a distant hunter had secured some meat.

That night they camped just off the road near the river. They carried the horses down to the river to drink and built a campfire. Once the horses were fed, watered, and picketed, they relaxed around the fire. BC, Lucy, and Emma all had a piece of jerky and were pretending to smoke cigars. An abandoned truck provided a tank of gas for the Power Wagon. The next morning, as they were getting ready to leave, the dogs started barking. They looked to see a covered wagon being pulled by a couple of horses coming in their direction heading east. Carolyn and Cathy took the kids out of sight, while Hawks and Dawson waited with their weapons ready. The man driving the wagon pulled his horses up when he got to where they sat by the road.

The man nodded. "I'm not looking for trouble. I'm just going home."

Hawks asked, "You traveling by yourself?"

"No, my wife and kids are in the back. My wife has a shotgun. We don't want any trouble."

Dawson agreed. "You won't be getting any from us. That's what we're trying to do as well. Can we expect any trouble ahead?"

"There's a crossing about a day's ride east and south of here. There're some men from the reservation, and they make you pay a toll. The toll is half your food. I'm fortunate that they at least left me with my deer rifle and horses. I had two elk quartered out; now I've got one."

Hawks asked, "Can we see the crossing before we get to it?"

"Sure, just watch the road signs. It should tell you when you are within a mile of it. You'll also pass an old Methodist church on the right when you are a couple of miles out. Be careful if you try to deal with them. They got people back off the road as backup."

Dawson gave him the thumbs-up. "Safe travels, we appreciate the heads-up."

They watched as the wagon continued. The wife and kids waved from the back. His wife was holding a shotgun.

Dawson asked Hawks, "What do you think?"

"I think we'll be playing cowboys and Indians tonight."

Dawson grinned and called to the girls, "C'mon out, we can hit the road."

Carolyn looked at Hawks. "Sooner or later, your luck is going to run out. I know what you're going to do."

Hawks gave her a wink, "We're not even married yet, and you are already reading my mind."

After traveling most of the day, they finally came to the Methodist church. It had not been used in quite a while, but they could camp out of sight behind it. Dawson went through the open back door and checked out the interior with the little daylight filtering its way in. There were a few hymnals and bibles in the racks behind the seats. The church office was ransacked, as well as the kitchen. Choir robes were strewn across the floor in a room near the office. It was sad to see the little church in disarray.

He walked back out and told them, "Nothing to see in there. It's abandoned."

Cathy said, "Do you think it's OK to build a fire?"

Dawson said, "The wind is not blowing in the direction we are going so I doubt they will smell the smoke. Unless they are sending out scouts, we are OK." They set up camp while Hawks checked his weapons and geared up.

Carolyn hadn't said much. "I don't like it. Your luck is going to run out sooner or later. We can't make it without you."

Hawks frowned. "You and I both know that there's only one way we're going to make it past that road block. It's no different than what we went through back in Crofton and Lady Smith. We're never going to make it home unless we can trick them or kill them. These guys are well past being tricked after these many weeks."

Dawson said, "I imagine they may be past the being surprised stage as well. I think we need to sneak down there and observe them from a distance. Maybe one of us can sneak around. It could be suicide going in there."

Hawks pointed at the river. "Unless we can find boats on that river in the next mile, we're going to have to go through that intersection. If they clean us out, we're dead. If they start shooting, the kids could get hurt."

Cathy and Carolyn came over to where Hawks and Dawson were making plans.

Cathy shrugged her shoulders. "What's the plan?"

Carolyn answered, "I know what the plan is. Hawks is going to sneak in and kill everything that moves."

Hawks gave her a stern look. "I am going to do what I have to do. There are three little kids that have to be cared for, no matter what. We can't take a chance on both of us men getting killed. The kids need their mothers."

Carolyn interrupted, "They need their daddies too."

Hawks gave her a hug. "I'm being the daddy. Of the two of us, I'm the most expendable. Dawson has youth and strength and is the best choice to take care of y'all if I go down. I don't fight fairly, and I always think of the alternatives. According to the map, this road runs between the mountains to the south and the river to the north. Two miles from here another road comes in from the northeast and crosses the river. This is a three-way intersection. I plan to leave here at two 2:00 a.m. I want to get there around 3:00 a.m. when most of them will be asleep and anyone on guard duty will be dozing."

Dawson pointed out, "I know we had our guard down a bit after we killed the men from the ski lodge. Unless they have dogs or perimeter alarms, a man may be able to slip in."

Hawks spoke up, "I want y'all to get ready to go by 5:00 a.m. If I go in and kick the door open, we're not going to have time to get packed and moving. I'm not going to start anything unless I am certain I can prevail. In the meantime, let's get some sleep." He fished around in their sack of jewelry and found two Rolex automatic watches. Handing one to Dawson, they set the time using Carolyn's pocket watch. The numbers glowed in the dark so he could readily see it. He pulled his shirt sleeve down over it to make sure no one could spot it in the dark. He remembered the idiots sitting in the dark smoking that made them easy to spot. It was 7:00 p.m., so he could at least get in six or seven hours of sleep.

Dawson lamented, "I finally made enough money to buy one of these, but I couldn't bring myself to waste the money. I don't need the watch; my Seiko automatic watch is still running. I'll take the first watch until Hawks heads out."

Carolyn piped up, "I'll take the next one. I won't be sleeping until he comes back."

It was another bright clear night with little wind, so Hawks elected to sleep under the stars. He was fully clothed, so he did not try to crawl into a sleeping bag but used some old cushions from the church pews for a mattress and covered up with a sleeping bag. He dozed off but was awakened when Emma crawled under on his right side and lay her head on his arm so he could cradle her. Carolyn crawled in on the other side. He knew that whatever transpired in the morning, he had to prevail. There was too much riding on his success. He watched as Dawson added some wood to the fire and fell into a deep sleep.

CHAPTER 43

Hawks woke to Dawson gently shaking his boot. Hawks gently repositioned Emma so she wouldn't wake. Carolyn stirred and got up with Hawks. Dawson pointed to the campfire. "I have a pot of coffee on the fire and some of our sugar cookies. They are starting to break up a little from all the handling, but they still taste really good. I also saddled you a horse. It will be safer for you to ride until you get closer. The horse can see better in the low light than you."

Hawks agreed. "Good idea. I don't need to stumble and fall off into a ravine. And I can hightail it back if I need to escape."

After kissing Carolyn goodnight and shaking Dawson's hand, he saddled up. He slung the rifle so that it rested across his lap. There were eight thirty-round mags in a vest under his coat. He wore his holster carrying a Browning High Power with two extra magazines. His large hunting knife was in a sheath on his left side. A canteen of water hung on the saddle horn. He gave his horse one of the half-eaten cookies and mounted up. Once he got away from the fire, his eyes became accustomed to the twilight. He didn't hurry the horse, so they traveled at a walk. He had on a pair of wool gloves and would pull them off if the shooting started. The temperature was in the twenties; fog came with every breath from him and the horse.

After an hour of riding, he came to within sight of the camp.

His horse's ears came up first. The horse knew something was ahead. He glanced at his watch; he was right on schedule. He tied his horse to a road sign post and proceeded on foot. He hoped a bear didn't show up. He figured she could break her bridle and leave if she came under attack. He stayed to the side of the road and made his way until he could see the intersection.

The road was blocked by a pole mounted on some saw horses. He was about three hundred yards out when suddenly all hell broke loose. Gunfire erupted from three sides as men hollered, dogs barked, and women screamed. A pair of horses came running by him, and he heard a dog yelping. He quickly climbed up an embankment to where he could overlook the camp. This embankment had been created when the roadway was blown out of the rocky side of the mountain. The dynamite drill marks were visible even in the twilight.

Once he was where he could see better, he could make out men moving. The gunfire had slowed down to occasional shots. Two men came running out of the camp and headed up the embankment where he was perched. They were virtually on top of him before they realized he was there. One of them got off a shot. Hawks felt the sting of a bullet as it clipped his ear. He reacted automatically as though no conscious thought gave his body orders. The next minute both men were dead, one from a shot from his Browning High Power pistol the other from a stab from his big knife. Hawks had plunged the knife in an upward angle under the man's ribs and into this chest cavity. He could hear the sucking sound of air as the man tried to take a final breath before the massive loss of blood killed him. Hawks pulled out the knife and wiped it on the dead man's clothes.

At that moment, in a strong Texas accent, a man said, "Thanks, I thought they were getting away." Hawks looked up to see a man holding an M14 rifle staring at him.

Hawks got up, "I didn't have much choice. They were on me before I could spit."

The man pulled out an old flashlight and shined it at Hawks. "Hold still, I want to see how bad you're hit." After looking at his ear, he said, "It just shaved off the very top of your right ear. I believe it will grow back. If not, you can let your hair grow long on that side. What are you doing up here?"

"We met a couple in a horse-drawn wagon who said a bunch of men from a reservation were shaking down everyone who passes for half of their food. I'm not letting a bunch of people steal our supplies. We need every scrap to make it home. What about you?"

"They don't just get supplies. I'm surprised they let them come through with the horses. They must have more than they can feed right now. They killed my brother and most of his family a couple of weeks ago. My nephew survived but barely made it back on foot. He had to swim the half-frozen river; he's still in pretty bad shape. We have a ranch north of here where we raise bison and have a guide service. We have a big operation, and there are a dozen of us cowboys up there. These idiots tell themselves that they are Shoshone Indians. They are no more Shoshone than I'm part of a Scottish clan. A bunch of them are Indian, but a lot of them are at most a quarter Indian. They are mostly dope addicts and alcoholics who have lived off government money their entire lives."

"How many are there?"

"At least two dozen, not including the women and children. I'm Bill Emrick."

Hawks shook his hand. "Glad to meet you. I'm Bill Hawks; everyone calls me Hawks."

Bill asked, "Is that an Indian name?"

Hawks laughed. "I think there's a thimbleful of Indian blood in me. Not enough to keep me from being a cowboy." They rifled through the men's pockets and took their weapons and ammo.

Hawks pointed down the embankment to where his horse was tied. "Let's go this way. I want to get my horse."

Bill followed him down to the roadway to where the horse was tied. They hung the dead men's rifles off the saddle horn and dropped their pistols and ammo into a saddle bag. Hawks took a moment to exchange the magazine in his Browning with a full one before they headed down the road to the intersection. Hawks could feel blood running down his neck behind his ear, so he tied a bandana around his neck to replace his wool scarf. The bandana would catch the blood before it soaked his coat and shirt. Once they reached the intersection, a couple of Bill's men came up.

Bill asked, "Did any get away?"

The older of the two men answered, "No, just the two you were chasing."

Bill pointed to Hawks. "They didn't get away. What about our guys?"

"We have three wounded; all three should recover. Smiley may have broken his foot when his horse stepped on it."

Bill asked, "How many did we put an end to?"

"We killed seventeen men and three women who were putting up a fight."

"How many are left?"

"There are two wounded men, seven women, and four kids. What do you want us to do with them?"

Bill looked at Hawks. "What would you do?"

Hawks pondered for a moment. "I'd shoot the men and send the women and kids packing. I'd give them enough supplies to get back to where they came from. If it weren't for the kids, I'd almost be inclined to kill the women too. I'm sick of being preyed on. I'm sure glad you guys were here to help. I don't know if I could have killed all of them by myself."

Bill looked at him. "Are you serious?"

"That was my plan. We are heading south. I am looking to get some boats or canoes and float down the Missouri."

Bill gave him a puzzled look. "That might work, but what are you going to do when you get there?"

"I haven't quite figured that out yet."

Bill pointed out, "Living off the land isn't going to be easy. How many of you are there?"

"There are two men, two women, and three small children."

Bill pointed to the north. "Our ranch is about thirty miles north of here. Go get your group and follow us up there. We have plenty to eat, and we have enough men to defend it. We don't put up with any crap from anybody, but we can sure use some like-minded people. We have comfortable cabins you can stay in until we can locate some boats if you decide not to join us. Go back and get your group. We have a mess to clean up here, so it will be a while before we head back."

Hawks said, "Thanks, we should be back here an hour or so after daylight."

Hawks handed over the weapons on his horse and headed back. He caught up to the two horses that had run from the battle and led them back to the church. When he got back, everyone was up and waiting.

Carolyn ran to him. "We heard gunfire. What happened?"

Hawks took the three horses over to the picket line and secured them. "I had help. Some cowboys from a ranch got there just before I did. They cleaned them out. I only had to handle two."

Carolyn noticed his bloody ear and face when he got near the light of the fire. "You're hurt. How bad?"

Hawks grinned. "My ear may be funny looking for a while. I just hope it doesn't affect my boyish good looks." Emma didn't say anything. she just clung to his leg and cried happy tears that he was OK.

Dawson asked, "How many were there?"

"There were twenty-one men and ten women. I'm not sure how many children. Nineteen men and three women were killed outright. There are two wounded men. I don't expect to find the men alive when we get back. The cowboys have a ranch thirty miles north of the intersection. They've offered to take us in until we can locate some boats. They are bison ranchers and hunting outfitters; they have food and cabins for us until we move on."

Dawson responded, "That sounds too good to be true. Do you think we can trust them?"

Hawks shrugged. "They had every opportunity to kill me and take my horse and weapons. They did not come across as needing us or our supplies. The men at the intersection had murdered the owner's brother and family. The only survivor was his nephew, who is still laid up. At any rate, they know we are up here. If we don't show up, they can easily find us. I'm not prepared to take on a group of seasoned cowboys. They'd chew us up and spit us out if they had a mind to."

Cathy, who had been listening with Carolyn, said, "I think we and the horses are weary from traveling. This may be a good opportunity to rest up and explore the river in the area for boats."

Dawson said, "The worst-case scenario is that we swap the Power Wagon for enough horses and tack that we can all continue on horseback. We all know that the Power Wagon could give out at any time, and then we'd be stuck with not enough horses for all of us to ride."

Hawks agreed. "We can walk and lead horses, but it is a long walk to Missouri and even further to south Louisiana. Let's take a leap of faith and pray that this is a lucky break."

They pulled out at the crack of dawn, leaving the old church behind. It was probably one of the Methodist churches that was a casualty of the woke revolution several years earlier. Hawks had a small bandage over the top of his ear to keep it from rubbing on his hat. His wool scarf was drying on one of the saddles after the blood had been rinsed from it. When they reached the intersection, there was a pile of bodies to act as a warning for anyone who may have the same idea of stopping and robbing people.

Bill Emrick gave them a wave and came over as the Power Wagon came to a stop. "You've quite a rig there."

Dawson grinned. "I'm Dawson Stewart. This is my wife, Cathy, and our two kids, BC and Lucy."

Bill held out his hand. "I'm Bill Emrick. We're about to wrap things up here."

Hawks came riding up. "Bill, this is Carolyn and my little girl, Emma. We've decided to take you up on your offer."

Bill grinned. "Great news, all we have to do is crank up an old tractor and hook it to a hay trailer so we can transport our wounded."

Hawks asked, "What about the wounded Indians and the women?"

"Sadly, the two men didn't survive their injuries. Four of the women and their children elected to go home, so we sent them walking with food and water. The other three were captives and will be joining us. I didn't mention it earlier, but I am the Mormon Bishop up here. I don't know what religion you are, but you are welcome to worship with us."

Cathy spoke up, "We're Christians, can you preform weddings on non-members?"

Bill gave her a sly grin. "No, but if you are willing to join our church, I can. We are Christians just like other Christians. We just have a different doctrine. The name of our church is the Church of Jesus Christ of Latter-Day Saints."

Cathy looked at Dawson. "Sure thing, my Catholic mama can use the exercise rolling in her grave."

Hawks had overheard and looked at Carolyn. She nodded yes. "My grandparents on my dad's side were Mormon."

Hawks agreed. "I think it's a good idea. I've worked with Mormons on a big project in Utah. They were all forthright hard-working people. My mother made me prayerful, and I went with her to the Baptist church while growing up. I've felt funny running around acting married but not being married."

Bill smiled. "It's settled. We should be able to take care of all this Sunday. These days I try to rush important stuff. You never know what's going to happen that can change lives drastically."

Hawks asked, "I must ask you something. Can you tell me the date?"

Bill looked at him. "It's Tuesday, March 18th."

Hawks reacted in disbelief. "We've been so busy surviving, I lost track of time. I knew it was probably sometime in March because we've had a bit of a thaw."

Bill answered, "Up in this part of the country, we can still get a late blizzard. I wouldn't try to head south for another month. If you get caught in six-foot snow drifts, you and your animals are going to die unless you find shelter. There are farms and lodges all over this country, but getting to one may prove to be impossible. We've grown accustomed to plowed roads and emergency services; those days are over. It's frontier justice, we've even had to take on remnants of the police and military."

Dawson lamented, "The first thing they did was try and confiscate our food. Later a group of them, all armed with military rifles, pistols, and gear killed our families. I killed the bastards; their remains have probably been cannibalized by now."

Hawks agreed. "They quickly pull out their title as if they still have authority. Everyone we came in contact with had one thing in mind and that was to take what we had."

Soon they had all the horses saddled and everyone loaded

up. The old diesel tractor with the wounded men brought up the rear. The Power Wagon followed the riders. It took them most of the day to get to the ranch. He had to stop and gas up the Power Wagon a couple of times. Once at the ranch, Bill sent some of the hands to show them where the three guest cabins were located behind the main ranch house. Just as Bill said, they were comfortable, three-bedroom, one-bath cabins.

"We have a natural spring-fed water well. We're close enough to Yellowstone that it puts out warm water. Just remember the pressure can get low with so many of us using it, so forget long showers unless you do it between midnight and dawn."

The three rescued women took the third cabin. They left the Power Wagon and trailer loaded and took the packs and saddles off the horses. They took them up to the stables and turned them out in the corral with the other horses.

Dawson asked Hawks, "Do you think we'll be able to pick them out from the others when we get ready to take the trail south?"

"Sure, ours don't have shoes."

Bill came out to where they were watching the horses. "You guys get settled and rested tonight. If you like, you can help us with guard duties. I'm fixing to spend some time with the three gals in the third cabin. We need to know everything we can about that crowd we wiped out. They could just be a wing of a bigger organization. They probably know by now what happened."

Hawks agreed. "We need to know who's head of the organization. We may need to make a surgical strike."

Bill headed back toward the cabins. "Follow me; I'm going to head down there and visit with the ladies. My wife, Violet, will be down shortly to see if there's anything they need."

Hawks asked, "Do you mind if I sit in?"

"No, I think two will be better than one. Two of us may be better at reading them than just me."

Dawson commented, "The one thing I can't do is read women. I need to get back to our cabin where one of the women I can't read is waiting for me." They laughed and headed down the path to the cabins.

Carolyn came out to the path. "The cabin is perfect. I have a fire in the woodstove, and it's toasty in there. Emma and the twins are having a good time."

Hawks pointed to the third cabin. "I'll be back in a bit. Bill is going to interrogate the three ladies and wants me to sit in. His wife Violet will be by here in a few minutes."

Bill said, "If you see her, introduce yourself and tell her to give me about thirty minutes."

Dawson headed toward his cabin. "Is Cathy in our cabin with the kids?"

Carolyn nodded over her shoulder. "No, all the kids are busy ransacking our cabin. Cathy was going to start cooking."

"Great, I'm going to grab a shower."

Dawson came in the back door to find Cathy fresh and clean; her hair was still damp. He took her in his arms and gave her a kiss. "I feel safe for once. I'm going to get a shower."

"Hurry up, I'm getting ready to cook dinner, but you get desert first." He disappeared into the bath, and she turned to the stove where she started a pot of water to boil.

Hawks and Bill went down to the ladies' cabin and knocked. A brown-eyed girl opened the door. "Come in, we've been expecting you." They walked into the room and found the other two young women standing next to the woodstove.

Bill spoke up, "Ladies, I hope you are finding everything you need. We'll have you up for dinner in a bit. I came down here not only to check on you and get you settled but to find out what happened to you. I'm Bill Emrick, and this is Bill Hawks; you can call me Bill and him Hawks. What are your names?"

The young girl who opened the door answered, "I'm Helen Jernigan."

Another young lady with darker brown hair spoke up, "I'm Billie Wilson."

She turned to the last lady who stepped forward, "I'm Lena Robinson; my friends call me Tootsie."

Bill said, "Let's sit at the table." He lit the kerosene lantern hanging over the table, and they all gathered around. "Can you tell me what happened?"

Tootsie spoke first. "I lived about thirty miles south of here. My husband and I had been married two years. We lived next door to my parents on our family ranch. The men came through and just murdered my husband, parents, and brothers. They tied me up and threw me in the back of an old panel truck. I was six weeks pregnant and lost the baby when they beat me up. I have just one question; can I borrow a weapon? I want to kill as many of them as I can." Bill and Hawks listened to their stories. All were of lives ripped apart by ruthless men. All three women had tears dripping down their faces as their anguish was laid bare.

Hawks commented, "I pray that you can get some peace."

Billie spoke up. "There's got to be some way we can fight back."

Hawks asked, "You can fight back. Can you tell us about the ones we haven't killed?"

Tootsie asked, "What do you want to know?"

Bill started, "How many more are we up against?"

"They have or had three groups. You took out one of the groups. One group is busy cleaning out farms, ranches, and towns around this corner of the state. The other group is at another intersection on the other side of the county. Their headquarters has a dozen men just this side of the reservation. It's led by Alfred Sanson. He made up an Indian name. He calls himself Red Cloud and swears he's the grandson of a Shoshone chief. I heard some of them say that his grandfather was an alcoholic drug addict. He's a warlord, not a chief."

"Can you show us on a map where he is located." All three nodded yes. Bill fished out a folded map from his pocket and circled the locations they pointed out with a pencil. "What were their plans for you three?"

Helen spoke up for the second time. "We were there to cook, clean, and haul things. They made it clear that we could either sleep with them or work for them. There were a bunch of women who gave in and acted like their concubines. We had to wait on them hand and foot as well. In fact, I want to get a shot at a couple of them who made our lives miserable."

Bill asked, "Do you think they will come for us here?"

Tootsie answered, "I would bet my life on it, they know you are here. I overhead them talking while they were drinking and smoking dope. They were planning on coming here as soon as the second group gets back from their run. Once they find all the dead, they'll be pissed."

Hawks commented, "Their arrogance can be their weakness. If they are overconfident, it will get them killed."

Bill asked, "How are they traveling? Are they on horseback or do they have vehicles?"

Billie said, "They are using an old school bus, a panel truck, and some old motorcycles."

There was a knock at the door. Billie opened it up and met Violet. Bill introduced everyone and excused himself and Hawks. They headed back down the path. Bill spoke candidly to Hawks. "You are in danger here. I can send you up in the hills until we see how this works out."

Hawks summoned him to his cabin. "Let's look at my map so we can see what we're looking at." He called out to Carolyn, "Are my maps here?"

She pulled them out of his backpack. "Here you go." The kerosene lamp was already lit over the table so he spread it out so they could see. Bill showed him on the map where they were sitting and where the intersection was where they had the shootout.

Hawks pointed to his map. "It looks like that bridge crossing the river is the only one for a hundred miles east and south of us. The next bridge must be seventy-five miles in the other direction. If we blow the bridge they have to go around, that will delay them."

Bill pointed out, "They'll just murder and rob folks on the trip. I'd rather catch them in an ambush and kill them. I realize it doesn't sound Christian, but I'm not taking prisoners or giving them a chance." Hawks grinned, "If we can catch the majority of them in that bus crossing the bridge, it will be a massacre. All we have to do is leave a broken-down vehicle on the bridge. They'll have to slow down or stop to move it. Four or five men with rifles can massacre them. It looks like the days of riding painted ponies are behind them." Carolyn came out with some biscuits cooked in the woodstove.

She had a jar with honey and hot coffee. "Here's a snack for you guys. Cathy is cooking and should have supper ready in an hour or so."

Bill said, "We Mormons aren't supposed to drink coffee, but I'm making an exception this time. It was a long night."

Dawson watched from the bed as Cathy got dressed. She turned and caught him watching. Smiling, she came back and gave him a kiss. "Relax while I finish supper."

He rose and dressed. "I'm going over to see how Hawks and Bill are coming along. I bet Hawks is about ready to pass out. He's been up over twenty-four hours and counting."

"Tell Carolyn I'll have food on the table in an hour."

He gave her a peck. "Will do." He pulled on his coat and

headed out of the door. He walked the path back up to the first cabin and knocked on the door. Carolyn answered, "C'mon in, you're just in time for biscuits and coffee."

Dawson smiled. "I haven't had real biscuits in a while."

"Thanks to Bill, we now have flour and honey; I splurged on the coffee. Hawks has got to be running on empty right now."

Hawks gave him a rundown on what they faced. Dawson nodded in agreement. "We get to kill some more bad guys. I know you think I'm crazy, but I am at the stage where I relish killing them now. I suggest we immediately man the bridge with as many men as possible. Do you have a couple of old trucks that we can use to block the road? We can put them going in opposite directions and not side by side. We want it to look like they both were caught on the bridge. When the bus shows up, it will have to stop and try and push one of them out of the way. We'll let the motorcycles through. We can kill them here at the farm or when they turn around to find out why the bus wasn't following."

Bill said, "That sounds like a great plan. I'll get my ranch hands working on it now. I'm sure my manager will have some more ideas. I want men on the bridge without delay. Can we use your Power Wagon to drag one of the trucks? That old tractor we found can drag the other."

"Sure thing, we'll get it unloaded."

CHAPTER 44

It had been a busy two weeks at the ranch. The bridge was staged, and hidden shooting positions were set up on both sides of the river. Six men with M4 rifles and plenty of ammo covered the bridge at all times. The weddings came off without a hitch. It was now a waiting game. Hawks and Dawson took up duties on the ranch and with duty at the bridge as well. The three ladies were taught to shoot, and they helped around the ranch too. They were soon hanging out with some of the single ranch hands. Nature was taking its course.

Dawson sat in his blind on the southeast side of the bridge. It was hard not to doze. From where he was positioned, he looked down on the bridge. He was startled when he heard the sound of a lone motorcycle. It tooled down the road and had a bit of a backfire as it slowed and turned on the bridge. The rider stopped and got off to look in the staged trucks. As agreed, no one fired. If this was a scout, they didn't want to reveal their plan. The rider got back on the bike and headed in the direction of the ranch. After about ten minutes, he came riding back and returned in the direction from which he came. Hopefully, he would report the bridge was open so they could plan their revenge.

As planned, one of the ranch hands on the opposite side of the bridge left on his horse at a fast lope heading back. Ten miles down the road, he changed horses, went another ten miles, and mounted the last horse. He rode into the ranch yard and fired off a couple of rounds in the air. The entire ranch burst into action. Horses were quickly saddled and men prepared to head out.

Bill came out. "As planned, this looks like it. Make sure you have food and water and plenty of ammo. The wounded and ladies will guard the home place and be the last line of defense. We've got children and all our supplies to see us through. Show no mercy because we will receive none from them."

Alfred Sanson, a.k.a. Red Cloud, sat in his office surrounded by replica bow and arrows, animal skins, and other make-believe Native American decorations. His hair was long enough to pull it back into a ponytail to augment his costume. He heard the motor-cycle pull up outside and waited until the rider came in. "What did you find?"

The rider's hair stood on end from being disheveled by the removal of his helmet. "I didn't see signs of anyone. We can easily cross the bridge. There are just a couple of broken-down trucks on it. We can easily push them aside with the bus. We may even be able to drive around them."

Alfred asked, "Are the guys rested up from the last run?"

"They should be. They found a few more women. Do you want me to get the guys from the road down south or do you think we can handle it?"

"I think we can handle it. There can't be that many. The gals that made it back said there were some wounded, so they won't be fully manned. Get everyone together. If we leave now, we can be back in time to grill some bison steaks. I'm sure they already have a couple of carcasses ageing. Tell the guys they have a bunch of women up there as well. That'll stir 'em up."

The rider said, "We've got several of those warrior women types with the side-shaved heads. I'm sure they will be excited at the prospect of fresh women as well." Alfred pulled out his rifle and strapped on his battle belt that included his pistol, magazines, war axe, and hunting knife. He put on his hat with what appeared to be an eagle feather and walked out to the parking lot where the bus was pulling up.

He pointed down the road. "Let the motorcycles lead. If they draw fire, we can stop, spread out, and take them all down. Kill everyone but the women." He climbed up into the bus and took the front seat after the ones sitting there jumped up and went to the back when they saw who was coming in. The men had been drinking. You could smell the liquor in the bus.

Alfred stood up and hollered back, "I better not catch anyone drinking or doping until after we get back."

One of the men said, "F'you, no man tells me when I can drink."

Alfred poleaxed his skull with his battle axe. The man collapsed where he sat. Alfred put his foot on his chest and pulled the axe free from his head. He looked around. "Anyone else?" No one uttered a sound.

Alfred turned around and headed back to his seat. "Throw that garbage out the back door once we get down the road. I don't want him stinking up the parking lot." Absolute authority was all these human jackals understood.

Hawks let his horse hang back from following Bill and the ranch hands as they headed toward the bridge. He still considered himself a novice, even though he stayed on his mortally wounded horse back at the hunting lodge. He caught up with them while they rested their mounts. There was a small stream, and they let their mounts drink a bit. They had to keep moving and pace their mounts. If the bus and men got past the bridge, then it would be imperative they get there in time to back them up.

Dawson heard the motorcycles before he saw them. He knew

it was coming. He laid out several magazines on the rocks around his blind. As expected, four men on motorcycles crossed the bridge and weaved around the two trucks and disappeared down the highway. Soon the bus showed up followed by the panel truck. They waited until the bus had stopped while trying to weave past the staged truck. The panel truck pulled onto the bridge behind the bus.

From where he sat, he could see into the cab. He took his rifle and shot the driver and passenger. It rolled forward and hit the bus. He then started round after round through the bus windows at every body he could see. He turned back to the panel truck and shot out the rear duals on the side next to him. The other shooters riddled the bus as well. The truck had the back door of the bus pinned shut.

Gunfire came from the bus, but it was not directed fire. Several men poured out of the bus door, but his fire put them on the ground. One man tried to crawl under the bus, his body jumped as bullets from his and the bullets of the ranch hand on the opposite side of the river hit him. Blood ran out of the bus and pooling under it. He checked, and he had run through five full magazines. As an afterthought, he dropped a fresh magazine in and riddled the panel truck's cargo body in case there were any men in there.

The four men on the motorcycles ran full into Bill, Hawks, and the ranch hands while they were resting the horses. Eight men opened up on them. Two went down, and the other two managed to turn and head back toward the bridge. They made it back to the bridge, but they didn't make it back across. As they sat, watched, and waited, a lone individual waving a white handkerchief limped out of the door. He wore a hat with a feather. He held his battle belt in his hand and dropped it. He died with his hand waving the handkerchief. The final bullet through his head took him directly to the happy hunting grounds.

When Bill, Hawks, and the ranch hands arrived, they carefully approached the bus to make sure there was no sign of life. It was riddled with bullets, and the odds of anyone surviving were remote. One of the ranch hands volunteered to go in. "They killed my little sister and her family. She was the only family I had. Please, let me go in."

Bill agreed. "I don't blame you son. I want you to shoot every one of them in the head; do you understand?"

"Don't worry; I know what to do." The young man went in and emptied three thirty-round magazines before he came out and went to the bridge rail and threw up over it.

Bill put his arm across the young man's shoulder. "Good job, now let's get busy cleaning up this mess."

Dawson and the other shooters came down to the bridge to where Hawks watched. Hawks looked around to Bill. "I have a suggestion. They have one last group at that other intersection. I think we need to hit them tonight before they are alerted that these idiots aren't coming back. I say we go through these guys' headquarters, lock up their women and children, continue on, and kill the others tonight. If not, we're going to always be waiting for them to show up and attack one day."

Bill called all the men together. "Guys, I think we need to continue and wipe out the rest of them down at the south intersection. I think eight of us can take care of it. I want volunteers. I would prefer men who don't have children back home." Every hand went up. He called out the ones who didn't have children or pregnant wives. "Everyone else return home."

"If we don't come back, don't try to rescue us; just make sure there are no surprises at the ranch. We're going to leave this blood bath just like it is for anyone else who thinks they can come this way. Let's round up all their weapons and ammo and put them in the armory back at the ranch."

Dawson and Hawks loaded up a bunch of rifles and packs of ammo and headed back toward the ranch. Hawks asked, "Do you think they can finish them off?"

"If these guys can't do it, I don't who can."

"What do we do now?"

"What else? We'll ask the two women we can't read if they're ready to continue on the TRAIL SOUTH."

ABOUT THE AUTHOR

Ken Gallender is from the Deep South and spent summers of his life roaming his grandfather's farm in the Louisiana Delta. Here he hunted, fished, and spent countless hours walking dusty turn rows. Bit by ants, stung by wasps, chased by cows, and riding in the back of pickup trucks down dusty gravel roads fill his memory. He developed a love of dark water and cypress trees in the oxbow lakes that dominate the region. He watched huge trees carried south in the turbid waters of the Mississippi River. An everyday sight in his life was huge tugboats with a string of barges traveling up and down the river. He has spent winters in Alberta, Canada, and on Vancouver Island feeling the sting of minus 20-degree wind on his face and the squeak of powdered snow under his feet. His description of firearms and their use comes from actual experience. He reaches into his memory and uses these experiences to breathe life into his scenes.